THIS FOR CAROLINE

Doris Leslie

SAPERE
BOOKS

THIS FOR
CAROLINE

Published by Sapere Books.

24 Trafalgar Road, Ilkley, LS29 8HH

saperebooks.com

ISBN: 978-0-85495-419-3

FOREWORD

In presenting this life of Lady Caroline Lamb, which, although a novel, is based entirely on fact, I have endeavoured to portray her as some of her contemporaries have given her to us in their letters, memoirs and journals. Chiefly known for her association with Byron, she has become the object of vilification for the poet's more recent biographers, who depict her as his evil influence and him as her unwilling victim. As both were highly imaginative it has been suggested that Caroline's infatuation for Byron was largely cerebral; and as they are probably the most famed and defamed pair of lovers in the nineteenth century, much that has been written of them is either apocryphal or grossly exaggerated.

It is from the numerous recollections of those who knew her personally that I reconstruct her life. Much of the dialogue and many of the scenes, therefore, are authentic.

I am deeply indebted to the Earl of Bessborough, Professor Aspinall, and Messrs John Murray Ltd for their permission to reproduce a few excerpts from the letters of Lady Caroline, Lady Bessborough, Lady Spencer and Lord Hartington in *Lady Bessborough and Her Family Circle.*

I am also grateful to Lord Brocket for his interest in this book and his valuable information concerning Brocket Hall.

PART ONE (1795-1812)

There is a tide in the affairs of women,
Which, taken at the flood, leads — God knows where.

Byron, *Don Juan*

ONE

On an April morning of rain and shine in the year 1795, there drove up to a house in Hans Place hard by the tollgate of Knight's Bridge a cumbersome yellow coach, its panels emblazoned with a coronet and strawberry leaves. This impressive equipage, drawn by four stout greys, halted at the door of Miss Rowden's Select Academy for Young Ladies, as proclaimed upon a signboard swung above the portals.

On the box beside the coachman in purple and cocked hat, a footman, identically liveried, unfolded his arms and, with careful attention to his white-stockinged calves, descended.

The pull of the door-bell was instantly answered by a diminutive page, of whom the footman, in an imitative fashionable tonnish drawl, enquired, 'The Laideh Caroline Ponsonbeh?'

At which, from the hallway, emerged an elderly virgin in rustling black. So wide were her skirts and so narrow her shoulders, she resembled in shape an isosceles triangle; or so it may have appeared to one small astute observer who followed in her wake. Not that this youngest of all Miss Rowden's Young Ladies had any more knowledge of Euclid than had Miss Rowden herself, since the Academy's curriculum sparsely covered the use of the globes, a smattering of French, orthography, and the reading (expurgated) of the works of William Shakespeare, for whom Miss Rowden professed a penchant. But being of an inquisitive and acquisitive mind, the Lady Caroline Ponsonby had, upon occasion, leafed through her brothers' school books, digesting less of the diagrammatic content than of the bawdy marginal comments on and caricatures of their tutors.

'Take her ladyship's baggage,' commanded Miss Rowden, indicating a hair-trunk that the page ineffectually endeavoured to hoist.

'Her laidehship's baggage,' the footman coldly corrected, 'will be called for latah in the day.' Never let it be presumed that the duchess's coach should be emburdened by her ladyship's hair-trunk.

'My dear, my very dear Lady Caroline!' Miss Rowden sidestepped to reveal a skimpy child in a sky-blue pelisse with a boyish crop of ash-blonde curls. 'This is indeed for me a grievous parting,' pronounced Miss Rowden with no evidence of grief.

'And for me, ma'am.' That soft rejoinder in a little monotone carried the suspicion of a lisp. 'I have watered my couch with tears, as the psalmithst has it, for my instinct — since we all have instincts —' the elfish grin that hovered at the corners of her mouth belied the artless upward glance from fawn-dark eyes — 'is regretfully to leave this sheltered cloithter for a broader, higher thphere.'

'Sphere,' came the sibilant echo. 'Guard your S's. I cannot sufficiently impress upon your ladyship that careful enunciation is the hallmark of the nobly bred. Repeat after me for one —' Miss Rowden allowed her voice a carefully simulated break — 'one last vocal exercise: "Swee-eet are the uses of adversity."'

'Sweet are not, if you'll excuse me, ma'am, the uses of adverth — adversity,' was the gentle contradictory reply. 'For, having so often to repeat the quotation, I sought the word in my dictionary and found it gave adverse as hostile, adversity, misfortune, and Adversary, the Devil. So it seemth that even

Shakespeare can go wrong sometimes. My duty, ma'am,' she curtsied, 'and may I be forgiven my mith-deeds and mithbehaviour. I can't help it if my tongue slips my S's, being too big for my mouth like James the First of England'th, only when he spoke he slobbered, which I don't. I exthpect I'll grow out of it when I grow up, unless I die young of that disease called Death. God bless you, ma'am. We shall meet again. In glory. If not before. Perhapth.'

And, leaving her instructress visibly appalled, she tripped past the page holding open the door, gave him as near as made no matter to a wink, and, ignoring the proffered escort of the footman, ran down the steps into the coach.

At an upper window a dozen young faces were gathered to watch her departure. She waved to them, calling, 'Goodbye, goodbye! Good riddance! Parting is *such* sweet sorrow — but I'll not say goodbye until tomorrow. I invite you all to Devonshire House and we'll have cream buns for tea. The duchess's cook makes exthellent cream buns and he'll bake me a birthday cake with eleven candles on it. My dear good aunt will make you very welcome. You'll love her, and you'll hate my cousins as much as they hate me. Oh, look. There's a rainbow and the sun is come to thpeed me on my way. Sh*ine out, fair sun, till I have bought a glass, That I may see my* sh*adow as I pass.*'

The footman slammed the door; the coachman cracked his whip; and the coach rattled over the cobbles, bearing Caroline away to a 'broader, higher sphere'.

A sphere which had its limitations. Devonshire House, that elaborate temple into which the child Caroline so suddenly was jettisoned, had reached its zenith in the day of eighteenth-century *fin de siècle*. Second only in Augustan splendour to

Carlton House, this great palace of the Cavendish family occupied a site in Piccadilly fronting the Green Park. Led by the Prince of Wales as First Gentleman, a pageant of exquisite frivolities was presented in a glamorous over-crowded *mise en scène:* a scene of alcoved intrigues, ephemeral and fleeting, where the pendulum of lightest love swung to exaggerate depths of passion bordering on melodrama, to vanish as a breath on glass, and then forgotten.

But beyond the cultivated intellectual patter that embraced with like exuberance politics and poesy, the joys of faro, dicing, and the more subtle savour of the senses, only a perceptive few were haunted by the spectre of revolutionary unrest, of doom swift-dawning, that wafted its fetid breath across the Channel from the howling streets of Paris. Still less of these few heard or heeded the thunderous orations of Mr. Fox, 'the friend of Liberty', and closer friend of Georgiana, Queen Regnant of Devonshire House.

A curiously labyrinthine *ménage* was this wherein the child Caroline would lose, or find, herself. Her mother, Henrietta, Lady Bessborough — sister of the duchess, and suffering from ill health resultant, possibly, on vertiginous high living — had been medically and conveniently advised to take a prolonged rest from her responsibilities, maternal and marital. Though her charms were on the wane, Lady Bessborough had still managed to secure a train of ardent admirers on whom she lavished, each in turn, wholehearted emotional interest.

In her fifty-first year she confessed, *I am courted, followed, flattered, made love to … and for seventeen years I have loved, almost to idolatory, the man who probably loved me least of all.* This was Lord Granville Leveson-Gower, who returned her 'idolatory' by marrying her niece. She was, however, far from her fifty-first year when she rendered her small daughter to the equivocal care of her sister.

'A sacrificial deprivation,' she deplored, 'but what would you? My failing health will not permit me to give my Caro the fullest attention incumbent on her tender youth.' And since it was evident her Caro had benefited nothing from Miss Rowden's tutelage, where could she be better placed than with her mother's 'beloved Georgiana'?

Where better indeed?

The house of Lady Bessborough's beloved Georgiana was filled with a miscellany of children: the duke's heir and two girls by the duchess; her son, traced to Lord Grey, one of her many admirers; and two daughters of the duke and Georgiana's bosom friend, Lady Elizabeth Foster. There was no false restraint nor squeamish sentiment in the haphazard ideology of these patrician Whigs. The children of Devonshire House came and went at intervals, each attributed to a variety of parents, each with different surnames, and all accepted with tolerant forbearance by the duke.

Not so was Caroline accepted by her cousins, other than the little boy, Lord Hartington, who, from the moment of her entry to the household, became her willing slave. But her descent on the Devonshire dovecote, to cause among the hens thereof considerable stir, was a case of the cat among the pigeons. That she, a little impudent hussy, should lay down the law to them, mimic their voices in her silly affected childish lisp, be forever spouting Shakespeare and airing her views, and telling such lies, too, and chasing the pages to borrow their suits and dress up as a boy — and her language! The words she came out with, learned from her wicked eavesdropping, ear to keyhole, at the back-stair doors!

Thus the litany of Lady Harriet, the younger Cavendish girl, sent to the duchess by her suffering sisters some few weeks after Caroline's arrival.

'We've borne her tantrums as long as we can, and we can't, Mama, bear them any longer. Of course with you she's your little angel — but with us! If you could only see and hear her in her tempers, you've no idea. She screams and rages if she doesn't get her way and calls us horrid names and see, Mama, what she did to me this morning.' Harriet exposed a plump round arm on which were engraved three scarlet crescents. 'That's where she flew at me and dug her nails to draw blood just because I told her she talks too much about herself. She talks of nothing else. It's I, I, I, all the time. I'll be p-poisoned,' was the sob-impeded declaration, tears coursing down the pasty cheeks of Harriet. 'And when in self-defence I held her hands or she'd have clawed my eyes out, she called me a b-bandy-legged bitch.'

The duchess leaned her lovely head against the cushions of her couch and, gazing at the painted nudities of gods and goddesses at play upon the ceiling, said, 'These continuous complaints are excessively fatiguing, and I cannot but believe, my dear, of gross exaggeration. There are doubtless faults on both sides, yet you must realise that Caro — younger than any of you girls — is a highly excitable child. Dr Warren, who examined her at the request of your aunt, reports her remarkably intelligent, advanced beyond her years and very sensitive. She must, the doctor says, be humoured. Your aunt and I had excellent reports from Miss Rowden on her conduct. She was a favourite among her schoolmates and is indeed of a lovable nature, one who gives love in return for love. I greatly fear this rancour against your sweet little cousin is prompted by

—' the duchess shook a playfully admonitory finger — 'by a *soupçon* of the green eye, shall we say?'

'So! You think I'm jealous? Well, and if I am, what daughter wouldn't be to see herself pushed down to second place as I and Georgie are in our mother's love? Yes, you talk of love in return for love, but what love do you give us? You give it all to her, that d-deceitful lying bragging little —'

'Ssh!' The admonitory finger was raised again. 'How dare you speak so to your mother?' Though the words were vehement the tone was not. The duchess never was easily ruffled. While she spoke she looked upon her plain and dumpy daughter, thinking, *She grows more than ever like a pie. How did I happen to come by her?* A question oft recurring, that was inevitably left unanswered.

With cooing calm she said, 'Let us hear no more of this tittle-tattle, darling. Go back to dear Caro with love in your heart. It is love, remember, that makes the world go round.' The duchess glanced at an ormolu clock on the mantelshelf. 'And don't — I beg you, dearest — *don't* repeat me these nauseating tales. Little birds in their nests should agree.' A ravishing smile was offered to Harriet's scowl, and with no diminution of that same smile which, accompanied by indiscriminate kisses to butchers, bakers and the *hoi polloi* of Mr. Fox's constituents, had won him a majority vote in a past election, she added plaintively, 'You have given me the megrims. Just hand me that mirror beside you.'

Harriet, snivelling, lifted from a sofa table a cupid-wreathed porcelain looking glass.

'Hold it up that I may see myself.' Georgiana closely scrutinised her beautiful reflection, rearranging her fashionably tousled red-gold curls cropped in the latest *victime* style brought over from revolutionary France. 'I look awful,' cooed the duchess. I can't bear the sight of me. You may give me a kiss, my poppet, and go.'

Her poppet reluctantly pecked at her mother's peach-bloom cheek. 'Then you're d-determined,' she whimpered, 'that Caro shall live here and torture us?'

'Torture? Come, come.' Georgiana had discovered an infinitesimal spot on her nose. 'What a place to grow a pimple! I can't put a patch on the tip of my nose. Take away the mirror and then take away yourself. I am expecting a visitor any minute to discuss matters of more moment than your tale-bearing nonsense.'

'Well, so you don't seem to mind if I'm m-mauled by a young savage. I'm sure I wish,' wept Harriet, 'that I may drop down dead.'

'So long as you don't drop the mirror. You tire me dreadfully,' murmured the duchess. 'Do go.'

With bulging lower lip and sniffs and mutters Harriet Cavendish went.

As she passed through the hall, a stout paunchy man with a blue stubble of beard on the first of his chins was admitted by a footman and conducted by the butler to the door of the duchess's boudoir. Harriet slid behind a Corinthian column to hear her mother's greeting, sweetly tuned: 'My dear, dear Charles! How good of you to come so promptly.'

And the reply in that catarrhal fruity voice which held spellbound his supporters in the Commons and rasped unpleasantly upon the ears of his Tory opponents: 'Madam, at your bidding I would come to you from Hades, but in this case no farther than from Carlton House.'

'Wading through alcoholically flavoured Stygian waters?'

A laugh like a carillon of bells trailed the duchess's query; then the door silently closed, the butler withdrew to his sanctum, and Harriet, still snivelling, took herself upstairs to meet her cousin Caro coming down, bearing a weighty silver dish. At her heels came the boy Hartington, half-hidden behind a pile of greasy platters on the topmost of which reposed the remnants of a meal.

'We've had our dinners,' announced Caroline, 'and there's nothing left for you. I hope you've had a satisfactory session with my aunt and have perthuaded her that I am past redemption.'

A violent shove from Harriet caused her to let fall the dish and its contents with a clatter of metal on marble, and a lackey guarding the wrought-iron entrance advanced to retrieve the spilled carcass of a fowl.

'Take the plates from his lordship,' ordered Caroline, 'and if there's anything left besides bones you can give it to Lady Harriet. She's missed her dinner — not that it matters seeing she's so fat. It'd do her good to go without her dinner for a week — Ow-ooh!' This yelped ejaculation was wrung from her as Harriet's fingers endowed a vicious nip to her cousin's upper arm. 'Scorpion!' screeched Caroline. 'May the devil roast you on a grid and serve you to his imps in hell!'

'She'd carve up in juicy portions,' chuckled Hartington, a cherubic pink-and-golden boy, and received from his sister a tug of his hair and a cuff on his ear to turn it red.

'Sow!' yelled Hartington. 'You ugly pig-faced sow who goes sneaking to Mama to have Caro sent away.'

'Hah!' snapped Harriet. 'So she's been teaching you her keyhole tricks, has she? And don't you shout at me, you little beast. Mr. Fox is with Mama. Just let him hear you. What'll he think?'

'He'll think what I think, that you're a pig-faced sow,' with parrot-wise reiteration jeered her brother. 'Come on, Caro, let's slide down the balusters.'

'No!' cried Harriet, 'you'll fall and break your neck. Caro, don't you do it!'

But neither child heeded her, and Caroline, knee-gripping the broad marble balustrade as if on a hobby-horse, was followed gleefully by Hartington with whoops and hunting calls of 'Tally-ho! A Fox! A Fox, halloo there! 'Ware Fox!'

'Those noisy children,' sighed the duchess as the racket without penetrated to the intimate communion within. 'What to do with them all I do not know. Hart will go to Eton — but the girls! And now I have Caro Ponsonby thrust on me by my sister — quite a handful, so precocious. Dear Charles, do tell me — I am all agog to hear the latest news of the second Mrs. Prinney. Lord Malmesbury says she *smells*! It would seem his *trop de zèle* has sent him sniffing at Her Highness. How long do you think *this* marriage will last?'

'Hours and hours,' responded Mr. Fox, 'unless the rumour that he has begot him an heir may be proven.'

'So indecently soon, to bring about a wailing and gnashing of the Fitz's false teeth?' The duchess exposed her perfect own in her illuminative smile. 'Tell me some more.'

Crossing a knee Fox rolled a relishing eye at the reclining Georgiana, noting that her figure, despite a tendency to increased *embonpoint,* still retained its luscious curves, her hair its reddish sheen of gold, untarnished.

'Just this much more,' Fox amusedly reflected. 'The prince is about to take his fair princess to Brighton, where Lady Jersey, whose condition is of equal interest, has also retired. According to the ubiquitous Walpole, HRH is floundering between wind and water. Of the two pregnancies conjecture gives the smallest as a tennis ball, and the largest as a dropsy.'

'Fox! You'll kill me!' cried the duchess. 'Is it true?'

A shrug of heavy shoulders, a twinkle of those treacly black eyes set beneath jutting brows, accompanied the answer: 'As true as my proposed sale of the life interest in the Duchy of Cornwall in settlement of the prince's debts.'

Her Grace's smile lingered. '*Et tu, Brute?* And what does our Prinney have to say to that?'

But what their Prinney had to say to that was left for the moment in abeyance when the din outside rose in lusty volume to terminate in a scream from the duchess's daughter. 'I *knew* that would happen. Serve you right!'

'And you wrong. Take your pig's trotters off me and go boil your face,' from the duchess's son, capped by sepulchral recitative from the duchess's niece:

'Avaunt! And quit my sight. Let the earth hide thee. Thou hatht no thpeculation in those eyes which thou dotht glare with!'

'Oh, Lord! What is it now?' bemoaned the duchess. 'They have been so much more troublesome since our sweet Caro came. What ought I to do with them, my dear Charles? Say.'

Her dear Charles said, 'What you ought to do with them — which you will never do with them, but what I would do with them — is spank them good and hard nor spare the rod. Supervision, discipline, is what they need.' And which neither governess nor tutor were more than temporarily disposed to give, since none could be retained in permanent charge of the children of Devonshire House.

Thus we find that, though served on gold and silver, they waited on themselves, carrying trays and dishes from their quarters to the kitchen. They had no knowledge of life beyond their own four walls, knew only two strata of society, the rich and the poor — who, so they had learned from sporadic reading of the Scriptures, were always with us. Yet none of them had ever seen 'the poor', unless glimpsed from coach windows on their drives through London streets, or in the villages of Holywell, the house of Lady Spencer, Caro's grandmother, or the Bessborough place at Roehampton.

Such visits to her father's rural home were all too rare for Caroline. She loved the country, loathed the town, and tells us that she much preferred *washing a dog or polishing a spur, or breaking in a horse to any accomplishment in the world.* She had it firmly she should have been a boy. Her mother, having borne three sons, had wished for a girl to find her wish fulfilled, with epicene result. *Half nymph, half Ganymedes,* was the inward comment of a certain young gentleman who first sighted the wild elfish little creature riding barebacked in a meadow of his father's house in Hertfordshire where she and her cousins were invited for a week. A momentous visit as it proved to be, though neither of the two concerned were at the time aware of it: indubitably not the child Caroline; nor, save for that one passing thought, was William Lamb.

On vacation in his final year at Cambridge, this second son of the first Viscount Melbourne, a sober, scholarly, elderly, young man, found the voluptuous charms of Duchess Georgiana less appealing than the more insinuating graces of her sister, Henrietta, Lady Bessborough.

The enjoyment of her ill-health was delightfully enhanced by the marked attention of the nineteen-year-old William, who, when launched by his mother on London society, became an instantaneous success.

Lady Melbourne was one of the lovely Georgiana's dearest friends; a friendship of gushing affection on the one side, on the other — if equally gushing — tempered by a cautious, contemplative eye not only to her own main chance but also to that of William, her favourite son.

The daughter of Sir Ralph Milbanke, a Yorkshire squire, she, at the age of seventeen, had ensnared and captured Sir Peniston Lamb, a man of greater means than parts, whose fortune derived from his forbear, a Nottinghamshire lawyer. He had died without issue, leaving his goodly estate to his nephew, Peniston's father, who subsequently increased his heritage by marrying a wife as wealthy as himself. His considerable affluence secured him a baronetcy; and on his death, his son enriched by unlimited cash, proceeded light-heartedly to spend it in hunting, drinking and wenching.

His marriage to Elizabeth Milbanke was advantageous to both. Of higher birth than that of her doltish husband, she ignored his succession of mistresses, and luxuriously installed as chatelaine of a mansion in Whitehall and Brocket, his Hertfordshire house, she set herself forthwith to procure him an Irish peerage and a seat in the Commons, where he sat for forty years and never spoke.

Her ambition thus partially satisfied, she allowed him his wine, his women and her body, while disposing of her favours to men of better breed. Among the many who fell victim to the lure of Lady Melbourne was George Augustus, Prince of Wales, with whom, as that arch-gossip Mr. Walpole had it, she *danced from night until dawn in a rather cow-like style*. If, after bearing her husband six children, her figure tended a trifle to the bovine, her vitality lacked nothing of exuberance. Her salon still attracted a distinguished circle, predominantly male. Nor, in her choice of lovers, did she scruple to annex the husband of her dearest 'friend'. Not for nothing was she dubbed the 'Thorn' among her feminine acquaintances; but one man only held her heart, and he, Lord Egremont, stayed faithfully unwed although the father of numerous progeny.

Not the least of them, so humour hinted, was Lord Melbourne's second son. That's as may be, but whatever her husband suspected he had sense enough, even when drunk, not to voice his suspicions lest 'his Betsy go pokin' her nose in a hornet's nest to be stung by his Sophie' — Mrs. Sophia Baddeley, on whom, and on every unlawful occasion, he showered more than a moiety of his wealth.

With a background such as this, and in a world where the chastity of women was disdainfully regarded as bourgeois sentiment; where the perfect expression of human relationship was dedicated to the pursuit of love esoteric, erotic, never platonic; where marriage vows were made to be broken and not the wisest of sons could know his own father, no wonder that young William Lamb was drawn into the siren web of Lady Bessborough.

Old enough to be his mother, she combined maternal interest with a warmer interchange of thought and feeling that could not fail to attract a ready response in a pliable, sensitive boy. She had reached a time of life when youthful admiration lends to ripened summer the dormant bloom of spring. So, at Brocket, William found his heart if not entirely possessed, exclusively monopolised. They walked and talked together, discussing current politics: the prince's debts, the latest news from the fighting front, the Reform, no longer a bogey to scare the more timid of Mr. Pitt's Tories, but a seed, scattered on hurricane winds through a war-tormented Britain smarting under the disgrace of recent defeat, to sow cataclysmic discord. The whinings of the underdog had become a predatory wolf-howl, and the flood tide of accumulative grievance was loosed in political meetings all over the country.

'Too shocking,' the lady delicately shuddered, and sheered away from the stark reminder of those starving thousands who, in that tumultuous period of gestation, would bring forth a gargantuan infant destined to father industrial revolt. 'Quite dreadful, so alarming,' murmured Lady Bessborough.

They were walking on the terrace that overlooked the lake. The sun blazed from a cloudless sky and on the lady's lightly powdered hair. She did not conform to the *victime* crop, nor had she yet discarded the mid-century fashion of dress — the hoops, padded petticoats and towering 'heads' — in favour of the newest innovation of classic simplicity suited only to the figure of a sylph, which the Junoesque redundancy of her ladyship's proportions most certainly were not.

'Shall we sit?' The day was unusually warm. Tiny beads of moisture bedewed the lady's temples; a faint odour of perspiration emanated from her armpits, undisguised by the scent of musk and amber. But her skin was faultless, and her pensively humorous smile enchanting.

William sat and gazed, enthralled. 'May I,' he offered, 'read you a poem I have written?' *Although you,* he thought and did not dare to say, *are a poem in yourself.*

'Ah, yes, pray do.' Their eyes met, and meeting found it difficult to disengage.

He did not read, he recited his poem, prefatorily declaring, 'It describes a transitional phase between this year and the last. You understand?'

She understood perfectly. 'The chrysalis emerges.' Her eyelids drooped.

He swallowed, braced his shoulders, and began:

'A year has pass'd — a year of grief and joy —
Since first we threw aside the name of boy,
That name which in some future hour of gloom,
We shall with sighs regret we can't resume...
...Exalted in the raptures thought can give,
And said alone, we then began to live,
With wanton fancy, painted pleasure's charms,
Wine's liberal powers, and beauty's folding arms,
Expected joys —'

'Hi! Hart! And all of you — see us take this jump! We're *off!*'

A voice, shrill and tuneful as a bird's, brought rhapsodic recitative to abrupt finale. William's eyes went searching. Beyond the glistening lake and low-hedged lawn, sloping to green meadowland gold-carpeted with buttercups, a group of children stood to watch a boy in bright blue pantaloons astride a racing pony. Distance lent kaleidoscopic movement to that colourful mosaic of green and gold, the eager forward thrust of the young rider's body as the little horse gathered himself to clear the high-stacked hurdle amid a burst of cheers from the onlookers. He, who rode barebacked, dismounted and came running, vaulted a wicket gate in the hedge and, skirting the lake, tore across the lawn to halt beneath the terrace. His short curly hair, sun-gilded, swept back from the pink-flushed forehead. Legs wide apart, he stood staring up at William looking down; but seen at such close quarters, the open-throated shirt clung, sweat-dampened, to define the small firm breasts of ... no boy.

William released a breath. 'What a lovely child! Whose girl,' he asked, 'is she?'

The lady unfastened a smile and said, 'She is mine.'

'Of all the Devonshire House girls that is the one for me.'

It went the round of the clubs to be floated into legend, this remark of William Lamb in jest — surely not in earnest? — concerning Caroline.

Between drinking and dicing the blades of St James's repeated it with chuckles and embellishment. 'Does the mother take kindly to playing second fiddle in the chamber music down at Brocket Hall?'

Lady Bessborough's reaction to that first encounter of these two whose stars had crossed was summed up with ineffable indulgence to her sister Georgiana: 'I do believe he thinks he is in love.' Or if not in love, irresistibly attracted — to a child of thirteen.

During the years that elapsed in the care of the duchess, Caroline's chameleon adaptability had assimilated to the full the flow of swift impressions. Inherently explorative, her insatiable curiosity was for ever seeking knowledge, not only of herself but of that life beyond the duke's seraglio: a life of shadows where figures passed and vanished in processional formation and, for her, had little contact with reality.

She was, as William found her, a creature of surprises, an engaging blend of protean impulse and naive sagacity; a wild tomboy who would ride cross-saddle like a jockey in her cousin's borrowed trews, who would chatter unceasingly, darting with firefly inconsequence from one topic to another; from the points of a pet dog to Dryden's *Ode* — or the latest invasion scare that had aroused the fighting blood of every man and boy in Britain.

'I'd have gone for a soldier had I been a boy — and would go now, if they'd take me. I could well pass for a boy in Hart's pantaloons, couldn't I, Mr. Lamb?'

He joyed to draw her out, sounding her on politics acquired at the keyhole of her aunt's boudoir in worship of her hero, Mr. Fox. Together they would drink damnation to the Tories, he in brandy, she in mugs of milk.

So unique a little oddity, imbued with puckish humour, was for William enormously appealing. Her delicious head of gold-tipped curls, gracefully poised on the long slender neck, had a transcendent ethereal beauty. But she was not strictly beautiful according to the overblown flamboyant standards of her day. Her eyes, wide-set, of a velvety darkness in bewitching contrast to her Saxon-fair colouring, looked out with ingenuous bewilderment from under faintly surprised eyebrows, as if to solve the riddle of life envisioned but as yet incomprehensible. Not the least of her attractions was her laugh like a song, and her voice with its soft lisping drawl.

If William were captivated, she, as eagerly reciprocal, dwelled in daydreams. Not ignorant, though innocent and still child enough to believe in fairy tales, she allowed imagination to run riot on the coming of a prince for her awakening. Cerebrally she fused and flamed to words unuttered, to unkissed kisses and the giving of herself to him, untouched. That she would have stayed untouched, in their rambles through Lord Melbourne's park with none but deer to follow them, is doubtful. William was no man of steel but a virile hot-blooded youngster, reared in an atmosphere of hedonic tradition that discouraged self-denial. Her excessive youth served as no deterrent, rather as incentive to desire. In three or four years' time, he hazarded, she would be equally desirous as she was desirable now.

He, too, indulged in daydreams, to find his idyll ended, his dream unromantically shattered. His girl developed chickenpox and, out of sight and hearing, was incarcerated in the nursery suite at Brocket Hall. It is possible, however, he was not left entirely disconsolate when, bidden Godspeed by her mother, he went jogging back to Cambridge in the coach.

A great era had passed; one greater still was in its dawning, but the birth of the nineteenth century gave to war-ravaged Britain little promise of that unparalleled achievement destined for the next hundred years. While the shade of Napoleon bestrode the whole of Europe, despite the unforgotten victory of '98 when a blind-in-the-eye undersized admiral had chased the little Corsican out of Lower Egypt to destroy his fleet in the Battle of the Nile, storm clouds still darkened the horizon.

Yet London, or at least a London bounded by Westminster Hall and Piccadilly, was not to be disturbed at, nor diverted from, the charming dissipations of a summer season by the threat of a death-struggle between the First Consul, Lord of the Land, and Nelson, First Lord of the Sea.

Night after night those famished hordes to whom war had spelled starvation, crept from their lairs to stand up-gazing at phantasmal shapes that passed and re-passed across uncurtained windows in the golden glow of candlelight. On flower-decked balconies couples, detached from the graceful weaving of the cotillion, would appear in momentary silhouette against the dazzling background of a world as far removed from that ragged herd of watchers as heaven is from hell. Few of the privileged, whose leisured carefree way of life encircled their existence, could have been more aware of those lesser beings down below than of a swarm of beetles in their cellars, unless with one likely exception.

He, as second son of negligible prospects, a cog in the glittering wheel of a pampered aristocracy, sought to probe beneath the infinite gradations of a new-born democratic movement whose cry was 'Liberty, Equality, Fraternity', a reverberant echo borne on the whirlwinds of revolutionised France. But William Lamb, product of the new intelligentsia, suffering from a surfeit of prodigal extravagance and disorderly example, was not yet to find his anchorage in uncharted seas of politics. He was to find it in a voyage more perilous from which there could be no retreat and no escape.

He was foredoomed.

TWO

On a summer's day in 1803, a *fête champêtre* was held in the grounds of Holland House. Situated in its vast green acres at Kensington, this historic home of the Hollands stood second only to Devonshire House in the running for the leadership of fashion.

Elizabeth Holland, ex-wife of Sir Godfrey Webster, had committed the unforgivable sin of being found out in adultery. Her marriage to Lord Holland, with whom she eloped, did not mitigate the scandal of divorce as viewed by the ultra-conventional ladies of society. But if those of the high *ton* refused to receive her, others of the highest were ready to excuse her indiscretions, since theirs would hardly bear investigation.

Georgiana Devonshire, her sister, Lady Bessborough, and William's mother, Lady Melbourne, were almost the only women of her world who accepted Lady Holland. Not that she cared a row of pins whether they did or did not. Nothing of a feminist, she made it a favourite rendezvous for men of intellectual Whiggism and culture, headed by Lord Holland's uncle, Charles Fox.

Yet those who met at that stately red-brick mansion were not drawn there by the wit or the charm of their hostess, since she was neither witty nor charmful. She owed her success with the men to her outstanding personality. Of a commanding presence — large-bosomed, outspoken, loud-voiced — her peculiarities may have been deliberately fostered to focus attention on herself. At dinner parties she would suddenly announce that all must change places, causing a general reshuffle and confusion. Or in the midst of a *conversazione* she would pull off her stockings and bid her page bring a bath of hot mustard-water to rub her legs, 'for the ease of my rheumatics', she would explain to the amusement of her guests, most of whom enjoyed her eccentricities.

Her easy-going husband, who may or may not have regretted his choice, shared this in common with his wife: both were indefatigable big-game hunters, delighting to stalk the latest lion, or, as in the case of William Lamb, lion cub.

So we see him on that sweltering June day driving in his curricle to Kensington. Conducted by a lackey through the great oak-panelled hall, he found the garden fête already well in progress. Lady Holland, as parsimonious as she was unpredictable, had on this occasion lavished much expense in outward show, with three brass bands on the lawns, all playing at once, and two marquees where trestle tables offered meagre sandwiches, tepid hock, claret-cup, urns of tea and coffee, and intermittent dishes of debilitated strawberries. These the younger contingent, sons and daughters of her guests, and a son of her own by a former husband, had almost entirely demolished.

William was received by his hostess in a wide-brimmed rustic hat and a girlish muslin gown, damped, as demanded by fashion, to cling and — with startling effect — to emphasise her generous proportions. She greeted William with the request that he would join the haymakers 'out there', pointing vaguely in the direction of an upward sweep of pastureland where, limned in bas-relief like figures on a frieze, workers toiled in the sun. 'We are short of labour owing to the cholera at

Chelsea,' boomed her ladyship. 'Half our men are down with it so you must all make yourselves useful.'

She turned to welcome new arrivals while William went in search of refreshment. Elbowing a way to a crowded marquee, he managed to grab from a passing footman's tray a tumbler filled with a pale liquid that might have been hock but proved to be water flavoured with lemon. After one sip he was about to set it down when someone jogged his arm, spilling the contents of his glass over his spotless white buckskins. A peal of laughter spun him round to find Caro Ponsonby beside him.

'Mr. Lamb, how do you do?' Her lips rounded to the syllables in that well-remembered drawl. 'I was told you would be here. I have been looking for you everywhere. How long — how long is it since last we met at Brocket? Years and years — four hundred years or four? You know I had the chickenpox? They thought it might be smallpox, but it wasn't and I've never seen you since. I've been in Paris. So now we meet again. I'm theventeen. You haven't changed. Have I?'

Slightly lost of breath, he said, 'I think you've grown.' Yet still outwardly a child, with the same boyish angles, those same velvety dark eyes, set wide apart in the small pointed face under the short cropped curls of ashen gold, the same slight lisp and all about her that magical quality of a creature not quite of this world. And at sight of her his heart gave a startled leap as the thought flashed through his mind that, although so little grown, unchanged, she was no child now but a girl in her unfolding between the bud and blossom.

'It is too crowded here. Let us go into the field. We've been working there to help the haymakers.' She slid a hand in his, guiding him across the tree-lined lawn, in and out of the massed throng where the fragmentary pattern of foppish pastel blues, pinks, buffs of men's long-tailed coats were scarcely more solidified against the green than the diaphanous gowns of the women. The gigantic hoops and padded petticoats of a former century had vanished. The new freedom of thought had brought freedom of movement along with the freedom of morals. But William, whose aesthetic sense might, in other circumstances, have been enchanted by that arcadian spectacle, rainbow-tinted, shimmering, the frills of a cobweb, laced cap edging the gently rouged blush of a cheek, had no eye for it.

'Quick, quick! Let us get away from here!' She had to shout above the cacophony of sound, the chorus of voices, the blare of the bands. 'Noise gives me a pain in my ears. There's a gate nearby into a field.'

By this time she had got him through the worst of the crowd; and now that the mêlée had thinned he could recognise isolated figures here and there. Sheridan, engaged in conversation with his host; and Sidney Smith in tie-wig and clerical black, both striving to out-talk the other; Sheridan with gesticulatory spread of his hands; Lord Holland, stout, stocky, beetle-browed, a younger edition of his Uncle Charles, guffawing with a throw-back of his head.

'Do let us listen to what they are saying!' cried Caroline. 'A duel of wits between Mr. Smith and Sherry is sure to be worth hearing.' Yet what they heard was only the tag of it to do with the prince's pavilion down at Brighton, 'capped by a myriad miniature domes, as if St Paul's,' said Sidney Smith, 'had gone to the sea and pupped.'

'Isn't he delightful?' rippled Caroline. 'I'll put that in my thought book. I keep a thought book in my mind — not for anyone to read, for there is nothing written yet. It's just a storehouse of my memories and they come running to my call. One day I will write them. Ah, there's Mama!' Her hand was still guiding him. Where — to paradise or to perdition? The whimsy took and shook him into laughter. 'Mama! See,' she shrilled, 'who is with me. I have found him.'

Drawn from politely rapt attention to Sir William Hamilton and his Emma, Lady Bessborough turned her famous smile on her daughter. 'Caro, my dear, pray consider your manners. Lady Hamilton, I beg you will excuse my little girl. She is always so impetuous.'

Lady Hamilton, whose beauty and figure, both somewhat over-ripened, were not shown to best advantage in a short high-waisted buttercup-yellow thinnest of cambric gowns, advanced like one of Nelson's warships in full sail.

'Verily, verily, so this is your little gairl?' declaimed her ladyship in ringing tones of liveliest amaze. It was generally assumed that the rich timbre of her voice had been induced by addiction to porter.

'We are going to make hay,' announced Caroline, rising from the bob to be warmly embraced by the lady.

'As I live, an elf, a sprite, an Ariel! What eyes, and what a mouth! If Romney could see her he would never let her out of his sight, but, alas, he wastes in melancholy under the Kendal roof-tree. Sweet gairl, your mouth would be a revelation to Romney, as, he avows, is mine. And here do I see the son of my good friends, the Melbournes? My dear young Lamb, you grow as handsome as your mother.' She opened wide her arms as if she would embrace him in his turn, a demonstration adroitly evaded.

'I find her just a little overpowering,' was Caro's comment on her ladyship's performance when the two had gained the hayfield and left the fête behind them. 'By her greeting of me you would think I had dropped from the sky, but she dined at our house only last week and said just those verily, verily very same things of my mouth and my eyes and Mr. Romney. I'd hate to grow older and fatter if I were a beauty as she is — or was. Shall we sit? It's too hot to make hay while the sun shines.'

They sat.

She did most of the talking; he was content to watch her small vivacious face with only half an ear for what she said in that soft drawling voice of hers.

'Yes, I've been in Paris with Mama, and we saw the First Consul — such a little yellow dwarf to cast a giant's shadow — driving through the streets with a mob of people cheering for the peace. But it's only a spurious peace, don't you think, this Treaty of Amiens?'

'It is pretty clear,' said William, roused from contemplation of her charming tilted profile, 'that Buonaparte does not intend to live on equal terms with any European Power. I give it a year.'

She plucked a sprig of sorrel and nibbled it, shaking her head.

'So much can happen in a year. For instance, me — and you.' She stole a look at him whose eyes had never left her. 'What will happen to us in a year? What *has* happened to us — in an hour?'

The implication suggested by those words, so carelessly spoken that he doubted she could realise their meaning, set his heart like a drum in his ribs, momentarily to deprive him of speech, while she, abandoning the stalk, gazed dreamily into the distance.

He told himself, *She is only a child in age, yet ageless as an elemental.* The tender curves of her body under the close clinging muslin gown were not yet shaped to womanhood, for she would never, he thought, be a woman; and made his voice firm to say, 'You may be married by this time next year.'

'I, married? To whom? To Hartington, my cousin — that boy?' She hunched a thin shoulder. 'Yes, he wants to marry me, and so does Godfrey Webster. See them there —' she pointed to the far end of the field — 'pummelling each other in the hay? They are at it again, fighting over me. They are always fighting over me. Hart is beautiful to look at but such a little ass. As for Godfrey — do you know him? He is porcine and clownish and has very ugly ears. I wouldn't marry either of them. I don't want to marry *anyone*, unless — if you —' she sucked in her underlip, then blurted, 'if *you* would wish to marry me — this year, next year, sometime — never?' She sprang up laughing, holding out her hands to him. 'Come along. We'll go. I've said too much, too little — not enough. I could say volumes and it wouldn't be enough to say what I would say to you, but it will all go in my thought book. You must forget my silliness. What's on my lung leaps out on my tongue — so please, please, *please* forget it!'

The westering sky poured a golden radiance on the hayfield, bordered by elms dark against the green serenity of undulating meadowland upswept to the heights of Notting Hill. The voices of the scythers, the shouts, thinned by distance, of the two boys tumbling each other in the unbound stooks, mingled with the evensong of birds.

Then, as they retraced their steps towards the house, he, below breath, said, 'There can be no forgetting.'

And he knew himself handfasted, sealed, surrendered.

Long past midnight she knelt on the window seat in her white-curtained room of the Bessborough house in Cavendish Square. All was still and drowsy. The city slept in silence undisturbed save for the occasional clatter of hooves and wheels on cobbles, and the cry of an owl in a treetop. Opening her casement she leaned out for air, her face uplifted to the star-pricked sky where a great yellow moon swam out from a foam of gossamer cloud.

'You,' she murmured, 'Artemis, Diana — you are sickly-faced tonight. The Greeks believed you goddess but you have never lived. You are a sun as yet unborn, which in some timeless time will burn red-hot and so burn up this world as I burn now, red-hot for him... Was I too precipitate? Should I have let him first declare himself before I opened out myself to him? I must — *must* have him... But suppose he won't have me? He was not at all forthcoming to my overture. God forgive me, I've the instinct of a harlot. Did I solicit him or didn't I? Why should I be ashamed or feared to tell him of my love? I'll die if he won't have me. Make him, make him have me...' She bent her head, crushing her teeth into her knuckles. 'Fool, you fool! This love of mine is tearing me to pieces.'

She rose from her knees, lit candles, drew the curtains and ruefully watched the reddening mark on her hand; then slowly began to undress. Stripped naked she stood adoring herself in the long cheval-glass, fingering her small firm breasts, smoothing her slender flanks. In the candleshine her flesh held a pale luminous transparency.

'How beautiful you are!' she whispered. 'And all of this is his. I give it all to you, my William. There can be no wrong in loving, for God is love. O, God, I pray you let him take me soon, soon. I cannot wait.'

But she would have to wait.

Months passed, speeding to a year, during which time they met at frequent intervals and with apparently no more between them than the mildest flirtation. They were often seen at the opera under the watchful eye of her mama, who, with Lord Granville Leveson-Gower and Lord Bessborough, a complacent cypher in the background, suffered William's attendance on Caroline with as much encouragement as would be given to a lackey.

Things were at a pretty pass when she, perversely, and despite her prayers and longings, gave him little hope that his tentative approach would be approved of or accepted by her parents, or by her. Moreover, he went haunted by the uncomfortable reminder of his calf-love for her mother. What a coil! *Off with the old love and on with the new,* he reflected grimly when, unable to endure this gnawing suspense, he made bold to present himself to Lady Bessborough with a formal offer for her daughter's hand. How, he wondered, would she take it?

She took it with glacial cordiality.

'My dear boy,' her smile regressed him to the schoolroom, 'Lord Bessborough and I cannot possibly entertain nor contemplate your suit. There are several reasons why we must reject it, but I will give you only two.'

And expansively she gave them, to sink him.

'She is bespoken — I tell you this in confidence — to Hartington, her cousin, and with our full approval. Also, neither her father nor I could consent to our only daughter's marriage to a younger son with no adequate means to support her. She is very young, and although you are some years older you have not yet shown any indication of that distinguished future for which Lord Bessborough and I had hoped you were destined — in politics or letters, or the law. You must surely realise that as a younger son you have at present no commendable prospects.'

'I — I — I have taken my degree in law,' he stammered from out of a dry mouth, 'and am now called to the Bar.'

'Good. Very good,' conceded her ladyship. 'The Bar and the Church are the most expedient professions for a younger —'

Say it again, inwardly groaned William.

She said it again. '— younger son. I do so much regret that Lord Bessborough and I cannot agree to your proposal. Put Caroline out of your mind and heart, dear William. She is not for you. Even were you in a position to support her in the circumstances to which she had been used, you are both temperamentally ill-matched.' And in coolest dismissal she gave him two fingers.

Fiercely red, he bowed over them, backed, and without another word or look he left her.

Had she intended to fling him at her daughter's head she could not have adopted more strategical means. Determined to overcome all obstacles he went in search of Caro to learn from her own lips this rejection of himself, and the truth — if truth it were — of her betrothal to her cousin.

He had not far to seek. He found her guiltily tiptoeing up the staircase, followed, waylaid her and caught her by the hand to swing her round and face him.

'You!' She professed wide-eyed astonishment. 'When did you arrive? I didn't know you were here.'

'Did you not? Then you must be hard of hearing, since this —' he touched her earlobe — 'bears the imprint of a keyhole.'

'William, you look very warm for so cold a day. I haven't seen you for an age. Let me show you my dear little, new little, spaniel pup. Come into my parlour.'

'Said the spider,' muttered William.

She led him to a cream-panelled room hung with curtains of flowery chintz. A golden-brown puppy came gambolling to greet her. She snatched him up to lavish him with kisses.

'Isn't he a darling? Godfrey Webster gave him to me. Don't do that, my angel.' Extracting from the puppy's jaws a morsel of her fichu, she set him down and moved towards the bell. 'I'll ring for tea.'

Losing his head, William heard himself say, 'I don't want tea. I want —'

'Wine?'

'I want you.'

He gathered her to him, and all the pent-up frustration of months was released in broken words, in pulsing throb and surge of sense and fevered touch, until a small convulsion shook her and in his arms she slackened and lay still.

'My love, my love,' he whispered, 'look at me.'

She stirred; her eyelids lifted. 'Do I dream? I have dreamt of this so often to die a hundred little deaths and die again, and now... my resurrection.'

He knelt, taking her hands to turn palm upwards and hold a lingering kiss in each. 'We'll be married, come what may,' he told her urgently. 'Younger son or nothing, and be damned to them! Yes, Caro, yes — you will?'

She freed herself, leaning over him to smooth the crisp black hair from his temples. 'I cannot say I will or won't, my handsome. How beautifully your hair curls.' She bent her lips to it, inhaling. 'You smell of apples and honey. You do not know me, William. You only know what you can see of me. You do not know my inner self, and nor do I, more than that I have a hellish temper. Let me warn you, I am one of the Furies incarnate when I am roused. Would you take to wife a wild cat that screams and claws and bites? I even bite myself when I'm enraged... oh, Lord, the pup! He's piddled.' She ran to seize the puppy by his scruff, ruefully regarding a wet patch on the Aubusson. 'Do you think it will stain? It's a very good carpet. You naughty, naughty — There then, there. Mother isn't cross with you, my baby, because you're only a baby — not yet three months old. We all did that at three months old.' Cuddling the unabashed infant she called William to her. 'Come here by the fire.' She slid to the hearthrug.

With their arms round each other, the puppy between them, they sat like a couple of children. Laying her cheek to his, 'Now that you're called to the Bar —' she said, and was interrupted.

'So you heard that too?'

'Well, of course. I knew you had come to ask Mama for me when I saw you arrive. I had one of my instincts. She was horrid to you, my poor Lamb. It isn't Papa who objects. He does what she tells him. I call them Voice and Echo. Mama is Voice. What was I saying? Oh, yes. Now that you are called to the Bar, a barrister full-fledged, I'll be your clerk. I'd look well in wig and gown — a Portia, and I could live with you in your chambers and none would take me for a girl. So you would learn all there is to know of me before we wed in Holy Church. It wouldn't be wrong, would it — to test our love to the uttermost, do you think?'

'I cannot think,' he replied dizzily. 'But this I know, that none can part us now. Tell me,' he put a hand beneath her chin, forcing her eyes to meet his, 'you must tell me. Are you bespoken, as your mother said, to Hartington?'

'Poor Hart.' She laughed softly. 'He is mad in love with me and always has been. My dearest and best Mama has set her heart — on Hart. You must pinch me when I pun. I abhor a punner. She would like of all things to see me a duchess, only she would have to wait a long time for that. The duke is strong and healthy.'

'In which case,' he said tight-lipped, 'if they should keep you from me, then, by God, I swear I'll take you off to Gretna Green, for I must and will have you. How do you suppose I have endured to see you spill your favours out to others while you withheld yourself from me?'

'Did you say Gretna Green?' She scrambled to her feet. 'William! Do you mean we will elope? I've always wanted to elope for the experience. How wonderful this is! Let us hire a coach and go now, this very minute.' She made for the door, then back again to him. 'You'll have to take me as I am, in these very clothes I'm wearing, with not even a toothbrush, lest my maid should suspect and go sneaking to Mama.'

'You won't need clothes,' said William chokingly.

'I am sure you're right.' Her eyes were dancing. 'I am at my loveliest with nothing on — as you will see.'

He clutched her to him. 'I cannot wait to see.'

'Oh, William,' between laughing and crying she whispered, 'my happiness is more than I can bear.'

His too, if denied him, was more than he could bear.

He walked to Melbourne House with his head in the sky, and wrote her a letter to have on record his formal declaration … *for that bitch, her mother,* thought he inexcusably, *and for all who run to read.*

But only one ran to read it. And how she read it over, slept with it against her heart, and brought it, crumpled with her kisses, not to her 'dearest and best Mama' but to her 'kind, dear Papa.'

Lord Bessborough, sunk in an armchair with a bottle beside him, was roused from a nap by Caro's tumultuous entrance. Sucking his wine-soured palate he turned a bleared eye on his daughter.

'Hey — what? An offer? From whom? Lamb? Which Lamb? Peniston? A mint o' money there when he inherits.'

'No, Papa, William. Who else but William? I hardly know Peniston. See, here is his letter. Where are your glasses? You can't read without your glasses. Let me read it for you.'

And she read:

'I have loved you for four years, loved you deeply, dearly, faithfully — so faithfully that my love has withstood my firm determination to conquer it ... has withstood all that absence, variety of objects, my own endeavours to seek and like others, or to occupy my mind with fixed attention to my profession —'

'Profession?' was his lordship's explosive interruption. 'What's his profession? A professional dilly-dally dilletante, hey? Don't bother me. Take this nonsense to your mother. She'll deal with it. All I know is that he hasn't a groat and looks like to have less because —' Lord Bessborough reached for the bottle at his elbow — 'shall I tell you for why? Because Melbourne has his doubts that he's his son. Hah! That whips you, does it?'

'Yes, it does!' She rounded on him, blazing. 'It's a wicked shameful libel. Who dares to spread such a report?'

'Nature, me darlin',' chuckled her father. 'If you take a good look at Egremont you'll see young William as his living spit.'

'It's a lie!' And, the demons of her rage released beyond control, she flew at his lordship to tear off his wig and expose a head as hairless as an egg.

'Here, ye little devil! What d'ye think that ye're about?' her father nervously expostulated, ducking to avoid renewed attack.

'I know what I'm about and I'll say what I'm about,' yelled Caroline, 'that were he the bastard of a blackamoor I'd marry him. I wouldn't care if he hadn't a farthing and I had to live in a sty. You've money enough for both of us, so why should *you* object? It's obvious,' she added meaningly, 'why Mama objects.'

Lord Bessborough blinked.

'Poor Papa!' And now her temper faded as swiftly as it flared, and she was in the giggles. 'You look so very bald. We can take it, then, as settled. He writes a manly letter, does he not? You should be proud to have him for a son-in-law. He will go far. He has great potentialities. Sheridan, Fox, Lord Holland, all,' she fabricated, 'are agreed that he should stand for Parliament. You should hear how they prophesy him as a rising star in politics, so please to tell Mama of my intention and show her his letter.' She threw it at him. 'Not that anything *you* say will move her one iota, but this *I'll* say, so mark me well: if you and she refuse consent I'll marry him without it. Here's your wig.'

And dropping a kiss on his baldness she dashed from the room.

Poor Caroline's Fate, wrote her mother to Lord Grenville Leveson-Gower shortly after this, *is probably deciding for ever.* She had *long foreseen and endeavoured to avoid just what has happened.* While admitting William's *thousand good qualities* — some of which in the past she had sampled — she *dislikes the connection extremely.* She dislikes *his manners, his principles, his creed, or rather no creed.* Above all does she dislike his mother. None the less, *his behaviour,* she says, *has been honourable and his letter beautiful…*

It seems that fate, more than 'probably deciding', had in fact decided to account for this sudden change of front. No longer could William be dismissed as an ineligible; his pecuniary prospects were assured.

By the unexpected death of his elder brother Peniston, he had now become Lord Melbourne's successor, and no matter that his father doubted his legitimacy, William — born in wedlock and accepted as his son — was entitled to the Melbourne peerage and its fortune. Meanwhile his position as such must be adjusted to meet his future state. Not that Lord Melbourne was eager to accord him the generous allowance allotted to his late indubitable heir; still, an income of two thousand pounds a year could not be regarded as inadequate. All was as it should be, Caroline in seventh heaven, and matters brought to the happiest conclusion in a box at Drury Lane.

William, invited to join them there by Lady Bessborough, sat, a silent spectator through the whole of the first act, on edge for the curtain to fall. No sooner was it down than he was up, to offer Caroline his verbal declaration. Lord Bessborough, warned by his wife what to expect, took himself off to the buffet, leaving her to sponsor proceedings.

They were brief. Unaware that Caro had shown his 'beautiful letter' to her parents, his proposal, addressed not to her but to her mother, was couched in a near repetition of those same stilted terms.

'For four years I have loved your daughter dearly, deeply, faithfully — so faithfully that my love for her withstood my determination to conquer it, but now I can no longer contain myself from opening my heart. Am I permitted a favourable answer?'

Glancing from the pale young lady to the blushful young gentleman, Lady Bessborough turned the light of her lovely countenance upon them and said with pensive grace, 'The decision rests with Caroline. I leave it all to her.'

What then occurred was duly reported to Lord Granville: *He followed me into the passage behind the D. Lane box, threw his arms round me and kissed me, saying, "The decision is in my favour, thank heaven!" No words can convey to you my confusion.* Doubtless caused by that exuberant embrace which happened to be witnessed by various men of her acquaintance. When the lady hastened to explain the cause of this singular behaviour on the part of Mr. Lamb, the news was in the clubs before the morning.

The succeeding weeks went joyously for Caroline.

'Now that Mama is reconciled to the marriage she accepts you,' Caro told him, 'as her "natural" son. I think she is delighted to have me off her hands. She will suffer no more tempers nor *sauvageries* from me. Do you know the name my cousins give me? "Little Savage". You, my soul, must set about to tame me — if you can. But 'tis not too late to withdraw, and if you *want* to withdraw I'll let you off.' She wrinkled her nose at him, her upper lip folded back in her impish grin. 'Why don't you marry my cousin Harriet? She'd make a far better wife than I could ever be.'

'There is no wife in all the world for me but you, while I live and though I die,' said William solemnly.

They did not know themselves ridiculous. They only knew themselves in love. She, the more demonstrative, may have wished him just a little less reserved, or less detached from her effervescent spontaneity. And although her family gave welcome, open-armed, to their prospective son-in-law, the Melbournes — and his mother in particular — doubted the wisdom of his choice.

Caroline, in Lady Melbourne's estimation, was an *enfant terrible,* whose total disregard for the conventions, her irrepressible eloquence and ungovernable temper required a firmer hand than William's to restrain it. Nor did she hesitate to impart her views on the forthcoming marriage to Lady Bessborough.

'I have never known the Thorn so thorny,' she confided to her sister. 'How will my poor child contend with such a woman? Yesterday she called on me, ostensibly to bring Caro her wedding gift, a diamond circlet for the hair. Much too ostentatious, more suitable for a play-actress than for a bride-to-be. And my dear, after several little *cuts,* what do you think she said?'

'I can't conceive,' murmured Georgiana, who also had chosen for Caro's wedding gift a diamond circlet and one perhaps even more ostentatious, as given to her by the Prince of Wales. She would have to give Caro the pearls she was keeping for Harriet — if she ever married, which was most unlikely — or perhaps the jewel-studded veil she had worn at her own wedding.

'She said,' Lady Bessborough induced a sob, 'that she hoped the daughter would turn out better than the mother and that William, like so many other husbands, would not be disillusioned.'

'All husbands and most wives are disillusioned,' cooed the duchess. 'But I think the Thorn's objection to the marriage is not so much that she disapproves of Caro as that she cannot bear to see her adored William head over heels in love with her — as once he was with you.'

Allowing a moment's pause for that little *cut* of her own to sink in, she sighingly continued, 'My poor Hart is quite beside himself at losing Caro. I do feel so very guilty in having encouraged him to hope for her.'

A hope too long deferred. Hartington's childhood infatuation for Caro had increased as he grew older, and now, although not yet sixteen, he had determined he would marry her as soon as he came of age. When her betrothal to William was announced he had rushed off to Cavendish Square and stormed into Caro's room, demanding, 'Is it true you are to marry William Lamb? You were promised to me. Everyone *knows* you were promised to me. I've loved you since I was … oh, Caro!'

Clutching at her hand, his cherub's face distorted, his hair on end, a hysterical torrent of words came pouring out. 'You can't — you can't! I forbid it! You are mine. We were made for each other, you and I. He can never understand you — you're so different from anyone else. He's so solid. So humourless, so dry! Think of all the fun we've had together — what fun we'll always have, all our lives, seeing the same jokes, loving the same things — dogs, horses — Caro, I love you — I love you even when you fight and scratch and bite. I love to see you in your tempers. D'you think he'll put up with your tempers? Caro, *don't* marry him — marry me!'

Flushed, tearful, incoherent, he was so painfully in earnest that her heart quickened to a vista of enchanting possibilities. They two — yes! Made for each other, loving the same things — all the fun they'd had together — she to guide him, he to follow, as he had always followed where she led. Then she saw his boy's face crumple, saw a golden sprout of hairs like a Lilliputian cornfield on his chin between a growth of adolescent pimples — he had not even yet begun to shave! — and she steeled herself to tell him with a lightness that belied the sudden catch in her throat, 'Darling Hart, I adore you and your tricoloured eyes. Did you know you have tricoloured eyes — hazel, green and blue? But you're too young to think of marriage. Besides, we're first cousins. We'd have idiot children.'

'You're more likely to have idiot children with him! Too young, am I? But not too young,' shrieked Hartington, 'to *kill*

myself. If you won't marry me I'll cut my throat, take poison
— kill him — or kill *you*, rather than he should have —'

He made a lunge at her; she backed behind a chair. He
kicked it over, seized a china ornament from the mantelpiece,
dashed it on the marble hearth where it splintered into
fragments, and was out of the room like a rocket.

Whether or not it was the shock of Hart's brainstorm, which
resulted in a doctor being called to pack him off to bed with a
soothing draught, or her own doubts and misgivings, released
by his criticism of her William — *solid, humourless, dry* — the
fact remained that her spirits sank to zero. She was moody,
melancholic, tormented by self-searchings.

Lying sleepless through the night after that scene with
Hartington, were they, she wondered, too much in love to see
beyond their mutual absorption in each other? Marriage was a
sacrament: *whom God hath joined together let no man...* But every
marriage, as she saw it, was put asunder. What if William
should tire of her, turn to fresh loves with all the petty
intrigues and hypocritical deceptions which seemed the natural
sequence of married life? That her uncle the duke had his
woman, Elizabeth Foster, living at Devonshire House, was
common knowledge — and her aunt accepted that serpent as
her friend to cover up her own affair with Fox. Yes, and how
once she had believed him to be the greatest man on earth!
Untidy, uncouth, and odiously fat, yet for all that a political
genius. And what of her own dear lovely sweet Mama? Her
liaison with Lord Granville had been going on for years, and
even when he was appointed Ambassador to Petersburg they
corresponded daily. And then there was Sheridan, always
drunk, whose amorous pursuit of her mother at dinners, balls,
the opera, had made her the talk of the town, and Papa shut
eyes to it, played high and drank deep and collected old prints.

No word of scandal had ever besmirched Papa, who adored her mother as did every man she met, and William not the least of them.

On all this did Caro brood, and was more than ever melancholic. Her mercurial dexterity of speech, her lightning wit, her laughter, were now so obviously forced when alone with William that he took alarm and her mother took advice.

So we hear how Lady Spencer, that dominant old dowager at Holywell, wrote to her daughter in answer to an urgent appeal:

As far as I can decipher your abominable scrawl you and Caroline will come to me ... Indeed I am most anxious to have you come for I am sadly afraid our dear child is in too great a hurry of spirits and I should strongly recommend her being as little as possible in Town in the interval... Roehampton, this place, and perhaps Brocket Hall, are all far preferable to London.

With which their 'dear child' entirely agreed. Anything to get away from Cavendish Square and the incessant invasion of milliners, mantua-makers, modistes in preparation of her trousseau; the continuous fittings, measurings, choosing of materials; the trying-on of caps and bonnets, of less interest to her than the selection of the scarlet-and-chocolate uniforms for her pages; all this may have induced that ambiguous 'hurry of spirits'. Then, at the last minute, Lady Bessborough decided she could not spare the time to accompany her to Holywell, but would come later to bring her back. Accordingly, attended by her mother's confidential maid, Mrs. Peterson, and with her spaniel, from which she refused to be parted, Caro set off in the family coach for St Albans.

On the lawn at Holywell House, in the shade of a cedar, an old lady sat in a high-backed chair. At her side stood a marble-topped table on which were placed a brass bell, a Bible, and Paley's *Principles of Moral and Political Philosophy*. On her knees reposed a volume of Blair's *Sermons*; on her nose a pair of spectacles; on her hair, lightly grey beneath its sprinkling of powder, a cap of Mechlin lace.

Her eyes, under dark level brows, when not lowered to her book, were continuously searching the distance where a screen of trees hid the long drive from the lodge to the front entrance; and, every now and then, between those brows, the smallest lines, as of impatience, came and went, leaving a forehead surprisingly unwrinkled. She wore a grey cashmere gown of a Quakerish severity fashioned in a style of fifty years before.

This was Henrietta, Dowager Countess of Spencer. Much given to good works, deeply religious, she possessed none of the beauty or charm of her daughters but a dry wholesome wit expressed in countless letters lamenting their propensity for high play and late hours, and imploring 'Harriet', as Henrietta was known in her home circle, to keep her heart *free from that life of dissipation* in which she seemed to have plunged; to *abandon vanity and folly* and dedicate herself to *the service of God* to whom she owed the *many advantages* of which she was possessed.

That these maternal exhortations had not the least effect in persuading Harriet to abandon vanity and folly and a life of dissipation, did not deter Lady Spencer's resolve to save her daughters from the Pit. She greatly disapproved of their interest both in politics and in leading members of the opposition party. She considered elections to be 'vile things', causing a lamentable waste of money, manners, temper, and begged them to fly to religion for support.

However, Caroline's engagement to William did appear to have satisfied her as to its propriety. *My head and heart are so full, my dear Harriet, that I can only say how fervently I hope your dear girl may be happy…* But she added a cautionary rider, *she must run some* risques.

Since Lady Spencer rigidly avoided London, Caro paid brief though frequent visits to Holywell and, despite the old lady's sharp tongue and keen eye that seemed to strip her naked to her soul, she had a deep if somewhat awed affection for her grandmother. Yet it was not without a certain trepidation — not having heard the dowager's views on her betrothal to William — that, after changing her travelling dress for a very transparent muslin, she presented herself to Lady Spencer on the lawn.

'You are late,' announced her grandmother, removing her spectacles to offer a cheek the colour of old parchment. 'I have been awaiting you these three hours. I expected your arrival at noon. Unpunctuality is a grievous fault. Life should be lived by method. Up with the sun, down with the moon. You look pale. Were you sick in the coach? You always travelled ill as a child.'

'No, Grandmama, I was not sick and I don't feel sick. Only thirsty.'

'You shall have refreshment.' The dowager waved her to a wicker chair. 'Tinkle the bell.'

Caro tinkled it and sat, hands demurely folded in her lap.

'I presume you have never read this?' Lady Spencer indicated the volume of Blair's *Sermons*.

'No, Grandmama, I confess I am more devoted to history. If you are thinking of a wedding present, dear ma'am, I would adore of all things Rollin's *Ancient History*, a most amusing and delightful book.'

'In twenty-four volumes!' The dowager looked down her nose, which was long and thin. 'You would require a wheeled bookcase to carry them about with you. As for delightful and amusing, I should have thought exactly the reverse. I had the whole set of them here, but I gave them to your Uncle Spencer for his library at Althorp. Ah, the tea.'

Two footmen approached bearing trays, followed by a page leading Caro's puppy, now almost fully grown. 'And what is this you have brought with you? A dog?' Had it been an elephant the lady's tone could have scarcely been more startled.

'Although an uninvited guest, I trust you will allow him to remain,' pleaded Caro. 'He is very sweet and good. He was given me by Godfrey Webster and I call him Edgar after Lady Holland's page because he looks so like him. The same mournful brown eyes. Both are orphans and very well bred. His mother died whelping and his father — well, I rather think his father ran off with another wife — I mean, *my* Edgar's father. But the other Edgar's father may have done the same.'

'More than likely,' caustically commented Lady Spencer, 'if associated with the Hollands. Does he mess? I won't have him messing on my carpets.'

'He is perfectly house-trained, Grandmama. The most loving and cleverest dog in the world. Die for me, darling.' At once Edgar rolled on his back, his four legs stiffly extended. 'Is he not clever?' cried Caro. 'I have taught him scores of tricks.'

'He should be trained as a gundog, not a circus dog. You will take tea?'

'Yes, Grandmama, if you please.'

'Tea for her ladyship. Lemon water for me.' The dowager waved aside a dish of cakes offered by a footman. 'Ratafias for you, my dear, and cream buns. These are made in your honour by the chef, with whom you are a favourite. A fork and napkin for her ladyship. Don't eat with your fingers, girl. You will have cream all over your gown. And what a gown! Nothing so indecent has been seen since Eve. Bless me, what's the matter with the dog?'

Edgar, sitting upright on his rump, uttered four sharp barks.

'He says, "I want my tea." He is a talking dog, Grandmama. See this?' Caro took a ratafia cake and threw it at Edgar to be neatly caught between his paws and swallowed. 'No! No more. Now say "thank you".' She was answered by two short barks.

'There are many starving children who would be grateful for as much,' remarked the countess, unimpressed. 'The dog is too fat and you are too thin. Another dish of bohea for Lady Caroline. You call it tea. In my day it was bohea, and a luxury at eighteen shillings the pound. Remove the dog —' this to the page — 'he is about to put up his leg on a rose bush.'

'If so, Grandmama, it is the first time he has put up his leg on any bush or anywhere. My precious one! What an event! I will mark it in my journal. *Today Edgar crossed the Rubicon between puppyhood and doghood and will never now look back.*'

'It is to be hoped he will not look back on my furniture if you bring him in the house. Take the animal away. I will not have him soiling the flower beds and lawns.'

And when Edgar was led off and the table cleared Lady Spencer, after gazing intently at Caro, dived her hand into a reticule suspended from the arm of her chair and drew from it a silver phial. 'Come here,' she commanded. Another dive produced a wad of cotton. Composing her face, Caroline rose from her chair, advanced, and was bidden, 'Kneel down. The grass is not damp but your gown is. A most dangerous mode to wet the muslins so that they immodestly define the figure, causing rheumatics, tertiary fever and phthisis. Kneel.'

Caro knelt.

'You have a fine skin, but it needs attention. You freckle easily and I perceive you scrub your face with soap. I have never used soap on my face in my life, and for near on seventy my complexion can vie with a girl's.' Pouring from the phial a pinkish milky liquid on to the wad of cotton wool, the dowager made several dabs at Caroline's forehead and nose. 'This prevents sunburn, freckles, blemishes and all vices of the skin. It is made from crushed strawberries. My own recipe. I will give you a bottle. Use it every night until your wedding night. Allow it to dry, and next morning wash with chervil water. You do not marry for a month, in which time your skin should be clear and smooth as a water lily. But always remember that the only intimacy you may *not* allow your husband is that of your toilet, although in my day it was the custom to receive gentlemen in our dressing rooms and dressing gowns, yet with circumspection, which is not practised now.' The lady replaced the phial, disposed of the wet cotton, and told her granddaughter, 'Sit there where I can see you, and tell me all your news.'

'There is not much, Grandmama, that you don't know already. Dun wrote to me yesterday —' she was referring to her brother, Viscount Duncannon — 'saying how happy he is that I am to marry William. He hopes you will approve and is certain you will love him when you know him. You do approve, do you not, Grandmama?'

'Of your William I know nothing more than that I much dislike his mother and her *ménage*. That his father is too fond of his wine and his women, which is almost universal among the men of today, and indeed of any day. However, I have gleaned from reliable sources that William Lamb is more soberly conducted than the average young man of his age who has nothing to do but wait until he steps into his father's boots. In this case I gather they will be comfortable and well-lined boots. I would have preferred an older peerage, an earldom, not a second viscounty as his will be, and of Ireland at that. 'Tis to be hoped he will not follow too closely his father's example of high play and low living. I hear he has in mind to stand for Parliament. If so, when he inherits, he, as an Irish peer, can remain in the Commons like his father before him, who, I understand, has never once opened his mouth.'

'William will open his mouth to swallow the House once he is in, Grandmama, as you will see. I prophesy that William will rise to greatest heights — Lord Chancellor of the Exchequer, or even prime minister, when the prince comes to the throne. He is much liked by the prince, and often at Carlton House.'

'I am sorry to hear it. So you have faith in his prowess. Keep it and encourage him to high endeavour. Marriage is a covenant in which man and wife are pledged to give each to the other the best of themselves. Your husband, to whom you cleave, must always have first claim on you. Read your Bible, child. Read the Psalms. Attend church regularly and learn to know that this life of ours is but a preparation for the day when we come to be judged. The sun is lowering. Go now to Peterson. Change your gown for supper and pray wear something less scanty. The vicar is joining us for prayers at eight o'clock.' The dowager rose. 'Hand me my stick, if you please. My legs are not so young as yours and need support after sitting. You may leave the books. The boy will fetch them. But take this and study it.'

She held out Blair's *Sermons,* which Caroline received with a murmured 'Thank you, ma'am,' and a mutinous underlip behind the lady's back. As she followed her grandmother into the house she was handed a letter from William.

I had intended, my dearest Car, not writing till I had heard of your reception at Holywell. I am much more anxious about it than I can express, and I listen for the postman's knock with cold hands and indescribable anxiety …

At Lady Stafford's last night the whole room successively wished us joy; the surprize is universal, as nobody had seen anything of it in the world, and that they look upon you I believe as only eight years old… But what words shall I use to express the Prince's rapture? For rapture it really was. He could do nothing but shake us all by the hands with a face rayonnant of delight and repeating: 'I am so happy, oh! but so very happy!'… I was not happy till I got home to your dear Mama with whom I talked of you till two o'clock.

Till two o'clock! The picture she conjured of those two whom she loved best in the world closeted together in close intimacy 'talking' — but surely not solely of her till two o'clock? — fretted her throughout the evening.

The vicar duly arrived to read prayers, with the whole household in the dining room, from butler to page on their knees, and Caroline on hers, deaf to the vicar's intoning, while she repeated in whispers her favourite psalm, the hundred and thirty-ninth: *'O Lord, thou hast searched me, and known me… Thou understandest my thoughts afar off… For there is not a word in my tongue but thou knowest it altogether…'* And kneeling there she prayed that she, and her thoughts, might be worthy for Him to know, which she doubted.

The service over, the staff dispersed and the vicar, with profuse apologies that he could not stay for supper, took his leave. Then for half an hour in the drawing room, Lady Spencer, between sips of camomile tea, questioned Caro on her trousseau and other equally feminine concerns.

'You must tell Mrs. Peterson to pack a medicine chest containing, among the necessary toilet requisites of which my strawberry lotion will be one, a jar of my especial unguent, most necessary for a bride's first — hem! — No, I myself will instruct Peterson. And now what of your undergarments? Your mama had a dozen of every article with my particular attention to woollen night-shifts for the winter and cambric for the summer. These were all made with long sleeves, but I was dismayed to see that both your mother and your Aunt Devonshire, when I visit them during their various indispositions, favour low-necked short-sleeved and immodestly semi-nude bedwear. Have you been measured for your wedding gown?'

'Yes, Grandmama. It is to be of white satin embroidered with sequins and pearls.'

Lady Spencer took several sips before echoing, 'Pearls. Imitation, I presume. Your father's high play at Brooks's will never run to oyster pearls. Any hint of gaudiness should be avoided. Your mama made a lovely bride in a simple satin with a daisy chain on the bodice embroidered in silver by myself. She had six layers of linen and organza petticoats and a hoop well padded. I cannot hope that you will wear even the flimsiest of petticoats, since from the present-day fashion it would appear you wear nothing under your gowns but your skin. Your mother was a beautiful woman. You do not much resemble her. You follow the Ponsonbys, but you lack your father's height, being small for your age and too pale and —'

'Plain?' prompted Caro meekly.

'Nothing of the sort,' energetically declared her grandmother. 'You have fine eyes, good colouring and *esprit,* yet you are too thin for my liking or your health. We must fatten you while you are here. Three pints of milk a day, fresh from the cow. It is to be hoped your mother will initiate you in your duties as a wife, which are more than to love, honour, and obey. You owe fidelity, loyalty and submission to your husband, for better or — for worse. I was *not* initiated, with result that I hid in a cupboard on my wedding night. I do not know which was the most to be pitied, your grandfather or I.'

Caro's lips parted on a quick intake of breath. 'I'm sure I will not hide in a cupboard.'

The dowager looked at her over her spectacles, set down her cup and rose. 'It is time you were in bed. Breakfast is served at eight o'clock. Prayers at seven-thirty.' A warm dry kiss was deposited on Caroline's forehead. 'Goodnight, my dear. Sleep very well. God bless you.'

For the first few days Caroline dutifully trailed after Lady Spencer in the gardens and to the cowsheds to watch the milking, in which the dowager took the keenest interest. Yet, for all Caro's delight in the country, time lagged and she longed for town and William, until, unexpectedly, he came; and with him, Duncannon. This was so delightful a surprise that she laughed and chatted excitedly all through dinner — which at Holywell was served at three o'clock — ate little, drank too much of the wine which replaced, for this occasion, Lady Spencer's special elderberry brew, and left the table in a state of near inebriation.

Later, while her grandmother took her afternoon nap, William and Duncannon joined her on the lawn where she sat with Edgar, and, still a trifle dizzy, she flung herself at each, embracing them in turn.

'Darlings! How wonderful to have you here. I have been inexpressibly bored and felt my lot to be that of the blameless vestal's, the world forgetting by the world forgot! Dun, you are handsomer than ever. Are you in love and in debt? For you know they are synonymous. Never one without the other — with exception of William, whose papa has paid up, howsoever grudgingly, for my betrothal ring and trinkets. Mama tells me you are courting Maria Fane — Ah! You blush, so you *are* in love — and that you intend to stand for Kilkenny, of which I know no more than its predilection for cats. So now you'll be in Ireland part of the year and we'll have two Parliament men in the family. But don't get in before William. Is that a new suit? No, Edgar, no! *Not* on the rose bush. You know your Grannie objects.'

'Still talking, Caro?' Duncannon tweaked her nose. 'You'll have to muzzle her, William.'

Said William, soberly, 'Her chatter charms me.'

And Caro thought, *Yes, now, but will it always? I must watch myself and pray. Are we to be happy? My love for him is a tearing pain. Love shouldn't hurt like this. There are too many aches in our love.*

And she said, 'Let's go for a ride. I haven't ridden since I've been here. There's the sweetest roan mare in the stables. I'm longing to mount her. I'll tell them to bring round the horses. Meet me at the front entrance.' She was for dashing off, but William stayed her.

'No dear, not today. Dun and I have rode from London, don't forget.'

'Oh! I did forget — how thoughtless I am.' She caught his hand to her lips. 'Forgive.'

Duncannon said, 'I'm game. I know that roan mare. I'll ride her. She's a mettlesome hussy. Too hot for you, my dear.'

'There's nothing of horse-flesh too hot for me. I'll ride her cross-saddle, only I haven't any breeks. I'll have to borrow the page's. Tomorrow, then, shall we? *Yes*, William, for I won't ride without you. Tomorrow, *please*, tomorrow.'

But there were no rides tomorrow, as William must be back in town and Duncannon with him, their visit being only for one night; and in those few hours Caro was not left an instant alone with him since Lady Spencer exclusively claimed his attention. However, for a few moments after breakfast before he and Duncannon left they did manage to meet in the rose garden, screened from the house by a hedge.

'Now, at last!' He had her in his arms. 'It has been torture to be kept from you. Your grandmama evidently considers it uncircumspect for an engaged couple to indulge in this — and this.'

His mouth closed on hers. She lay against his heart, soothed and comforted, all her doubts dissolved like a vapour in the sun. And as she drew away from him she said on a laughing whisper, 'You need have no fear that *I'll* hide in a cupboard...' And left him gazing after her in wonder.

THREE

The marriage of Caroline Ponsonby and William Lamb took place on the evening of June 3rd, 1805 in the drawing room of Cavendish Square, attended only by close friends and nearest relatives, with the exception of Hartington who was conspicuously absent.

The reports of the bride's demeanour during the ceremony present her in so violent a state of agitation that she flew at the officiating bishop, tore her wedding gown to rags, and was carried fainting from the room. When she was finally restored with burnt feathers and vinegar the service proceeded without further interruption.

This account of her behaviour, circulated for some unfathomable reason by herself, gained credence through the years, dramatically embellished from her own imagination. In point of fact no bishop but one Reverend James Preedy, Vicar of Winston, officiated, and Caro, suffering from nervous exhaustion due to a sleepless night crowded with those same uncertainties and fears that had racked her during the last few weeks, was in no fit state to fly at the bishop — had he been present — or at anybody else. We can take it that she was tearfully flustered and that her responses were almost inaudible, but there is no evidence of hysteria, no mention of a scene in her mother's letters to Lord Granville, who, had any such remarkable incident occurred, would have been the first to hear of it.

Lady Elizabeth Foster, writing to her son, refers to the bride only as *dreadfully nervous*, and to her bridegroom's manner as *beautiful, so tender and considerate.* And within an hour they were driving through the June dusk for their honeymoon at Brocket.

Whether she did or did not hide in a cupboard on her wedding night, William's tenderness and consideration must have been sorely tried; for despite scraps of knowledge gleaned from keyholes at Devonshire House or from Lady Spencer's attempt to initiate, she had been basically unprepared for her wifely obligations.

When dawn, like an attenuated ghost, crept through a chink in the curtains, she, still suffering from shock, bruised in mind and body, turned on her pillow to see her husband on his back, his mouth a little open and his jaw a little dropped, emitting slow long snores.

Laughter seized her, then she fell to crying, grabbed a handful of his hair and screamed in his ear. 'You're *snoring!* I'd never have married you had I known what you would do to me as well as that you *snore.* Stop it, I tell you — stop it!'

William, rudely awakened and striving to soothe, served only to bring on that fit of hysterics retailed by herself and performed not at the marriage service but in the marriage bed. He, having endured Tantalus pangs of passion fruits withdrawn at the first exquisite taste of them, sends an urgent message to Lady Bessborough begging her to come at once to Brocket, a singular plea on the part of a one-day-old bridegroom; but, as Lord Granville was duly informed, that visit had to be postponed since *Poor little Caro has been ill and would see no one, not even me…*

However, poor little Caro appeared to have sufficiently recovered within a week or two, for we find William writing to Lady Spencer that *although still nervous* Caro behaved to him *like an angel.*

It must have taken all his not inconsiderable pre-nuptial experience, after that first stormy night, to sustain his wife's angelic behaviour and lead her to responsive consummation, in which he seemed at last to have succeeded, for when her mother eventually arrived she records that they *flirted all day.*

Those were halcyon days for Caroline. There were no more hysterics. Under William's guidance she unfolded, was appeased. Together they would wander through the Hertfordshire lanes on those warm green afternoons, or lie in the long grass of a hidden glade to enjoy with sweet explorative caresses each facet of some fresh delight in the crowning of their love. Or, later, to return sedately to the gardens of the house, where he would read to her selections of the poets, preferably his own translations of the classics, while she sketched him, depicting a beautiful dark-haired Adonis with enormous staring eyes, arched brows, and the coy little mouth of a cupid's bow.

'You must have gipsy blood in you,' she said. 'You are so very dark. Lift your chin. No, don't turn your head. I want to catch your nonchalant, half-scornful smile that tilts up to your nose. You have the loveliest nose. Stop reading a moment. Part your lips. Your teeth are white as whitest coral, but I can't draw teeth. I'm not a dentist. Now you can go on reading. I haven't listened to a word. Don't read, my darling. Let's talk about us.'

They talked of little else with the delicious foolishness of lovers through time immemorial. Their future plans were nebulous. She would have and she *must* have a country house — 'miles and miles from London, because, my own dear, I cannot abide to live in London with its noise and its chatter and its whirl and its gossip, its spite and its malice and snatching of husbands and wives from each other. Are there any faithful husbands or honest wives in London? Are there, William? You should know.'

'How should I know?' A hot dusky flush mounted to his cheekbones at that mischievous insinuation. Would she never let sleeping love lie? Must she for ever be jibing him for that which, when she was yet a child, had been his first youthful passion — for her mother?

'Of course,' she quizzed him impishly, 'you wouldn't know. You're as innocent as I was once, until you made me the equal in knowledge of any matron in the land — or, come to that, of any courtesan, from whom, despite your prudishness, you must have learned all the tricks you teach me of love-play. And how I hated it at first — and how I love it now! Don't look so shocked. You should have been a parson — though you do make love divinely, which, had you been a parson, you never would have dared to do. But you need not fear, my Lamb, that I shall slip my traces so long as you ride me on a martingale... Oh, this dreadful drawing! I've given you a squint.'

She tore the page from her sketchbook and crumpled it into a ball to throw at him. He caught it deftly, smoothed it out, and gave it his earnest attention. 'It has its points,' he admitted, 'but you can do better than this.'

'No, not even Gainsborough could do better than this in justice to you, my handsome. I wish you were not *quite* so handsome, a constant menace to women. Ah, me, I wonder...'

Sighing, she let fall the sketchbook. Elbows on knees, chin cupped in her hands, her eyes, gazing distantly, clouded. He, always swift to sense her every quicksilver change of mood, asked, 'What is it now, my darling?'

'I was thinking... I'm just a little bit afraid of what will come of our living at Melbourne House.' For that was the arrangement until they could make a home together.

A bumblebee buzzed past William's head. He watched it dart and poise above a clover flower, there to cling with eager hairy legs while it probed for honey. He said, abstractedly, 'We shall have our own apartments.'

'Yes, but it won't be quite the same. Your mother doesn't like me, and she doesn't like Mama; nor does Mama like her. I want everyone to like me — no, to love me! I have so much love to give.'

'And I claim the whole of it.' He stretched a hand to her who sat just too far for him to touch her fair bent head where a slight breeze played with the gold-tipped curls. 'I'll be banker for your love,' he said, 'and pay you highest interest.'

She jumped to her feet. 'William! Yes! How rich we'll be on — say, ten hundred thousand pounds of love. And what will that amount to in each year? I can't do sums. I can't add two and two.'

'I can.' He drew her to his knees, looking down into her eyes. 'We two are one — for ever.'

'If only,' she whispered, 'our few weeks here could be one timeless day.'

But all too soon for them was their return to Melbourne House.

Their rooms on the first floor of the family mansion in Whitehall became the centre of the younger brightest set in town. There, night after night, they entertained or attended dinners, balls and routs. They were radiantly happy. To the envy of many and wonder of all, Caroline had become an efficient and charming hostess, and seemingly, a perfect wife: submissive, adoring, and withal so adored by her husband. And he, tolerant or disregardful of intermittent tantrums and attacks upon his person — it was said he carried the marks of tooth and claw upon his hands — was as much in love with her as ever. Women were envious, men covetous. None but did not wish himself possessed of this unaccountable, exquisite creature who, still more child than woman, could dazzle the eye with her fairy-like grace, her wit and her whimsical humour. There was no knowing what Caro Lamb, went the talk of her, would say or do next to shock or make an impression.

One stupefying incident created a furore, revived with juicy chuckles through the years when those who witnessed it were in their dotage.

It was during a dinner at Devonshire House that an enormous silver dish was carried to the table, and the cover lifted to disclose Lady Caroline impersonating Eve: a vision so startling, enchanting, breathtaking as to cause the ladies palpitations and the men to dream that night as no sane man should dream and keep his reason.

As for William, when he got her to himself, he delivered her a lecture to bring about a thunderclap.

'So! You emulate the antics of a slave-girl at the worst excesses of a Roman banquet.'

She pealed with laughter. 'Was Eve a slave-girl, or — come to that — a Roman? Your chronology, my poor Lamb, is post-dated.'

He did not laugh. 'You have shamed me and disgraced yourself. What possessed you to behave like a whore or a lunatic?'

'The spirit moved me,' she retorted, 'to uncover, not my nakedness, but yours — your prudery worn as the hair shirt of the hypocrite. I stripped you bare to wake the prig in you, at war with your desire for and your delight in me. You know that you and all the men, if not the women, enjoyed my little act.'

Said he icily, 'I see you know yourself for what you are. One who in her supreme egotism and self-adoration is an exhibitionist.' Nor did he know that he had coined a word used long after his time by those who sought to delve beneath the superficialities of mortal consciousness.

She, struggling with the fastenings at the back of her sheer muslin gown, shot him an impudent grin. 'I exhibited nothing of me that was private to you. I lay snug in the dish as a suckling pig — face downwards, admittedly rather a squash — and my rump was veiled in gauze, ready to be whisked off at the flourish of the carving knife. Oh, hell! I need eyes at the back of my head to unlace this thing. Unfasten me, please.'

He stood erect and glowering. 'I am not your maid. Ring for her.'

'I've sent her to bed. I can't keep her waiting up night after night, poor soul.' And, suddenly crimson, she flared in a fury, 'I'm sick, sick, *sick* to the stomach of your parsonic sanctimonious long face. Can you not understand that 'tis my breath of life to create a sensation and watch the effect on persons whom the unusual intoxicates as does a rare matured wine? I can heartily appreciate the worst excesses, as you call them, of the Roman orgies and their lovely sensuous slaves. I have the deepest admiration for the Romans. Their culture was far ahead of ours. They knew how to live unashamed, and joyously, and yet could produce some of the greatest thinkers and philosophers of all time. There's no shame in what I did, the shame lies in alcoved lusts, the favoured food of fashion — and that's alliteration, a worse sin than any little nonsense I performed tonight.'

A muscle tensed his jaw as he answered stiffly, 'The shame lies in your total disregard for the proprieties.'

'Be damned to the proprieties!' And after that the deluge, when she flew at him to hammer at his chest with her small fists. He caught her hands and gripped them in a vice while she aimed a kick at his shins, screaming, 'Let me go! Let go — you beast, you *beast*!' And, as ever when she lost control, the lisp was more pronounced. 'You and your pro-prietieth —' Another kick; and she wriggled free to stand before him, seething. 'You knew what I was when you married me. You've often said I'm an elemental. So I am. I am! I can't alter my nature. Well, you know what you can do. Throw me out. Send me back to Mama, which will delight your thorny mother who loathes the sight of me. I'll forswear our marriage bed and take me to a nunnery. And now — *will* you unfasten my dress?'

His mouth twitched. He restrained an unconscionable urge to take her by the throat and strangle her or tumble her, or both. She had turned her head over her shoulder; in her eyes were two sparks of mischief. She was so much the little girl that his heart plunged, and before he knew what he was about he had lifted her and carried her to their waiting couch…

'If all our quarrels should end this way,' she sighed in the aftermath of love's recuperation, 'so let us quarrel every day and night.'

It came about that this too often was to be. More frequent were their disagreements, their reconciliations less ecstatic. Yet she enthusiastically followed his political interests. When Pitt, England's premier, died, she saw tears in William's eyes despite his Foxite Whiggism. 'He died as he lived,' he said, 'with no thought for himself, only for the soul of Britain. His last words were, "My country! How I leave my country!"'

He left her doomed to another ten years of war, with that hashed-up coalition ministry dubbed 'All the Talents', too short-lived; for within twelve months they had lost their fighting leader, Fox, and with him went the hope of the Whigs. The Tory government had come to stay for near upon a quarter of a century.

But a greater loss for Caroline than her childhood's hero, Fox, was the death of her Aunt Georgiana. The duchess, who had been ailing for some time, was stricken with a fatal disease. None knew the serious nature of her malady, which had baffled the doctors, while, only a week before the end, Lady Spencer had written to Lady Bessborough concluding that her illness was *due to the old hopeless story of money difficulties.* The passion for high play of the duchess and her sister landed them incessantly in debt, and the harassed dowager was too often called upon to help her daughters, who dared not approach their husbands with their difficulties.

William, having heard from Lady Bessborough of Georgiana's latest 'hopeless story', told Caro how her grandmother had sent the duchess a draft of one hundred pounds, twenty of which she had been saving for the journey to visit her daughter's sick-bed.

'Poor Grandmama! How she bleeds herself for them. Why can't my aunt ask the duke for the money — or is he similarly pressed, spending all his spare cash on Elizabeth Foster, that snake who lies coiled round Devonshire House?'

'The duke has vast estates to maintain. He cannot be expected to pay his wife's gambling debts.' William glanced across at Caroline, who was seated at her escritoire nibbling a quill. Scrawled sheets of paper were scattered on the floor; the desk was littered. 'What are you writing?'

'A poem, or rather a letter in verse, to Hartington. Shall I read it to you?'

'Not now,' said William hastily. 'I think it would be a gracious gesture on your part to call upon your aunt. I hear from your mother that the doctors consider her condition to be serious.'

'No!' Caro flung down her pen and started up. 'I thought — we all thought it was just another of her vapours caused by the worry of her debts. Is it true? What has she?'

'Some internal trouble. She has been intermittently unwell these several months, as you should have known were you not so absorbed in yourself.'

Wincing at that thrust, she blurted, 'How should I have known? None of us, not even the doctors, has taken her ailments seriously. What a heartless wretch I am — and all of us! We thought of her so gay and lovely, never really ill. Even Grandmama didn't think so. What does Mama say of her condition? Have you seen her?'

'I have not seen your mother for these last few days, but I do strongly urge you to go to your aunt. I will order the carriage.'

'Won't you come with me?'

'If you wish, but I would rather not. I must get on with my work.'

He was busy with his translation of Ovid, but his chief interest lay in politics. For now, as the eldest son of his father, it was a foregone conclusion that he must enter Parliament. Already accepted by commanding politicians as their coming man, it only remained for him to find a seat. Meanwhile he marked time with the classics.

Caro went muffled in furs, for the March winds had beaten up the clouds in a sky heavy laden, threatening snow. The carriage drove briskly through the almost empty streets; in this part of London none stirred out of doors if the weather did not invite ladies to drive, or the bloods of St James's to stroll, shop-gazing. They preferred the warmth of their clubs, their wine and their gaming.

A mail coach rattled by from Charing Cross. Caro, who had never travelled in a public coach, was thrilled by the four spanking horses fresh from their stables speeding to the north, for this was the coach to Scotland. The coachman — fur-caped, rubicund, stout — lashed his whip at urchins running at the wheels in the hope of pennies flung from outside passengers, wrapped to the chins in rugs.

I must go to Scotland in a public coach, thought Caro, and wished that William had carried her off to Gretna Green regardless of consent that would only permit a conventional stay-at-home marriage. Not yet a year wedded and the gilt, she reflected, was wearing off the gingerbread, which, dare one say it, had a trifle staled? Then she shook herself. *You don't deserve to have the most wonderful husband in the world. Who but he would put up with you, who scratch and bite and kick, screeching like a banshee if you don't have your way? He's a male Griselda, but I'm not sure if his patience isn't as trying as hers must have been...*

And then she fell to brooding. Should she have married Hart, who laughed at and encouraged her frenzies? William didn't laugh at them. He would look anxious and pained and endeavour to soothe as if she were his imbecile child. Perhaps she was what Peterson would call 'not right'. Maybe the penalty of her outstanding gifts. No question, she complacently considered, but that she was gifted. Fox had always said so, according to Aunt Georgie. Some day she would turn her gifts to good account. Write a novel, or publish her poems... Pray God her Aunt Devonshire was not gravely ill.

She wished she had religion and could earnestly believe in prayer. Of course she prayed and said 'Our Father' night and morning, and read her Bible for the lovely psalms, but did she heed or understand the message of the Gospels? She knew there was a great Almighty Spirit who made Himself a man to die for us that we be saved from sin, but … were we saved? There surely was no greater sinner than herself, so utterly contained in her own petty small desires. She wished she had been born a Roman Catholic, the earliest and only living church as founded by Our Lord almost two thousand years ago and then reformed — or should one say deformed?

Yet we here in England, she said to herself, *persecute and ostracise the Catholics whose faith is followed by more than half the world, and proclaim an insane king as Supreme Head of the Church. There is only one head of the church, and he is God's Bishop, the pope. But this is heresy, and if you dared to utter it when Elizabeth was queen you'd have been hanged, drawn and quartered,* sans merci. *You'd have made a lovely martyr to end up as a saint. Saint Caroline. Don't be silly… Here we are.*

The carriage drove in at the gates of Devonshire House. Hardly waiting for the footman to help her out, she was down and up the steps in a trice. The door swung open. Of the butler who had known her all her life she asked breathlessly, 'The duchess — can she see me?'

'I will enquire, my lady.'

'No, don't. I'll go to her unannounced, unless — Find out if she is sleeping. I would not waken her.'

After an interval of impatience while she moved restlessly about the hall that seemed to be unnaturally silent, with no sign or sound of Hart or any of her cousins, she was informed that Her Grace would receive her.

It was some weeks since Caro had seen her aunt, and she was shocked to see her changed, almost unrecognisable, wasted to a shadow of her former self. Her lovely skin held a greyish tinge; her copper-gold hair hung dank and lifeless about her face, whose contours had sharpened; her mouth had fallen in; her lips were colourless. A maid who sat by the window rose as Caro entered, and whispered, 'Her Grace is drowsy, my lady. She has been in great pain. The doctor has given her a draught to ease her. Lady Bessborough has been with her all the morning, and will be returning shortly.'

From the rose-curtained bed came a faint voice. 'Who is here?'

'It is I, dear Aunt. Your Caro.' Throwing off her furs, she dropped on her knees beside her. What awful sudden thing had come to strike to swiftly at this joyous dazzling creature? Fear clutched at her heart. She reached for the pale bloodless hand, bereft of jewels, lying on the coverlet. How pitifully thin and cold to the touch.

Georgiana's eyelids quivered; lifted. In the blue sunken depths of those once brilliant eyes lurked a mute question as of a smitten child shrinking from some unknown terror.

With lips drawn back against her teeth she uttered feebly, 'Sweet of you to come. I am ill … very. There's some … pain. In … indigestion. We eat too much. You have come to live here with me, darling? I love … I love to have you here. So many children … so noisy. Have you seen Fox? We won the election … True Blue … and all of you. We sang it at the … party.' The lids drooped, sank.

'My lady,' the maid plucked at Caro's sleeve, 'Her Grace wanders in her mind. It is the drugs.'

Caro choked back her tears. She could not speak, could only chafe that pale wasted hand in both of hers, while her heart froze with a fearful dread, and a frantic prayer, unspoken: *She mustn't die. God, don't let her die!*

She died three days later.

'And with her,' sobbed Caroline in William's arms, 'the light has left Devonshire House.'

Lady Bessborough was inconsolable. She would see no one but Fox, who, himself in bitter grief, strove to comfort her. Caro, also barred from visiting her mother, heard from Mrs. Peterson how the Prince of Wales insisted on paying a visit of condolence to the stricken lady at Roehampton, forced his way into her room and talked so much and drank so much that he left her in worse case than before.

While the death of Georgiana had been a bitter blow to Caroline, she was too engrossed with her own affairs to mourn for more than a month. Life for her had become a fanfare of trumpets blowing, flags flying, a glorification of Caroline Lamb as the centre of a universe where the light of William's star was eclipsed in the blinding incandescence of her own.

The first excitement of his entry into Parliament as member for Leominster had waned; and while she and her fantods at first amused William, repetitive scenes and hysterics tended to pall. It was not all married bliss in the mansion of the Melbournes. Lady Melbourne's undisguised disapproval of her daughter-in-law was shared by the younger Lambs, who were not disposed to applaud her in those melodramatic farcical scenes she joyed to perform as leading lady. To William's brothers and his sister Emily, she was that 'horrid little beast'; to Lord Melbourne, an 'attractive young baggage who might well be bedworthy if she were dumb'; and to Lady Melbourne an unruly spoilt child totally unfitted to be her adored William's wife.

Faced with hostility on all sides, she was the more determined to shock and outrage those who condemned her. Appealing to William when 'Tried past endurance, environed, as I am, by hate,' she told him, 'For heaven's sake, then, let us go and make a home together. You surely don't intend us to live here for the rest of our lives, dominated by that porcupine, your mother, whose thorns are now prickles to poison our love. Why not take a house in your constituency? There are charming houses in Leominster — or why not your home county, Hertfordshire? I'd be quite content with a cottage, an acre and a cow, alone with you. William, be warned. Can you not see, can you not *feel* what is happening to us? Your mother with her lectures and your sister with her sneers — how dare they intrigue together, tearing me to pieces, watching, recording everything I do or say, that you may be notified and come to realise the hideous mistake you have made in taking to wife such an abomination as that awful Caro Ponsonby. How can you bear to see me tortured by your hateful family? I won't — I *can't* live here —' She broke into a storm of tears, flung herself on to a couch convulsively beating the cushions with her fists. 'I won't. I won't! It's killing me!'

'My dear girl,' he remonstrated, 'pray control yourself. It is out of the question that I should live in my constituency, or even in Hertfordshire. It is important that I live in London. How could I travel daily back and forth to Westminster from the depths of the country?'

'Parliament doesn't sit all the year round, and you don't have to sit all day and every day. You can come and stay with your doting mama when there's an important debate. What about members who come hundreds of miles to sit — like a lot of hens, and with as much cackle!' Then, seeing him stiffen, his lips tucked into so thin a line that he seemed to have no mouth, she flared again. 'Very well, if you prefer your odious family to me I'll take a house in the country by myself — a hovel, a barn, or a pigsty — anything sooner than submit to continuous criticism and active dislike from one and all of you... Take your hands off me!' when he attempted to placate. 'I know what I want and what I'll do whether you will — or you won't!'

His reply to that, with judicial weight of words, was, 'The chief reason against marriage is: however congenial two partners may be, they seldom act as one. By taking a wife, a man runs the risk of contracting what may prove to be an insuperable obstacle to his own opinions and ideals.'

'Ideals?' She wheeled round, crimsoning. 'You, the cynical materialist, to talk of ideals? How little you understand either me or yourself. Let us face it, then. If, as you say, we never act as one and I am the insuperable obstacle to your opinions, your idealism and your life's work and happiness, we must part. It is obvious that we are as fire and water. We cannot blend. The one burns, the other quenches the flame — to find what? Dust and ashes. So, my dearest dear, accept the fact that we hate each other. You are a Lamb, I the wolf in Lamb's clothing. Here's a mixture of metaphors! Fire and water, dust and ashes, wolves and lambs and what not. William, my love, my soul —' She sprang to her feet, holding out her hands to him. Her eyes, tear-filled, were dark as drenched velvet in the pallor of her face. 'Don't let us be like this together. We love each other madly, so why should we be cursed?'

'Cursed?' His eyebrows went up; his smile was a trifle crooked. 'How you delight to exaggerate.'

'Or star-crossed, if you more poetically prefer it. We ought never to have married. I was ready, you remember, to live with you and be your love, your clerk, your page, your... Ah!' A little shudder seized her, and a dizziness; she swayed. 'I am faint,' she breathed, and fell forwards into his arms.

Alarmed, he held her, gazing down at closed eyes, her whitening lips. Lifting her he returned her to the couch, fumbling beneath her corsage for her heart. Was this another of her acts? Was she ill, or … what?

And, as if in answer, her eyelids fluttered open. A sigh escaped her. She laid a finger to his forehead, saying, 'Let me smooth away these two harsh lines between your brows, my handsome. And don't glower at me like a Gorgon. This is not the first time I've "come over", as Mrs. Peterson would say; and gives a reason for it which until this month I doubted. But now I do believe, and can be almost certain that for all we hate each other I take back what I've said. We are not cursed. We're blessed, I hope, or will be … come next August.'

During the summer months the pen of Lady Spencer, was scratching away to her 'dear Harriet' concerning her two great-grandchildren; the one a girl born to Maria, wife of Lord Duncannon, the other a boy to Caroline, on August 29th, 1807.

Not ineptly was he named Augustus, less for his birth month than for his godfather, George Augustus, Prince of Wales, who offered himself to Lady Bessborough as sponsor.

While Caro lay in long protracted labour, William, in a frenzy, paced the hall, watched by his wife's pages laying wagers in pennies on the odds for a boy or a girl. There were four of them lined up in readiness to be despatched to the clubs of St James's with the news, all exactly dressed alike in the brown-and-scarlet liveries designed — and worn, upon occasion — by their mistress.

Lady Bessborough, in no less frenetic state than the anxious young husband, strove to distract her daughter, who bore her travail with surprising fortitude: no hysterics and scarcely a moan. 'Her courage,' sobbed Lady Bessborough over ratafias and sherry wine with William, 'sets example to us all.'

'One might believe,' thus Mrs. Peterson to a certain stout and starched indispensable party, 'that her ladyship was the first female of us all in like condition the way them two do carry on. I was with my lady when she brought forth the heir and each one after him, and Lady Caroline, the sweetest cherub out of heaven ever seen. Could you do with another drop o' porter to wash down the rabbit, Mrs. Stukey?'

And when Mrs. Stukey had done with the other drop of porter, in a Toby jug, to wash down liberal Welsh rarebit — to which she did full justice, as evinced by grateful belchings — she was moved to remark, ''Tis to be hoped that *this*, when it comes, which should be before mornin', will bring about 'appier conditions between the little darlin's pa and ma. I've heard tell her antics is somethink rampageous, of which he rightly disapproves. Only fancy attendin' a dinner mother-naked in a pie dish!

'Not mother-naked, so to speak, Mrs. Stukey,' corrected Mrs. Peterson with frigid loyalty, 'for I draped her myself in a gauze scarf wore over a pair of flesh-pink tights.'

'Which she must have shed, Mrs. Peterson, for one of my ladies — no names, don't ask me — of which I delivered with these two 'ands of mine prematurely — *saw* her as nature provided her parts and no hiding of them neither. And if I tell you, which you may not know if you wasn't at Brocket Hall last month, which I was not ten miles off for Lady — no names, dear, I beg — a still-born but nine already — that 'er ladyship was seen tearin' bareback in a pair o' breeks round the paddock at the 'all on a yearling, and she in her eighth month and askin' for a miss — and 'ow she got herself into them breeks, which must have been a giant's so big as she is — and dreamin', as she tells me last night, of a two-headed foal — pardon me, Mrs. Peterson, the rabbit *will* repeat — and I think I'll have me forty winks before I go to her again, so don't let me keep you, Mrs. Peterson. You look as you could fancy forty winks yourself. You'll know where to find me if I'm wanted.'

But whatever forty winks she may have fancied, Mrs. Peterson did not achieve them, for Lady Bessborough, who had never left Caroline for more than ten minutes during these long hours of her labour, was called away on a summons from Sheridan's wife. Fearing, from the urgent message, that 'Sherry' was dying, she drove to his house, leaving Mrs. Peterson in charge during her absence. She returned an hour later in greatest perturbation.

Mrs. Peterson met her at the door of Caro's room. 'Her ladyship is easier, my lady. The doctor's been and says it won't be before the morning. My lady, you look sadly put about.'

'I am, Peterson, I am. Poor Mr. Sheridan. It has been too terrible. Is her ladyship awake?'

From the bedroom came a fretful call. 'Peterson! Don't buzz out there. Is that you, Mama? Is Sherry dead?'

'No, darling. Drunk.' Lady Bessborough bustled in and, seating herself in her chair by the bedside, she told of the scene in Sheridan's rooms. 'He begged his stupid little wife to send for me, and she, thinking him *in extremis* at the point of death, did so. That's why I had to leave you, but I left you sleeping as I thought.'

'And was he at the point of death?'

'I have seldom seen him,' reflected her mother, 'so disgustingly raddled. He fell at my feet, clutching my knees, blubbering, beating his breast, tearing his hair and vowing that I am his one and only love. I was never more embarrassed, and his wife, poor soul, looked like to kill me. Only with the utmost difficulty did I make my escape after locking him in his room. And now, of course, his poor wife will always believe I am his mistress.'

'And aren't you?' regrettably enquired Caroline, turning on her side. 'Oh, dear! Don't make me laugh. It hurts.'

'My angel! I should have left you to your sleep.'

'I wasn't asleep. I saw you go. I was in a doze from the pill the doctor gave me. The pain comes in bouts and wakes me up. How beautiful you look, Mama. Such a lovely colour! There's no greater beautifier to a woman than to know she is loved, even by a lover who is drunk, and as this lover of yours is also a genius —'

'Hardly that, would you say?' her ladyship deprecatingly submitted, with a deepening of the lovely colour.

'I do say. As a dramatist, politician, *bon viveur sans pareil* I would emphatically proclaim him brushed with that magic which is the very essence of genius. I have a touch of it myself, and that, I think, is why I am so unconformable and odd, or maybe I'm a changeling. You didn't see, by any chance, a little green man with squirrel's eyes standing by your bed when I was born?'

'Dear heart!' Lady Bessborough laid a hand on Caro's forehead, smoothing back the dampened tendrils of hair. 'You are hot. You're sweating. Are you in pain?'

'Not now. I don't think this babe will ever come. God send *it* is not a changeling. I've no preference as to its sex. Dun has a girl and wanted a boy. I wouldn't care if mine were twins and one of each. By the size of me, it — or they — probably is, or are.' Her eyelids trembled. She closed them. The long lashes lay on the flushed cheeks like gilded crescent moons. 'I think I will sleep now, Mama, and so will you. Go to your bed, dearest.

That fat midwife, so very like a bolster, will relieve Peterson, but she won't be wanted yet. Goodnight ... or is it morning?'

Morning it was, and a few hours later all the clubs had it that 'Caro Lamb has been brought to bed of a remarkably large boy for so small a woman.'

At peace and tranquil, in a state of beatific wonder at this glory that had come to her out of unspeakable torture, she lapsed into lyrical verse over the squalling atom, hideous, greedy, crumpled, red, who pulled and sucked and gurgled at her breast while to her, its willing slave, as to all mothers of all time, it was beautiful as an infant Apollo whose:

> *...little eyes like William's shine*
> *How great then is my joy,*
> *For while I call this darling mine,*
> *I see 'tis William's boy.*

The christening in October was a tremendous affair that caused as much stir as if this scion of the Melbournes had been the son and not the godson of George Augustus, Prince of Wales. Invitations to the celebration party held at Melbourne House were handed in by footmen at the doors of the elect as though they were royal summonses. It may be that Lady Bessborough was not a little overwhelmed by the prince's offer, and that Lady Melbourne, equally gratified, spared no expense in entertainment of choice guests invited to meet His Royal Highness.

Only one of the Bessborough-Melbourne entourage did not receive an invitation, a deliberate slight that ricocheted. For, when the gala evening came, there drove into the portals of that mansion in Whitehall, brilliantly illuminated with fairy lights and flambeaux, a hackney coach from which its occupant, a trifle unsteadily, descended.

In the cream-and-gold salon the two grandmothers stood to receive: the one, razed of her thorns for the occasion, beaming with smiles, magnificent in purple; the other in dove grey, pensively sweet, her hair lightly powdered; and both in a blaze of jewels. The baby's mother, in purest white as for a bridal, bepearled, becurled, bewitching, fluttered here, there, everywhere, with a word, a quip, a laugh, a kiss bestowed in careless whimsy to flatter or confuse the recipient according to acquaintanceship or not.

Suddenly the doors of the salon were flung wide; guests, poised for the bob or the bow, expectantly hovered, when Sheridan, in full fig of fondant-pink swallow-tails, frilled shirt and white breeches, announced His Royal Highness's arrival, and himself as the prince's gentleman-in-waiting. Then, nose to knees, his body arched, he homaged profusely the royal godfather.

Uncommonly fat, artificially pale but none the less imposing, the prince, with his imperishable charm, acknowledged the curtsies of ecstatic women in high-waisted pastel-hued gowns; of men bending double to greet him; of his two hostesses billowing in waves of purple shot with silver, of satin grey reflecting iridescence from a hundred crystal lustres; and of the radiant nymph-like Caroline, who was raised, clasped, fervently embraced to the envy of all other aspirants to favour.

'How disgraceful of Sherry to crash in on us like that. I didn't invite him. Did you?' nervously enquired Lady Bessborough.

To which Lady Melbourne, holding her smile, but showing a thorn, made ambiguous reply to the effect that moths would be drawn to candles willy-nilly until the wick, in nature's time, burns down.

The acid response that tipped the tongue of Lady Bessborough was halted by the query of the prince, who, abandoning Caroline, demanded of these ladies with a languishing look and his still irresistible smile, 'Is it two bountiful beautiful Ceres I see here — or one? And this is strange on the part of my sight, which never plays me false before I've supped.'

That hint, unmistakable, disguised in royal badinage, was met with appropriate trills of laughter and an immediate signal to the assemblage. The prince, with a hostess on each arm, was conducted to the dining room; and when food and drink had circulated and been imbibed to repletion, royalty — and his self-appointed gentleman — departed with less pomp than vinous circumstance. Then hired musicians, two fiddlers, a cello, a harpist and a flute, were called on to play a cotillion until, when tired of prancing in overheated rooms, perspiring couples dispersed.

The evening was over; but the baby so auspiciously heralded into a world of every possible advantage that beauty, wealth and fame could bestow on him, slept undisturbed through the racket below.

Kneeling by his cot, his mother adored with a prayer of thanksgiving in her heart, that held, for all her happiness, a furtive fear. Was his head not a trifle too large for his body? His divine little head, its baldness now covered with a gold-tinted fluff, which, in the agony of parturition had torn her asunder? Yet would she not have endured a thousand times more pain for the heaven-sent joy of bearing him?

FOUR

During the first few months of his life the infant Augustus was Caro's sole engrossment. But when the novelty of this latest role as mother, performed with every tender nuance calculated to enthral an audience of avuncular Lambs and grandparental Melbournes, ceased to draw a full house, she began to seek other diversions. Nor can we entirely blame her for that.

William, now immersed in politics, had less time to spare for her or his son while he floundered in a sea of indecisions. Although officially attached to his defeated party, his critical mind surveyed a vista of advantages that might be gained from either factor, Whig or Tory. Accepted by the former as an asset, his somewhat ponderous speeches, despite welcome flashes of humour, had not so far struck any resonant note. He was liked, watched, approved by both parties for his modesty and reticence from the firework displays which other up-and-coming young members were wont to let off from the Opposition benches in true Foxite tradition. Yet, lost of their leader, their voices lacked the Jovian thunder that had awed the House and quelled the temerarious. Wooed by eminent Tories, William might have been won and coerced into the enemy's camp, but that he misdoubted, not only the advisability of changing horses midstream, but the effect upon his wife of such apostasy.

She, reared in the brilliant effulgence of Devonshire House, regarded the Tories as traitors to the Crown, the Constitution and herself; for that which Caro Lamb believed — were it political, tactical, strategical, or right or wrong — was and must be irrefutable.

William, cautiously avoiding politics, would air his views on moral, social or religious fallacies; or, wilfully to goad her for the doubtful amusement of inducing a scene, would tell of his earlier amorous adventures. These did not always achieve the desired effect unless well disguised in a mantle of scorn.

'If the retailing of your activities both in and out of bed with harlots — or the more exclusive wantons of our circle — before or after marriage, is intended to arouse me to jealousy, I hate to disappoint you, my sweet William. Your unsavoury exploits neither disgust nor dismay me. I am not squeamish and might be tempted to follow your example. As you kno I have never indulged in such *passe-temps* as those you so graphically describe, but there are many of your friends and mine who, were I to invite them, would enjoy to engage with me.'

Although this speech was delivered in tones that mocked his own rather pompous inflection, he should have been warned of the challenge implied. He was not. Her greatest charm for him lay in her childlike innocence, which, despite her *gamine* unconventionalities and temperamental tangles, she somehow managed to retain. It should, therefore, have come as a shock to shatter him when Lady Melbourne brought to William that, notwithstanding his belief in his wife's Lucretian chastity, Caro was encouraging the attentions of Sir Godfrey Webster, the son of Lady Holland by her first husband.

'And as everybody knows, my dear boy, except yourself who has never an ear for scandal, Webster is a rake-hell from whom no woman's reputation is safe. I could name at least three young girls, all virgins of the highest *ton,* who have been forced to retire to the country as a result of his — ah — attentions.'

William received this intelligence with vexatious equanimity. 'My dearest Mama, your interest, always centred in my happiness and welfare, is inclined at times to mislead you. Caro has known Godfrey all her life.'

'Does that condone her acceptance from him of a bracelet and a dog?'

'He gave her the dog before we were married. As for the bracelet,' said William, carefully sharpening the point of a quill with his pen-knife, 'I see no harm in her acceptance of it since they are almost like brother and sister.'

'In the sense, no doubt, of sister to a Pharaoh,' retorted Lady Melbourne; at which William glanced at her sideways with a look which brought a clutch to her heart and the thought that so might Egremont have looked in words unspoken.

But what he said was, 'Pray, Mama, excuse me if I continue these annotations for my speech *contra* Catholic emancipation, which comes up for debate again.'

Ignoring the hint, his mother returned to the rally. 'If you are so wilfully blind to your wife's conduct — or should I say misconduct? — you might at least consider me and the name you bear. Or has your infatuation for this impossible young woman died its natural death to account for your complete disregard for her consistently outrageous misbehaviour? The only excuse I can find for it is to assume she is out of her mind.'

His answer to that refuted any hope Lady Melbourne may have nurtured concerning the doom of his marriage. 'My love for Caro transcends infatuation. Whatever she is, whatever she does, is for me *sans peur et sans reproche*.'

'Caesar's wife, in very truth! My poor, poor boy!' The lady's vast bosom expanded to endanger the seams of her bodice. 'Your ostrich-headed obstinacy — or is it pride that cannot admit of a fall? — will bring about the wreckage of your life unless you come to your senses and see that wretched girl for what she is.' With which oracular pronouncement his mother retired, leaving him to his interrupted work.

Yet neither Lady Melbourne's poisoned darts, nor the frequent arguments that almost daily now resulted in a row between himself and Caroline, when he too would lose control and rage at her as she at him, could shake his faith in her fidelity. He loved her as he ever would, for all she was, and — the more, perhaps — for all that she was not.

The talk that buzzed about the name of Caro Lamb to couple it with that of Godfrey Webster was a delectable titbit for the gossips to seize, devour and regurgitate, fanning the flame of Lady Melbourne's resentment against 'this impossible young woman'. Had she thought that, by incessant bombardment, she would succeed in bringing William's errant wife to heel with full admission of her guilt, she was mistaken. Caro, though apparently subdued by admonitory lectures, threats, rebukes, had no intention of renouncing that which, contrary to rumour, was no more than a trivial flirtation.

That William accepted it as such and, as his mother told him, 'with inexcusable indifference', heaped fuel on the fire of the lady's indignation. For William's chief concern at the stir occasioned by Caro's latest impropriety was not on account of her alleged adulterous affair with young Webster, but that she should associate with one who had no more to recommend him than good looks, a good heart and good seat in the saddle.

Coarse-grained, coarse-mouthed and oafish, he was more at his ease in a brothel than a boudoir; yet Caro, always eager for any new experience, found the slow-witted Godfrey's admiration refreshing; his clumsy avowals amusing. And it may be that she turned to him as an anodyne, a consolation for the disappointment in 1809 of the birth of a daughter who lived but one day.

They were seen constantly together at dinners, balls, the opera, while William sat late in the House returning home to sup alone. The gossips were enchanted, Lady Melbourne fulminating, and Caro's mama, who endeavoured to make her see reason, served only to make her see red.

'If you can believe these calumnies with which the Thorn delights to prick me, then, Mama, I'm lost indeed. How can you listen to that woman's lies and spiteful innuendoes? You know that Godfrey has always loved me to distraction — or as much as it is possible for him to love anything more than his horses and hounds — but that doesn't mean I reciprocate his adoration or would forswear my marriage vows for him. My heart bleeds for poor Godfrey,' Caro declared with a heavenward roll of her eyes. 'The son of a woman divorced who has never cared for nor given him a mother's love, no wonder he fell into bad company. I set myself to save him and I think I have succeeded. He drinks less, and if he's to be believed, he no longer frequents certain houses of ill-repute favoured by the bloods. In fact he now leads, thanks to me, so exemplary a life that I'm hoping he'll take holy orders. A hunting parson is always an asset to a parish — and in any case, Mama, you of all women have no right to upbraid me on account of these unwarranted suspicions. I'll say no more because we know — do we not? — *why* I must say no more.'

This artless appeal, offered with the least suggestion of a smirk, aroused in Lady Bessborough an urge to lay hands on her daughter. Restraining herself, she uttered in a tremble, 'You have said too much.'

'I, who have said so little? What a wretch I am, and what a bitch is *she,* although the epithet is entirely inapposite since the female of the canine species is a noble creature. I often wonder why we use the word as a term of opprobrium when applied to the female of the human race. However, I digress. I was about to say that she, that old witch, that old besom — old in years to me though not to you, Mama, nor to the very young men who always seem to adore elderly women, as witness the prince, who, though, young no longer, has succumbed to grandmotherly charms — I was about to say — how I do run on, to be sure! — that my mother-in-law would give every hair of her head to wreck my marriage but she won't — she won't — she *won't!*' Hysteria soared with each crescendo, to bring down the curtain on a dramatic finale. 'I'll drag her through the courts! I'll let the world know how she has maligned me, she who is the queen of petty intrigue from Prinney to a certain noble peer who shall be nameless, unless Papa goes blurting it forth as he did to me when William came a-courting. So! Let her do her damnedest, she, who'd whip me at the cart's tail for a harlot or see me hanged as yet she may — she may! For she *incites* me,' shrieked Caro, 'to murder!'

With which she hurled herself on to a couch to give her usual performance of beating the cushions with her fists, and with more than customary violence, as if they were the face of Lady Melbourne. Her mother hastily retreated, meeting William in the corridor as she went out.

'Go to Caro,' she bade him in agitated whispers, 'she's in one of her fits. I entreat you to take her to Brocket, and for mercy's sake persuade your mother not to harry the poor child with her wicked accusations. We all know she delights to disdain the proprieties, but that Lady Melbourne should bruit abroad such libellous indictments against her is more than she — or I — can bear!'

More too than William could bear when the lady fell to sobbing on his shoulder; and with Caro in her 'fits' that could be heard throughout the house; and a to-ing and a fro-ing of a maid with sal volatile and feathers to be burned, and a page with a bottle of brandy, and another running with a letter in his hand.

Relinquishing his tearful burden, William led her to a seat, snatched the note from the page, opened it, read it, tore it across and returned it to its envelope saying, 'Take this to your mistress with my compliments.'

'William, how rash of you!' panted Lady Bessborough, 'She will bring the roof upon our heads.'

'So be it. We'll be buried together in the debris,' was all William had to say to that.

'These scenes,' moaned the poor lady, 'will be the death of me.'

'But think how tedious our lives would be without them.'

'She behaves like one possessed, and you encourage her. She has been very much worse since her marriage.'

'She stages these scenes for my diversion,' smiled William. 'She is a creature of infinite variety.'

'I would prefer less variety and more enduring peace,' Lady Bessborough replied, covering her ears at a shriek from Caro's room. Rising, she swept down the stairs, calling over her shoulder to William, 'I hold you responsible for this latest *crise*. You and your mother between you have conjoined to break her heart — and mine!'

'So you see, my dear Godfrey, all must be ended between us.'

'There's been nothing between us to end,' returned the stoutish, pink young gentleman, precariously seated on a flimsy chair that creaked beneath his weight.

'I wrote you a note this morning which was intercepted by my husband, although it is not he who objects to our friendship. He knows me and loves me too well to misjudge my interest in you, but the world is always ready to condemn the innocent who suffer for the guilty.'

'Umm,' mumbled Sir Godfrey, sucking the tortoiseshell handle of his cane. ''Tisn't my fault,' he suspended attention to the tortoiseshell to say, 'that we *ain't* guilty. You know what I want and what I've always wanted. How's the dog? Come 'ere, you!' He snapped fingers at Edgar, who had risen from the hearthrug, leisurely advancing to inspect Sir Godfrey's boots. 'That's a fine dog, that is. Is he good with guns?'

'He is not gun-trained. You gave him to me as a pet, you remember, and my precious pet he has been — until yesterday.'

'What 'appened yesterday?'

'I thought he'd run mad. He growled and showed his teeth at Augustus, whom he adores and of whom he has never been jealous, and then he began to foam at the mouth.'

'Who?' Godfrey's eyes goggled. 'Augustus?'

'No, my poor idiot, Edgar — as if he had the rabies, and I felt it to be a judgement on me for having shown an interest in you that by the ugly-minded could have been misconstrued.'

Shaking his head Godfrey pondered. 'I can't see how you make that out. He don't look as if he's got the rabies.'

'Of course he doesn't, because he hasn't. I only thought he had.'

'I expect he was hot,' suggested Godfrey brightly. 'They often dribble when they're hot. You should see my bull-bitch. Brings up froth like whipped cream when she's hot. She's in season now or I'd ha' brought her with me. It'd never do, would it — or would it? — to cross a bull-bitch with a spaniel. She's out o' Rosa by Crib. Best blood in Britain. Might serve this feller of yours to her and see what comes of it. Start a new breed. What?'

'Quite so,' Caro rose from her seat, 'but Edgar shows no interest in the women of his kind. And now, if you'll excuse me, I must ask you to go.'

'To go?'

'I said go. I am dining, for my sins, down below.'

'Down below?'

'I perceive this duologue tends to the rhymed couplet at which I am adept, but for your better comprehension I dine with the Melbournes, and that's as near to hell as I hope I'll ever be. Adieu. Farewell. Goodbye.'

'Well, I must say —'

'Don't say. Silence is golden — or in your case, my dear *fratello,* pinchbeck.'

She gave him her hand. Very red, he bent over it, blurting, 'I *will* say! I love you, Caro, and you know it. You can kick me down and kick me out, I'll love you here and hereafter just the same. Always have and always will, although you tear out me guts. I used to fight Hart for you when we was codlins. How's Hart, by the way? Is it true the duke's goin' to marry Bess Foster?'

'Heaven forbid! Who told you that?'

'Heard it at Boodle's. It's all over town. Well —' he straightened up — 'I'd best be off. It's clear you don't want me, but you know where I am if you do. And if you're in any sort of trouble, which you're bound to be all your life long, you've only to call and I'll come. I'll be waiting.'

He turned from her, took his cane and his hat, and went, yet not before she had seen a moisture trickle from under his eyelid. Poor Godfrey!

Sentimentally she sighed, then, of a sudden, made a dash for the bell-rope. To the footman who came in answer, she said, 'Tell my maid to pack bags and baggage for a week. We leave in the morning for Holywell.'

It was a spur-of-the-moment decision. William, late from a session, found her asleep and stood in his nightshirt shading a candle, looking down at her where she lay; so young, so small, curled there in their great bed, the merest child with those cropped yellow curls! Then, seeing her lashes wet on her cheeks, he drew in a breath and slid to his knees; his lips touched her forehead. Her eyes opened for an instant. Dazedly she smiled, then slept again.

Snuffing the candle he got into bed carefully, lest he should wake her, and lay staring into the dark. Although to his mother he had loyally upheld her innocence, he was not altogether convinced that her flirtation with Webster had stayed within the bounds of those ethical proprieties he demanded of his wife and, by frequent insistence, had been the cause of their many tempestuous scenes. He recalled how, too often, he had delighted to tease her by recounting his own extra-nuptial affairs for the satisfaction of feeding his pride in the knowledge that she loved him enough to be jealous, for all her protestations to the contrary. Yet now, in these few years of their marriage, his political life allowed no time for feminine entanglements even were he so inclined. But that she had risked damage to her good name and his by her latest indiscretion with 'that damned asinine lout of a Webster' — so to his inner man did he apostrophise him — shook his self-esteem more than it shook his faith in her.

After a night of irritable wakefulness he overslept to find it full morning, his bed bereft of Caro, his valet with his breakfast and a scrawled note from his wife.

I think lately, my dear William, we have been very troublesome to each other; which I take wholesale to my own account and mean to correct. Condemn me not to silence and assist my imperfect memory.

That touched him; how often he told her to guard not only her tongue, which was too long, but her memory, which was too short. She could not even remember to date her letters, which she would invariably head: *Heaven knows what day…* With a twitch of his lips he read on.

I will on the other hand be silent of a morning, entertaining after dinner, docile, fearless as a heroine in the last volume of her troubles, and strong as a mountain tiger.

She begged him to come to her at Holywell and left him with *that pretty little Augustus of yours for your comfort.*

The man was made of steel who could resist her when she chose to be tenderly contrite, but … docile? He doubted. Fearless? He conceded, and all of the tiger, or tigress, who could never be tamed. However, it required every effort of his will not to call for his horse and go pounding after her to Holywell. That, though, was impossible in view of the agitation in the Commons concentrated on British military efforts in the Peninsular War.

Discouragement was great. A certain hot-headed young general, Sir Arthur Wellesley, who had led the first British force of nine thousand men to the Peninsula to throw the French out of Portugal, had been supplanted by veteran officers coming from England with an army of thirty thousand under Sir Thomas Moore. His daring advance had saved Cadiz and Lisbon to threaten Napoleon's flank in Spain, but a cannonball killed him at Corunna, and the return home of Moore's forces, who had failed to hold Lisbon, gave the faint-hearted to fear that Napoleon would not only be unconquered but unconquerable.

Unlike the majority of Whigs, who clamoured to abandon the Spanish campaign, William supported Tory military aggression. Wellesley, again in command, had brought off with flying colours his victory at Talavera, to get him a peerage and be acclaimed the nation's darling as Lord Wellington.

But no matter that the British army had now got a fighting leader, well matched to grapple with that little Corsican, ruler of all Europe, the plight of the war-scourged working class had become increasingly acute. The gilded youth of England, Whig and Tory, were united in one effort to alleviate the sufferings of the starving underdog.

So, with all this disturbance on the political front, William shirked further disturbance at home. Although tempted, he was wise enough to let his Caro go; she would not stay in the rarefied atmosphere of Holywell for long. She'd be home, he guessed, inside a month.

She was.

Lady Spencer, busy in her garden filling a basket with September's bloom of roses, heard the approach of wheels in the drive.

'Go, see who it is,' she told the page, who was almost entirely extinguished by the Michaelmas daisies his lady had cut and given him to carry. 'Lay the daisies there,' she pointed to a rustic bench in a thatched arbour at the end of the rose walk, 'and wipe your nose ... no, not on your sleeve. Haven't you a handkerchief? Then use it. Mercy, child! Not that dirty rag. Come here.'

From her reticule Lady Spencer took a pad of cotton wool, vigorously applied it to the page's button nose and bade him, 'Blow.'

He blew.

'Take it and throw it in the dustbin, then come and tell me who has arrived. Make haste.'

Making as much haste as his short legs would allow, the page ran off and returned in five minutes with the breathless announcement: ''Tis — the Lady — Caroline, m'lady.'

'Bless my soul! And not a room has been slept in for a month. Take this.' She handed him the basket. 'Ah, there is Miss Trimmer. Go you and wash your face. You look like the sweep's boy... Trimmer, if you please, have a warming-pan put in the blue room for Lady Caroline. One cannot rely on these housemaids. I delight to have my granddaughter here but I wish she would advise me of her coming. Has she brought her woman with her?'

'No, Lady Spencer, only Edgar, I...'

'Edgar?'

'The dog, ma'am.'

'Oh, the dog.' Diving a hand in her reticule, her ladyship produced a bunch of keys. 'You know the key of the linen chest? The forget-me-not-embroidered sheets for Lady Caroline, and find an old blanket for the dog. She, deplorably, allows it to sleep on her bed.'

Adjusting her spectacles, Lady Spencer peered through them at the pale countenance of her *dame de compagnie,* a recent acquisition to the household staff at Holywell, and one time governess to the children of Devonshire House.

'You have a most unsightly pimple on your chin, Miss Trimmer, and with a white head to it,' was the result of her ladyship's survey. 'Do not attempt to squeeze.' Another dive into the reticule brought forth a pot of ointment. 'Apply this night and morning to the spot. It is infallible. I fear your blood, my dear Trimmer, is poor. You shall drink a pint of porter *per diem*. I insist.'

'Lady Spencer, you are so, *so* kind, I don't know how to thank…' Miss Trimmer's voice dwindled; she rarely finished a sentence, or if she did she would repeat it, as it were, in paraphrase.

A hipless, breastless, narrow little person was Miss Selina Trimmer, with timid hare's eyes, a small mouth and a large nose which, it would seem, had assimilated all the 'poor blood' in her body, or at least in her face. Long association with unruly pupils had induced in Miss Trimmer an air of perpetual apology as if for her own insignificant existence; for, as Caro not ineptly described her, she was:

Like a fair fruit that has not been tasted,
Its sap and bloom and all its flavour wasted,
Droops our Selina on her virgin tree
Unloved, unloving any living he.

And at dinner that same afternoon: 'I trust, I do sincerely trust,' Lady Spencer dipped a peeled walnut into a glass of cowslip wine, 'that you and William have not fallen out again.'

'No, Grandmama, we have fallen in again.'

'I do not follow you. I may be obtuse. Drink up your porter, Miss Trimmer. Don't sip it. *Drink* it.'

'Yes, Lady Spencer, I do. I find it very… Porter is a most stimulating beverage. A strength-giving tonic. I am more grateful than I can…'

Caro said, 'It will fatten you, Selina, that's why the common people call it stout. Emma Hamilton has put on a dozen stone in weight, all due to porter.'

'A pity you do not take to it,' pronounced her grandmother, 'but Lady Hamilton lost most of her fat when she went into mourning for Nelson. By "fallen in again", as you concisely put it — you young people are so terse — what, may I ask, do you suggest?'

'I suggest, dear ma'am, that marriage is a steeplechase run by two riders. They may, with any luck, clear the first, the second and the third of their hurdles but they often come a cropper at the brook. It is then for the one who flounders up the bank, mud-besmirched, to hold out a helping hand to his, or her, mate before he, or she, is sucked under.'

'Hmm.' Lady Spencer shot a penetrating glance at Caro, who was picking at a bunch of grapes. 'There is no fear, I hope, that you will be "sucked under". I much dislike your metaphors.'

'But not inappropriate, I think.'

'*Too* appropriate.' A lace-edged napkin was delicately offered to Lady Spencer's lips. 'As for this mud which besmirches a name that was once most dear to me —'

Caro glanced down at Edgar to slide him a marshmallow from the silver dish beside her. 'Do you allude to me and to my name, dear ma'am?' she supplemented to the lady's pause.

'No. For once, and for your chagrin, I do not allude to you or to your name. I would not feed your dog sweets if you value his digestion. I allude to my son-in-law, the duke. Even to my seclusion here has come the buzz of his intended marriage to the woman who for years betrayed the trust of her dearest friend, your aunt and my beloved daughter. Trimmer, I beg you, look up and count ten.'

Miss Trimmer, whose poor old nose was turning puce in the sudden fit of choking that had seized her, managed to gasp through her paroxysms, 'I — I — one-two — ow-ow — Crumb. Wrong way. Three — ouch!'

'Too great a shock for her to hear of the duke's intention,' whispered Lady Spencer in a hissing aside. 'She adored your aunt, as who did not? A glass of water for Miss Trimmer. What does your mother think of it?'

'I haven't asked her. None of us has mentioned it, not even Hart, but I understand it is in all the clubs. Poor Selina, let me pat you.'

'Ouch — ow — your ladyship is too — I — I — ow — I would not — ouch — put you to any —'

Caro, who had risen to administer several thumps to Selina's narrow shoulders, said across the flustered lady's head, 'I must write to Hart and hear what *he* thinks of it. She's a wily one, that serpent. As for my uncle, may I die if I ever speak to him again. Better now, Selina?'

'Better — bett — much recovered. Thank you,' to the butler. 'Thank you, Lady Caroline. Dear me, how embarrass … such a thing to happen. Never before do I remember…'

'Then, if you will excuse me, Grandmama, I will write at once to Hart so as not to miss the post.'

'Very well. The vicar is coming for prayers and to supper. And must I forever implore you to wear something more substantial in my house, whatever you wear in your own, than this film of sheerest gauze?'

'I promise you, *chère grande dame,* that I will appear before the vicar in black bombazine, six flannel petticoats and a heavy woollen shawl which, so soon as my letter is written, I'll drive to St Albans and buy.' On her grandmother's forehead she planted a kiss, remarking, 'How prettily your hair grows here.' She smiled at the wilting Selina and, with a grin for the white-haired butler at the door, was gone.

'Always,' observed Lady Spencer, 'when Caroline leaves the room it is as if the candles were guttered to their wicks. You may snuff them,' to the footman; for winter or summer, day or night, there were candles on the table at Holywell.

'*Such* a ray of sunshine,' sighed Miss Trimmer. 'So bright and ... as a child, too, so clever. She outwitted all her cousins. Never at a loss for...'

'Coffee on the terrace,' Lady Spencer said.

From Lady Caroline Lamb to Lord Hartington:
With a cross heart, a bad pen, red ink & no time I write these few lines my little kind cousin. I have read the Rights of Woman, am become a convert, think dissipation great folly, & shall remain the whole year discreetly & quietly in the country...

Which she may have intended when she dashed off this letter, one of several written to Hartington from Holywell; then she follows it up with one dated incorrectly, in view of Hartington's reply dated the same day:

Oct. 11th 1809
I lament that you think it such an annoyance to write to your first & best friend ... The last letter I wrote to you my good gd mama chose to send & observed there were rather strong expressions in it. It was all about what I now find is declared and however little right I have to censure that old witches (sic) conduct, I shall never hear her called by the dear name she has assumed without regret & disgust ... I detest such petty artifices as Bess employs. If she will be wicked let her be so in the face of day, but

when I think of the deceit, plot, iniquity & wiles this serpent has made use of, I shudder at the thought: & you have begg'd her pardon & advised her to take this step. Oh hypocritical Hart, fret & storm behind, & fawn on that wily woman when before her … moreover I am as cross as patch at the triumph of hypocrisy & the petty intrigues I see everywhere carried on. I am sure the Melbournes knew of this long ago & I am sure also my good cous. that you told old Bess you would not disapprove of it. Oh she is a deep one! she has flummeried up a certain young Marquis from his cradle … This mistress of yr papa's knows how to throw her chains about you…

God bless you dear vain angry cousin. You once loved me as I always shall you, write or not write…

From Lord Hartington to Lady Caroline Lamb:
Oct. 11th 1809

I do not mind your accusations because I am sure you do not mean what you say about what I feel for you, which you must know is always and everywhere the same, and if you knew the happiness I felt at the prospect of seeing you at Chatsworth, and the rage I shall feel if you won't come you would not have thought so ill of my silence … The thing in your letter that shocks, provokes and makes my blood boil, is this incredible marriage, and your letter is the first that has told me of it.

My Gmother's representations I thought were exaggerated by her fears, and hardly till I see it can I believe that the woman could have the assurance to take that name always so sacred to us … Do, dearest Car, tell me that you did not mean any of the bitter things you said … and write directly for until I hear from you again I shall not have peace by day or rest by night. And now forgive me, & beg my pardon, dearest of wild young women, I will write to you every day in the year for the future if you wish it. God bless you, dearest.

Marriage was in the air, for no sooner had the storm occasioned by the duke's secret wedding to that 'serpent' subsided, than the family was embroiled in the news of the engagement of Harriet Cavendish to Lord Granville Leveson-Gower. How Lady Bessborough received the shock of this is not recorded, but one may believe she accepted it with unruffled outward calm and inward ebullition.

Neither she nor Caroline were at the wedding ceremony, from which it seems that both were deliberately excluded. Caro took it, so she wrote to Hart, as a personal affront; but she had more to trouble her than the marriage of her cousin to her mother's lover, or her uncle, the duke, to his mistress. Her adored Augustus had been taken ill, not gravely, though her vivid imagination exaggerated as a hopeless fatality the feverish chill that flew to his chest. Day and night she sat by his cot, eating little, hardly sleeping, watching, praying, fearing, not so much for his present condition as for that of his future. It was as if, in making a mountain of a childish molehill, she sought escape from the ever-haunting spectre of a truth she dared not face. This lovely 'William's boy' of hers — unless a miracle could save him — had something wrong with him. In his fourth year he could scarcely speak more than three words; yet he was beautiful and sturdy, physically strong, although all his movements were lethargic. No light shone from his eyes, dark-clouded as if a curtain had been drawn across his mind. He seldom cried, and, unhappily, he seldom laughed. His mother showered toys on him, coaxing him to play, but he soon tired and would fall asleep, showing little interest in the games she would devise for him. He slept too much, more than other children of his age; and sometimes, in her agony, she would pray that from such unnatural heavy sleep he would not wake.

This was her tragedy, a thing she would never to herself acknowledge, let alone discuss with William, who may also have suffered, as did she, each hiding from the other a bitter grief and disappointment that must go unshared. For, according to the doctors whom both, in confidence, consulted, he might well grow out of it. The king's own physician offered hope. He had known many such cases when delayed development in nonage had developed after puberty. There was no reason to believe the boy abnormal…

Yet it was there, the horror of it, a canker rooted in her heart, and always the recurrent question: Was it she from whom he had inherited this blight of what she dared not believe could be incipient insanity? Or was he, as the doctors unconvincingly assured her, merely behind for his age? A healthy sign, they said. Better far he should develop late, as often was the case in a too-advanced intelligence, than suffer complete derangement in manhood, as witness His Majesty the King, who had shown such promise as a youth, and now, alas…!

Small comfort this, since all the world knew that the king, after several relapses, was now pronounced incurably insane.

'Will he die?' she asked Dr Warren, in attendance on Augustus.

'Die? I wish I had as good a chance of making old bones as he. You go to bed now, Lady Caroline. You must rest. Your boy is in no danger. The bronchial tubes are clear, the cough subsiding.'

She was eventually persuaded to be taken from their sleeping child, who lay flushed with health, not fever; and to Hart she poured forth a thanksgiving.

Friend of my heart accept this letter,
The child thank God is rather better
But spight of Doctors drugs & pill
has been most wonderfully ill
'Tis true he did not wheeze or Hoop
But yet we thought he had the Croupe
His breathing was so short & thick
We were oblig'd to make him sick...
So that I may in safety say,
The inflamations giving way...

*It grieves me not to see you but I have scarcely been out of the boy's room
& am so full of nursery jokes I hardly know how to write sense...*

What than summer sun is brighter
What than feathery down is lighter
What more burning is and chilling
What more beautiful if willing
What so turbulent if crost
What so seldom found if lost
As what tyrant power we prove,
Call it what we will, 'tis — love.

PART TWO (1812-1814)

Man's a strange animal and makes strange use
Of his own nature and the various arts,
And likes particularly to produce
Some new experiment to show his parts.
This is the age of oddities let loose,
Where different talents find different marts...

Byron, *Don Juan*

FIVE

In a room in his castle at Windsor, his eyes bound by walls of darkness, dwelled an old man, blind and deaf. At his window he would sit, grateful for the warmth of the sun he could not see, ears strained for sounds he could not hear. That lost confused identity that once had been a king would trouble him no more. It was sunk in a world of mysterious dimensions.

His son, who for more than twenty years had stood by as understudy to his father's leading part, had now been called upon to play it in an age of magnificence unparalleled. An age of wealth and power, of social and ideological phenomena, of industrial revolt; of an implacable enemy at grips with the flower of English manhood in that struggle to the death on land and sea; an age of victory triumphant to reverberate for centuries to come while England lived.

But that higher stratum of society, ruled by the regent who represented an era unique in splendour and essentially his own, was the lesser half of a kingdom divided. They whose nights were spent in gaming rooms, or beneath the dazzle of candelabra when they whirled to the waltz, the latest craze of fashion, knew nothing of — or, if they did, cared less for — the inhabitants of those nether regions where men whose daily bread depended on the labour of their hands were deprived of their livelihood and of life itself, with the coming in their midst of the Machine.

In the industrial centres and in particular at Nottingham, the installation of the new-fangled stocking frames which enabled one man to do the work of ten, had resulted in widespread riots. Mobs of starving weavers and knitters who, for generations, had followed the trade of their fathers in their cottages, were joined in unanimous revolt to seize and break these infernal instruments that they believed to be of the devil's own contrivance to bring ruin on them and their homes. Men and women, driven to desperation by the cries of their famished children, battered down the doors of mills and factories, setting fire to the frames to light the sky with clouds of molten copper.

Beyond the oaks of Sherwood Forest, Newstead Abbey, on the outskirts of Nottingham, reflected in its windows that same fiery glare. From his library the owner of the abbey saw a crescent moon turn crimson.

'Are the gates of hell flung open?' he enquired of one Robert Dallas, a kinsman whom he had invited for a week or two to run through the proofs of a poem he had written. Solemn, sober-faced, something of a novelist was Dallas.

'It must be the frame-breakers again,' said he. 'The dragoons have been called out, I hear, to quell them. They won't. They will fight to their last axe and hatchet, to the last drop of blood. I'm minded to spill mine with theirs and all strength to them.'

'I trust,' was the reply, 'you will do nothing of the sort.'

'Are you afraid I'll burn before my time? Or if I do not join them bodily I will be with them in spirit. Do chuck aside those damned proofs, they are very badly printed and I'm very badly paid. I think Barabbas must have been a publisher. I will read you something of more interest than my pilgrimage — of grace, or should I say disgrace? See that?' He waved a hand towards the window.

The night is now a blaze, the moon a sun…
Their breath is agitation, and their life

A storm whereon they ride, to sink at last,
And yet so nursed and bigoted to strife,
That should their days, surviving perils past,
Melt to calm twilight, they feel overcast
With sorrow and supineness, and so die
Even as a flame unfed, which runs to waste
With its own flickering, or a sword laid by,
Which eats into itself and rusts ingloriously.

'You'll not find that in those proofs for it is not written yet — save in my head. So, Dallas, listen. I will read you my speech.' He turned to search in a bureau drawer and pulled out a sheaf of papers, thumbing them through. 'Um-um-um — where are we? I'll not give you the whole of it, only that which will harpoon my fish-faced brethren. Have you not observed how like to fishes are the faces of some noblemen? They'll be more fish-faced than ever when I tell of the monstrous doings here in Nottingham and round about. I will tell them how men with blackened smoke-grimed faces run hunger-mad battering the doors of those pot-bellied overseers, their masters, who send the cavalry to mow them down with their women and skeletal children. I'll tell them — God! Dallas, how you stare. You, too, are like a fish who has come out of its natural element, the water. Have we survived the Flood to be submerged again? Not dust unto dust but slime unto slime, since *I was made in secret and curiously wrought* … Hah! that's true enough, I am indeed most curiously wrought. Now, Dallas, give me your attention. I'll read from these notes and then revise and learn them off by heart, for I cannot make a speech unless I write it. I dread to speak in public. Always did. Even when at school my voice never seemed as if it were my own but another's, a familiar who sits on my shoulder and makes me say what I would not…'

Yet, some few weeks later, when there limped into the House of Lords a pale young cripple with a beautiful stormy face to champion the cause of the workless, he held his peers spellbound. Whether or not he were prompted by a 'familiar', he delivered his oration unsparing of gesture and with an eloquence that smacked of the stage.

'My lords, never, in the most oppressed provinces of Turkey, did I behold such squalor as I have seen in the very heart of a Christian country. The convulsions I have witnessed must terminate in death since these men are liable to capital conviction for no other crime than that of — poverty! But do you believe, my lords, that these famished wretches who have braved your bayonets will be appalled by the gibbet? No! They will fight, they will pillage, burn and plunder for their rights — they who *have* no rights!'

He created a furore to bring down the House, broke away from those who would detain him to congratulate or argue, and joined Mr. Dallas, patiently waiting outside in the rain under a dripping umbrella.

'Not a hackney to be had,' he was informed.

'Then we must walk.'

They walked to the rooms in St James's engaged by the ubiquitous Dallas for him who had come to London to seek his fortune — and to find his fate.

'I must, I positively *must* meet him! I'm dying to meet him. You must arrange it,' insisted Caroline, who had ordered from her bookseller, on the day of publication, the first two cantos of a poem that was to ring the name of its author round the world. 'I know of nothing more romantic than that he, hitherto unheard of, obscure, impoverished, should wake one morning to find himself famous — overnight! Not because of his theatrical speech about the machine-breakers, but because he is a genius: an undiscovered genius. I may say *I* have discovered him, for until I read and raved about his poem, no one else did. Or did you, Rogers? What is your opinion of it? Not that your opinion matters to me one iota. I hold my own views, and as a poet myself, though a minor one, I consider I am as competent a critic as are you.'

'Since my opinion would appear to be superfluous, 'twere better I withhold it,' commented Mr. Rogers, an emaciated exquisite with a malicious smirk, an undersized body, and a beautiful house full of beautiful things overlooking the Green Park. A literary lion much favoured by the *ton,* he was a banker-poet of considerable wealth and no mean parts, whose connoisseurship and glib tongue had gained him access to that inner circle of society which might otherwise have looked askance at one who started life shovelling money into a till as a clerk in his father's bank. He was a bachelor not from necessity but from choice, because, as he was wont to say, a wife would encumber his collection of Old Masters and new mistresses.

'So you will bring him here to me, or me to him,' commanded Caroline.

'This very evening,' Rogers said, taking snuff from a trifling gold box preciously enamelled. 'He attends a rout at Holland House.'

'To which I am invited and did not intend to go, but now I will. I'll fetch you at nine o' the clock and will not let you out of my sight until you have presented him to me, when you may leave us.'

'It shall be done.' Flicking invisible snuff from his sleeve with a morsel of a handkerchief redolent of *peau d'Espagne,* Rogers rose to bow. 'I am enchanted to be at your ladyship's disposal. *Au 'voir*, madame. *À bientôt.*'

In a white-and-gold anteroom curtained in red velvet, a stream of guests lined up to be greeted by Lady Holland, resplendent in turquoise sarsenet and a turban of silver crowned by three nodding ostrich plumes, these held in place by a silver fillet — 'which should bear the motto *honi soit* in diamanté, since talk gives it the lady aspires to the host of Carlton House,' cattily purred little Rogers, to receive a nip from Caro where her fingers rested in the crook of his arm.

'Keep your eyes alert, if you please, and your tongue from speaking guile. Is he here?'

'I do not see him, but 'tis early yet and he is always late.'

'You will never see him in this crowd. Is he tall or short?'

'Of medium height.'

'Caroline, my love! *And* Mr. Rogers. Delighted.' With a kiss for her and a smile for him that looked to split her face in two, their hostess waved them on into the ballroom, where couples revolved to the strains of *'O du lieber Augustin'*.

'You will waltz?' offered Rogers.

'No, you must watch for him. Let us sit here. You can see him through the archway when, or if, he comes. And if he doesn't I will kill you.'

'To die at your hands, madame, would be the happiest of deaths for me,' replied Rogers, a quizzing-glass actively employed.

Caro's sandalled foot drummed the polished floor. 'I long to dance but daren't for fear I miss him.' Her eyes strayed, searching each newcomer who passed under the pillared archway. Myriad candles in crystal chandeliers lighted the heads of those who, with the fanatical intensity of dervishes, followed the ritual of the dance derived from Austria to sweep the Continent and take London by storm.

'*Ach, du lieber Augustin, Augustin, Augustin,*' Caro hummed to the music. '*Ach, du lieber Augustin, alles ist...* Look, Rogers, my aunt, the duchess, who comes to prance away her crocodile tears while still she mourns my uncle wearing the royal purple. Does she, too, aspire? Will this poet of yours never come?'

'If he doesn't I will fetch him from his rooms and drag him here by force,' declared Rogers, 'if need be.'

'Were it needful he be dragged to meet me, whom he would certainly know must be among these *invités,* I would not demean myself by waiting on his whim for more than half an hour.'

The room, hazy with dust rising from the powder sprinkled on the floor to render its surface slippery as ice, had become overcrowded, overheated. The sweating fiddlers and pianoforte player, thumping out the measure above the hiss of pumps and slippers, the tinkle of laughter and buzz of men's voices, were given scarcely one minute's respite before a chorus of '*Encore!*' from untiring enthusiasts set them off again.

Caro unfurled a fan. 'I feel quite giddy watching their convolutions, which are much more fatiguing to the onlooker than to the participant. I waltz every morning after my ride, and with such boundless energy that what little solid flesh I have upon my bones has melted. Rogers, I am thirsty, fetch me something to drink... Aha! See who's here. My cousin, Devonshire!' Gleefully she hailed him. 'Hart! What a joyful surprise. I thought you were at Chatsworth... Yes, Rogers, orange water, citron water ... sewer water if there's nothing else, since our hostess's parsimony is such that she well might send for carriers to bring it from the Thames, but have it iced and quickly. Do you know my cousin? This is Mr. Rogers, Hart, who writes such charming verses.'

'I have not yet had the pleasure of acquaintance with Your Grace.' Rogers, low-bowing in gratified obeisance, could not fail, though he hobnobbed with the peerage, to be impressed by introduction to a duke.

'A drink, Rogers,' entreated Caroline, 'if you can force a passage to the buffet.'

'Is that your latest acquisition?' Hart enquired as Rogers reluctantly withdrew.

'He's not my latest. I've known him ages. He's my special gossip and can be quite amusing with a spiteful tongue and a volatile pen. He likes to model himself on Horace Walpole, but he never will achieve that incomparable mixture of vivacity and wit, yet he has coffers full of money and ineffable good taste for one who started life as a bank clerk. Enough of this. I must have all of you. Give me your news, sweet Hart. How pretty you are, prettier than ever since the strawberry leaves have sprouted. Your stepmama is here, you know.'

'I ought to know,' Hart dismally rejoined. 'She made me bring her.'

'Perfidious Devon! Are you to be always at her beck? And will you let her live in your houses for ever?'

'Not if I can help it.'

'You *must* help it. I feel sick every time I pass through your portals and see her snakily encoiled on your sofas in place of her whose memory we cherish and adore. The very sight of her there causes me to vomit. Why don't you send her to Chiswick?'

'I did, but she won't stay. She says it's damp. I, too, must have a drink. These rooms are infernally hot. Is your appendage still struggling at the buffet?' Hart stared mournfully around and then at her whose eyes were everywhere for everyone, but not for him. 'I've had you on my mind, Car,' he said, 'to that degree of anxiety and fret that I can't sleep o' nights.'

'Do I weigh so heavy lying on your mind while you toss and turn in your lone bed? Poor Hart, we must find you somebody to share it.'

''Tisn't true! Tell me, Car, that it's not true.' He caught her hand savagely to crush the small ringed fingers.

'Don't!' She snatched her hand away. 'That hurts.'

'Not so much as you hurt me and hurt yourself. You are so heedless, headstrong, crazy as you ever were and ever will be, and I love you for it, my wild one, but the world is a censorious unkindly beast and talks of you to make my blood ferment. It has come to me at Chatsworth of your doings, which I must believe unless you swear that what they say of you is lies. For what I heard, God damn them, did so infuriate me that now when I go out with the guns I miss each shot. I'm cock-eyed with worry over you.'

'So that's why you sent me no pheasants this year, and William is too busy in the House to go shooting. I see that I must mend my ways if I'm not to be deprived of game — I mean the feathered kind.'

'Caro!' His cherub's face clouded and he burst forth with, 'Tell me, I *will* know. What is he to you?'

'What is who — or whom — to me? I never was grammatical.'

'That jackass Webster.' A muscle tightened in his jaw. 'I had the most almighty row at Boodle's with a fellow who spoke of you as no man has any right to speak and live. I'll allow he was raddled, full as a goat, but that's no excuse.'

'*In vino veritas*?'

'No!' denied Hart wildly. 'The truth is not in him nor in his wine. He can hold his drink to put me under. I called him out — 'twas the night my father died so suddenly to knock me flat — and of course we couldn't meet next morning, but I made him eat his words, the hog!'

'I hope they worked as an emetic. Who is this hoggish gentleman?'

'No gentleman, and of a name I choose to forget, but he only voiced what every man in clubland says, and I can't wing them all.'

'My brave good honest knight, my little Don Quixote, don't — I entreat you — do *not* tilt at windmills or come at pistol- or sword-point with babbling swine, and don't go chasing after Godfrey. He's more sinned against than I am sinning. I suppose 'tis not the slightest use that I avow my innocence, which none believes but my dear Lamb, who has an angel's heart and knows his Caro inside out, as you do not.'

Taking her hand again, Hart turned it palm upward to kiss. 'You have never,' he whispered, 'given me the chance to know you as *he* knows you — inside out.'

'I wish … I wish…' she murmured and caught her lip under a tooth with a sigh.

'What,' he steadied a shake in his voice to ask, 'do you wish?'

'For the moon. But, more immediately, that they would play some other waltz than this everlasting *"Augustin".'*

Their moment of tension had passed.

Hart, releasing a breath, looked towards the archway, where a group of women fluttered like a startled flock of multi-coloured birds. 'Is it your escort who causes this commotion?'

Rogers, with a tumbler of orangeade, frosted to its brim, dodged excited ladies posturing before a youth of remarkable beauty and a mouth too womanish for any man, yet hard as though the skin of it were grafted upon steel. His hair, beneath the candlelight, glowed like burnished bronze.

'I see,' disdainfully Hart answered his own question, 'it is not your mincing escort but some play-actor fellow Lady Holland has inveigled from the boards of Drury Lane.' He glanced aside at Caro, who had lifted her fan to hide the ebb of blood from her cheeks, leaving them marble-white in the surge of emotion that seized and overswept her. She had risen to her feet and stood transfixed, her breath quickening between her parted lips, her eyes drawn to him whose gaze carelessly voyaged among that rosary of blondes, brunettes and *rousses,* turbaned heads and creamy shoulders. Then, as his roving look stayed to rest on Caro, it seemed in that one second's pause to stab her heart and hold her, 'as if for all the world,' so she afterwards recalled, 'I were some rare night-flying moth he had pinioned to dissect.'

She saw him disengage from that bevy of adhesive women, saw him advance with halting step and jaunty head upflung as though defiant of attention to his crippled foot.

'Lady Caroline,' Rogers at her elbow, 'allow me to present —'

A crashing chord from the pianoforte drowned the rest of that, while a stentorian voice announced, 'Your Grace, my lords, ladies and gentlemen, there will be now an interval for supper. Pray conduct your partners to the dining room.'

There was a general thronged movement to the door; but, as he who was presented bowed profusely, she had seen his smile, mocking, bittersweet, with lips turned down, his eyebrows arched; and panic gripped her in a nameless dread. She slid a hand, as for protection, in her cousin's, who was taking measure of this 'play-actor fellow', to note that his coat of raven blue, ill-fitting, required a brush; that his hair, too closely curled, framed the face of a girl — or, he grudgingly admitted, an Adonis.

Caro, in a high-pitched drawl, said, 'Take me to my carriage, Hart. I'm hideously bored.' She moved away.

'I think,' Hart told her when they were out of earshot, 'that you need not have been quite so abrupt.'

'He frightened me.' She was still very pale. 'I dislike the way he looked, as though to strip me naked.'

'Which I've no doubt that he, as others have before him, would lose his soul to do.'

'Dear Hart, you're coming on! You'd never have dared say that to me before you were a duke. He's wickedly handsome, is he not? And mad, bad, and — dangerous to know.'

''Spite of that, all of which I grant him,' Hart assented, glumly, 'you *will* know him. 'Tis a combination that should appeal to you.'

'God forbid!'

'So that is the much vaunted Caroline Lamb. She baas like a sheep, speaking up to her name; she's too thin for my taste and her manners are atrocious,' said Lord Byron.

William had not returned from the House when Hart, who insisted on accompanying her to the door, left her with a warning.

'Let your intuition be your guide. You have judged him well — mad and bad, indeed! He's a mountebank, a charlatan who has made a hit with this — what does he call it — Child something?'

'Harold.'

'Why Harold? Is it to do with a Saxon king?'

'Darling!' She stood on her toes to pull his face to hers. 'You are so utterly, adorably ingenuous. There's not another soul in town who would confess to ignorance of *Childe Harold*. Everyone has read it, and if they haven't they will say they have. For myself, I consider it the greatest poem since Pope's *Iliad*, not only for its bold originality but for its passionate energy and glowing utterance. He is unsurpassed by any writer of any period in any age. But never fear, my pretty coz, that because I adore *Childe Harold* I'll transfer my adoration to its author. Let my disappointment at this first sight of him reassure you on that score. You are right, he *is* a mountebank, a conceited puppy, that much without a word exchanged between us I fully realised. I sickened at the way those women grovelled to him. Well might he disdain them and their ecstasies. Thank God that I'm no victim of Byronic fever. It is a great mistake to meet in the flesh an author one admires. The reality bears no resemblance to the image created by a fantasy too fond.'

'Methinks,' Hart told her stolidly, 'the lady doth protest too much.'

'I could go on protesting until dawn, such is my antipathy against him as a person, yet I'll read every word he writes if he ever writes or publishes again. This may be a sudden flash sprung from some smouldering spark that will die down and never be repeated. So … goodnight.'

But, having sent her maid to bed and gone to hers, she lay awake, her thoughts chaotic. Why, she furiously asked herself, did she turn her back on one whose genius had fired her with longing to possess and be possessed by him? Why had she not acknowledged that briefest introduction with the usual banality — 'Charmed to meet Lord Byron whose brilliant, glorious, inspiring, magnificent, romantic and sublime, etcetera —' The string of adjectives hurled at him by those fools of women was inexhaustible. She should have joined the chorus to cap it.

'Charmed'? Yes, bewitched. The man's a wizard or the devil, and I a greater fool than any, for I love him and loathe him and I fear him.

Mad, bad, and dangerous... So her diary testifies in those hackneyed words of hers inscribed under the date of their first meeting.

And, staring into the dark, she restlessly reiterated, *Why, why, why did I not seize the opportunity to impress him with my wit, to outwit him who, unless mounted on his hobby in the Lords to inveigh against the Frame-Breaking Bill, and, according to Papa who heard him speak, was, if not lacking in loquacity, theatrical. He's more beautiful than I had dreamed. His lameness lends enchantment to that air of melancholy which I'll wager is assumed to excite those gushing idiots to offer themselves for his taking, as brazen bold as doxies. He can never have enough of their fulsome adulation to feed his vanity and of which he'll never sicken ... God! Let me sleep!*

She couldn't sleep. She thumped her pillows, which felt as if they were stuffed with flint, not feathers. Shapes formed behind her quivering eyelids; faces disembodied swam against a night-blue curtain pricked with minute astronomical stars that scintillated to converge into a pale moon face, gigantically swollen, which bore down upon her, its eyes wide, its mouth a blood-red chasm to suck her in and swallow her ...

She shrieked, she fought, she struggled ... and she heard, 'There, then, there. Too much excitement, my darling. Wake up.'

She said dazedly, 'I've been awake for hours. What time is it?'

'Past three o'clock,' said William. He was in his nightshirt and night-cap: its tassel dangled, bobbing, on his nose; which she found to be ludicrous and pealed with laughter, eldritch, shrill; and, laughing, couldn't stop.

'Quiet now, quiet. You are overwrought.' William blew out the candle and got into bed, drawing her into his arms.

'No, William, no. I'm sleepy now…'

'Sweet love, I love you, let me love you… Yes! I must…'

His mouth crushed down on hers. She resisted, helplessly, then, of a sudden, yielded with a passionate intensity that delighted and surprised him. In all her moods and vagaries he had never known her touch such heights of exalted and complete abandon, until, exhausted, she lay still and scarcely breathing.

Presently she stirred and, yawning, said, 'Light the candles. I shan't sleep now. The birds have started. Can you hear them? There's a book beside you on the table … yes, *that* book. The latest poem by this latest poet, Byron. They say it's quite remarkable. I haven't read it yet. Have you?'

Two days later, when riding through the leafy glades of Kensington to test the paces of a new young mare, she turned in at the gates of Holland House.

'I will call upon her ladyship,' she told the groom. 'The mare pulls like the devil and is sweating like a pig. Take her to the stables and rub her down.'

The groom dismounted her and led away the horses. She unfastened the coat of her habit. The cambric shirt beneath it was damp with the heat of her body. A footman flung open the door, bowing her in. Handing him her hat with its white ostrich plume, she asked, 'Is her ladyship at home?'

'Yes, my lady.'

She was conducted to Lady Holland's boudoir and effusively embraced. 'What happy chance has brought you here, my love?'

'A raging thirst and a mare with a hard mouth. Pray excuse the dirt and dust I deposit on your carpet. My habit, as you see, is foam-flecked. I had all to do to hold the mare. She goes like the wind and I think she has winded herself, if not me.' And, to the two men who, on her entrance, had risen, 'Ah, Tom Moore, and my good friend, Rogers.' She extended a hand to each.

Lord Holland, who had not risen, heaved his huge bulk out of a chair to offer her wine. 'This will quench your thirst.'

'It will not unless I drink a gallon. Citron water, if you please.'

Citron water was supplied, and interrupted talk resumed. 'We were discussing the Nottingham riots,' blandly announced Lady Holland. 'Our poet has distinguished himself with his maiden speech.'

Sipping lemonade, Caro asked in an affectedly childish voice, 'Was it a nice speech?'

'Nice?' Up went Lord Holland's black-shelved brows. 'Nice is scarcely appropriate to anything Byron says, does, writes, or is.' Passing his glass of brandy back and forth beneath his nose, he said, 'It was a forceful speech but he will never make his mark in politics. He can speak only when he has a subject nearest to his heart to expound, of which his favourite,' he chuckled, juicily shrugging heavy shoulders, 'is — himself. Politics and poesie are little in agreement; besides which, though I allow he's enormously gifted, there is that about him which will never raise him to the greater heights, for, as Burke gives it, *A king may make a nobleman, but he cannot make a gentleman.*'

'It is surely not essential for a politician to be a gentleman,' democratically corrected Lady Holland, who reclined on a sofa, her legs outstretched, exhibiting ample feet and rather too much leg. 'But let me remind you that the Byrons, or Burens, came over with the Conqueror.'

'The fifth Lord Byron,' purred Rogers with a show of teeth, 'was tried for murder by his peers.'

'So I've heard.' This from Moore. The son of a Dublin grocer who had made money enough to send his son to Harrow, he had got himself received by fashionable hostesses in virtue of his pretty erotics under the pseudonym of Thomas Little. Although at the same school as Byron, he, nine years his senior, had left before Byron set foot on the Hill. 'There's madness in the family,' supplemented Moore, taking snuff.

'Yes,' Lady Holland nodded, taking snuff in her turn to leave deep orange stains in either nostril, 'that one may well believe. Madness is the twin of genius. He is obviously unbalanced, as witness certain stanzas in these first and second cantos, which are autobiographical. Such gloom and melancholy is almost maniacal, but none the less — superb! He is the poet of the century.'

'The century,' said Caroline, 'is only twelve years old. There will be better, greater poets than he before the end of it. And let me say here and now that I'm sick of *Childe Harold*. 'Tis an abortive birth. It reads like nothing so much as a travel book in verse for the benefit of schoolboys who will be making the Grand Tour... Please,' she held out her empty tumbler. Tom Moore sprang to take it from her. 'Fill it up again, Tom. Lord! I'm hot.'

She wriggled out of her tight-fitting coat and sat there in her frilled shirt, her riding skirt hitched over one arm above her knee-high dusty boots. There was a scratch on her cheek where a bramble had caught her, a smudge on her nose, beads of sweat on her forehead. Taking her refilled glass from a footman presiding over a table laid with drinks, sandwiches and fruit, she was about to drain it when the butler from the door announced: 'Lord Byron.'

The tumbler slipped from her hand and fell to the floor, unbroken on the moss-thick carpet. A page picked it up and bore it away.

Clumsily, with dragging foot, the visitor advanced and bowed to his hostess, who met him open-armed.

'My dear, my dearest Byron! This is indeed a pleasure unexpected.'

'At your service, madam. I drove out to Richmond for a breath of country air, and could not pass your gate without a sight of you. There are primroses along the way, and daffodils are trumpeting their welcome to this first day of spring. I lay in the greening bracken and fed the deer from my hand. I always carry something in my pocket for my horse or any creature that may cross my path, but there are not such pretty hinds here as in my park at Newstead.' His eyes travelled from his beaming hostess to Caro, who was mopping lemonade from off her shirt front with her handkerchief.

'Caroline, my love, may I present Lord Byron?'

For an instant their eyes met. He bowed with mock humility while she continued to bestow marked attention to her riding skirt.

'This presentation,' Byron said, 'has been already made, and by Lady Caroline rejected. May I ask why?' The question was to her, demanding answer.

'You may ask.' She dropped the sodden square of lawn. 'There is nothing to prevent you. Speech is free.'

'Yours, I think.' He retrieved and offered her the handkerchief.

She snatched it from him, rolled it into a ball and flung it down again. ''Tis drenched and useless now. Page! Tell my groom to bring the horses. Lady Holland, pray forgive me that

I go. I am unkempt, untidy and unfit to be received by you in such a filthy state.'

She got upon her feet, bobbed to Lady Holland, and ignoring Byron, kissed fingertips to the three other men and fled.

'You see,' remarked Rogers as the door closed behind her, 'she sits here with us in all her disarray like any urchin, but the moment my lord appears she flies to titivate. She will be back again, for this —' he held up her discarded jacket — 'and you'll perceive a transformation.'

Sure enough, within ten minutes there she was, coatless but clean, her cheeks rice-powdered, touched discreetly with the hare's foot, her boots well brushed, her riding skirt well ordered by Lady Holland's maid.

'I forgot my coat — Ah! Thank you, dear Rogers, you are always so attentive, and I — always so forgetful. You will attend tomorrow morning at my waltzing party?' It was more command than invitation.

He bowed. 'With all my heart.'

'And you, Lord Byron,' she said softly. 'I would be delighted if you, too, will join us.'

'I thank you, but I do not waltz.'

A flush wavered to her face. She could have bitten out her tongue to see his glance significantly drop to his maimed foot. She rushed in with, 'Later in the day, then, or the evening, if you will.'

'At any time of any day at your ladyship's command or,' his smile was one-sided, 'your caprice.'

'Tomorrow then, at six o'clock.'

Again she went, but this time she gave him her hand.

Punctually at six the following evening Byron arrived to find her playing with Augustus in her salon. She ran to greet him with embarrassing effusion.

'Byron, at last! I have longed to tell you how I read and re-read the glorious pictures you unfold in verse until I am intoxicated with their beauty. With you I:

'...sail'd, and pass'd the barren spot
Where sad Penelope o'erlooked the wave;
And onward view'd the mount, not yet forgot,
The Lover's refuge, and the Lesbian's grave.
Dark Sappho! could not Verse immortal save
That breast imbued with such immortal fire?
Could she not live who life eternal gave?
If life eternal...

'No, the rest eludes me though I have it in my mind, but no words to express what I feel for your superb epic. How wearied you must be of rhapsodies, yet not even the most crustaceous of carping critics — forgive alliteration, 'tis an artifice to which I am addicted and endeavour to correct in my own poor verse and prose. I was about to say that not even Grub Street hacks, themselves disgruntled authors, poets, poetasters — what you will — that scrape a living by attempting to destroy a brother penman who has won the laurels they covet, and that is why they so often tear to rags the work of established writers who are as far above these worms as is the sun above the earth — yes! but they will offer plaudits to the garbage of scavengers who never will be read, or if read cast aside, forgotten — I say that even such as these, who spew their verbal vomit in so-called 'literary' circles, must kneel to damn with faintest praise — Lord Byron!'

He was very much taken aback. Though accustomed to panegyrical enthusiasm from feminine adorers in these first weeks of the *Childe*'s publication this eulogy, delivered not in her usual muted lisp but in a high-pitched flow of words that seemed still to find some difficulty with their sibilants, deprived him of response to it.

He stood in silence. What new trickery was this? A creature of caprice, indeed, an *originale*, the like of which he had never yet encountered. Physically she failed to attract him. The antithesis of all he had hitherto admired, in no way did she conform to the voluptuous charms of those Eastern houris he had sampled on his 'pilgrimage'; or to that lovely girl he had found in Athens with her raven hair and golden skin, of whom he wrote:

Maid of Athens, ere we part
Give, oh give me back my heart!

Which he had never lost to her, although he fancied that he had — and, to impress her, did, very slightly, stab himself with the point of his dagger, which to his chagrin left her unmoved and, despite his pursuit of her, intact; or, again, the more mature appeal of his half-sister Augusta, whom he seldom saw — she was married to a colonel of dragoons, and a few years older than he — but they had always corresponded during and since his Harrow days; and each time they met she had grown, for him, more lovely.

Then there was the unforgettable Mary Chaworth of Annesley, his first love, whose father's estate marched with Newstead. Her he had madly adored, at fifteen, his 'Morning Star', as he named her who led him on to let him down. She gave him a ring and a picture of herself that emboldened him to hope she would marry him when he left school, until he overheard her telling her maid she wished 'that stupid lame boy' would cease to pester her — as if she 'could care for a cripple!'

That finished him. He returned to Harrow a disillusioned adolescent, with the seeds of cynicism prematurely sown and a deep-rooted conviction that girls were the devil. Always hyper-conscious of his infirmity, he now went armoured in hostile arrogance against his schoolmates who had delighted to torment him when, as a nervous sensitive new boy, he had hobbled round the playground with another crippled child of his age. But the bullies soon learned to fear Byron's hot retaliation. His own sufferings from the fists and jibes of his fellows had made him the champion of those weaker than himself.

His courage and his beauty soon prevailed to win him hero-worship. Among those whom he befriended was a bashful, pale little boy, small for his age, one Robert Peel, destined to scale and achieve the apex of political heights. Yet never in these youthful days did he seek the love of girls.

He had thought Mary Chaworth had broken his heart, but she had barely bruised it. And since fame had singled him for favour, with every woman his for the asking, he, who could pick and choose, had never chosen, until...

Watching the eager flush that mounted to her words, he judged this little Caro person different from any woman he had ever known or wished to know. That faint suggestion of a lisp, those close-cropped curls, her eyes wide-set under faintly surprised eyebrows and so unexpectedly dark against the primrose hair and pallor; that boyish body — much too thin, he might believe her elfin-boned — yet that very boyishness had for him an epicurean appeal as of some Sicilian shepherd lad, a golden-headed Lycidas beloved of Theocritus. And all of this and all of her, combined with that superlative reception of his work, enlivened his interest in this bizarre young creature. While fully aware of and amused by her egocentricities, he did not realise or would not admit that they met on mutual ground. He, too, was the centre of a self-erected stage whereon he postured, as did she, in rivalry to take the curtain call. It may be that her arrow-swift perception had already visualised the human comedy they were ordained to play each for their devastation.

Narrowly he watched her when, having exhausted her vocabulary of adjectival praise, she turned to the child who sat where she had left him on the hearthrug surrounded by his toys and bricks, his eyes vacantly fixed on Byron, his mouth open.

'Come, my darling, come to me.' So this was yet another facet of her versatility, this tenderness, unfeigned, for once undramatised.

She went to him who, at her coaxing, did not budge, but still stared with a glazed blue empty stare. With difficulty she lifted him — he was heavy for his age — carried him to a couch and sat him on her lap. His head of tumbled yellow curls lolled on her shoulder; a lovely boy, but Byron noted with a painful twinge that the beauty lay in feature only; the eyes were blank, and from those fallen lips came no answer to the mother's blandishments. More painful still was it to see and hear her laugh and chatter to him, with every now and then a glance at Byron, uneasily defiant, as if daring him to notice her child's disability.

'See! We are building a castle to make Augustus king of it.' She was down on her knees with him again, guiding his hands to place the bricks. 'Lord Byron will help us. He lives in a castle, too.'

Slowly Augustus turned his clouded eyes on him who lowered himself on to the floor, his foot with its unsightly boot tucked under. And so with the mother and her hapless boy, Byron forgot himself in pity for the pair of them.

'You will dine with me?' she asked when the nurse came to take the child from her. ''Tis bedtime now, my precious one. Kiss Mama and say goodbye to Lord Byron.'

Again that staring look; no kiss for her who showered kisses upon him, only a gurgling from those fallen lips that spoke no word as he was borne away.

He heard her sigh, and, as she moved her head to give an order to the footman at the door, he saw a tear steal from under her eyelid.

'His lordship dines here — but you have not said you will. My husband sits late at the House and I do not care to dine alone, so — will you?'

Yes, he would, to prove himself a disconcerting guest. When offered soup: 'I do not take soup.' Salmon was served. 'I do not eat fish.' Barsac was poured. 'I do not drink wine.'

'Tokay, brandy?' she suggested.

'Thank you, no.'

Chicken was offered and again refused, followed by saddle of mutton, dismissed with a wave of his hand and the lofty information: 'I eat neither fish, flesh, nor fowl.'

'Good heavens! Then what do you eat — or drink?'

'Soda water, cabbage, dry biscuit, toasted bread. No fruit.'

'Cabbage for his lordship, toast, biscuits and — potatoes. Can you eat potatoes?'

Yes, he could eat potatoes. 'But steamed, not fried or roasted.'

'It would appear,' said she, 'that after all, I dine alone. For how long have you enjoyed this hermit's diet? Do you suffer from impaired digestion as result of your travels in Turkey?'

'There is nothing wrong with my digestion. I practise self-denial and self-discipline for the good of my body and soul.'

Your self-denial and self-discipline, if practised anywhere or for anyone, save for my benefit, she told him silently, *is nothing but a pose. I'll wager you'll demolish a point steak when you get home.* And to a hovering footman she said, 'Soda water for his lordship.' A murmur in her ear from the butler, and apology from her. 'I fear you must wait for the cabbage. There is none in the house. They have sent out for it. Or would you —' with a little grin — 'prefer a carrot?'

'Potatoes are sufficient.'

'Not for me. I will take the chicken.'

Thereafter conversation languished while he munched cracknel biscuits and potatoes, and she toyed with chicken and sipped wine. And when the sweet was served, 'Will you not,' she asked him, 'change your mind?'

'I never change my mind.'

'I will remember that, and although you eat nothing but biscuits and potatoes I will make you eat your words.'

'Is that a threat?'

'Or,' she slid a look at him, 'shall we say — a promise?'

Later, in the drawing room, she enlarged on that remark. 'You see —' she took a bonbon from a silver dish to nibble; her teeth were like a squirrel's biting into it. 'You see, I know you, Byron. I know that you detested me the moment that we met, as I detested you. Never in my life have I experienced such antagonism for any man or woman, not even my mama-in-law, as I felt for you at sight — you whom I so longed to meet, and which is the more remarkable in that the thought of you obsessed me to exclusion of all else when I read your poem on the very first day it was published. May I tempt you to a fondant? They are stuffed with cherries soaked in cognac. Or let me order you a sandwich; you must be hungry.'

'I am.' His eyes weighed on hers. 'But not for food.'

Her breath quickened. 'My thoughts run on so fast I can't keep pace with them. What was I saying?'

'That you detested me at sight, as I detested you.'

The colour rushed into her face. 'It would seem, then, that we hate each other.'

'I think most certainly we do. The ruling principle of hate creates for its pleasure the things that it annihilates. Therefore we, to each other, are anomalous and, were we not, I should have loved, not hated you at sight.' He got to his feet with a glance at the clock. 'You will forgive me if I leave you now? I must to my work, which has been interrupted.'

'By your evident unwilling attendance upon me.' She also rose, her temper rising with her. 'Go then, and be damned to you, unless...' That sudden flash, swift as summer lightning, passed to leave her words suspended on a breath.

'Unless,' low-voiced he finished for her, 'you will have me ... stay?'

A tremor shook her body. Her hand went out to his, drew back and was engulfed, her mouth possessed, herself surrendered to the moment's madness. There was something pagan in the pressure of her slight flanks to his, in the urge and sting of her questing lips, and in the flood of passion that consumed her till she lay in his arms, limp and spent.

'You have lava in your veins,' he told her dizzily, 'not blood, and your heart is a volcano.'

''Tis you,' she whispered, 'who cause it to erupt.'

SIX

All London watched and babbled of her conquest, or of his. Which of the two had come to see and conquer, the Lion or the Lamb? 'And did they,' giggled the bucks of St James's, 'lie down together?'

Gossip, circulated by the indefatigable Rogers, hotly denied that they did. He, not she, had been ensnared. 'Artemis pursuivant and as chaste,' he tittered, 'for although that she's inflammable, capricious and exotic, she also is astonishingly naive. And no matter that they both may flaunt it to the contrary, I'll swear if they have met in the tilt-yard of love's tourney, *she* has not fallen in combat.'

Rogers was probably right.

Supremely egotistical and with superb interpretation of their respective roles in the drama-comedy they set themselves to play, they shared the honours of applause from a full house. Yet, notwithstanding 'the lava in her veins', she still retained, as Rogers had surmised, a something arrested, almost virginal, an ineffaceable reminder of the child Caroline who dwelled in daydreams, and whose senses were always more passionately roused by imagined ardours than by their consummation.

It is likely that William, who understood her so completely, knew just how far he could allow her to ride on a free rein before she plunged headlong down a precipice. From his distance he kept a watchful eye on her that, to the more malicious, was an interim *sub judice* against the time when her long-suffering husband could bring the force of legal action to bear upon his wife who dishonoured his name.

Loudest in dismay and disapproval of this *scandalum magnum* was the Lady of Melbourne House, while the two principals, regardless of the havoc they had wrought, made no effort to disguise their part in it. He, who might have paused before he endangered his meteoric rise to fame by following the affair to its finale, was not halted in his stride by Lady Bessborough's attempt to circumvent his pursuit. With her usual sweet tactlessness she told him Caroline's affections were engaged elsewhere and that Webster's infatuation was now wholeheartedly returned.

That decided him. He would brook no rival for his dominance of her at whose feet he flung himself with wildest demonstrations of love, jealousy, and hate of any other man on whom she bestowed the smallest interest.

Together they were seen at every notable function in the height of the London season; at the play, the opera, dinners, balls, and each morning at the waltzing parties held in her salon. There Byron, who could not dance, would sit biting his nails to the quick, a gloomy spectator of those who whirled to the measure thumped on the pianoforte by a long-haired hired pianist purporting to be Austrian but born in Seven Dials.

Among the pairs who tripped it to the count of 'One, two, three,' presided over by an equally long-haired dancing master who played the fiddle and led eager novitiates round the room, alternately beating time with his bow and squeaking the tune on the strings, was a round-faced, round-eyed, snub-nosed young woman.

She caught Byron's attention by seeming to have wandered into that fashionable milieu by mistake. She was dowdily dressed, had a fine complexion, mousey hair, pretty feet and good ankles. So much he cursorily noted, and, finding his attention fixedly returned, he glanced aside. Some lady's companion he took her to be, and saw she was partnered by 'that Devonshire boy', who had been waltzing almost exclusively with Caroline, and on whom he 'glowered', as Hart afterwards reported, 'with a positive man-eating tigerish glare. I had a feeling he would pounce on me at any moment and tear me limb from limb.'

When the dance ended and the couples dispersed, some to their carriages, some to the buffet in the dining room, the girl who had been waltzing with Hart was presented to Byron by Caro as 'my cousin, Annabella Milbanke'.

Closer inspection revealed her to be not pretty but well formed, small, slight, yet not too thin, with an intelligent forehead and a generalised impression of a higher opinion of herself than of Caro, whose introduction she primly corrected.

'I am cousin-in-law to her ladyship. William Lamb is my cousin.' And, sketching a curtsy to Byron, she begged Lady Caroline to excuse her departure. 'I am due to wait upon my aunt, Lady Melbourne, who is driving me to Richmond, where my parents are temporarily in residence.'

Another bob to Hart, who resolutely stayed when she had gone and was bidden by Caro, 'Darling, will you not also leave us? I'll not answer for the consequences if you don't, with you and Byron at daggers drawn. I am no pacifist to call a truce between you.'

Hart took the hint and himself away; and no sooner were they left alone than Byron, seizing her hands, swung her to him and swore, 'By God, I'll make you pay for this.'

Her eyes widened. 'Why, what have I done?'

'Who knows what you've done, or will do, from day to day — or night to night? Do you think I will stomach seeing you revolve in the arms of every man, and, more than any, with that seraphic Devonshire lad who has the face of a lass and the brains of a louse? What's he to you?'

'My cousin, and his brains — though he doesn't air the knowledge they contain — are superior to some who may be over generously gifted with the gab. Let go my hands. You are too violent — let me go, I say, or I'll —'

She aimed a kick at his shins; he all but slipped on the polished floor, recovered himself and released her. 'You seem to be prolific in cousins, with little respect for the maimed and the halt.'

'You harp too often on that theme to gain my sympathy. You are perfectly aware that your disablement, in conjunction with your beautiful face — if only I could paint it! — is less a liability than your strongest asset.' Then, seeing him whiten and wince at that thrust, she flung herself into his arms and implored him to forgive her. 'I say such awful things — you know I never mean them. You are my all, my love, my life, which I would gladly give to you and die for you.'

'I would sooner that you lived for me.'

'I do, I do!'

'You don't.' A vein like a cord stood out on his forehead. 'Your professed love is but an aggrandisement of your own self-love. I, the pet of fashion,' he spat the words at her from lips curled back against his teeth, 'coveted by every woman, must be possessed by you who will have all that is new and rare — for the moment.'

'You brute, you beast, you devil!' Her hands climbed to claw his eyes; he held her from him at arm's length.

'Aha! My little wildcat. Is this the faerie sprite, the elf, the Ariel eulogised by Rogers, Tom Moore and sundry others, whom you tease to the verge of surrender and then withhold yourself to madden them as you would madden me — to fall before you to be your creature and your clown? But I know your tricks. I'll not jump through your hoop at the crack of your whip. Yet, while you and I find each other vital to the mutual seduction of our minds if not our bodies, I demand my rights — of which one, that may seem trivial to you but not to me, is your promise never to waltz again, for I insist that I share all your pastimes, and from this one in particular I am debarred.'

'Good heavens!' She snuggled up to him. 'Of course I promise — cross my heart. Never from this moment will I waltz again —' *in your presence,* she added silently — and said, 'But my sweetest Byron, you speak of my aggrandisement. Surely we both suffer from the same complaint, only yours is the more virulent. I would call it *folie de grandeur!* And, forestalling his fierce retort to that, she put her lips to his and held them there, until, when he was roused to frenzy, she withdrew from him and whispered, 'No, not now, not yet. Are you so greedy? Wait, my love. Let us not take all our delight at once and so find nothing left...' And sent him from her fuming.

Such scenes as these were frequent, and even more absurd. Rogers had all to tell of their incessant quarrels, to which he often would be called to bring about a reconciliation.

On one occasion when, according to her account of it, Byron had reduced her to a state of nervous prostration by his taunts, threats and demands, she performed her usual tooth-and-claw act, first on him and then, having left her mark in a scratch on his cheek, dug her teeth in her hand to draw blood, screaming, 'You torture me, torture, torture me! And I submit to it, poor fool that I am — I'll promise, yes, I promise never to waltz again.' He, it seems, had come to one of her parties to find her whirling in the arms of Godfrey Webster, and this despite her former vow. 'I'll shut myself up here and never stir out of the house, except in my carriage with the blinds drawn down, and I'll wear a yashmak, or whatever they call it, like your Turkish women, only love me, *love* me! That is all I ask of you, love, love, love!'

He stood over her menacingly. 'You said you would give me all of yourself. I'll not take you divided.'

'Then you shan't take me at all. Would you have me as your harlot?'

'I would have you as my wife.'

Divorce! Was that in his mind? To what lengths would he be prepared to go in order that his vanity be satisfied?

Rogers and Dallas declared that this besotted pair had confessed, independently to each of them, that they had undergone a mock marriage in her drawing room with exchange of wedding rings and all the rest of it; but as both, Rogers said, were such consummate liars, neither he nor Dallas were impressed by the evidence produced in Caroline's album with Byron's signature and her own scrawled beneath it as Caroline Byron.

Talk was rife around their names from Carlton House to the stews of Seven Dials. How, if he were the guest to a dinner or soirée to which she had not been invited, she would rig herself up as a page and wait for him at the door among the link-boys until she saw him come out, when she would dart into his carriage and drive with him to his rooms.

The story may have had its origin in an episode recorded by Dallas, who gave it that one day, when Byron, in his study at Bennett Street, St James's, was reading to him Canto Three of *Childe Harold*, a *fair-faced delicate boy of some thirteen or fourteen years, wearing a page's livery of scarlet velvet and silver lace* arrived with a letter which he handed to Byron. He was immediately, said Dallas, hustled into the bedroom adjoining, partitioned by folding doors. Yet he had glimpsed a tip-tilted profile and a crop of yellow curls. It needed no vivid imagination to penetrate the disguise of this pretty boy, even had Dallas not overheard a tirade in that well-known lisping voice, capped by Byron's overheated tones. Not wishing to intrude on what was evidently heading for a violent row, Dallas left them to it and departed.

But not always were these two engaged in farcical quarrels or dramatic demonstrations of undying love or hate. Nor could there be any plausible reason why she, who professed to defy the conventions, should choose to visit him disguised as a boy — whether Byron's mistress or not — when those before whom she paraded her passion were firmly convinced that she was.

It might have surprised them could they have known how, when not engaged in theatrical postures, they conducted themselves as more rational beings; that he found in her a ready listener, for he too could talk at interminable length to out-talk her; of the two he was possibly the greater egoist. His infatuation for Caroline — it could scarcely be called love, but no less emotionally virulent than hers — was increased by her eagerness to imbibe all he had to tell of his early youth.

With the heavy-headed, heavy-eyed Augustus on his knee he would recall memories of his father, Captain Byron, that rip-roaring young rake who had married his mother, a wealthy orphan, one of the Gordons of Gight. His first wife had left her husband, Lord Carmarthen, afterwards Duke of Leeds, for the gallant captain, and inherited, on her father's death, a barony in her own right together with four thousand a year.

She gave him a daughter, Augusta, and died, and with her died her life interest in that useful four thousand a year.

Nothing daunted, the widowed Captain Byron sought about to find another heiress. Catherine Gordon not only had money, 'which my father,' said Byron, 'proceeded to burn,' but was also of royal descent through Annabella Stewart, sister of James the Second of Scotland.

He enlarged with pride on the bloody feuds and raids of the Gordons of Gight, who for centuries had terrorised the Highlands. 'I am sprung from a breed of kings and brigands,' said he grandly. 'The ballades of the north resound with the courageous exploits of my clan. Almost all of them died a violent death — some in battle, some on the scaffold, few in their beds. And some swing on a branch of my family tree. They were a murderous lot. There was a Gordon of Gight sentenced to pay the extreme penalty for killing five children who barred his way to the lands he had fought to possess. On the day of his hanging, the wife who adored him, and whom he deserted, begged the king for his royal pardon — and got it. I bear the mark of Cain handed down to me from both sides. The record of the Byrons is not exempt from violence.'

Caroline nodded, turning up her eyes. 'God knows I've proof enough of that. There is more Scot in you than Sassenach. *Nurtured in blood betimes, his heart delights In vengeance, gloating on another's pain,* and — although you so brilliantly describe it, and I rejoice to read how you deplore that bull-fight you witnessed in your Spanish pilgrimage — these attributions to the matador are just as applicable to you. Go on, my bonnie Highlander. I enjoy to drink your words but you prefer wine, having renounced your ascetic diet of late. Help yourself.'

A table with bottles of Beaune, Barsac, Madeira and brandy invited. Carefully depositing Augustus on a sofa, where he quietly sat as he had been placed, Byron poured liberal brandy into a glass and proceeded, 'Before I go on, as you command, you must allow for poet's licence in the suggestion that the heart of the Scot in one or any of my race, gloats upon another's pain. We delight in vengeance for injury, yes, and while we punish we forgive — but we never forget. Will you not take wine?'

'No. Tell me more of the Byrons. Were many of them gallows-meat?'

'Only one, so far as history relates. Biron, or Buren, came over with William of Normandy. His grandson fought against and conquered the Saracen under Richard Coeur de Lion in the Third Crusade. My ancestor was knighted on the battlefield for valour. Our motto is *Crede Biron.*'

'Trust Byron,' she murmured. 'Yes, one may — with reservations.'

Discarding that remark he swallowed more brandy, set down his glass and took again on his knee the staring Augustus. With a touch tender as a woman's, he smoothed back a strand of the silken gold hair that had fallen over those wide unblinking eyes, and gazing, not at Caro but as if at some inner focal point envisioned by himself alone, he mused, 'The fifth baron was a madman, or damned near it. He committed murder, indulgently called homicide by his peers, who tried and acquitted him.'

'So,' she nodded, 'I have heard.'

'Yet what you have not heard,' he flashed her his bitter smile, 'is how he delighted to torment his wife. Rumour gave it that in the end he threw her in the abbey lake and drowned her. Certain it is she mysteriously disappeared. He consoled himself with a kitchen slut who soon made a shambles of Newstead. When bored with her — our inamoratas never last for long —'

'Am I,' she interrupted, 'to take that as a warning?'

'You may take it as you will. I state a fact.'

'Are you bored with me?'

'My sweet Caro, could I be bored with you who make hungry where most you satisfy, only that you never satisfy. I was saying that the fifth baron, not undeservedly dubbed by his tenants the "wicked lord", was a great one for racing. Not horses. Cockroaches. When tired of his woman he would sit for hours in his cellar watching his numerous stud race over his body, and if they lagged he would whip them up with a straw. They swarm in the basement to this day. I sent a man there to exterminate them but they always return. It is said they are seeking their master. I went down there once to see — and saw. The walls and ceilings of their domain were black with them.'

'Don't!' shrieked Caro. 'I'll be sick.'

Byron smiled. 'I was.'

She never tired of hearing what he had to tell, although she guessed that much of it was pure apocrypha. He spoke with disparagement of his mother, who had died the year before he came to London.

'She was exceedingly foolish and fat. Lord! How fat she was, and no beauty. Such good looks as I possess, which you and others extol, I inherit from my father, as handsome a devil as ever broke a woman's heart and her bank at the same time. She was a courageous soul, but for all her royal blood she looked like nothing so much as some overblown blowsy tradesman's wife. My father made her life a living hell — as do all the Byrons with their lawful wives, but she adored him.' He lifted his chin, meditatively rubbing his knuckles against it. 'And we,' he said, with that same bitter smile, 'adore our mistresses.'

She gave a little shudder. "You are cruel!'

"Of course. To enjoy the acme of pleasure with the woman of the moment, one must give her the acme of pain.'

She flexed her fingers, and, looking down at them, echoed, 'The woman of the moment. Is that all I am to you?'

'Why,' he jerked out impatiently, 'must you always be so personal? You turn everything inward to yourself. I was speaking of my mother, poor wretch, left with a crippled child, no money, no husband — he was supposed to have committed suicide. He deserted her, as we all do, fled to France, and became involved in the revolution. None knew if he were fighting for the French or spying against them for England, with no thought of her or of me. How the Fates must have delighted in the *coup de maître* to make me — whose mother could never in her wildest dreams have hoped or imagined that the heir of that old maniacal dotard would suddenly die without issue — to make me the immediate successor to Newstead and sixth baron of my line.'

'How wonderful!' breathed Caro. 'Your whole life is a romance. I must write a novel of you. What a joy it must have been to your mother when you came into your own.'

'Joy?' He uttered a short laugh like a bark. 'I told you my great-uncle's whore had made the place a shambles. It would have cost a fortune to render it habitable. But to me that grey and lovely Gothic edifice, glimpsed through the oaks of Sherwood, was the palace of a fairy prince and I the lord of it — at ten years old. It mattered nothing to me that all my mother possessed in the world was a hundred and fifty a year. That old ruffian, my great-uncle, had wilfully ruined his son whom he loathed, and was, I think, unaware of my existence.'

'How,' she asked, 'could your mother afford to send you to Harrow?'

'By badgering the officers of the Civil List for a grant to educate me during my minority.' He began fretting at his thumbnail. 'I was horribly ashamed of her when she came to visit me at Harrow, because she was so enormously fat. I dread to think that some time or other I will inherit her too, too solid flesh. That's why I am careful of my diet.' And with startling irrelevance, still biting his thumbnail, he added, 'I was fifteen when I first fell in love.'

'Tell me,' she demanded, 'of your loves.'

'They are legion. I cannot enumerate them, but of the many that engaged my heart for a day, a night, a week, a month — only one has held it.'

'Yes,' her breath came fast. 'Yes! Say it, Byron, say it! I am the only woman you have ever loved.'

'Ever? For ever?' Relinquishing his thumb he pursed his lips, opened them again to speak, and at that moment Augustus, who, quietly sitting where Byron had placed him, had fallen asleep, toppled off the sofa on to the floor, and woke with a muted yell.

'My angel!' Caro flew to him, but not before Byron had lifted him into his arms.

'There, there, you are not hurt. Big boys don't cry.'

'He never cries. Give him to me.' Caro took him and sat protectively glaring over the ruffled golden head. 'So enthralled are you in talking and boasting of yourself, of which you talk and think of nothing else, you let my darling fall.'

'He isn't hurt. You aren't hurt, Augustus, are you?'

No answer more than a gurgling sound from that moist red open mouth.

'He shall have cream buns for his tea, my blessed one.' Caro kissed the drooping head. 'Pull the bell, Byron, for Nurse.'

He got up and limped to the bell-rope, turning to say, 'You asked me if you are the only woman I have ever loved. There is one — but not you — whom I love more than any other and possibly more than myself.'

'Who?' She replaced Augustus on the sofa and sprang to her feet, her face aflame. 'Who *is* she, if not I? Who?'

He walked to the door, opened it, said, 'My half-sister Augusta.'

And without another word or look he went.

Augusta! This was the first time Byron had spoken of his sister by his father's first wife. Caroline longed to meet her.

'I have heard of her, of course. Her brother is now the Duke of Leeds, and her mother ran off with Captain Byron, who gave her hell. According to Byron they all desert, drown, or unmercifully ill-treat their womenfolk, who invariably fly from them. But I can't think why I have never met this sister whom he, apparently, adores. So odd of him to keep us apart, don't you think?' This to William, who, from his pinnacle and with amused tolerance, watched these pseudo-lovers play their parts, as in a series of episodes performed to an eagerly expectant audience awaiting each entrance to be followed by alarms and excursions.

'A possible reason why you have not met Mrs. Leigh,' he suggested, 'is because she prefers a placid existence with her husband and children at Six Mile Bottom near Newmarket to the turmoil of a London season, when not in waiting on Queen Charlotte.'

'A lady-in-waiting to the queen, is she? He never told me that.'

'There is much,' said William succinctly, 'that Byron has not told you.'

She came to perch herself on his knee. 'My own Lamb! Don't you mind — don't you *care* that I am madly in love with him?'

'I would care very much if you were *not* "madly" in love with him,' was the somewhat staggering reply.

'What do you mean?' She jerked up her chin. He cupped it in his hand, turning her face to look down into her eyes.

'Because the mere fact that you admit to be "madly" in love proves that this hysterical passion you profess to entertain for that remarkable young man is just another of your many emotional fantasies.'

'It is no fantasy, but —' she puckered her brows, considering — 'shall we call it an obsession?'

'More likely,' he smiled, 'a delusion.'

She put her lips to his ear, nibbling it, and whispered, 'William, I adore you, and you adore me in spite of all. You do — don't you?'

'If I did not I would have left you long ago, yet, my charming, I confess that at times you try my patience beyond a Job's endurance.'

'Dear heart. I can see a glory glowing round your head, and when you die you will go straight to heaven while I sizzle down below. As always, you are right. What I feel for Byron is an emotional delusion, and not to be taken *au grand sérieux*. At the same time I fear that this 'hysterical passion', as you call it, is a form of bedevilment. The moment he enters a room my flesh *creeps* — I go cold, and then so hot, that I can scarcely breathe, and my heart beats to kill me. I am magnetised. The man's a wizard, or one of Satan's minions… Oh, don't quirk your mouth in that satirical smile of yours. You dissect me and all my moods as the great Dr Hunter dissected his bodies. You should have been a physician.'

'Perhaps I am — a physician of the mind.'

She paid no heed to that and rattled on, 'But what you *must* believe, if you believe naught else, is that I am yours as faithfully and chastefully — is there such a word? — as on our wedding night. You do believe that, don't you?'

'Against all rumour, all hopeful conjecture, all scandal that soils your name, and mine, I do believe it,' William put her from him saying wryly, 'to make of me — your fool!'

'No, no!' She flung herself at him. 'My hero! You know me so utterly for what I am, only what am I? Wasn't it that marvellous French poet, François Villon, that rascally whoremonger, ballad-monger, thief and superb genius — greater even than Byron — who said *Je congnois tout fors que moymême* — "I know all but I know not myself"? Yet you, William, know me and trust me, thank God. I'll leave you now to your work, which engages you more than I do or ever can, for politics are your life.'

But despite her protestation of fidelity and his acceptance of it, he was not wholly reassured. His mother was for ever beseeching him to remove his wife from dangerous proximity.

'Take her to Lismore, the Devonshire place in Ireland. When far from sight and sound of Byron she may come to her senses, if she is not entirely bereft of them. The poor deluded creature believes that Byron returns her adoration. He does not. Already he is on the track of sweeter and more gentle quarry whom he can coax to his call.'

'I am well aware of that, Mama.' William gave her a long searching look. She returned it with a smile.

'I refer to my niece. Your cousin Annabella.'

'You are always so perceptive, dear Mama.'

Yet something in his acid tone, besides his sharpened look, caused her eyes to wander while she still retained her smile, saying coolly, 'I have to warn you, my dear boy, for your own sake. I dread to think what fresh outrage she will commit were she to know of his intent towards Annabella.'

'Intent?' Up went his eyebrows. 'This is news to me.'

'I thought,' his mother said softly, 'that you would welcome, as do I, so happy a solution to Caro's Byromania. A marriage with the heiress to your uncle Milbanke's thousands would secure for Byron the desire of his heart, which is for —' she slightly paused — 'for no woman, but for the restoration of Newstead. It is evident he is interested in Annabella. He confided to me that he finds she has much variety of intellect behind so demure and quiet an exterior. There is attraction in contrasts. She is diametrically opposed to Caroline both in her physical and mental attributes. None the less, I would advise you to take your wife away, and I am confident that Byron would be only too delighted to be rid of his tiresome adhesion.' She swept from the room, leaving William at his desk, his thoughts adrift, his pen idle.

Too often of late had his pen been idle, notwithstanding that in the spring of that year which had brought to town the Byronic fever, political London had been equally turbulent. The assassination of the prime minister, Perceval, in the lobby of the House of Commons had caused the Whigs to hope for a general election. Now that the regent was firmly established, and in view of his Whiggish predilections, it was generally assumed that the Opposition would be recalled to leadership.

Yet, as time went on, it became more and more evident that their confidence in the prince's support was weakening. He dallied; he toyed with his fancy for a coalition government composed of his friends, with Sheridan and other of his favoured ironies to the fore: those who would be likely to deal with and disperse his avalanche of debts.

Then, while he kept the Whigs on tenterhooks, Lord Liverpool, most exclusive of Tories, was summoned to kiss hands at Carlton House. The crisis was over; the Whigs were out and the Tories in for another fifteen years.

Bitterly did Lady Melbourne upbraid her precious William.

'You could have taken Cabinet rank had you exerted yourself to support Canning in a coalition, who himself told me he had the greatest faith in you. And now what have we? That old woman, Liverpool, the regent's toady with his Tories trailing after him, and you with your great future, gone, retired, lost.'

Yes, unwilling to risk losing his seat in the forthcoming election, he had decided to renounce it. He would not stand for Parliament again in Opposition. But of this, his ultimatum, delivered to his mother, Caroline knew nothing until it was an accomplished fact.

Lady Melbourne might have taken William's retirement more hardly were it not for an equally engrossing and personal concern.

At sixty-two she still retained the magnetism that, since her early days, had lured a succession of lovers in her train. It must have caused the Thorn some malicious satisfaction when, having arranged, as if by chance, various meetings at Melbourne House between Byron and Annabella Milbanke, his interest in the niece proved to be considerably less than his interest in the aunt. From her point of view an amusing and opportune *contretemps* for the baulking of the Caroline affair, it needed but small effort on her part to turn his attention to herself. While she lacked the arresting beauty of Georgiana Devonshire or the wistful charm of Henrietta Bessborough, Elizabeth Milbanke conformed more to the Byronic ideal of voluptuous full-blooded womanhood than did the slenderly spriteish-fair Caroline — or Annabella, the prim little blue-stocking who attended lectures on science and would discuss with Byron, for his boredom, the density of the earth with the pedantic precision of a geological professor. She was not pretty, but her virginal spinsterish graces and airs attracted by force of contrast to the women he had hitherto known and enjoyed to the full, 'and who,' as Lady Melbourne crudely put it, 'you run through like a dose of salts.'

Her coarseness of speech when alone with him was an added attraction to Byron. He delighted in what he called her 'masculine mind'. 'A perfect union between the sexes,' he told her, 'can only be achieved if the woman possesses at least twenty-five per cent of the male element in her mental capacity, by which token the man whom she chooses to be her life partner should be equally endowed with the same percentage of woman in himself. There is nothing more tedious to me than the hundred-per-cent female with her coy and skittish femininity.'

'Which is what you find so tiresome in Caroline?' was the Thorn's hopeful suggestion, to be hotly refuted.

'No, you are wrong, and you have Caroline wrong. Her distinct masculinity, or rather boyish adolescence, which is paramount in her hybrid mentality, accounts for much of her unorthodox behaviour and is, for me, one of her strongest attractions. One might believe her incarnate from some exquisite hermaphrodite attendant on and loved by the Lesbian, Sappho.'

Thereafter Lady Melbourne forbore to mention Caroline save to sing her praises, and achieved the desired effect of ramming her down his throat until he sickened and said, 'I can swallow no more of Caroline Lamb. She is an ineffable *poseuse*. I much prefer the society of men, providing they, like Rogers and Dallas, have enough of the female in them to satisfy my urge for the sympathy of an intelligent woman — such as yourself, or, in lesser degree, your pedantic little niece, the Princess of Parallelograms. She has a certain masculine approach to the subjects she discusses *ad nauseam* with me, that, although she bores me to extinction, is a welcome contrast to the vagaries and superficial erudition of Caroline.'

All of which was excellent; and although the Thorn continued to encourage this latest, and youngest, of her retinue, she delighted in her capture. What a *coup* to have snatched him from the arms of William's wife — that wretched girl who had caused them all such misery and shame! And what a match for Annabella, could she bring it off, and who, Lady Melbourne realised, was not easy to suit or to be suited. Meanwhile it charmed her to know that she, in this autumnal second blooming of her life, was as desirable to questing young manhood as in her springtime.

So now gossip had an ample choice of titbits to pounce upon, select and chew and chuckle over, heads together, in the clubs and salons of St James's and Mayfair.

'How does Caro William take the transfer of her beau to the mother-in-law's string? Was there ever so piquant a triangle as this?' buzzed the ladies who flocked to Devonshire House, where, bereft of its queen, and despite Hart's objection, her uncrowned successor held court.

The latest news conveyed by the duchess, reclining at her ease in Georgiana's drawing room, gave it that 'Caro is doing all sorts of imprudent things for — and with — Byron. He vows he will go back to Naxos and then her husband can sleep in peace.'

'He sleeps in peace now that he no longer sleeps with her,' was the verdict of Harriet Leveson-Gower, who claimed to know a good deal more of her cousin's intimate life than Caro knew herself.

Lady Bessborough, to whom every latest scarifying news of Caroline was carefully relayed by Harriet and others of the family, including the Duchess Elizabeth, hurried back and forth between Byron and her daughter with tears and entreaties, imploring them to be done with this 'foolishness' which she fully realised was nothing but a 'dangerous flirtation' that had been cruelly exaggerated by wicked scandalmongers into *une grande passion*. Let them resolve never again to give the slightest opportunity for these evil-minded carrion to swoop upon a purely innocent relationship. Let them consider *her,* if not dear William, who had suffered with such forbearance and dignity this lamentable *affaire.*

Nothing could have been more likely to exasperate the pair of them than Lady Bessborough's tearfully well-meant endeavours to bring this 'lamentable *affaire*' to an end which only succeeded in bringing it to a head.

Caro, infuriated by her mother's interference, and suspicious that Byron had tired of his thraldom, was for ever watching and following his movements, even to the extent of forcing an entry to his rooms, not this time as a page, in which guise Fletcher, his valet, had already recognised her, but in the smock of a wagoner, purporting to have come from Newstead with a basket of vegetables and fruit.

She was allowed in, and confronted Byron at his desk littered with Canto Four of *Childe Harold,* accusing him of fornication with her mother-in-law, 'whose morals are as easy as those of any she-cat.' To Fletcher, overhearing at the keyhole, there then ensued between the two 'the most almighty row', as retailed in confidence to Mrs. Peterson, who gleaned from him news enough to bring her mistress, Lady Bessborough, to the verge of a nervous breakdown.

'I hate scenes,' Byron confided to Dallas. 'I shall be forced to snap the knot, although her mother, that silly sentimental fool "Lady Blarney" (his name for Lady Bessborough), has done her best to tie it with her provoking well-intentioned and ridiculous advice. Honestly, Dallas, I regret that I ever allowed myself to be inveigled by and involved with the fair one. I am bound immensely to admire her husband for his acceptance of and attitude towards me and his wife's absurdities.'

Of which her latest absurdity was this storming of Byron's rooms in the disguise of a carter. 'I fled from her appalled,' recounted Byron, 'and left her screaming on the floor.' Dallas may or may not have believed his version of the story that was soon all over town.

'Their imagination,' twittered Rogers to his circle when he heard of it, 'soars to incredible heights. While Byron swears that he has never had her, she, to all and sundry save her husband, swears he has.'

Yet, apart from surmise and conjecture, it was certain that Caro's extravagant conduct not only delighted the tattlers, but caused the gravest alarm to her mother and William, who tardily came to acknowledge the danger for which she was heading.

Lady Melbourne would have seen to it that Byron's pursuit of other attractions was common knowledge even had the scholarly and virginal Miss Milbanke not entrusted to Caroline a set of verses she composed for Lord Byron's perusal — 'If you, dear Caro, would kindly submit them to him with whom you are on such amicable terms...' The prim button mouth unfolded to a smile less artless, Caro was constrained to think, than artful. It speaks well for her that she did not fly at Miss

Milbanke when she presented her verses, one of which, entitled *Byromania,* she made 'dear Caro' promise not to show him, for, 'I am sure he would not at all approve of nor agree with my opinion of him, which is as candid as I hope it will be private — to you. I will read it for your better comprehension of my somewhat cramped calligraphy. It is satirical, as you will hear, and I trust your ladyship will be amused.'

And in her precise little voice Annabella read:

'Woman! how truly called a "harmless thing",
So meekly smarting with the venom'd sting.
Forgiving saints! — ye bow before the rod
And kiss the ground on which your censor trod...
See Caro, smiling, sighing o'er his face
In hopes to imitate each strange grimace
And mar the silliness which looks so fair
By bringing signs of wilder Passions there...
Then grant me, Jove, to wear some other shape
And be an anything except — an Ape!'

Her ladyship was *not* amused, and we may believe that only by an immense effort did she refrain from bringing 'signs of wilder Passions' impressed by her nails on Miss Milbanke's rosy cheek. Indeed, with commendable generosity, she promised to present Byron with the remainder of Annabella's poems, well aware of their poor quality and that they were too insignificant for him to waste his time reading them.

Nevertheless the various rumours of his strayed affections could not be ignored, particularly as his chief feminine interest was centred now in Lady Oxford, whose amorous promiscuities had placed her beyond the pale of convention. Only Lady Holland, that most liberal minded of Whig

151

hostesses, who did not enquire too deeply into the intimate lives of other women since her own would not bear close investigation, would receive her. But Caro, always ready to excuse those who heaped her with flattery, found in Jane Oxford a sympathetic friend. She could even overlook the lady's vulgarisms in favour of her sentimental attitude to love. She had a slight aptitude for the classics, had taught herself Latin, a smattering of Greek, could quote Horace, Aurelius, and, incorrectly, Homer, read much and assimilated little. For Caro she professed unstinted admiration and wrote letters couched in terms that were almost those of a lover.

Although William heartily disapproved of the acquaintanceship, Caro continued to court her until Byron appeared upon the scene. In her forties she still retained the dairymaid prettiness of dark curls, retroussé nose, and ripe luscious lips of Hoppner's portrait. She had also retained a variety of children by a variety of fathers, known as the Harley Miscellany from the pamphlet issued by the library promoted by her husband's famous ancestor, Robert Harley, first Earl of Oxford under Anne.

The strain of hearing, fearing, watching Byron's latest infatuation for this elderly siren had taken its toll of Caroline's overwrought nerves.

'She is behaving like a lunatic,' reported Dallas, Byron's shadow to protect him from the dreaded importunities of one whom, again according to Dallas, he 'begged to be spared from meeting until we are chained together in Dante's *Inferno.*'

Caroline's jealous suspicions, now forcibly aroused by the many who levelled at her from every direction darts tipped to sting with tales of Byron's latest pursuit and capture of Lady Oxford, brought her to a pitch of uncontrollable frenzy.

Rogers, next to whom at Holland House she happened to be seated during a dinner to which Byron and his lady were also invited, was horrified to see Caro glare across the table at Byron whispering in Lady Oxford's ear... 'Then, of a sudden,' so Rogers gave it to his cronies at his club, 'she lifted her empty glass and 'pon my life and honour, she bit, yes, positively *bit* a slice out of its rim, cutting her lip to spurt blood on her gown...' When he at once called a footman's attention to the 'accident', saying, 'You have served her ladyship with a cracked glass' — 'to save her from more scandal,' giggled Rogers — 'damme if she didn't scream *haute voix* for all to hear, "Don't you blame the footman. I have swallowed a great lump of it and I hope it kills me!"'

When William was given report of this episode from his mother, who brought Caro's every outrageous performance to Byron and him, he, in conclave with Lady Bessborough, now agreed that Caro would have to be removed. At once. To Ireland. Her mind, he feared — but dared not convey his fears to her distraught mama — had become unhinged. Her exaggerated passion for Byron and her violent behaviour must, he thought, be indicative of some serious mental disorder.

'We must get her away,' he told Lady Bessborough, 'as far away as possible — to Ireland. And if you cannot go with her I will ask Hart to take her. I should have sent her long ago had I followed my mother's advice, but go she must.'

'But go she mustn't!' Caro burst into the room. 'I heard you dispose of me as if I were a parcel. "I should have sent her long ago had I followed my mother's advice." Huh! Your mother's advice — whose sole purpose in life is to tear us apart and degrade me with her wicked lies — and you'll "ask Hart to take me"! I wish to God he *would* take me and *had* taken me, as he wanted to before I married you. I should have married him, not you — you mealy-mouthed parsonic —!' She choked; her face became suffused with the ominous blood rush that presaged a storm; and it broke.

Lady Melbourne in her room below heard piercing screams; heard running footsteps down the stairs and through the hall; saw from her window William, bare-headed, dash into the street, heard him hail a hackney, jump into it, and be driven away.

'What now?' Her husband, also aware of the racket above, and a tempestuous sobbing, not Caro's but her mother's, drowned by a fresh outburst of shrieks, poked his head round the door of his wife's boudoir. 'What's all this to do?'

'Can't you hear what's to do?' rasped his lady. 'Your son's wife is raging — as usual. Just listen.'

He listened. Caro's voice rose again to yell in a volley of words.

'I'm going. He said I must go, so I'm GOING. I'm leaving this Melbourne — no, HELLborn House — for ever! Never to set eyes on it or its vile inmates again. I hate — I HATE them all. I'm sick to death of Lambs and my Lady Mutton most of any — I'm off, I'm *off*, I'm OFF!'

At which Lord Melbourne, roused from his normal sloth and galvanised to action with remarkable vigour for his size and weight, sped up the stairs and into Caro's room, where he found her screaming and kicking her heels on the floor, and her pale mother imploring her to calm herself, which had the immediate opposite effect. Caro sprang to her feet, raised her fists to smite the air and, had Lady Bessborough not ducked her head, she would have smitten her as well.

Redoubling her shrieks, 'I'm going, *going*,' reiterated Caroline, 'to Byron!'

At which Lord Melbourne, followed by his wife, who likely may have prodded him since he, of all the family, had hitherto taken a lenient view of Caro's 'tantrums', seized her by the shoulders, shook her with some violence, and shouted, 'Go then, and be damned to you — if he's fool enough to keep you, for I won't!'

When William returned, bringing with him Dr Warren, whom he had fetched from his house to administer a palliative to Caroline, he found Lady Bessborough in the vapours, his father in his cups, and Lady Melbourne commanding half a dozen footmen and Caro's little pages: 'Go, all of you, search every road and alleyway, particularly by the river banks. Oh, William, my dear boy, *and* Dr Warren! But, Doctor, I fear you come too late. She has gone.'

'Vanished!' sobbed Caroline's mother. 'She tore out of the house just as she was, in her flimsy gown, no cloak, nor bonnet, and see — it has started to rain. O, pray God she has done herself no mischief!'

'The Thames will be dragged,' briskly stated Lady Melbourne. 'This is a terrible shock to me,' she added with no visible sign of shock nor anything more than relief. 'My poor William, we are doing all that is possible to find her. She cannot have gone far. If she is not back within the hour we will inform the constables. Doctor, do you think,' she lowered her voice, glancing aside at the weeping Lady Bessborough, 'that she may deliberately have fallen in the river?'

'I think nothing of the sort,' was Dr Warren's emphatic reply. 'Her ladyship is far too intelligent and,' he in his turn dropped his voice for the benefit of Lady Melbourne's ear alone, 'far too fond of herself to run any risk of losing her life. And since it appears that my patient is not immediately available for my medical advice, I will, with your ladyship's — and your lordship's — permission,' he bowed to them severally, 'take my leave.'

While this was going on, Caro, bonnetless and in her 'flimsy gown', her hair in curliest disorder, was speedily making, not in the direction of the river but for Pall Mall and St James's Street, bearing northwards. Few pedestrians were abroad at that time of day, with the *ton* at their luncheons and the townsfolk at their work. Regardless of the downpour of rain she sped up Bond Street; her breath came fast; she halted to regain it with a hand to her heart and one eye on a passing hackney cab. She called to the driver: 'Hi! Please, will you take me to —' then remembered she had no money with her, and sighting a jeweller's shop opposite, she bade him, 'Wait for me here.' She darted across the road, pushed open the door, and announced to the young man behind the counter, 'I am caught in the rain without an umbrella or a purse, and I want to go to … Newmarket,' the first locality that occurred to her. 'I have called a hackney to take me to Charing Cross, where I can book a seat in the coach, but I have no money with me having come away in such a hurry — so stupidly forgetful!'

Luckily for her this was a jeweller whom she had never before patronised. 'I have here a ring.' She drew it from her finger. 'Is it possible that you could buy it from me or allow me to borrow a few pounds on it?' She leaned across the counter to tell him confidently, 'You see, I have run away from a cruel stepfather who keeps me under lock and key at the horrible hotel where I was brought only yesterday to be married to a nauseating rich old man whom I detest and, oh, I must go back to Doncaster — I mean Newmarket — so please, oh, please, please help me!'

Help her? The young assistant would have gone through flood and fire to help her, having fallen in love at first sight of this adorable unknown who stood shaking the raindrops from her primrose-fair curls, whose lovely eyes were fixed imploringly on his to offer him the ring drawn from a finger 'like a white rose-petal', he sentimentally observed. He fancied himself as something of a poet, had devoured *Childe Harold,* bought in its first week of publication and read all one night in his lonely bed over a greengrocer's shop in the High Street of Mary-le-bone.

The ring was an opal set in a circle of diamonds. Although but a mere apprentice to this well-known firm of jewellers, he had a keen appreciation for — and, despite his youth, a well acquired knowledge of — the value of a jewel. He took the ring, saw the stones to be of finest quality; yet in duty bound to his employer he refrained from expressing his opinion.

Blushing dreadfully when he encountered those velvety dark eyes, he mumbled, 'If Miss will — er — excuse, I will ask my…' and, detaching himself from the lure of those eyes, he opened a glass-panelled door at the rear of the shop, marked PRIVATE, and dived within.

Caroline began to shiver. She was wet. Her gown, with little more than a chemise underneath it, was drenched; her sandals sodden. She would catch her death of cold, but what of that? Let her die and be done with this misery of love and life. 'For love and life are to me,' she murmured, 'indissoluble.' She must get away, out of this odious London. Far away. Abroad. To France. Or Italy. Yes, she would travel incognito, as English governess in some high-born Italian family, to teach the younger children and seduce the eldest son. Or she would go into a nunnery. Take the veil. Or take poison. Death would be her solace. To sink into oblivion and wake to a birthday in heaven... If only to goodness this young man would hurry up!

He hurried up within five minutes. His blush was fading, but his ears were red. 'We can allow you twenty guineas on the ring, Miss ... er ... um, if to your approval?'

'Very much to my approval. Are you buying it from me?'

'No, miss,' the blush returned, 'we will lend you the sum of twenty guineas to be reclaimed at your ... at your convenience.'

'At my convenience! How sweet of you to be so generous without any fuss at all. I have not the least idea how much it is worth but I am sure a great deal more than twenty guineas, though I wouldn't *dream* of asking you for more, you are so kind and so good-looking. Is this is what is called "pawning"? I've never pawned anything before, but since you are so accommodating I will collect all sorts of things to pawn in future, and I'll always think of and remember you as *mon oncle.*'

'...?'

'French for "my uncle". I have heard that pawnbrokers are called uncles — I can't think why.' She smiled to ravish him. 'One hears such strange and silly things, doesn't one? But neither you nor your shop, which looks to be so stylish, should ever be referred to as a pawnbroker or its equivalent establishment. I think you are a very charming young man and I wish I had the time to improve on our acquaintance.'

'S-s-so do I,' stuttered he whose name, although she asked and was given it, is of the least concern to us and of no concern to her. But she had her twenty guineas, and because she had no purse she bought one of netted silver for three pounds from the enamoured young assistant with a reduction of a shilling on each guinea 'in consideration of your honoured custom, miss, that you may rest assured of my — of —er — of

our best attention, miss, at —er — at — now and at all times.'
For which she warmly thanked him, turned at the door to blow
him a kiss and left him in a state of rapture.

During this transaction the rain had ceased; the sun, dodging
the clouds, blazed forth from a blue transparent sky and
reflected pools of azure in road puddles. The pavements were
almost dry but she was not; her gown still damply clung, her
feet squelched in their satin sandals. Into the hackney, patiently
waiting, she jumped and told the driver: 'Go to … anywhere
you like, via Kensington or Timbuctoo or hell!'

With an indulgent grin for the whimsies of the high-born,
recognised as such by one whose fares were culled from
Mayfair and St James's, he whipped up his horse and rattled
over the cobbles bearing her westward. Past Knight's Bridge
turnpike and the market gardens of Brompton went the cab at
an even trot, and down a side lane into the village of
Kensington. There, struck by a sudden reminder; she called to
the driver: 'Pull up! There used to be a Dr Grayson here. I
wish you to find out if he still lives in Kensington and take me
to him now.'

Dr Grayson, she recalled, attended Miss Rowden's young
ladies, and although the Select Academy had ceased to exist
there was no reason to believe that Dr Grayson did not.

A passing milkmaid bearing her empty pails slung from a
pole across her shoulders, having filled the jugs of villagers,
gave the desired information. 'Sure, Dr Grayson lives way
along 'ere, the corner house at end o' the 'igh street.'

The hackney coachman who deposited her at the doctor's
door was told again to wait, 'while I write a message that I wish
you to take for me on your way back to town.'

The boy in buttons who came in answer to her knock informed her that the doctor was on his visits and would be back at four o'clock.

'Very well,' she said. 'I will stay here till he comes.'

She was conducted to an anteroom and asked for pen and paper. These supplied, she scribbled a note, slipped it in an envelope, ran out to the hackney, gave the man a guinea and bade him, 'Deliver this at once to Lord Byron in Bennett Street, St James's.'

He drove off and she went back to the waiting room, there to leaf through the pages of the doctor's medical books and find, according to the symptoms of various diseases, that she was suffering from inflammation of the bowels, a malignant tumour of the brain and an acute attack of ague with its attendant chill and fever. She shivered and was hot, burned and was cold, and believed herself about to die.

When the doctor, a balding, pouter-chested little man in a bottle-green coat and grey kerseymeres, did at last arrive, she greeted him with, 'Ah, Doctor, I doubt if you can save me. I am resigned to walk through the valley of the shadows having made my peace with God. As you see, I am desperately ill. For years I have suffered from a flux of blood to my head which causes me to fly into tempers and say and do extraordinary things and — I think you don't remember me at all?'

The doctor assumed a pair of spectacles the better to scrutinise his attractive young visitor, whose voluble introductory speech had given him to diagnose some nervous disorder; at the same time, recognition dawning, he said, 'Did I not attend your ladyship when you were a pupil at Miss Rowden's school?'

'You did — for the stomach ache — but Miss Rowden would hate to hear you call her Select Academy a school — or, as I, in those days or even now unless I keep a guard upon my S's, would call it, "thcool". How clever of you, Doctor, to recognise me after all these years. I must have considerably changed. I am now a wife and mother.'

He bowed. 'As so I have heard. Yes, indeed, Lady Caroline, I have followed your career with the greatest interest.'

'Yes, my career and my affairs, even the most private, are of greatest interest to everyone … ah — t'chew!' she sneezed. 'I seem to have caught, besides my other maladies, an abominable cold, and as I happened to pass your door on my way to … or rather coming from — a-ah-excuse me … a'tchew!' she feigned another sneeze while she paused to improvise, 'from — ah — Richmond, where I have been visiting some relatives of my husband, Sir Ralph and Lady Milbanke, who are staying there *pro tem,* I thought that, as you, dear Dr Grayson, knew and treated me long ago for my childish ailments, I would call upon you now for your professional advice.'

He bowed again, his eyes, like lamps behind the spectacles, searchingly upon her. 'Which I shall be honoured to give, if your ladyship will come into my surgery. Allow me…' He opened the door for her, and led the way to a room at the end of the hall.

Having stated a plausible reason for her visit, she rapidly decided that the doctor's house, situated in the purlieus of Kensington village, might be an excellent hide-out where she could remain undiscovered while she made further plans for her departure, if not from life, most certainly from London. She had now in her possession from the pawning of her ring sufficient money to take her to Paris, if not to Italy, where the idea conceived of travelling as an English governess presented delightful possibilities. It would be dreadful, of course, to leave

Augustus, though she left him with an admirable nurse, and it would only be for a month or two, just long enough to make Byron realise his loss, and William also, who, she thought had shown himself so utterly indifferent to the fact that she loved another as much as, if not more than, she loved him... Or had he, too, ceased to care? But she must not allow herself to dwell upon so terrible a thought as to lose the love of both the men who meant so much to her. 'O! that way madness lies; let me shun that...' So for the immediate moment she must seek the doctor's sympathy and his opinion on her state of health. With which end in view she induced a violent fit of coughing accompanied by genuine sneezes.

After a careful examination, the doctor pronounced her to be suffering from a severe chill; she should take to her bed at once. As to her complaint of a flux of blood to the head, he could find nothing symptomatic of any serious disorder, but to allay this discomfort as reported by her ladyship he would advise she be bled by cupping, or the application of leeches.

'No!' screamed Caro. 'I would sooner die of a tumour on the brain than have leeches stuck all over me. No, Doctor, I will not be bled, but...' She had already decided that she must confide in him who, she gathered, was not to be gulled by imaginary ills. 'But,' she continued, standing before him, the picture of injured simplicity, 'I am in direst straits. I have been driven to desperation by the cruel treatment of my husband's mother, Lady Melbourne, and since a patient must have no secrets from her doctor, I must tell you the absolute truth. I have *not* been visiting the Milbankes at Richmond.'

'Quite so.' Dr Grayson, with the smallest of smiles, drew forward a chair and begged her to be seated. 'I was perfectly well aware of that,' said he.

She sank down into the proffered seat. 'And the rest of my tarradiddles too. You doctors see far more than bodily ills. You can penetrate the innermost recesses of the mind. You are a very clever doctor, sir, and should not be tucked away here in this village. You should take a house in Harley Street, where all the fashionable doctors seem to migrate. I must ask my father, who owns some property thereabouts, to find you a house to rent, nearby to Cavendish Square. Now, Doctor,' as he opened his mouth to speak, 'if you will hear my confession and not scold me nor bleed me, this is the fact of the matter.

'I have left my husband and my child — God forgive me! — but only to bring Mr. Lamb to his senses, of which he of late would appear to be bereft. He must choose between his wife and his doting, possessive and odious mama. You needn't look so shocked, my dear sir —' so very like a wise and startled pigeon, a carrier for choice, pouting his chest and nodding his head, she mentally parenthesised — 'even the highest of the high can be odious, but my mother-in-law behaves to me as she were the lowest of the low. So I am teaching her, as well as my husband, a lesson, that they may come to value and respect what they are likely to lose, and — ah-ah-a'tchew! — I may not be suffering from apoplexy, Doctor, but I have indubitably caught a hellish cold, because I ran out on the spur of the moment — there was the most appalling shindy going on at home and I couldn't stand it any longer. My papa-in-law positively bellowed at me: "Go, and be damned!" So I went forthwith, just as I was, in this muslin gown, and it came on to rain and, as you see, I am drenched. So I hired a hackney and told him to drive me to — to you, whom I remembered as so very kind.' Which was near enough to the truth to satisfy her and to gratify him. 'And if I may be permitted to stay in your charge until I am rid of this pest of a cold, and as you have ordered me to bed and I cannot go to bed, having no bed to which I can go unless you take me to yours — pray do not misunderstand me — I mean to whatsoever bed your wife — I presume you have a wife? — may offer me, I would be eternally grateful.'

The doctor, who had no wife, she having died some years before, was now in sorest straits. He had a married daughter down in Devonshire; he had a housekeeper, three maids, a cook, and a 'Buttons', but none of these inmates of his household could, in his opinion, suffice to act as chaperone to this notorious young woman who, on her own admission, had left her husband and her home to seek clandestine shelter with him. Had he, in his professional capacity, any right to be a party to her escape? Should he not at once inform her husband of her whereabouts?

While he hesitated he was lost.

'I know you will not refuse me the bed you prescribe for my cold as prevention of more fatal consequence. I am sure I am sickening for a fever. A neglected cold can lead to a consumption. May I ask you to order me a hot mustard bath for my feet to draw the cold from my head and a hot drink of rum and lemon, which I abominate, but I realise its beneficial qualities — ah-a'tchew! And if I am well wrapped in blankets to sweat it out of me — you see, Doctor, I am a mother and have nursed my darling little son — oh, how it breaks my heart to leave him! — through every kind of illness. I am a wonderful sick-nurse, so please, *please,* Doctor, put me to bed and keep me safe from wicked cruel invasion till I'm better. I am in such need of comfort and — and k-kindness.' With which, covering her face, she fell to sobbing.

What could he do, poor man, but pat her shoulder paternally and tell her she could rest assured that a room and bed would be placed at her disposal, and — this a sudden afterthought as sop to the conventions — he would procure her the service of a nurse. Whereupon, cutting short her tearful thanks, he hastened from the room to send 'Buttons' for the nurse on whom he was wont to call in cases of emergency; and while thus busily engaged he was not aware that another unexpected visitor had just arrived.

Caroline, impatiently prowling the surgery, was halted in her perambulations by the sound of hooves and wheels scraping the cobbles. Peering through the curtains she saw a cabriolet halt at the doctor's door, saw the occupant give the reins to the groom who had come to assist his clumsy descent, and waited to see no more.

Out at the front door, down the steps, she flew to meet him with hysterical cries of, 'Byron! Byron! No, oh! Yes… It *is*! O, God be praised. You have sought and found me. Come, come quick. We'll go from here. We'll go at once to … Paris!'

SEVEN

Seated on the lawn at Holywell, Lady Spencer laid aside a sheaf of correspondence. To Miss Trimmer, who diligently hovered, she said, 'My good Trimmer, sit down. I cannot stand your flutterings. It is natural that you should be anxious. I too am anxious to hear the latest news of Caroline and this unfortunate débâcle at Melbourne House, which I am certain is no more than a storm in a teacup ... and here are the teacups. Pray, Selina, occupy yourself with them and leave me to tell you in my own time what my daughter Harriet conveys to me, or as much as I can read of it in her latest illegible scrawl.'

Miss Trimmer, very pink in the nose and pale in the face, offered a timid apology. 'Indeed, I ... your ladyship must pardon ... I have been so disturbed to hear that Lady Caroline ... but more than relieved to know she...'

'Pour the tea, Trimmer. Page, pass me the ratafias and don't sniffle. It is a deplorable habit, or else you suffer from a chronic rheum. Use your handkerchief. No, Thomas,' to the footman, 'not those coconut cakes. They give me indigestion. Is there any currant bread-and-butter?'

There was currant bread-and-butter, duly served to her ladyship, who bade Thomas and the page, obediently using a not very clean handkerchief, 'Go, both of you. I will ring when we have finished. Selina, if you please.'

Her hare's eyes bolting, Miss Trimmer set down her cup and expectantly waited.

Taking up one of the letters she had placed on the table beside her, Lady Spencer went on, 'My daughter gives me an incoherent account as to the cause of all this pother. She writes she has received a delightful — the word might be letter, note or gift — from Lady Caroline. It is quite impossible to decipher, but I gather there is hope, now she is at Brocket with Mr. Lamb and Augustus, that all will be well. The boy's breathing is not so good as it might be, which I observed, as I told you, Trimmer, when he was with us here.'

'Yes, indeed, the poor child, your ladyship did mention…' Dolefully Miss Trimmer shook her head.

'Yet,' continued Lady Spencer, 'I feared to draw Lady Caroline's attention to the fact lest she should take upon herself to doctor or diet him. Instead I wrote to Dr Warren asking that he should give Augustus a thorough examination and report to me, which he has done and finds nothing radically wrong more than abnormal lethargy for his age, which we already know.'

'Ah, yes,' sighed Miss Trimmer, 'alas! But,' she added with false cheer, 'he may grow out of … children do … I have often seen how…'

'Drink your tea, Selina. I hope you may be right. As to my granddaughter, I regret to tell you that her outlandish behaviour, in particular during this last year, is, according to Dr Warren, symptomatic of a certain instability of mind… Yes, Trimmer?'

'Never,' with startling vehemence uttered Miss Trimmer, 'can I recall any signs of instab… No evidence, whatsoever, of any such symptoms when I had the honour of instructing … in all my situations as instructress of the young, never did I find a more … intelligent responsive pupil with a positive thirst for knowledge and great literary appreciation. She could recite *verbatim* the works of Shakespeare and…' Miss Trimmer's momentary courage evaporated with her voice.

Lady Spencer nodded her head. 'We are all aware of Lady Caroline's singular gifts, and your perspicacity and sympathetic approach to the problems that beset young children. It always surprises me how you, who are so timorous a conversationalist, did prove yourself to be so excellent a governess. I was astonished when I visited the nurseries at Devonshire House to see how well you managed your unruly charges, even though they learned nothing from you at all — to this day neither Caroline nor the duke can spell — at least you stayed the course longer than any of your predecessors, and the children were devoted to you.'

Miss Trimmer, taken with the flushes, murmured deprecatingly, 'Your ladyship is too, too kind. I have always endeavoured to ... the devotion, if any, on their part is wholeheartedly returned by...'

'The divers reports of Lady Caroline's uncircumspect conduct,' adjusting her spectacles Lady Spencer referred to another letter, 'are, I do not doubt, much exaggerated if not entirely false. Trimmer,' looking up over the spectacles, 'do, I implore you, eat some bread and butter or a tea-cake. You don't eat enough for a bird and are pitiably thin. I do not endow these tales with more than a fraction of credulity, and I believe that dear warm-hearted girl is utterly loyal to her husband, whom she loves and who as yet loves her... Yes, Trimmer, what did you say?'

What Miss Trimmer, surprisingly, had said but did not dare repeat was, 'Hear, hear.'

'Moreover,' continued Lady Spencer, with a sabre-edged look at the pinkened Miss Trimmer, 'I would, despite her many indiscretions, be prepared to swear to her innocence in a court of law were I called upon to do so, which, pray God, I never will be. As for that dastardly poet with whom she has entangled herself, peer of the realm though he is and of most dissolute descent and repute, he deserves to be horse-whipped, which, were I of the age and sex to do it, I would readily undertake. Duelling at pistol-point — they crossed swords in my day — is still a gentleman's prerogative and Lord Byron, for all his ancient lineage, is no gentleman. He is a scoundrel.'

To which, and again with unusual emphasis, Miss Trimmer agreed to the effect that she was entirely of her ladyship's opinion. 'I have attempted to read Lord Byron's much-praised … which while I recognise its indubitable merit I found to be … not to my … and if one may venture somewhat too … outspoken, too vigorous, too…'

'You're less of a fool, Trimmer, than you appear to be,' condescended Lady Spencer, and would have enlarged upon that when she was stayed by the sound of wheels in the drive. 'Go and see who has called,' she commanded. 'It can't be the vicar, he always walks here. It may be Caroline from Brocket or my daughter, Harriet, from town. They will,' her ladyship said fretfully, 'descend upon me without a moment's warning as if Holywell were a hostelry, although they know they are welcome as life, provided the beds are aired.'

But as Miss Trimmer turned to go and see, she was hailed by a voice shouting, 'Hallo there, Selina! Ever fresh and evergreen.'

The owner of the voice was revealed in a rush down the steps of the terrace to embrace the flustered Selina with a bear-like hug.

She, palpitating, disengaged to curtsy and, in a bleating *tremolo*, to say, 'Your… Your Grace! What a happy … her ladyship will be delight… And how well, if Your Grace will pardon personalities, you look. I declare you have…'

'Grown? Of course. You tell me so every time we meet, by which reckoning I should now be eight feet high. And don't, my precious Trimmer, ask me when I am going to be married because you are so far the only person who never does pose me that unanswerable question — unanswerable since the one woman I have wished to marry cannot marry me as she is already a wife. And how well *you* are looking, dear Selina. You grow younger as I grow taller. Ah, you blush. It makes you look quite pretty. I declare I might even forsake my self-sworn celibacy if you blush at me like that. How is the granddam? Not too perturbed by Caro's latest naughtiness?'

'Her ladyship is very well, thank God. Has Your Grace had … tea?'

'No, I have not. In fact I've had nor bite nor sup since ten o'clock this morning. I had much business to do and no time to eat, and came post-haste from London to say goodbye to Grandmama before I leave for Ireland.'

'Ireland!' Miss Trimmer clasped her little mouse hands. 'When does Your Grace…?'

'The day after tomorrow. I am taking Caro and my aunt with me to Bessborough. William will follow later.'

'Dear me, this is very… Her ladyship will be… Would Your Grace care for a rump steak or a dish of chops? Tea is not sufficiently substantial for…'

'Anything you care to give me I will wolfishly devour. Aha, my grandmother has seen me. Don't get up, Grandmama.' He dashed forward, dropped on one knee to carry her hand to his lips and received her kiss dry and warm on his forehead.

'My darling boy! What a joyful surprise. Trimmer, see to His Grace's bed. You will stay with me, dear Devonshire, for a week or so, will you not? I have seen too little of you lately.'

'Only till tomorrow, ma'am, I fear. I leave for Ireland on Thursday. I have come to say goodbye. Caro is at Brocket. She sends all sorts of messages and love to you by me and begs you to forgive her for not coming in person but Augustus has not been very well — no, nothing to worry about, just one of his colds, but you know how she fusses over him.'

'Sit, my dear.' Lady Spencer indicated a chair. 'I will order fresh tea.'

'No, please do not, Grandmama. Selina is about to produce the fatted calf. I'll go in presently and eat it.'

'Caro, how is she?'

'She is well,' was the prompt reply. 'And William has shown so much sympathy and generosity to her over this deplorable affair that I revoke all I have ever said against him, though I still maintain that Caro would have been happier with me. Had she been my wife I would never have let her go astray, seeking other loves. She would have had a surfeit of mine.'

His gaze slipped past the old lady's eyes, fixed on him with something in them of the adoration of the Magi for this, her favourite grandson.

'So I often think,' she said, low-voiced. 'Yet though you might have been well matched I would never have agreed to a marriage of first cousins.'

'For the sake of the children's health?' he asked. 'But William is of no blood kin to Caro and they have — Augustus.'

'For their shared sorrow,' sighed his grandmother, and added briskly, 'Now, go indoors, dear boy, and have your meal. We do not sup till eight o'clock, and here comes Miss Trimmer, who will take you to your room. I expect you would like to wash after your journey.'

Later that evening, when prayers had been said and supper was over, Hart briefly gave Lady Spencer the facts of Caro's disappearance and her return to Melbourne House: how that she had sent a note to Byron, bidding him a last farewell, with no address, no inkling where she was, 'having forgotten,' Hart said, 'that Byron would question the driver of the hackney coach as to her whereabouts. And so soon as he heard she was with this doctor at Kensington he drove off and fetched her back. She went with him quite quietly in the end, although she begged him, at first, to elope with her to Paris. My aunt wrote all the facts to Leveson-Gower, and my sister Harriet came running to Devonshire House next morning with the whole bag of tricks hurled at my head.'

Lady Spencer, who during this recital had held herself in, now let herself out. 'What a thing to do — to go pawning her ring, poor rash misguided girl! I am thankful Byron had the sense to bring her home. Paris. Good heavens! I trust she will find these repeated eccentricities are favoured by none but herself. So what is the result of this fantastic escapade?'

'The result of that fantastic escapade, dear Grandmama,' Hart told her, 'is a streaming cold and her agreement, after pressure, to leave London *pro tem* for Ireland. Byron is at Cheltenham to drink the waters. He is always in a state about his health and goes in fear of inheriting his mother's avoirdupois. With the Irish Sea between them, well out of sight and mind, Caro may come to *her* senses — we hope.'

As all concerned with Caro hoped, when she, Augustus, her parents and William embarked at the end of the month *en masse* for Ireland. Hart had gone ahead and was at Lismore.

After a week or so at Bessborough, during which time Caro rang the changes from deepest gloom to wildest hilarity, she decided she would prefer to stay at Lismore, a few miles away. Her mother, anxious to avoid recurrent brainstorms, did not attempt to dissuade her. 'She must be humoured at all costs,' she told William, 'as much for my peace of mind as for hers. Don't you agree?'

William heartily agreed. There was excellent salmon fishing at Lismore; but Lord Bessborough flatly refused, he said, 'to be carted from pillar to post,' and would stay where he was. And why, he wished to know, could that girl of his not be content with his house but must needs go off to that dilapidated barrack of a place?

Scarcely a barrack, but dilapidated certainly, though Hart was bent on modernising much of it. Gaunt and grey, once the stronghold of the Earls of Cork, Lismore towered high above the lovely Blackwater river whose rapid stream churned a silver foam at the foot of the castle's walls. Directly faced by the Knockmele mountain, highest peak in that range of lavender-blue hills stretching eastwards, Caro was offered, on this her first visit to Lismore, promise of exciting mystical adventure. In the shadowed gloom of vast apartments hung with faded banners, tapestries, and ancestral portraits staring eternally down at armoured effigies, might be glimpsed the ghosts of the past when Lismore, erected on the site of an abbey in the reign of King John, had witnessed the storming of the castle by rebels in the year 1643.

Over the entrance gates were emblazoned the arms of the first Earl of Cork with the motto *God's Providence is our Inheritance*, but... 'There are no ghosts,' complained Caro. 'Hart swears it isn't haunted and I say it ought to be. He is too material to see what may be seen. The servants tell me the first earl walks in the tower that overlooks the garden. I shall watch for him by moonlight.'

She also found fault with Hart's taste in decoration, which was none of hers. 'You have made these beautiful rooms look like the parlour of a maiden aunt, with rosebud chintz, casement windows, and panelled doors instead of solid oak against stone walls. And the place is full of damp and rot.'

For her further grievance, Harriet Leveson-Gower was there installed as hostess to her brother's guests.

'She looks terrible,' was Harriet's opinion. 'Her eyes are starting from her head, she is worn to a bone and pale as death. What on earth possessed you,' she asked Hart, 'to bring her here? Why couldn't she have stayed at Bessborough?'

'She was miserable at Bessborough, and if you object to her looks and her company you know what you can do — take the next boat back to England. I didn't invite you to come, you invited yourself to spy on her and report to the Thorn and make more trouble. And I'll thank you,' Hart threateningly added, hot as Harriet was cold, 'to show some consideration for and sympathy with Caro, whom you have always disliked.'

'With reason,' his sister tartly rejoined, 'and William gives her all the sympathy and more than she deserves. He is an angel of forbearance and I only hope and trust he won't forbear too long. As for our aunt, Caro has almost been the death of her. You know — or don't you know? — that before they left London the poor soul broke a blood vessel and almost died of it as a result of that wretched girl's wickedness.'

'If that is so,' Hart said, 'that "poor soul" our aunt, looks remarkably well for one near to death. She dances jigs like a ten-year-old, drinks rum punch with the tenants and Caro's adorers, has affected an Irish brogue and sits up half the night writing reports of all her doings to your husband.' A reminder that Harriet would have wished to forget.

'I speak only for your good,' said she with acidulated magnanimity, 'and I warn you that wherever Caro is trouble follows. So take heed.'

Whereupon Hart regrettably made answer: 'Go shut you your potato jaw!' to send Harriet hurrying to pour out her account of it in letters to Granville, her sister, and the Thorn, who was doubtless not displeased to learn that *I hate her character, her feelings and herself when I am away from her but she interests me when I am with her, and to see her poor careworn face is dismal.*

Yet, however dismal her 'poor careworn face' appeared to Harriet, William was apparently unaffected by it. *He laughs and eats like a trooper,* is Harriet's account of him. She, it seems, was the only dismal member of the family at Lismore, since the young sparks of the neighbourhood found Caro's effervescence irresistible as she strove to outrival her mother in jigging, or entertain the company with quips, wisecracks and recitations of her poems; and one evening she infuriated Hart with repetitive complaints of 'damp, and fungus growing on the walls to have us all rheumatic when we're thirty, and Mama, who has reached the age when she refuses to tell it, will be walking on crutches, God forbid! And if I'm not mistaken I have here a distinguished visitor to bear me witness.' She jumped to her feet, ran to the door and flung it wide saying, 'Come in, my lord. I knew you would not fail me.'

A hush fell on the room. The men, sipping rum punch, looked expectantly over their tumblers at the open door that admitted no visitor, no sign of one. Lady Bessborough, at her tambour frame, stayed her needle in mid-air. Hart, his back to the grate where a log fire burned, muttered, 'Now what the deuce?' while Harriet, shrugging and whispering, said, 'A delusion. I've told you — she's out of her mind.'

And still nothing happened until Caroline, taking two candles from their sockets, held them on high and bade the unseen visitor, 'My lord, why do you hesitate to claim your rightful heritage? You are king of this castle which your ancestors have held for centuries past, and the duke, my cousin, is an interloper. Out with him — and you, my lord, come in!'

And there came, or rather hopped, in, amid shrieks from the ladies and guffaws from the gentlemen, a remarkably large and active frog.

'You see?' She wheeled round on Hart, who was shaking with laughter. 'Don't you dare say this house isn't damp. This gentleman here — Hi! Where is he?'

'Run to earth,' shouted Hart, 'after him, fellows. Tally-ho — a frog-hunt!' There was a general scrimmage, but the visitor had vanished.

'I'll tell you this,' said Caro, when the laughter had subsided, 'that his frog-like appearance is misleading. He is actually the scion of an ancient lineage dating back centuries to the Egyptians. If you know your Bible you will recall a plague of frogs that descended upon Pharaoh. Beware lest they plague you,' she pointed a finger at Hart, 'the usurper of their castle and their land. They have already begun to plague *me*. This very gentleman, who is now in temporary retreat, visited me in my bed last night. While I could name a dozen bedmates more attractive, evidently he could not.'

Yet not always was she laughter-making. She had her moods when that soft green plaintive land imbued her with an echo of its melancholy. Often she would walk alone down into the village where barefoot, ragged children played and scrambled in the dirt for the pennies she flung; and women in the doorways of their miserable hovels stood, stared, and blessed her as she passed handing each a silver coin.

There was an old man, too, in whom she delighted. He played the fiddle, was much in demand at wakes and weddings, and was almost always to be seen seated on a bench under a sycamore outside the village inn with a glass of ale at his elbow and a mongrel dog at his feet. He had long greyish hair falling either side of a long and narrow face. He gave the impression of being altogether long and narrow, very upright for his years, which he told her were older than time. He had a sharp pointed nose and eyes so pale under bushy grey eyebrows that they seemed to have no colour, like the white eyes of the blind.

She had first seen him followed by a swarm of children dancing to the tune he played. Up the village street they followed him who led them to the church, and in they went, Caro after them, to sit throughout the Mass: a children's Mass. The old man played the organ and the children sang: '*Gloria in excelsis Deo, et in terra pax hominibus bonae voluntatis. Laudamus te, benedicimus te, adoramus te…*' in their clear shrill young voices.

'Charming, charming,' she whispered, tears springing to her eyes to see those little ones go to the altar steps to receive the sacrament. Light from a stained-glass window filtered through, gilding the hair of Our Lady, at whose feet a row of candles blossomed like gold tulips.

The blessing was given, the children filed out, and he who played the fiddle was off to the inn and his pint. Caro waylaid him. 'Who taught you so tunefully and sweetly to play? You are very gifted.'

'Sure,' he replied, 'it was God who gave meself the gift. I played first fiddle — violin as they call it — in the Dublin orchestra. I was schooled in Dublin for me music as a boy.'

'What is your name?' she asked.

'O'Brien. And yours?'

'Mine is Caroline.'

'Och, 'tis a lovely name, and a lovely girl to wear it.' He looked into her eyes, smiling with his. 'Will ye sit ye down and take a glass with me?'

She sat her down under the sycamore and took a glass with him, brought by a girl, bare-legged, black-haired, her face like a sun-warmed peach.

'Will ye be visitin' the duke at the castle? Ye come from England by the voice of ye.'

She nodded. 'Yes.' She stooped to pat the dog who had come padding after them. 'Your dog, is he?'

'Sure, he's mine and all I have since I buried me wife and me daughter who had honey-gold hair like yours and eyes dark as the lough under rain. Do ye know poetry?'

'A little.'

'I could tell ye some poetry I've written here and there. I'd have made a book of it but I'm bone lazy. Now there's a mortal sin indeed is sloth, may God forgive me for it. Come now and I'll tell ye a tale. There was a child the first-born of a woman 'way there,' he gestured vaguely, 'beyond Wexford. A miracle it was, and she a wife of twenty years long past her prime. And to the babe where he lay in his cot came a couple from the hills, a man and woman. The man he kissed the child and said, "I'll give you music that your heart will never want for the joy of it all the years of your life, nor yet be lonely. And I'll give you," says he, "the words to write the music you make, words that are songs to be sung by them that come from under the waters and over the mountains rising up to the heavenly choir." That's what he said, and then the woman — it would be a woman, bad cess to her! — she made on the head o' the babe the sign o' the Black Pig o' the Valley than which there is nothing more heathen. So what in the name o' darkness can a man do at all that is marked with the sign o' the Pig? For there must always be a fight in his heart against the badness of sloth in him and the urge for to bring forth in blood and sweat the labour of his soul's creation that he needs must go begging for a groat and him playin' in the gutters for his potheen and his books of verse unwritten and his songs unsung. And if you disbelieve the truth I'm telling ye go ask me auld Aunt Mary at me home in County Wexford. She'll vouch for it and living still past ninety. She was there and saw those two with her own squint eye that holds more than mortal sight in it.'

'Write me a song,' said Caro, 'and make me some music, and I'll have your soul's creation bought for all the world to hear.'

He shook his head; his pale eyes dilated till their pupils were black against the whites of them. 'No, lady, no. The music that I make is not for nor of your world. 'Tis of my world, which none may enter save the chosen.'

She returned to Lismore full of it.

'A poet lost and buried here, one who plays the violin like an angel. His bowing is masterly. What is he?' she asked of Hart. 'Do you know him? O'Brien?'

'O'Brien? Yes. One time hack writer on a Dublin rag, swills ale all day and is drunk all night, when he is not hauled in for poaching. He has been in and out of gaol half a dozen times. I've stood bail for him more than once. You'll find him or his replica in every inn of every village, and in every town in Ireland.'

They all rejoiced in Caro's convalescence from Byronic fever, which appeared to be more than ever contagious in London.

'We must let her see,' was Hart's advice to William, 'that we treat the whole thing as a joke, then she, too, will see it that way, which would be the best possible cure. This Byron craze is an epidemic. It attacks young and old with equal virulence, but I've heard of no fatalities as yet.'

'Yes, but —' William looked up from a leather-bound wallet of flies he was sorting for fishing — 'if, as in Caro's case, the prognosis is favourable, there is always the danger of relapse.'

179

At present, however, the danger of relapse appeared to be receding. That she wrote to and received letters from Byron was no secret, since she would read them to all who cared to listen. The first of these, couched in terms of undying devotion, is of doubtful authenticity; indeed, Harriet would have it she had written it herself. Among other ardent protestations, he tells her that nothing he could say, do or ever had said and done could possibly convey his real sentiments towards her, his only love; and he vows that no other woman could ever hold *that place in my affections which is and shall be most sacred to you till I am nothing...* In a postscript he adds that he does not care who knows this, and tells her to make what use she will of it, for he is hers *most freely and entirely to obey, honour and to fly with me if you will...*

But she had flown from him and, to all intent, was in no haste to take flight with him again.

Lady Melbourne, at pains to let her know by way of Harriet, would have it Byron had told her he had written 'all manner of absurdities to keep her quiet'. Which may have accounted for this latest absurdity.

William, who, throughout the whole affair, had maintained an attitude of whimsical tolerance, did not regard this interchange of letters as indicative of an unconquerable passion, but rather as the natural sequence of their enforced estrangement. He had never been impressed by the physical beauty of Byron or by his affectations of the *Childe Harold* pose. While admitting his brilliance — modified, however, by superficiality — he graded Caroline as the more sincere in her emotional reactions. Yet now, with the danger of propinquity removed, was her apparent return to norm to be taken as a healthy sign or a deliberate deception?

Time would show.

Time did show, to bring about calamitous upheaval.

With Caroline safely out of the way, Lady Melbourne could enjoy to the full Byron's professed admiration. Thankful for the opportunity of widening the breach between him and William's troublesome young wife, she duly reported to Caroline that Byron had definitely stated he no longer cared for her and welcomed this temporary separation as a means to a permanent end. Moreover, she broadly hinted that his affections were transferred to another.

This nameless other to whom she alluded was not herself, as she believed, but Lady Oxford, which must have been as shattering a blow to the Thorn as it had been to Caro.

These various communications wrought havoc on her tormented nerves. More frequent were her paroxysmal outbursts, her rageful scenes and sleepless nights when she would wake William demanding that he take her to London or post-haste to Dublin and leave her there to die, 'or I,' she screamed, 'will hasten death myself!'

She jumped from the bed, lit a candle and rushed to the window. Fumbling with the latch, she wrenched it open. 'See! The Blackwater is in high spate. Down there in those rapids I'll find surcease from this misery of life. I'll make a lovely corpse floating on the river.'

Hysterically laughing she began to scramble over the low sill and was caught back, with some violence, by William.

'Stop this foolery or I'll lay you across my knee and give you the hiding you deserve and have never had. But do you play me these tricks again, my girl, you'll have a sore bottom for a week!'

At which inexcusable utterance, that, for a moment, silenced her, lips parted ready for another scream, she fell instead to laughing, and stood on her toes to wind her arms round his neck.

'William, how I love you! Not a living soul but you would dare say that to me, and I adore you for it. Yes, thrash me till I'm sore and cannot sit. I would enjoy to be thrashed — caned as if I were a schoolboy, which is all I am *au fond* and you know it. But what you *don't* know — or do you? Yes, you do! — is that I'm possessed by a demon at these times when the moon is at the full as now. Look!'

She wriggled free of him who held her and again ran to the window, where the curtains swelled to the wind. The night was wild, draped in a beggar's cloak of a cloud with the moon high-riding. 'You see! Here she comes — how fat-faced she is tonight, as if she had sucked into herself all the milk of humanity without its human kindness! She looks a regular bloated old witch with nothing in her of the chaste Diana. And when she is like this, wide-grinning, smug, self-satisfied, her effect on me is so baneful that I feel if I don't get her out of my blood I'll run mad — *mad*!' Raising her hands she fisted them to beat the air and turned on him, eyes glittering in the light of the candle; and then, in a voice of a sudden passionless, she childishly asked, 'Is that what is meant by being moonstruck, would you say?'

He would not say; but he took and lifted her and laid her on their bed, smoothed the tousled curls from her wet forehead and whispered, 'Quiet, my love, lie quiet. The moon is a world in embryo and thus cannot disturb you.'

She jerked up her head from the pillow. 'In embryo? What's that you tell me?'

'I have often thought,' said he, 'that the moon, after incalculable millions of years, may evolve into a world maybe inhabited, even as this world, God-created, has evolved from slime and darkness as given in the Scriptures. That cold pale orb out there in eternal infinity is too remote to affect you, my darling, nor any being on this earth, although you may not be far wrong to believe it feeds upon this planet as a babe suckles at its mother's breast.'

Her eyes were wide upon him. 'William, what a wonderful thought! If that were so it might account for much that is incomprehensible, beyond our understanding... Lunacy derived from *luna,* moon-ridden, meaning that certain individuals, myself *not* excepted, are more vulnerable, more sensitised to the moon's demands. I used to think it was a sun unborn.'

'Think no more of moon or its demands,' said William, 'think of me and my demands and that I love you and I want you, which is all you need to know and to believe.'

So, curled close within his arms, soothed and comforted, she slept at last.

'His sympathy and patience,' Lady Bessborough declared, 'set a heart-rending example to us all. No man but he would tolerate her vagaries.'

But even William's sympathy and patience were frayed to a raw edge when Byron, having ceased to write or to answer any of her letters demanding a reason for his silence, sent a reply of such sadistic brutality that she lost every vestige of control and for a few days her mind was completely unhinged.

It is the letter reproduced in her novel, *Glenarvon,* written and published after the final breach between them, in which she figures as the love-wracked Calantha, Lady Avondale.

I am no longer your lover; and since you oblige me to confess it, by this truly unfeminine persecution, — learn that I am attached to another...

(Which had already been confirmed by the rumours circulated by the Thorn.) *I shall ever continue your friend, if your Ladyship will permit me so to style myself; and, as a first proof of my regard, I offer you this advice, correct your vanity which is ridiculous; exert your absurd caprices upon others; and leave me in peace.*

    Your most obedient Servant,
    Byron.

The shock of this unmitigated insolence undid all the good that the respite in Ireland and William's tact and care of her had done. After the first blinding impact of the blow came repercussion.

Mrs. Peterson, who was with her at the time when Caroline read the letter, could vouch for it, and did — to Lady Bessborough — that she stood 'like an image turned to stone, then staggered and would have fallen in a faint and so white I thought her dying, but that I laid her on the couch and forced brandy down her throat till she came to.'

It is likely the letter, dropped from her hand in her momentary lapse of consciousness, was recovered by Mrs. Peterson and read not only by that estimable woman, but by all the family at Lismore.

Hart, in a fury at this insult to his darling, was for taking a boat there and then to England 'to slit the fellow's guts and string him up. Shooting is too good an end for that misbegotten cur.'

William, as usual not to be committed either for or against 'that misbegotten cur', was more than ever tender with his wife. She, when revived from her fainting fit, sent Peterson out of the room to fetch her mother and, in her absence, provided herself with William's razor. When Lady Bessborough arrived she was brandishing it within a few inches of her throat.

'You may tell him,' she shrieked at the poor lady, 'that he has murdered me by proxy. I do the work for him that his words have done for me — with this!'

It speaks well for Lady Bessborough's courage that, though driven almost frantic during these last weeks by Caro's frenzies, she managed, at this terrifying moment, to stay calm and collected. With remarkable presence of mind she seized her daughter's hand, and, turning the razor to her own throat, said quietly, 'If killing must be done, kill me.'

It had the desired effect; the razor fell to the ground. Mrs. Peterson, who had followed her mistress into the room, picked it up and bore it away.

Caro, baulked of her horror scene, substituted in its stead a fit of convulsions, beating her head against the wall, writhing on the floor with kicks and screams and vows of vengeance on that 'monster of cruelty, may he rot in hell!'

She was got to bed, purged, plastered, given laudanum to ease the pain in her head caused by repeated bangings, and was eventually induced to sleep the clock round.

Lady Bessborough, herself on the verge of a breakdown, had also taken to her bed attended by Peterson, who, when Caro's maid had been sent on some errand, took the opportunity of 'speaking my mind to you, my lady,' she said, 'by your leave.'

Beak-nosed, lantern-jawed and loyal to the bone was Mrs. Peterson, who spoke her mind with no mincing of words to the frail, pale Caroline, whose little body seemed to have shrunk on receipt of Byron's letter. Her eyes looked enormous, darkly shadowed in the pallor of her face.

'It breaks my heart,' thus did Mrs. Peterson unburden, 'who have known you, my lady, before you was born so to say, since I watched your mother growing big with you for the full nine months, and this I'll swear, that you'll be the death of her as sure as fate if you go givin' way to these screaming bouts to bring to her another spit o' blood. If you could see her as I do when she turns to her old Peterson, her eyes drowned in tears and her dear head on my breast crying heartbroken, "O Peterson, what can I do to save my poor girl besotted as she is with Lord So-and-so" — no names is ever mentioned, my lady being on her guard against them ear-to-keyhole Irish sluts of housemaids. I wouldn't trust 'em an inch, I wouldn't, not after I sees my best pair of yellow garters on the legs of that one what does my room — yes, slipped down they did, being too big for her — but I said nothing to the housekeeper, not wishful to make more trouble for His Grace.'

'Well, what,' asked Caro wearily, 'did my mother say, O Peterson?'

'Her ladyship, she says,' bridled Peterson, chin up, 'that noble lord without a name what plays so fast and loose with you — and this is what *I* says and not your sainted mother — does either of you ever think of Mr. Lamb, so kind and good a husband, and what he must feel to see you in your tearing tempers raging after his lordship? Oh no, none may cross you, my lady, nor deny you what you want and what you'll have. Forgive me that I speaks so bold who dandled you upon my knee from your first month, but speak I must and will, for her dear sake who bore you and almost died of it, so long in labour was she, with three doctors at the bedside and thinkin' all 'ope gone of life for you which God be thanked was saved.'

'Pity I *was* saved,' muttered Caro. 'I'm only a curse to you all.'

'Nay, now, my little lady,' urged Peterson. 'I should never have spoke as I did but for her, that pure saint —'

'Not so much of the saint, and not so pure neither,' put in Caro *sotto voce*.

'— who grieves to break her heart for you who should be a blessing, not a curse to her, and that good gentleman your husband, and your child. Forget his lordship who is so changeable as any weather-cock — and you too, my lady, if I may make so bold. A few months ago it was Sir Godfrey and now it is this other has turned your head and made you scare your angel mother out of her life with that razor, and oh, Lady Caroline, pray to God for strength of mind to behave as you ought, for this is dreadful.'

'*You're* dreadful,' blazed Caro, 'coming at me with your long face and your homilies. You forget yourself, woman — no, you don't — you don't! You have every right to lecture me, you good dear thing. How wicked I am! Do you think God will forgive me? I have no strength of mind. Byron has weakened my will. He's a wizard, a devil, and I'm caught in his claws but I won't be his creature — I won't, I won't! I hate him, *hate* him, hate him!'

She began to beat at the pillows in another of her screaming fits that sent Peterson hurrying for sal volatile and brought William from a room below. Striding to the bed he took her by surprise and by the shoulders, saying hardily, close-lipped: 'I've had enough of this. You've gone too far and I have not gone far enough.'

Silenced, staring up at him, she caught back her breath on a sob to ask, 'Wha — what do you mean?'

'I mean that short of spanking you I am taking you,' his eyes rested upon her with a softness that belied the curt announcement, 'to Dublin in the morning. You can tell your maid to pack.'

He had thought that to get her there and keep her there in fresh surroundings for a while, would give her some new interest in the not-unlikely acquisition of an equerry at the Viceroy's Court; but so soon as they arrived at the Dolphin Hotel she took to her bed in a state of melancholia.

There were no more hysterics, no scenes, no threats of hurling herself out of windows. She lay, scarcely speaking, refusing to eat. Her mother, as usual, was frantic and believed her to be dying although William suspected another of her acts in which she gave a good impersonation of herself in a decline: heartbroken, fading away, gently slipping from life into eternity.

Better every ill to prove
Than own the pains and joys of love.

She had written that in one of her letters to Hart, and repeated it to William in a whispering wan little voice when he sat at her bedside.

'I will call in a doctor to prove your every ill,' said he unsympathetically, case-hardened.

'My ills,' she murmured, 'are incurable. I will have no doctor.'

But a doctor, determined William, she must have, who advised she be bled although from the look of her, so pale and lifeless, it would seem as if the blood in her veins had ceased to flow. She submitted with a patient martyrdom that deceived no one except her mother. Convinced her end was near, Lady Bessborough insisted she return to England, and in November they were back again in London.

'Still very subdued yet calm and more rational,' was William's report of her. But not so rational as it would appear when, despite all opposition, she resolved to see Byron and extract from him an explanation of his 'monstrous wicked letter'.

Yet, once free of her, he was not to be caught in her clutches again. Moreover, Jane Oxford, who had him tied securely to her apron-strings, would offer unlimited favour only on condition that he remain leashed.

While Lady Melbourne encouraged his decision to escape from Caroline, she must accept with what grace she could muster his adherence to a rival — though far better, the Thorn may have reasoned, that he be enslaved by the redoubtable Jane than by that 'dreadful young woman', William's wife. She may also have foreseen that Byron would tire soon enough of his elderly charmer and seek more placid, fresh and youthful virgin soil to cultivate and to enjoy the fruits thereof.

That her niece Annabella had refused his offer dismayed Lady Melbourne not at all. She was well aware that this prim little blue-stocking had not entirely discarded thought of Byron, if not as a husband, as a man of whom she wrote in her journal:

There is a chivalrous generosity in his ideas of love and friendship, and selfishness is totally absent from his character … When indignation takes possession of his mind — and it is easily excited — his disposition becomes malevolent. He hates with the bitterest contempt, is inclined to open his heart unreservedly to those whom he believes good *even without the preparation of much acquaintance.*

Had he opened his heart unreservedly to her whom he 'believed good'? From her guarded edifice Annabella watched the fantastic comedy between her cousin's wife and Byron, which was rapidly turning to drama. She had heard various reports of Caro's suicidal reaction to his final letter; the razor episode had become such common knowledge that it was now stale news.

In the few months after Caroline's return to London further interesting reports of her were circulated. Along the Ladies' Mile in the park, on those green springtime afternoons, when the carriages and coaches halted at the barriers, where promenaders formed a delicately colourful mosaic against a background of bright tulips in the flower beds, a buzz of Byron and his 'little Lamb' was on every lip.

'My dear Lady X, did you know…? Did you hear…? Can you believe…?'

''Tisn't possible…!'

'It is, I vow, so may I die…!'

'You really mean to say…?'

'I do not say, the picture-dealer says…'

'Yes, my love, a forgery. She must have traced his writing, and with what pains to do it!'

'A picture of and by whom?'

'Of himself, of course, and by some obscure artist. She would not go to such lengths for a Holbein, but for him, ah, yes!'

It was all over town: how Caro Lamb had sent a letter purporting to come from Byron not, as talk would have it, to a picture-dealer, but to his publisher, John Murray, in possession of his portrait and demanding its immediate return. So exactly did she forge his hand that even an expert in graphology might have found it difficult to differentiate between the true and false.

Nor was this all. In her frustration, jealousy and wounded pride she vowed vengeance upon him by every incredible means. She had the buttons on her pages' liveries engraved *Ne Crede Biron* — 'Do Not Trust Byron'. She bombarded him with letters, imploring his return to her. She begged for a lock of his hair in a bracelet. He complied with a lock of his valet's hair of a similar shade to his own. This deception occasioned much mirth when related to his friends, not omitting Lady Melbourne.

Thinking to turn her from her fruitless chase of Byron, William took her down to Brocket. There it was hoped she would recuperate, enjoy her rides, her rambles in the country and the admiration of neighbouring young men, ever-ready aspirants as successors to her inconstant swain. But she gave them nothing of herself more than invitation to the waltz.

She did, however, devise a singular performance for the entertainment of the county and the villagers. This, her *pièce de résistance,* took place in the park at Brocket Hall.

The month of May had brought a heatwave with a burgeoning of blossom, a creamy lace of hawthorn in the hedges, white and pink candles glowing in the chestnuts along the avenue. When evening spread a bridge of dusk between night and the dying day, a group of village children, exactly dressed alike in white, were assembled round a bonfire stacked high. On this was placed an effigy, grotesque in its life-sized resemblance to Byron, stuffed with straw and wearing a velvet coat with open-throated shirt topped by a mask that Caro had carefully modelled. Dragging the thing after her she arranged it in a sitting posture on the pile, to a chorus of delighted shrieks and giggles from the children and her pages, of whom she refused assistance.

'I am the high priestess of this sacred rite. I will give you the signal,' she said to her favourite page. 'You shall sprinkle the faggots with this.' She handed him a bottle containing an oily liquid. 'You others, light the tapers when I speak the word, and we will see — what we will see!'

The young gentlemen of the neighbourhood arrived to find her greatly in her element. Relegated to a circle of seats some distance from that which she was pleased to call the 'sacrificial altar', they were strictly enjoined not to utter a word but to 'watch and pray'.

She wore a transparent gown over flesh-pink tights; a floating scarf hung from her shoulders and was held at her wrists by loops of cord so that, as she spread her arms, it gave the impression of wings. Fairy-like she fluttered, dancing round the enthroned figure that seemed in the half-light to be alive. Then, turning to her group of boys, she bade them, 'It is taper time. Light up! Set to!'

They set to with much excited will, and when the wood began to crackle and flames to lick at the feet of the object in a pair of William's slippers, she took from a basket carried by a page a handful of necklaces, bracelets, rings, various gifts from Byron to her, along with his letters — though not the originals. Those she was careful to keep; these were copies.

One by one the ornaments and letters were flung into the leaping blaze that soon became a furnace. Gathering the children round her she stood in their midst and, drilled by her, they sang:

'Burn, fire, burn, while wondering boys exclaim,
And gold and trinkets glitter in the flame,
Ah, look not thus on me so brave, so sad,
Shake not your heads nor say the lady's mad.'

But it was not the little girls and boys, participants in this game contrived, as they believed, for their amusement, who thought the lady mad. Accustomed to garden fêtes and fairs at Brocket, they regarded the performance as no more than a belated Guy Fawkes celebration. Her admirers were no less lavish in applause, with music and dancing on the lawn to end the revels.

Yet when news of that carousal filtered through to Melbourne House it was viewed by the Lambs as further indication of her derangement. 'She must be kept under restraint,' was her mother-in-law's verdict, which William attempted to do by insisting she remain at Brocket in the care of Mrs. Peterson.

This mandate, that she rightly guessed originated from the Thorn, brought about another hysterical fit and her immediate departure from Brocket in defiance of detention.

To William she said, 'You and your mother will not be content till you have me in a padded cell. Must I be labelled a lunatic because I choose to give a children's party?'

There was no arguing with her. She would never accept criticism, nor admit herself wrong.

'Very well then,' sighed William, 'back to London you go.'

Back to London she went, loud in abuse of Byron, with vows to 'ruin and destroy him' alternating with letters imploring him to grant her an interview.

Still under Lady Oxford's dominance, he was adamant; he would not see her.

'No matter how she threatens,' he swore to Dallas, striding up and down his room at Albany where he had moved from his chambers in St James's, 'I'm damned if I'll be drawn again into contact with that creature. She has worn me out, has made me a laughing stock and target for the gutter press. Think you how she must have studied my handwriting to deceive Murray and get that picture from him.' Then, throwing back his head, he burst out laughing. 'God, she's a wonder! Her impudent audacity delights, while her infernal persecution fills me with such abhorrence that though I love no other woman I will hate her to the last hour of my life!'

Dallas, who had listened time and again to similar tirades, was inclined to discredit Byron's 'abhorrence' of 'that creature'. He let him rave and went his way with one last word of warning: 'Beware lest she light another bonfire to burn you!'

But no sooner was he gone than Byron, at his desk, dashed off a letter to her. *I am not ignorant of your determination to obtain what you are pleased to call revenge,* he wrote, reminding her of those repeated threats to 'ruin and destroy' him. He believed her capable of performing all her menaces, yet, *as once I hazarded everything for you I will not now shrink from you. In your actions you hurt only yourself but is that nothing to me who wished you well?* She might settle as she pleased the arrangement for a 'conference' — and if still she persisted in meeting him again, he agreed it must be so.

And so it was.

Pacing the floor of his study, his eye on the clock, his thumbnail fretted almost to the quick, he awaited her arrival, timed for three o'clock. When at last she came — half an hour late — she wore, for some reason best known to herself, her page's costume.

She stood there in the doorway, admitted by Fletcher, who discreetly withdrew but, at his master's command, stayed within earshot. And at this sight of her all the hate Byron felt for 'that creature' surged up in a storm of passionate desire. He loathed her, he despised her, he wanted her, he loved her...

'Yes,' the words broke from him on a breath, 'God help me, yes! There can be no release from her.'

She saw his lips whiten as they moved, yet heard no sound from them, and went to him, a pale wisp of a girl or, bewitchingly to devastate — a boy, in her purple velvet tunic and green pantaloons, her eyes dark and drowned in a sudden rush of tears. With an impatient gesture she rubbed the cuff of her sleeve across them and said chokingly, 'I'm not crying. Are you?'

He was. A sob tore at his throat and he took her. She let herself be taken, held close, content, appeased. And all the ache and longing of these tortured months were for her as they had never been. For him? He could not say, could only wonder at himself, 'who am rooted in you, lost in you, spellbound by your devilry.' Dragging his mouth from explorative delight of her he managed to articulate, 'I did not ask for this. I did not wish for this. I had thought to have been done with you.'

She raised herself on tiptoe to lay her cheek to his and tell him, 'You never will be done with me, not while you live nor when I die.' Disengaging, she released herself to button her tunic that he had torn apart to find and kiss her breasts. 'I feel so strangely dispassionate,' she said, 'as if in this moment you had killed me. I may have died, and this, then, is our hell together: that we may never know the joy of ultimate possession. I was not meant for womanhood. I'm wrongly fashioned. God's hand slipped when making me.'

He turned from her, went over to the mantelshelf and, leaning his arms upon it, bowed his head to them. She saw his shoulders heave. A faint smile came upon her lips — was it of triumph? — when she heard him say, flinging out an arm in an exaggerated gesture, his face still hidden, his voice tear-muffled, 'I've been a swine, a brute. I can never hope you will forgive me.'

She went to him then, not touching but close enough for him to hear her whisper, ''Tis I must be forgiven, not by you but by my God, for having loved you more than I love Him. I'll leave you now. We cannot, dare not, meet again.'

His head lifted; he wheeled round on her savagely.

'What is it that wars with all I feel for you, all that eye, ear, heart and tongue could seek, all that I admire, exalt, despise, and yet to know I am entwined by your accursed sorcery, *with* you and *in* you as if by some astral umbilical cord, so that when we are lost to each other I think I will bleed internally, eternally. Hah! You stare. You have the eyes of a gazelle, soft, dark, melting, yet your look penetrates as if you read what's written in my heart.'

'The print,' she said with that same smile, 'is too small. I should need spectacles, rose-coloured.'

'But my heart, perverted, long destroyed, is open and the print is large enough for you to read my epitaph: *He hurt none but himself and her.*'

'Byron, don't — don't torture me!'

In that stifled cry was all the pain, the anguish she had suffered, or had thought she suffered; for even now these two, in this last act of their love drama, played each their roles with a flamboyant eloquence that was yet to reach its climax. As for him, in some close recess of his mind, every word he spoke to her he stored for future reference.

He knelt to take her hands in his, crushing her rings into her fingers, gazing up at her as if to impress upon his memory each feature of her face: her swimming eyes, her loosened mouth, warm, bruised and reddened from his touch.

'Friends meet to part...' His brow furrowed as if grappling to recapture from some erased palimpsest an errant verse, 'Love laughs at faith — true foes, once met, are joined till death, and so — farewell!'

It was all intensely touching. She wept, he wept. He kissed her fingertips, opened the door for her, bowed her out and rang for Fletcher. 'For God's sake, brandy! Her ladyship has done for me.'

'Very good, my lord. You will take the brandy neat?'

'Yes, neat and strong, but very strong, for I am very — weak.'

Weak he was when predatorily pursued and captured, even while he fought and struggled to be free of her, hurling every weapon of abuse in his armoury to soil her name. He inundated Lady Melbourne with innumerable letters inveighing against his 'Little Mania', as he called her, *whose bitterest enemy,* he said, *could not wish her such a fate as mine to have her now thrown back on me.*

But these repeated declarations of hate were unconvincing. That they had met was common knowledge; that they would meet again was certain, although he had sworn they would not. The incurably romantic Lady Bessborough may have hoped the affair would end in a tender heartbroken renunciation of their 'love', which would develop into a firm and lasting friendship such as hers and her 'dearest Lord G…'

'My Lady "Blarney"', Byron to Dallas reported, 'is horrified at my lack of romance. Yet it is she, if you but knew, who is responsible for the whole affair. From the beginning when, for my sins, I fell victim to the fascination of that absurd little dangerous and maddening creature who should have lived in Greece two thousand years ago — she has the quality of some demi-virginal *hetaera* — in those early stages of my infatuation her mother told me that my love, — for love it was at first — could not, nor never would be, returned. That raised the devil in me and now the "Blarney" professes horror and disgust at my behaviour to her precious sweet pet Lamb.'

But not so disgusted as was William, who had taken to himself Byron's rejection of his wife's renewed advances.

'I stand between two fires,' Byron laughingly complained to Lady Melbourne. If I speak to her, *he* is insulted; if I speak to him, *she* is insulted. Was ever man in such perverted humour wooed? But never in such humour to be won.'

It is possible he enjoyed the notoriety that Caro's 'persecution', as he defined her chase of him, had caused. Since the furore occasioned by Cantos One and Two of *Childe Harold* had died down and Cantos Three and Four were yet to come, he may have welcomed the publicity that cried her name and his on every tongue. Yet even he, whose meteoric triumph was still a novelty to wonder at, retreated, battered, from the scandal focused on the pair of them with which all London rang in the following July.

It was the night of a ball held at the house of Lady Heathcote, one of the many hostesses who, although not of the most exclusive inner circle led by Carlton House, was sufficiently within its outer bounds to send cards to the regent's intimate friends, if not to that First Gentleman himself.

This lavish entertainment wanted nothing of extravagance as demanded by *le beau monde,* of whom many were invited and a number came. Sheridan was there, out at elbows, out of pocket, notwithstanding that the regent had paid his latest debts to the tune of three thousand pounds. With a brandy-sodden eye on watch for Lady Bessborough, who, disappointingly, was absent, he held audience with a spread of charming hands and Irish brogue.

Dallas was there, Rogers, and Hobhouse, who had been at Cambridge with Byron and accompanied him on his travels as faithful close a confidant as Dallas. The son of a Bristol merchant, a staunch Whig and Nonconformist, a classical scholar and dabbler in verse, Hobhouse was equally determined to protect Byron from the onslaught of Caro as her vacilating lover half-heartedly was not.

The Ladies Melbourne and Oxford were there; the exquisite Jane looking fifteen years less than her admitted forty which was nearer forty-five, with her ravishing complexion and pert retroussé nose. The Thorn, who bragged of her age as sixty-two, wearing on her beautiful white hair a Regency cap crowned by three nodding plumes, was magnificent in amber faille. To those not aware of the rivalry existing between these two beauties, both idolising if not reciprocally idolised by Byron, it might well have been assumed they were the most devoted friends. On their entrance, and by one accord, they gravitated to the group surrounding 'Sherry'.

He appeared to be in greatest form. No matter that his lilac-coloured kerseymeres were threadbare at the knees; that his sage-green swallow-tails were at least five years demode, that his cream marcella waistcoat lacked a button, he, as always, failing Byron, was the centre of attraction, while the women buzzed around him with one name paramount.

'Is it true that Byron and *son petit agneau* are again *engloutissement*?'

'Ah now,' sparkled Sheridan, 'is he not known to be too much of every lady's man to be the man of any lady?'

A chorus of feminine laughter and appreciative chuckles from the men approved this quip, with a challenge from Hobhouse.

'One might suggest that every lady would delight to be his woman.'

'As what woman in the world would not?' countered Sherry. 'A youth of remarkable parts and possibilities if he don't fritter his gift in too-facile verbiage.'

'Is not his facility one of his most outstanding gifts?' Jane Oxford lifted limpid eyes to ask. 'Look at the fluence and ease with which he writes.'

'Yes, but,' Sherry flashed her his irresistible smile, 'easy writing makes damned hard reading.'

'I do not write easily.'

Byron had joined them. Immediately the women clustered round him while the men, with exception of Hobhouse and Dallas, moved away. And watching their withdrawal, to know himself deliberately cold-shouldered, his brow darkened. So it had been all these last few months with the men of Caro's set. Headed by Hart, a faction was forming against him.

'Byron!' Lady Heathcote bore down upon the group, dispersing his flock of devotees. 'I did not see you arrive. How shockingly remiss of me not to receive you.'

'The remission, dear lady, is mine. I ask your pardon for my late arrival.' He bowed over her hand and was led away to partake of refreshment. In the adjoining ballroom musicians were playing a waltz. As Byron, with Lady Heathcote on his arm, limped to the buffet where Sheridan already was sampling champagne, Caro, ethereal in clinging crepe no whiter than her face under her primrose-fair curls, approached him and stood in his path. Their hostess, with an uneasy glance from the scowling young gentleman to the pale young lady, said, 'Lady Caroline, are you not dancing?'

'Yes, I will dance if —' to Byron she made a mock curtsy — 'his lordship permits. I presume you do not now object that I waltz?'

'With every man in the room,' he replied. 'You were adept at cutting a caper before I was cutting my teeth. It would be my pleasure to watch you.'

She turned from him, her lower lip caught under; and, sighting Hart at the buffet with Sheridan, she called, 'Come, Devon, waltz with me.'

They waltzed, and waltzed again. She kept him at it until, panting, he protested, 'Dearest life, I am not a tee-to-tum. I've a stitch in my side and my head's in a whirl. Let me rest.'

'Dance, dance!' she cried. 'You will dance with me until you drop.' Her eyes went voyaging over his shoulder to see Byron with a woman, a stranger to her, making for the supper room. At that moment the waltz came to an end.

'Now, my poor puffing grampus, you may rest.' She released herself from Hart. 'I am in need of refreshment, so are you.'

She steered him through the archway, trailing Byron and his lady, tall, full-bosomed, bronze-haired with a mouth made for laughter. They were both laughing at something he had murmured in her ear as they took their seats at a table laid for two.

'Who is she?' whispered Caroline.

'Augusta Leigh, his sister… No, Car, you can't.' She was making full speed for their table. Hart pulled her back. She rounded on him.

'Leave me be. I will!' She darted forward and, as Byron gave an order to a footman, she bade him, 'Place a chair for myself and His Grace. Will you not,' she addressed herself to Byron, 'present me to your sister?'

His face stormy, he rose, effected the introduction; and Hart, bowing to the lady, said, 'My duty, madam, but I fear we intrude.'

'No, indeed!' cried Augusta in a clear high voice. 'I am delighted to meet Lady Caroline, of whom I hear so much. Pray join us if you will, dear Duke. I and my brother meet so seldom, and there is all to tell each other now I am here in London in waiting on the queen. I am *such* a country bumpkin.' She laughed wide and loud, showing a double row of strong white teeth and the red cavern of her mouth down to her uvula. 'There is so much to do buying clothes for myself and night-shifts for my husband, and the opera — 'tis a great treat to be in London but not to wait upon Her Majesty. Hush! That's as near to treason as no matter — but how we are bored!' She threw up her eyes. '*Ennuyé* to extinction, sitting in a circle of funereal madams with their everlasting chat and Handel's *Largo*. Her Majesty will have Handel every night because of the poor king who used to play him on the organ. Oh dear, oh dear!' More laughter. 'And our naughty sweet young future queen the only ray of sunshine in the morgue — who *will* expose her pantalettes with frills and legs stuck out to give Her Majesty heart failure... Darling, did you hear?' She tapped Byron's fingers clenched upon the table, his knuckles whitening. 'Please pay attention. I was telling Lady Caroline that Princess Charlotte insists she shows her drawers — the most delicious madcap of a child, admiring her ankles to dismay that poke-nosed governess of hers, not my sister-in-law, the Duchess of Leeds, but the other one, Lady de Clifford. "My dear princess, you are showing your drawers." "I d-don't care if I do." She has an adorable stutter. "Your Highness's drawers are too long." "The D-Duchess of Bedford's are longer!" Are those quail? I adore them.'

Byron, still standing, told the footman who had brought chairs, 'There is not enough room for four seats at this table. Your ladyship,' he bowed to her, ignoring Hart, 'will permit that I leave you with my sister and the duke?'

'I have no intent,' Hart said with ice, 'to incommode you.' And to the garrulous Augusta, 'Your servant, madam.'

Then … it all happened in a second.

Caro, who had taken a glass from the table, crushed it between her fingers with such ferocity that it broke into fragments. Blood spurted. Augusta screamed. 'She's cut herself. See, she has a dagger!'

She had dropped the glass and seized a knife. Striking an attitude she pointed it at Byron as if about to thrust.

'Do, my dear,' he drawled, 'but be sure you strike at your heart, not mine. You have struck there already.'

'To hell with you — I'll strike again!' she flung at him.

'Come, Hart.'

She swung round and ran off; her gown was splashed with crimson drops. Hart caught her arm.

'Caro, you little fool. What have you done?'

'The glass broke and it cut me. That woman, his sister, or half-sister, or whatever — he told me once she is the only woman he has ever loved. How she gabbles. Is she always so hare-brained?'

'Yes, very vague and crinkum-crankum. You're hurt! There's blood all over you.'

She gave a nonchalant glance at her gown. 'It looks much worse than it is. Now pray don't make a fuss,' for he had grabbed a passing page.

'Call a maid to attend her ladyship with bandages and a basin of warm water. Caro, come into this anteroom. I'll bathe it.'

'Dear soul, it's nothing. Just a scratch. I always bleed pints even for a pinprick, yet I appear to be so bloodless. Perhaps that's why. Yes, come away, everybody's staring. And now they'll say I'm a homicidal, suicidal maniac to make a thing of it.'

And make a thing of it they did, in Mayfair and St James's and in all the clubs, with a damnifying article in a scurrilous rag known as *The Satirist*. Of the different versions floated far and wide, much was guesswork, very little known. The current and most favoured imputation would have it she attempted to stab Byron with a carving knife and when he parried her attack she stabbed herself, and was carried away in a swoon from loss of blood.

In her account of it — nearer the truth than any — she admitted having taken up a knife to threaten him in jest, that she had cut her fingers, not with the knife but with a glass of delicate crystal that broke in her hand. The glass, she said, was cracked. She may have used considerable force in her rage at Byron's churlish reception. Her hands, though small, were strong from hard riding, which gives her explanation plausibility. As for Byron, he made nothing of the incident more than scornfully to label it 'another of her tricks'.

Lady Melbourne, who never ceased to harass William with this 'disgraceful episode', saw it as, 'the last straw to break your over-burdened back'.

'I am not, Mama, a camel, though I may be ostrich-headed,' was all William had to say to that.

The Thorn, who had come upon the scene just too late to witness it and had snatched her from the maid's ministrations in the anteroom, made the most of how that Caro, determined to infuriate Byron by waltzing when she had promised she would never waltz again, had flown into, a passion and vowed to expose him there and then in public for his abominable treatment of her.

William, however, discredited these various rumours as nothing more than mountainous molehills, reminding his mother and his sister, Emily, loud in condemnation of Caro, 'You know she enjoys to indulge in melodrama. She swears the whole thing was a joke, and I'll thank you,' he adjured them, 'not to circulate these horror tales that have resulted in letters of condolence to me from compassionate ladies all over the country — not excluding you, my dear mama and Emily, who seem to have little more to do than, by your good intent, make trouble for Caro — as if she, poor darling, could not make trouble enough for herself.'

Saying which he left them and went to his wife.

He found her with Augustus, on the hearthrug in her boudoir, patiently endeavouring to teach him his alphabet from a brightly coloured picture book.

He stood in the doorway watching these two, in all the world most dear to him; and this, his only son, would, if he lived, grow to manhood with a mind arrested in his seventh year... Was that a curse, he wondered, or a blessing? — for the mind of a child is, or should be, filled with thoughts of happiness, unsinful and unhurt.

When I was a child I understood as a child, I thought as a child, but when I became a man I put away childish things... This wife of his had not and never would put away childish things. She too, like their boy, was in part arrested, immature, unevenly balanced; yet each enchanting facet of her changeful personality reflected a brilliance as of starlight.

'No, my precious, no,' he heard her say. 'B is for bull, not for cat. See, here is a bull, a fine handsome fellow, isn't he? You remember him at Holywell? Great-Grandmama loves her good bull. Now you tell me. B is for — what?'

Augustus sucked his thumb, made an effort to speak, looked up and saw his father; his mouth widened to a smile showing a gap where two milk teeth were lost. Lifting a hand he pointed, mumbling, 'Ba — da — da — ba.'

'Why, William!' Caro sprang to her feet. 'I thought you were in conclave with your mother about me. We are learning our letters. Augustus is so clever, he has taught me four words. A for apple, B for bull, C for cat, D for dog — and here *is* a dog, our Edgar, who is getting fat for want of exercise.'

The golden spaniel, supine upon a rug, stirred in his sleep, opened one eye and got up to greet William, who stooped to fondle the long silken ears.

'He'll get plenty of exercise when he goes again to Brocket.'

'To Brocket?' echoed Caroline. 'When?'

'Tomorrow, if you will.' He crossed to the hearthrug, lifted the staring Augustus in his arms and sat with him on the couch. 'You will want to go to Brocket with Mama, Augustus, won't you?'

The wide blue empty eyes gazed up at him; the heavy head nodded. William laid his lips to the soft fawn-gold curls so like his mother's, who answered for him quickly.

'Of course he'll want to go to Brocket. He loves to be at Brocket, and so does Edgar. We'll take him for long walks in the woods, and only think what a wonderful surprise will be waiting for Augustus! Shall we guess what it is? Look, I'll show you.' She leafed through the pages of the picture book. 'See, H is for horse, but for you, my love, a very *little* horse — P for pony. I have bought you the sweetest little pony, and you'll soon learn to ride him in the paddock. So to Brocket we go.'

And to Brocket they went. William followed after; but that fatal incident at Lady Heathcote's ball was not allowed to die its natural death. The scandalmongers seized the opportunity to hurl at Caroline their accumulated garbage, to label her an outcast, a wanton in her shameless abandon. That she, who, hitherto, had kept her rantings and ravings and adulterous associations private to all but her suffering husband and his family, should, at a social function so far forget the decencies as to create so shocking, so vulgar and disgraceful a scene, could only be excused, if excuse were found, by declaring her insane.

Thus ran the verdict to destroy her last illusion; no longer could she see herself a heroine, torn by an imperishable love, but a woman who had cheapened the name she bore, to make it a byword of ridicule from Carlton House to Grub Street.

But at Brocket with William beside her she was shielded from the poisoned darts of public opinion; and to him she turned for comfort, pleading forgiveness, to be readily forgiven — but not by the Lambs. They, one and all, were badgering William to obtain a legal separation from his wife. He could no longer, they insisted, endure the disgrace her conduct had brought upon him and on them. To all of which he listened, and curtly let them know that nothing they could say or do would alienate him from his wife in this her greatest need of him. Byron, he insisted, was the villain of the piece: Byron, who had taken advantage of one so highly impressionable and whose first approach to him had been appreciation of the poet; not the man. That she had never been his mistress in the fullest sense, despite the probability and evidence against her, he believed. He may well have been right, knowing that her harlequin susceptibilities would lead her to indulge in vicarious imagination, more satisfying in that visionary world of hers than was reality itself.

Meanwhile Byron, now quit of his 'Mania', and always in search of flamboyant adventure, found himself committed, beyond his strangest dreams, to a love of which in a passion of remorse, or of lyrical rodomontade, he wrote:

Earth holds no other like to thee,
Or if it doth, in vain for me...
The very crimes that mar my youth
This bed of death attest the truth;
'Tis all to late, thou wert, thou art,
The cherished madness of my heart.

Madness it was to infuse him with its invidious slow virus: a blend of guilt and joy and danger isolated from all other loves that had gone before or would come after.

Not only were they bound by the ties of blood relationship, sharing the same reckless daredevil of a father, but in Augusta he recognised, with narcissistic satisfaction, a similarity of feature. Yet here resemblance ended. There was not and never could be any intellectual contact between them. Augusta, let us face it, was a fool; which for him, however, did not detract from, rather did it add to, his delight in her. No argumentative deep reasoning nor sharpening of wits were required of Augusta, as demanded when competing in rapier-edged discussion with a Caroline or Lady Melbourne; or his lovely 'Aspasia', Jane Oxford, who would spout her imitations of Sapphic odes at him in lamentable Greek; so unutterably boring. There was nothing of Sappho or her odes about Augusta. What a relief to be entirely relaxed, at ease with her; to meet her in his rooms or in hers at St. James's Palace, knowing that not the most watchful inquisitive eye could impute to those fraternally innocent sessions an offence to the proprieties. As brother and sister they could enjoy each other's company all day and every night, untouched by censorious suspicion.

Throughout that month of August, when London was deserted, he and his 'Goose', his pet abbreviation of her name, were continually together. For to her he was still the little 'Geordie' of his toddling stage. In her company he was a child again to be teased, to laugh at and to joke with; and in her he could confide all the misery he had suffered during his intimacy with that dreadful 'pest' of his, 'that Caroline', and his other affairs in Greece and Turkey, unsparing of erotic details. She was never shocked at anything he had to tell her of himself and his amorous adventures. It is possible these highly coloured reminiscences prompted the inception of *Don Juan,* while she, on her part, had much in her rambling inconsistent way to tell him of his early life from babyhood.

On the death of her mother, a peeress in her own right who would have been Duchess of Leeds had she not been divorced by her husband, Lord Carmarthen, for having left him for the rakish Captain Byron, Augusta, shortly after her father's second marriage, was handed over to her grandmother, Lady Holderness, just before the birth of 'Geordie'. 'And such a lovely baby you were,' she said. 'I adored my little brother. I knew you before you knew yourself, when I lived with your mother, who was a good mother to me.'

She had kept every one of his letters from Harrow and produced a bundle of them tied with pink ribbon. He read them all again and agreed with her that they were 'quite wonderful … the unripened fruit of genius.'

When he was nineteen and Augusta twenty-three she married her first cousin, Colonel Leigh, with whom, so she wrote to her brother, she was very much in love; to which the disillusioned ex-Harrovian, bereft of Mary Chaworth, cynically replied, 'Love, in my humble opinion, is utter nonsense. Had I fifty mistresses I should forget them all in a fortnight and bless my stars for delivering me from the hands of the little mischievous blind god.'

'You would hardly say that today, my darling, would you?' quizzed Augusta slyly, when that letter was re-read. And then she went off at a tangent to do with her court duties; the regent's blood-letting — 'so stout he grows he looks to have a dropsy, and so tightly laced that his belly rolls up to his chins. And as for Princess Charlotte, refusing — did you ever? — to retain a governess. She doesn't object to the duchess or Lady de Clifford as ladies-in-waiting but as governesses, oh dear no! Such a letter as she wrote to Prinney. He showed it round to all of us. *Young people of my age cease to have governesses — at seventeen.* The regent is in a howling rage and forbids her to see her mother, poor soul. There's certain to be a divorce. She — the Princess of Wales — does such outrageous things and is really rather dreadful, not very nice in her person. Her ladies say she's not particular to change her underclothes — you can't wonder at Prinney, who is so fastidious.'

All of this Byron greatly enjoyed, laughed with her and heard how her husband was fretting to have her home again — 'left there alone with our three children, but such a *glee* to be in London once in a while, so much to see and do.'

She spoke of his mother, who had died three years earlier, 'and who loved you as much or even more than I did, but could not begin to understand you. How you used to fight with her in your tempers — so naughty! — I remember how once I saw you punch her in the breast. I wonder you didn't do her a mischief.'

'I loathed my mother,' Byron said. 'She was coarse and fat and common.'

'Not common, never!' denied Augusta. 'She belonged to one of the oldest families in Scotland, though I'll admit she was fat, but so good to you and me, and don't forget she had a hard struggle to keep you on a pittance after our father ran through her fortune and died leaving her with almost nothing.'

'Yes, and I was put to grammar school in Aberdeen before she obtained a grant for Harrow. Poor wretch, she must have suffered hell when she found I was a cripple.'

'You were her only thought and care. She spent all she had on surgeons and had a special boot made for you when you were five, by the great Dr Hunter.'

'And much good that did,' retorted Byron glumly.

It was balm to his ultra-sensitivity to be able to discuss his disablement with Augusta, who never looked and looked away embarrassed, as did others feigning elaborate disregard of his foot in its 'special boot'. She accepted it as part of him, returning his demonstrations of affection with equal fervour. Yet it is doubtful if her pride in and devotion to this brilliant young brother was anything more than elder-sisterly love. Augusta, if a fool, was essentially a prude, an aristocrat with a bourgeois mentality. His tales of various conquests, and of the girls he had seduced in the Near East, she could countenance, but that she would lend herself to an incestuous relationship is beyond reason.

The monstrous offence with which this brother and sister stand accused in the eye of posterity has never been proven in fact. *In an age of oddities,* as he admits, he *has made strange use of his own nature,* to account for much of the Augustan legend.

The worst possible construction was put upon these indiscreet disclosures of a perverted passion for his sister, with which he regaled Lady Melbourne, Hobhouse, and that chatter-monger, Rogers. It was only a matter of time for the Thorn to offer Caroline the information she had gleaned. More than ever determined to secure Byron for her niece, Annabella, she judged precisely the effect these appalling revelations would have upon Caro to achieve the desired final breach between the two; and with fullest satisfaction to herself.

From the series of shocks Caro had sustained during these last few months, she emerged despairfully resigned to realise not only that she was discarded — she could have accepted defeat, having long foreseen it — but that this god-like being whom she had idolised could be guilty of a crime which, even to her elastic conception of morality, must be viewed with horror and disgust, completely shattered her.

And the Thorn, having now done her damnedest, had left the field clear for Annabella.

Not quite yet. In the first flush of his adoration for Augusta, Byron followed her to Six Mile Bottom, and stayed there the whole of September. Before he left London, Caroline, determined to stage one last spectacular farewell, called at his chambers; he was out. She told Fletcher she would wait.

In the study on a table was a book sent by his publisher entitled *Vathek*. Idly scanning the pages she saw it to be a lurid romance of illicit love between an Eastern princess and a caliph, with frightful descriptions of hell's torments where they suffered eternal punishment for their unrestricted sins and evil passions… *So like ourselves,* she thought, *but what unmitigated trash!* She could do better than that. And in this moment it is likely that the theme of *Glenarvon* was conceived, when, after waiting over an hour for Byron, who still did not return, she scribbled on the title page, *Remember me,* and left it lying open there for him to find.

He found, he read, and in a burst of rageful laughter wrote:

Remember thee! remember thee!
Till Lethe quench life's burning stream.
Remorse and shame shall cling to thee,
And haunt thee like a feverish dream!

Remember thee! Ay, doubt it not.
Thy husband, too, shall think of thee:
By neither shalt thou stand forgot,
Thou false *to him, thou* fiend *to me!*

So, for immortality, in these hackneyed lines he brands her whose only shame and sin was the shame and sin of loving … where love could never be.

PART THREE (1814-1828)

When lovers parted
Feel broken-hearted,
And, all hopes thwarted,
Expect to die;
A few years older,
Ah! how much colder
They might behold her
For whom they sigh!

Byron

EIGHT

In the spring of 1814 the French, sickened of war, destitute, famished, laid down their arms. Napoleon, the unconquerable, was conquered.

Great were the rejoicings throughout Britain. In London joy-bells pealed from every steeple; every house in every street blazed with candles, fairy lights and flambeaux. Never had been seen or heard such a tramping of feet, such a flying of flags; displays of bunting and illuminations coiled like a glowing snake around the city to proclaim a nation's massed hysteria at the deliverance from twenty years of war.

That same victory summer saw the Regency attain the apex of its splendour with the visit of the Allied Sovereigns to England. And, on the very day that the regent drove in state to meet Louis XVIII, exiled king of France who kept his impoverished court at a house near Aylesbury in Buckinghamshire, the little Corsican, who had grappled with and held all Europe in his clutch, set sail, escorted by a small British fleet, for the Island of Elba.

Throughout those sun-dazzled months of June and July, festivities, balls and banquets were organised by rival hostesses, each competing with the other regardless of expense to entertain the regent and the Allies; but only a few achieved their goal.

The regent, suffering from gout, a recalcitrant daughter, and the failure at his first attempt to obtain a divorce from the wife he detested, was in no mood for revelry.

With dutiful compassion and commendable patience Lady Bessborough, whose sympathetic ear had for years received his confidence and intermittent adoration, heard of the miseries His Royal Highness had endured in his marriage to the Princess Caroline.

Unlovely to look at, unpleasant to touch, unsavoury to his sensitive nostrils, she was no bedmate for him, he declared, who worshipped beauty. He could never forget his horror and disgust at his first sight of her, too utterly different from all he had ever been led to expect by the highly flattered miniature sent to him from Brunswick depicting a laughing Primavera. And what did he find? A heavy-jowled vulgarian who never washed below her waist! Cruel. Cruel! Not that it mattered. One 'damned German Frau' was 'as good as — or as bad — as another.' But how to be rid of her, with a host of supporting Whigs and Brougham at her back, and no evidence proven of adultery? Not even though accused of having borne an illegitimate son, that perfectly revolting child, William Austin, whom she called 'Willikin', whose origin and parentage were confusedly obscure. They said his father was a Russian prince, a Deptford sail-maker, a mangle-turner, an Italian organ-grinder and heaven knew what else. And why, in the name of Beelzebub, the regent raved, should the defence have won the case to vindicate her with the fact that her snotty-nosed bastard was hers by adoption and proven son of a Thameside laundry-maid? It was nothing short of blackmail, with threats of disclosure to the world by publication of a full report of the proceedings against himself. How, he reiterated, to be rid of her? *How?* Would not his dearest Lady Bessborough advise? He wept. He beat his breast, he clutched his beautiful Neronian curls, he wished he were 'eighty or ninety, or dead.'

Lady Bessborough, with sighs and plaintive murmurs of commiseration, might well have echoed the wish. The anxiety occasioned by *ye dagger scene of indifferent memory*, as Byron dismissed the incident at Lady Heathcote's ball, was of no indifferent memory to her. She went in dread of some latest scandal attributed to Caroline, for, as Lady Melbourne had it, 'she was like a barrel of gunpowder ready to take fire at the most trifling spark.'

That she did not take fire from the numerous and by no means trifling sparks rained on her from the conflagration that burned sky high after *ye dagger scene*, may have somewhat disappointed Lady Melbourne. Nor, when Byron's engagement to Annabella was about to be announced, having been privately known for some weeks, did Caro stage a grand renunciation act. On the contrary she appeared to be uncommonly subdued. 'The calm before the storm?' suggested William's sister Emily, now Lady Cowper. But not even the most distant thunder could be heard; the family sky remained cloudless. Caro alternated visits with Augustus to Brocket, London and Holywell. There she stayed till the turn of the year. Lady Spencer's failing health had given rise to alarm. Caro, who saw the gradual enfeeblement which her grandmother's indomitable spirit refused to admit, feared that this New Year would be her last.

It was. In the March of 1814, she died. Caro mourned her deeply.

'Yet she is undying,' she told Hart, 'the living symbol of an ageless age. Her letters breathe forth the life essence of the eighteenth century. There are few, so few, left of an era unsurpassed in productivity of art, of literature, but not, with us, of music. We are an unmusical race. We leave that to the Latins and the Teutons. How strange that those guzzling fat

Germans could produce a Beethoven. Well, she is gone... Poor Selina. She must come to me or go to you. We'll not desert her, will we, Hart? Promise?'

Hart promised. 'She can live at Chiswick and keep house for me there.'

'Yes, and some of the time I'll have her with me at Whitehall and Brocket if William agrees.'

William would have agreed to anything, so thankful was he at her return to norm. She had her moods, still variable, and violent outbursts of temper, but none of these lasted for long. She was writing a novel. That much he knew; but when he asked to read it she refused.

'If it is ever finished then you may. Until then — hold your peace.'

'So long as you hold yours, I will.'

That she was now immersed in her novel gave William optimistically to hope, despite his family's conspiracy to part them, that their marriage might yet be saved. With Byron betrothed to his cousin, the tongues of gossip silenced and his wife quiescent, he could resume his studies and consider re-entering Parliament.

Caro, meanwhile, performed this latest role of novelist with her customary zest. She must not, she bade her servants, be disturbed. Trays of food were ordered to be placed in the rooms she was likely to use, that she might eat if, and when, she wished. Otherwise she would attend no meals; William must sit at table alone. Any mundane interruption, she said, would destroy the fluence. To William's intense relief she was certainly holding her peace, scribbling away at her desk, diving into dictionaries, revising, discarding, rewriting.

'I strive for perfection,' she confided to Rogers, one of the very few who was allowed to know of but not to read this *magnum opus.* 'Prose comes to me harder than verse. I can scribble rhymed couplets in letters galore, yet to write descriptive narrative as I would have it written is hell's torment.'

Rogers, who had come to her bursting with news, could scarcely contain himself till she had finished before blurting, 'Byron's *Bride of Abydos* is now published — as you know.'

'I do not know.' She gazed at him wide-eyed. 'Ought I to know? What is it about?'

He returned her look with a quirk of his lips. 'Do you mean to say you haven't read it?'

'I can't read everything that every poet publishes, not even were it penned by the greatest. Is it, as ever, autobiographical?'

'All writers,' smiled Rogers, 'tend to offer fiction as autobiography and autobiography as fiction.'

'Which, then, is this *Bride of* whom — or what?'

'Of Abydos.' Rogers tapped a snuff-box. 'It deals with a singular subject, that of a brother and sister, Zuleika and Selim, who love each other to the verge of madness. The scene is laid in Greece or Turkey, somewhere in the Near East — I forget — and the theme is of incest. A somewhat imprudent choice in view of recent circumstances. I expect you have heard that Augusta gave birth to a daughter last April, named Medora at Byron's request? And now the boys at Harrow are asking Augusta's nephew — one of their schoolmates — if his aunt Mrs. Leigh is the Zuleika of the poem.' Rogers, still smiling, took snuff and added, 'Byron is really rather naughty. At Lady Holland's house, before a roomful of people, he let forth that he is passionately in love with a woman who has given him a daughter and that he chose for her the name — Medora.'

'What are you daring to say!' cried Caro, blazing. 'Even your adder's tongue should be shamed to dart such venom.'

Delicately Rogers sneezed into a silken handkerchief, with which he brushed specks of snuff from his lapel. 'Pardon me. The *soupçon* of a cold. But, dear child, pray do not take me at Byron's word nor my tongue as the harbinger of venom. I quote merely what our friend is so foolishly reported to have said.'

'And what a parcel of scrubby schoolboys have said.' Rogers shrugged his immaculate shoulders.

'They all read Byron, Harrow's hero.'

'A fine hero — if he has spread this filthy rumour, which I will not believe — though you are not the first to tell me, the Thorn has been on its tail for weeks. And should you repeat it,' Caro seized a cushion from the sofa where she sat, 'I'll have you in the courts for slander, you little purring cat!'

At Rogers's head she flung the cushion. He ducked; it missed him and landed on the mantelshelf and on a Dresden shepherd and shepherdess entwined. They fell together, broken, in the grate.

Rogers rose and knelt to pick up the pieces, deploring, 'A pity. Such a graceful pair of lovers but undivided still — in parts.'

'Go!' screamed Caro, 'and never let me see you here again. Why did you come to smash my little darlings? Yes, 'tis you who broke them, or caused them to break — with your evil talk and tales — damn, damn and damn you, go! Get out!'

With gentle haste Rogers got out, fearing, when she lifted from her desk a heavy paperweight of Bristol glass, that it would follow the cushion to be hurled at him.

It was; he just managed to slip through the door before the crash.

She wrote no more that day, but at night she was back at her desk; and when, as often, inspiration failed she drifted to the organ, a gift to her from Hart. She played it remarkably well, to keep the whole household and William awake until cock-crow.

At dawning he flung himself out of bed and went to her where, in the small room she called the 'music chamber', she sat in her night-shift at the open window, teeth chattering for the night was chill with mist rising from the river.

'Come away!' William urged, 'come to bed. Have some consideration for the servants and for me if you have not for yourself — sitting there half naked. You'll catch your death of cold.'

"'Come away, come away, death,"' she crooned. 'Listen, I will play for you a funeral march of my own composition. This is what I wish to be played when they carry me to my grave.'

'You will be carried,' said William firmly, 'to your bed — this minute.'

She let him lift her bodily from the stool; and, sliding her arms round his neck, sighed contentment. 'Kind you are, so kind, my dear good Lamb. Did I keep you awake? The servants shall have a holiday tomorrow. We will all stay in bed.'

Exhausted, she slept so soon as her head touched the pillow, to wake refreshed at sundown; and wrote all night and all the next day, and the next.

The celebrations in honour of the Allies brought her once again into the limelight at a masquerade. It was held at Wattier's club, with a marquee designed to accommodate fifteen hundred guests; actually more than two thousand arrived, among them the Duke of Wellington.

Caro elected to go dressed as a boy; William refused to go at all. Byron, back again in London from Newstead, went as a monk attended by Hobhouse as an Albanian. The duke came in uniform with the concession of a mask that did nothing to disguise his monumental nose.

Jostled, crushed, ecstatically surrounded by Columbines, nuns, goddesses, and Eastern houris, many of whom, overcome by the heat, were borne away fainting, the duke, his face bathed in sweat, declared to Captain Percy, his aide-de-camp: 'Damme! Here's a squeeze. I've known it hot enough in the Peninsula but this is a foretaste of what we may expect down below. I'm off to Almack's. Hey? What? Who?' He jogged young Percy's arm. 'Who is this lad?'

'This lad', being slight and small, had wriggled his way through the 'squeeze' to bow before the duke, hand on heart, and to say in a soft lisping treble, 'Your Grace, I crave your pardon for thus addressing you but at the risk of your displeasure I have to tell Your Grace that to exchange one word with the nation's hero will be the supreme moment of my life.'

'Hey? Much obleeged, I'm sure.' The duke's eyes, like gimlets, bored through his mask; his nose twitched; he rubbed the tip of it. 'But look 'ee here, my boy, what are you doin' up and about at this hour o' the night? If you were mine you'd be in bed.'

'As Your Grace suggests, so will I be honoured,' replied the wide-eyed innocent.

'Goddamme!' roared the duke, 'what have we here? Why, you little jackanapes, you'll find your neck inside a wooden collar if you —'

His Grace, empurpled, choked; young Percy turned his head to hide his splutters.

'Indeed, Your Grace,' the urchin's grin revealed a flash of teeth, white as peeled almonds, 'if I have unwittingly offended by overplaying of my part, I beg you to remember that this is a masquerade, and disguise a condition of the entry, at least that is how 'tis stated on my ticket, which I see Your Grace strategically ignores. None of us would wish to miss the opportunity to glimpse if not to speak with you, and were Your Grace incognito you might be overlooked. So may I,' he pulled off his mask, 'present myself, since there is none to do it, and forgive me if I overheard, but — are you off to Almack's?'

The duke was not off to Almack's.

And in the Ladies' Mile once more the tongues were wagging.

'Did you ever…? Did you see? She snaffled him, accosted him, brazen and bold as you please…'

'A harlot has more modesty… Yes, my dear, the two of them together seated on a sofa underneath a palm. My love, I vow I saw it, so did everyone… The duke red as a turkey, and with a bottle between them, was feeding her strawberries out of a dish turn and turn about, one popped in her mouth, one popped in his…'

'Yes, and she unmasked for him and looked to be undressed for him in her page's costume. Florentine she called it, after Botticelli.'

'After anything in trews, my dear. But honestly, *could* you have seen her in those green tights, *skin* tight, right up to her — well — if they had split!…'

'No, I didn't hear what time she left, nor did I see her go…'

'Unlikely that she went alone.'

Unlikely, yet she did, and before midnight, leaving the duke disconsolate with a dead bottle and an empty dish upon his knees beneath the palm.

But of all these spicy titbits bandied to and fro from the carriages in Hyde Park on that June afternoon, a *bonne-bouche* more tasty than any was to be savoured by none, for none knew or saw or guessed that she so 'brazen and bold' had escaped from the duke before midnight. She refused to stay for supper, excused herself and went, and was driven straight to Byron's rooms in Albany.

There Fletcher, aroused from his bed and half asleep, allowed her to wait for his lordship on the plea that, 'He knew I would be here. He told me to come and would follow shortly. He has a book of verse to give me sent by Miss Milbanke.' An impromptu that the semi-dormant Fletcher was easily persuaded to accept.

She waited … and she waited; and, curled up in an armchair, she fell into a doze, to wake and find him standing there.

Divested of his monk's habit and cowl, his hair on end, his shirt and the loose bow-tie he affected unfastened, he stared down at her, who, half awake, stared up at him.

'I had to come to say — if you will listen to me, please —' she spoke disjointedly, rubbing the sleep from her eyes — 'that the most appalling tales are told of you. Should they reach the ears of Annabella, poor girl, who loves you more than I have ever thought I loved to idolise —' She uncoiled from the sofa and got up, stretching her arms above her head, stifling a yawn. 'I'm most dreadfully tired. I've slept less than three hours a night for three months and then only on laudanum.'

Swaying where he stood, he broke out with, 'Why not take an overdose an' quit this life an' me?'

'I would, I would! — but that I fear to lose my soul and God's forgiveness and all hope of life to come.'

'Pah! How can you, an intel'gent woman, believe that hocus-pocus?' His speech was slurred; he licked his lips and said, 'Who's God? Wha's God? An eph-ephemera. Man's image born of's vanity. Won' accept he's no more than mortal flesh that corrup's, decays, an's dug into the ground to moulder till its res' — its res'rection. Who wan's to rise up from the grave where one may rest in peace? When I'm dead — I'm dead. Death's the twin brother of life and lovin' kind to those who welcome him.'

'No, Byron, no! She seized his hand and held it between both of hers. 'You are immortal. You will live for ever in your great work as poet though you die as man.' Her face, uplifted, paled. 'You used not to think nor yet to breathe such blasphemy as this. May God forgive you. By what evil influence are you possessed? Is it brandy or the devil that speaks for you?'

He snatched his hand from hers. ''Tis I — I who speak. None other. I am that I am and don't you perform a pietistic act on me. The part doesn't suit you in that dress, my fair Herm-Hermaphrodite. And, going to the table set with wine and glasses, he poured himself a drink and gulped it down.

'Byron, I must tell you this.' She spoke quietly and clearly. 'I, who loved you, for my undoing, and love you still, although I know you now for what you are —'

His smile slipped; he turned on her. 'What am I? A showman, a crippled clown, a sawney at a fair. Walk up, walk up, lad'es and gents. See the great Lord Byron in's cap an' bells who'll write you a poem turned out piecemeal for a penny. Walk up, walk up!' A raucous laugh burst from him. 'Well, what'll you say? What tales will you tell? I'll tell *you* one, shall I? Come here.' He snapped his fingers at her as if calling a dog to heel. 'Come here, you li'l bitch, my li'l love — I love you like this as a boy. Had I known you in Sicily three thousand years ago I'd have loved you as no woman could be loved … Daphnis, the shepherd son of Mercury. Aha, I know the tales that are told of me. I follow strange abortive loves in search of the abnormal. I'm enamoured of my sister. I have a daughter

225

by her, yes? Medora... Well, i'ss true! She is my life, my soul, my sin, my hope, my all, my doom. Augusta.'

'You're drunk,' whispered Caro. 'You don't know what you say.' And gaining voice she screamed at him, 'There's no word of truth in this awful thing you would have me and others believe. No more than that which you declared was love for *me.*' Her hands were fisted at her sides; her face was drained of colour, parchment-white. 'You hide behind a *papier-mâché* facade which you decorate with every conceivable and inconceivable perversion to make a peepshow for the shallow-minded to gape and point at and proclaim you the greatest poet of all time — which you are not. Pope is greater far than you can ever be.'

He whipped round.

'Ah, yes! That I grant you, and he, too, was beautiful and more physically deformed than I — a hunch-backed dwarf.' Twirling the stem of his empty glass he set it down and added: 'And he, too, had you all on your knees in worship.'

'For the gifts,' she said, 'that qualify you and that hunchbacked dwarf for a throne upon Olympus.'

'Gah!' Again he uttered his derisive laugh. 'How you bleat and blather to make of me a god conceived by the Musae, daughters of Jupiter — nine of 'em, and every one a virgin to mother me. I should be hydra-headed. Is that what you would say?'

'For God's sake,' she cried, 'hear me! If I never speak again you must — *must* — hear me, unless you are too brandy-soaked to heed *this* that I would say. On no account must Annabella know what they tell of you. I believe, maybe too fondly, that marriage with her will be your saving grace, but I will *not* believe that you and Augusta have committed —' She caught a hand to her mouth, choking back the word she could not bring herself to utter. 'From what I have seen of her, though she were weak enough to succumb to your devilish desires, she is too —'

'Straight-laced?' sneered Byron.

'Too innocent, as are you — yes, you!' she flung at him. 'I know how it pleasures you, as it pleasures me, to shock the world, and always to invent some fresh alarming *bêtise* to horrify and raise a cyclone to blow away the last shreds of hypocritical respectability, the fustian of those who are guilty of the same sins of which *we* stand accused. The more outrageously we shock, the more devilment that we devise, the greater *coup* it is for us. You have not yet outgrown your student days. How you and your fellow undergraduates at Cambridge must have joyed to bait the Provosts! Wonder 'tis you weren't sent down, as I'd have been were girls allowed at Cambridge — as perhaps they will be one day. I, too, joy to bait the Melbourne sheep-fold of my Lady Mutton — I, the wolf in her Lamb's clothing. She, whose grandmotherly interest in you might well be called in question. You were ever attracted, with an almost Chinese reverence, to age. I am too young for you. Yet we came together like two stars and clashed and fell apart. We both wished to be the brightest luminary in our constellation. Instead of which we find our luminescence overcast, eclipsed, each by the other.'

'My poor Caro, how you talk and say nothing. And how much and how little do you know of me, or of — yourself.'

He took her by the shoulders, propelling her towards the door. 'Go now, my little demon prince, my pretty boy, my Daphnis. The old pleasures turn stale and the newest strangest pleasures are offered in exchange for pride, fame, ambition, love, all that makes life bearable... Yet there is no joy the world can give like that it takes away. Now go.'

He fairly pushed her out, and stood watching the door close noiselessly behind her. With dragging step he crossed to the table, poured himself another drink, drained the glass, flung it down and stamped his heel on it, grinding the fragments into the rug with his surgical 'special' boot.

Then at his desk he sat, took up a quill and wrote:

The flowers and fruits of love are gone;
The worm, the canker and the grief,
Are mine alone!

A dry sob escaped him; he flung aside the pen, laid his head on his arms ... and slept.

In the spring of the following year the nine months' wonder of the Byro-Caro-mania had ceased to be the chief topic of interest among the *beau monde*. Shaken from their haphazard acceptance of life as they had lived it in a shifting confusion of parties, balls, routs; of gaming, dicing, dancing and loving, with butterfly insouciance for a day, a night, an hour, their little world, revolving in its elegant exclusive sphere, was of a sudden halted in its orbit.

While Europe licked its wounds from the ravages of war, that for twenty years had thundered back and forth across the Continent, a solitary prisoner caged in the Island of Elba watched the horizon, his telescope glued to his eye, and re-shaped his plans... From that barricaded fortress the British Governor sent warning messages to London and doubled his guard.

Yet still the coaches, carriages, chairs, blocked the route along Pall Mall to Carlton House. Night after night, the regent, garish, florid, fat with the star ablaze upon his chest, bowed his famous bow extolled as 'that concentration of all grace', and stood to receive his guests in his rose satin drawing room festooned with carven flowers and a frieze of august Caesars, no less regally imposing than himself. But at the end of that victory year came cataclysmic disaster to annihilate the joy of it.

Napoleon had slipped his guards at Elba and escaped!

What now of that glorious premature peace and the million nameless graves of those who had died in its cause? Gone with the whirlwinds of March in the first of those Hundred Days.

Once more the youth of Britain sprang to arms. Once more from Dover's cliffs their wives and mothers, sisters, watched the troopships cross that narrow trough of sea to meet the advance of a small grey-coated figure with his revitalised cohorts behind him, spurred by the promise that his eagles were soaring to swoop upon their enemies beyond that strip of water.

Caro and her mother were with those who watched and waited for news of Frederick, the younger Ponsonby son who had seen active service under the then Lord Wellington at San Sebastian. Anxiety for her brother was now Caro's chief concern. She had finished her novel and had spent the autumn quietly at Brocket with Augustus.

When, in the previous December, Byron's engagement to Annabella Milbanke was officially announced, she had accepted, with surprising resignation, the inevitable; nor did she make any efforts to obstruct it.

Byron, daily expecting to be bombarded by volleys of letters or herself in a fury on his doorstep, received a charming little note of congratulation, relayed to the Thorn as: 'Coals of fire. Ought I to be abashed, remorseful, conscience-stricken? Should I answer it or not?'

229

'If you answer it,' was his future aunt's advice, 'you are asking for more trouble. Never trust her in this chastened mood. She lies in ambush waiting to spring out on you and drag you to her lair.'

'Perhaps you're right,' he agreed. 'I fear this unnatural quiet more than all her storms.'

A fear unfounded. With touching naivety Caro wrote to know if Annabella would accept a wedding gift from her, which was duly, if coolly, acknowledged.

She had withheld from William that meeting with Byron in his rooms after the masquerade, when he had accused himself to her of that on which she dared not dwell. Yet always she went haunted. Should she warn Annabella, that argumentative, intelligent, so tiresome young blue-stocking, who must have known of his many promiscuous loves? Though surely so damning, repugnant a rumour involving Augusta, her soon-to-be-sister-in-law, would have been rigidly kept from Byron's prospective bride?

It was common knowledge that Augusta had stayed with Byron at Newstead in September after the birth of Medora. While there Annabella wrote promising to make his happiness *the first object in life*, and to trust him for *all I shall look up to and love*.

Augusta had repeated it to Lady Melbourne as 'the prettiest letter she had ever read', which the Thorn promptly retailed to Caro.

Lying wakeful in the night with William snoring at her side, she, for once forgetful of herself, was in a torment of anxiety and doubt. How in the name of sin could any woman for whom his letter was the 'prettiest she had ever read', be so heedless, so utterly indifferent to or unconscious of her guilt as to commit incest with her brother?

'It makes no sense,' moaned Caro to the darkness. What should she do? Ought she to have warned Annabella of some frightful secret in the life of him whom she so blindly loved? But had she attempted to enlighten that besotted 'Blue' she would not have believed her. Would have said it was another hallucination of her distorted mind; that she was raving mad! Yes, this the latest machination of the Thorn to harass William with repeated fears for her sanity. She had overheard, ear to keyhole, the ever recurrent family discussion in which William was advised she be put under restraint.

Tossing and turning in a fever of wakefulness, 'They will have me in Bethlem,' she said aloud, 'before they've done. That's what they want, all of them, William too. God, I hate them! Love your enemies. I don't. Lord, William, how you snore.'

In the dim light of the bedside candle she saw his face on the pillow. He lay on his back, his lips loosened in sleep. 'Had I known that you snore,' she muttered, 'I'd not have married you. Yes, I would, you know I would. I love you … love you. Why does it hurt to love? You don't love me, you can't. I'm such a bitch, a vile-tempered harridan, and yet … there's no one in the world for me but you. You know that, don't you? *Don't* you?'

She seized hold of a lock of his hair and unmercifully tugged as if to tear it from its roots. He woke, blinked up at her, said in the dazed voice of one dragged from a dream, 'What time is it?'

'Time for the birds to sing matins.'

'Damn you!' He sat up, rubbing his sore head. 'What the devil have you done to me? It hurts.'

'I'm sorry, sorry, *sorry* … I can't sleep. Darling, listen. I have a fearful weight on my mind. Should I have confessed to what was told me in secret? It's something Byron... No, I can't. It is too dreadful. I'm hag-ridden with the thought of it. I ought to have told you and I didn't. I just couldn't. I didn't honestly believe it. You see, had I told you, well — you might have stopped the marriage but I didn't dare … Please listen. Are you listening? He, Byron, told me he is in love with his sister and has a child by her.'

'Oh, that.' William dismissed 'that' with a thump of his pillow. 'Pay no attention to his fantasies. He — ah-a-ah,' yawning widely, 'has told the same hair-raising shocker to Mama, to Rogers, to the Hollands and heaven knows who else.'

'Yes, I *know* he has told everyone, and Rogers and the Thorn told me. I didn't believe them till I heard it from Byron himself — and I can't believe it now, but I do feel *someone* should have warned Annabella before marriage of this awful thing which is too —'

'— serious,' he interrupted, 'to be taken seriously. Now for heaven's sake stop talking and go to sleep, or let me.'

He laid himself down again, rolling over to present her with the back of his head. A finger of dawn slid through the curtained window. Shapes and colours in the room took on a lifting greyness; somewhere in a distant farmyard across the silent river the first cock crowed.

'So now,' she said, ''tis morning. Sleep on, my love, but I cannot.'

She got out of bed, flung a wrapper round herself and went to her boudoir. Taking the manuscript of her novel from her bureau drawer she scanned its pages, wrote and rewrote certain passages, signed her name to it and pulled the bell.

To the footman at the door, 'Bring paper and string,' she said, 'and make a parcel of this — in my presence. I won't have it read in the servants' hall. Then take it to an address I will give you.'

The address she gave him was that of John Murray, publisher.

The Ladies' Mile was deserted. Shutters were up at the houses in Park Lane, blinds drawn at the windows of Mayfair. On the steps of Belgravian mansions unpowdered footmen in shirtsleeves, smoking purloined cheroots, sunned themselves and discussed the latest news from Brussels. Butlers, divested of their swallow-tails, aired ladies' lapdogs in the Green Park, where, under the watchful eye of nurses, children played and, politely, romped.

From desultory exchange of talk between these guardians of the young, a stranger in those parts might have gleaned the reason why, at the height of the London season, these haunts of fashion would appear to be devoid of their inhabitants.

'Yes, my lady's there. She writes to me regular in a fuss about my two who was both well over the measles when she went, they only had it slightly, and she says as how my lord and she was at the Duchess of Richmond's ball when a message come from headquarters to say all officers must report at once for duty. They could hear the roar of the cannon from the French advance as plain as plain, my lady said. Don't pick your nose, you naughty boy, or you'll have Boney after you.'

'Boney can't be after me,' came the piping answer. 'Boney's a prisoner of war.'

'Quick, ain't he?' was the verdict. 'I've heard it's worms when they do that. Mine never did.'

"Worms, no, a nasty habit, that's all. Look, here's Mrs. Stukey. Who's her latest, I wonder? Good morning, Mrs. Stukey, how's your new arrival?'

'Not arrived, my dear, and not expected for these four months yet. I call in every week across the way. Have just come from there. She's doin' very well.'

Mrs. Stukey, more than ever like a bolster, paused in her walk to mop her face, saying, 'My, 'tis hot enough to roast a sucking pig.'

'So it's Lady Byron, is it?' was the obvious conclusion drawn from Mrs. Stukey's thumb-jerk to a house in Piccadilly. "Fancy that! So *she* won't be going to Brussels then?'

'Maybe not. He's going there next week without a by-your-leave to her. 'Ere, I'll have to sit, I'm that sweaty in this heat. Had pork chops for me breakfast and do they bring up the wind! Could you make room on the bench for me if I can manage to squeeze in?'

Emanating an odour of perspiration, Hollands gin and onions, Mrs. Stukey managed to squeeze in. 'Yes,' she continued, 'he come to her this morning when I was with her there and said he'd be goin' off to Brussels and never so much as asked me how she was. 'Eartless is not the word for it. And fat! You'd not believe how fat he's getting, always so inclined, and she, poor mite, there's nothin' of 'er. Could you know,' Mrs. Stukey dropped her voice, 'what Miss Minn her maid has told me of their goin's on right from the weddin' night, and how 'e said to her — if you could fancy such a brute, poet or nothin' and a handsome face, no question but handsome is as handsome does, I say — and 'e says to 'er that if they had a child 'e would strangle it and now he's pleased as Punch because she's breedin'. And as for 'im and that sister of 'is —' Mrs. Stukey raised eyes and hands to heaven.

'What of him and his sister?' was the eager prompting. 'One hears such tales. Are they true?'

'Never,' declared Mrs. Stukey, 'would I sully me mouth with the abominations I've 'eard to do with *them* but Miss Minn she did say as 'ow his sister Mrs. Leigh is the wickedest-lookin' cat she ever saw to make Lady Caroline quite saintly by her side. And this I'll say of her ladyship for all her goin's on and I should know having brought their one and only into this world of sin with a head on him so big as an el'phant's to kill her if it hadn't been for me and all to do before the doctor come and not a murmur from her neither. For meself I've always said and always will that Lady Caroline has got 'er a bad name undeserved from jealousy, 'er being so clever and so admired of the gentlemen and so lovin' of that poor simpleton, that boy of hers to break your 'eart. I knew how it was from the moment 'e first hollered and a fine job, too, did I 'ave to make him use his lungs.'

'Just imagine! So his lordship's off to join her there in Brussels,' was hopefully added to Mrs. Stukey's pause.

'Maybe, maybe not, but she's not there to meet him. It's her brother Mr. Frederick who I love,' declared Mrs. Stukey, 'as me own. Was I not wet-nurse to him, 'is mother bein' poorly and no milk? Yes, it's him my Lady Bessborough and Lady Caro's gone to see.'

'To see? He's not yet buried, then?' was somewhat ghoulishly suggested. 'Mind that ball there, Master Ponsonby. If you throw it over the hedge again I'll not go fetch it for you… Yes, I heard as how this one's uncle was among them killed at Waterloo.'

'Never, God be praised,' loudly denied Mrs. Stukey, 'wounded nigh to death but while there's life there's 'ope, as so Mrs. Peterson she wrote me. She's gone with Lady Bessborough and her ladyship and Mr. Lamb to nurse him.'

'London,' sniffed her audience, 'is like a tomb with them all off to Brussels and jollifying even on the night before the battle…'

'Well, I'm sure, Mrs. Stukey, I'm much obleeged to you for livening us up but I must be taking my two 'ome for dinner. Come, children. Pick up your ball, Master Ponsonby, and if you'd like to join us, Mrs. Stukey, there's a broiled fowl, I ordered it meself, and treacle tart to follow and a rarebit.'

'Now I take that very kind,' conceded Mrs. Stukey. 'I could do with me dinner. It's quite a walk from 'ere to my lodgin's Chelsea way, and I was ever partial to a rabbit. Don't 'e grow then, my own poppet?' Mrs. Stukey, rising, enfolded in her ample arms the grandson of the Bessboroughs. ''E's one of mine, you know,' she told his nurse, and, if she didn't know, it was not for want of telling.

Soon the grass of the park, no longer green but yellow-scorched, was bereft of children and their nurses, while from number thirteen Piccadilly Terrace a young girl at her window stood gazing out across those empty spaces bordered by trees, spinach-dark against the white-hot blue of the sky. Of what was she thinking? Of those first weeks of her marriage? Of her agonising disillusionment as bride? Of his frequent reminder of some terrible secret that preyed upon him and which he dared not divulge? Of his savage threats and reproaches charged with deliberate cruelty: 'I am more accursed in my marriage than in any other act of my life. I will live with you if I can until I have got me an heir. Then I shall leave you.'

Well, now she had got him his heir… It *must* be a son, not a daughter. That much she could give him. But what had she done, in what way had she failed as wife? She believed he had loved her once; had pursued her for these two years, at first against her will and then … that first night.

She sank to her knees on the window seat, heard again, as too often she had heard his voice recalled with that same inflection of positive dislike or mockery … or loathing. I hate to sleep with any woman, but you may if you choose.' That his greeting to her for their bridal bed. And later…

She strove to comfort herself that he spoke in his sleep, just aroused from a dream to see the firelight flickering across the crimson bed-curtains when he cried out in a voice to terrify her: 'Good God, I am surely in hell!'

Why think of it? Why torture herself with nagging memories to break her heart: of Seaham, her home, her parents and their happiness in what had seemed to be her joy in love given and returned? And now she was bearing him his longed for heir. Surely that would bring him back to her. He had never meant, could never mean, so bitterly to hurt her. Yet there had been some cherished moments. That time when he, more than usually restless, troubled with nightmares, had wakened her by striding up and down the room brandishing a pistol. She had gone to him, made him sit, and knelt to lay her head against his heart. 'You should have a softer pillow than this,' he had said. And she: 'I wonder which will break first, yours or mine.' And she had felt his tears on her cheek and his hand stroking back the tumbled hair from her forehead, and the touch of his lips on hers.

Rising from the window seat she crossed the room to look at herself in the wall-mirror. What did he see in her face that he had once professed to love, his 'Pippin' he called her for her rosy apple cheeks. What did she lack? The face of her cousin's wife, Caroline Lamb, rose up before her, delicious with its ash-gold hair cropped short like a boy's, the dark wide-set eyes; yet behind all that spiritual elusive grace so keen a wit, so scintillating an intelligence that illumined every word she spoke in that childish lisping voice of hers, to irritate as much as she enthralled. Yes, *she* had been Byron's obsession once, and now he could not bear the sight or sound of her. How often had he sworn that Caro Lamb was his bane, his bugbear, his curse? *But now I have you, and hope,* he had written that to her just before her wedding, *which is as much as mortal man can ask.*

She leaned nearer to the looking glass to see herself as he would see her… No, not pretty. Nothing of the airy-fairy grace and loveliness of Caroline. Yet, despite all she had suffered in these few months of marriage, her reflection offered no sign of grief or of pending motherhood in its round young fulness. A calm and placid countenance, 'As of a schoolmarm,' she whispered with acrid humour and a suspicious brightness in her eyes of tears unfallen, wrenched from a heart still unbroken. 'Only perhaps,' again that little whisper, 'slightly cracked…'

A footman entered bearing a silver salver; on it a letter from Caroline. Although addressed to Lady Byron it was written to her *Dearest Cousins'*, undated but the postmark gave it as from Brussels, July 7th, 1815.

She had been in 'hours of agony' until the news had come to them that Frederick was doing well and said to be, thank God, out of danger. She had heard that our troops had entered Paris, that Louis XVIII had been declared king, and that some fighting had occurred at Versailles. They were 'dull and dreary at Brussels, no books, no letters, and so soon as Frederick could be moved he would be brought home.' She and William would likely stay in Paris *en route*. How delightful if Annabella and her husband could join them there!

Byron came in while she was reading it. She held the letter out to him; he took it from her; a wry smile twisted his mouth as he scanned it.

'Unlike her usual effusions. There's some devilment behind this, that's sure.'

'Shall we go to Paris?' suggested Annabella.

'We?' He tossed the letter back to her. '*You,* certainly not, in your condition. I may or may not go. It depends.'

'On what?'

The questioning analytical look which accompanied that brief question aroused his smouldering antipathy towards this young creature to whom, on the first day of their marriage, he had said, 'Once you had it in your power to save me from myself. What a dupe you have been! It is enough now that you're my wife for me to hate you.' But then he had burst out laughing and she believed him in jest... He was, she told herself, just an adolescent; a mischievous naughty boy who happened also to be a genius, and genius is akin to madness. But in the depths of her she feared for him; and a still small voice within her said, *He is the most terrible and yet the most lovable of husbands.*

'And now,' he harshly demanded, 'what does that puzzled little line between your brows signify? Why do you always strive to unravel some sinister meaning from every word I say, which to me is so infuriating? That line engraved upon your brow — it deepens. Did I carve it there with my devilish sadistic brutality? Hah! And now I've coined a word for you to wonder at. *Sadistic.* Do you know, or don't you know, of *le Marquis de Sade* who died last year and lived a life from which I might have learned much? I wish I could have known him. But *retournons à nos moutons* or, if you will have it, *à mon agneau.* Yes, I go to Paris. Not with you.'

And to Paris he went, arriving the day after the Lambs had left for London. Harriet Leveson-Gower was one of the many who flocked there from Brussels after Waterloo. With her usual caustic criticism of Caroline's behaviour she reported her as 'in a purple riding habit tormenting everyone'.

One can picture her in that purple habit cantering in the Bois attended by an admiring cavalcade, a veil floating from her velvet hat; and *Poor William*, according to Harriet, *hiding himself in one small room while she assembles her lovers in another*.

From the same indefatigable source, whose pen could never have stopped scribbling, Caroline had been taken ill and calling upon doctors in every town through which she passed on her way to Paris in the belief she was dying. Yet she still looked remarkably healthy. 'Poor William', however, appeared to Harriet as 'worn to the bone'.

Immediately on arrival at their hotel, the Meurice — again our informant is Harriet — she sent for another doctor who, surprisingly, proved to be the Duke of Wellington. Whether the duke's visit, in a medical capacity, were by intent or by mistake on the part of the messenger is uncertain; but that the treatment prescribed was eminently successful is evident from the sensational accounts of various eye-witnesses.

At parties, balls and dinners she flaunted her latest conquest. Soon the whole of Paris had wind of the affair; for wherever she went, with or without the duke, she attracted, as ever, universal attention. The Parisians, unlike the *ton* of London, were enchanted with *cette belle petite anglaise* whose *espiègleries* revived their jaded husbands to a *verve plus agissante* in favour of their own too well-worn charms.

All kinds of talk, as might only be expected, followed her from Brussels: how she had deliberately 'set her cap' at the duke, had chased after him from a dinner party across the Place Royale wearing nothing but the flimsiest of scarves, resulting in a feverish chill. Hence that frequent summoning of doctors.

William, as remarked by the Parisians, was the most devoted of husbands. They might, went the general opinion, have only just been married, so much in love they seemed to be. A delightful picture of marital felicity went the round of the salons, how that Caroline, alighting from her carriage at the door of their hotel, was lifted in the arms of her husband and carried over the threshold as if she were a bride. It had been raining and this gallant gesture on the part of William had doubtless been performed to avoid the wetting of her feet in their thin sandals.

The news of Byron's imminent arrival caused, however, a rift in the conjugal lute. All arrangements for the return of the Lambs to London had been made, but so soon as Caroline learned that Byron was on his way to Paris she immediately decided not to leave. In vain did William plead with her, to induce another brainstorm and the wreckage in their room at the hotel of every china ornament and piece of *bric-à-brac* available. One after another vases from the mantelshelf, pictures seized from walls, candlesticks and table lamps went flying. William, too, went flying, never, he vowed, to return.

That pulled her up. She flew after him along the corridor to catch him by his coat-tails, imploring his forgiveness. 'I didn't mean it — I promise you I didn't. We'll go at once — sneak out before they make us pay the damage. Oh, what did I do! We *must go*. Now! Order a diligence. We won't stay to pack. I'll leave my clothes and you leave yours as security. I'll have to take my jewels, but my sable fur and muff will more than bear the cost of those trumpery things I've smashed. William, dearest heart, cast out these seven devils that are in me. It is all because of Byron — he *breeds* devils, and they take possession of me at the very whisper of his name. I won't — I will *not* see him. *Retro me, Sathanas.* He'll come and find me gone.'

He did.

On her return to London at the end of November Caroline heard that Byron and Annabella were about to part. The threatened breach between them had been expedited by the birth, not of Byron's longed-for heir, but of a daughter.

There could be now no prospect of reconciliation. Letters from Caroline to Byron would appear to have been prompted as much by a genuine impulse to bring about a truce between the two as by one last effort to recapture his attention to herself.

I scarcely dare to hope that I shall not offend, she wrote, *although I cannot presume to think that anything I say will have any effect.* She begged, as one who had 'loved him with a devotion almost profane', that before he was driven to desperate extremes he would believe her ready to swear it was she who had circulated these wicked rumours concerning himself and his sister.

Though such rash promises had no effect whatsoever on Byron, who ignored every one of her letters, nothing daunted her determination to see him again. With his wife and her baby well out of the way — Annabella had gone to her parents in Suffolk — she may have hoped to storm his citadel with happier results. Opportunity was offered when Murray, Byron's publisher, showed her a set of verses he had written, sobbed out on tear-blotted paper 'while suffering,' Murray said, 'from one of his liver attacks and an overdose of calomel'.

Moreover the house in Piccadilly was tenanted by bailiffs making inventories of all his goods and chattels. Having spent in one year considerably more than his wife's income on rent, servants, horses, carriages, and with insufficient from his poems to keep the duns away, he was now up to his ears in debt.

Hounded from his study by the gentlemen there in possession, he took refuge in his bedroom and, in a welter of self-pity, wrote the famous lines to Annabella:

Fare thee well! and if for ever,
Still for ever, fare thee well:
Even though unforgiving, never
'Gainst thee shall my heart rebel.

Though the world for this commend thee —
Though it smile upon the blow,
Even its praises must offend thee,
Founded on another's woe:

Fare thee well! — thus disunited,
Torn from every nearer tie,
Sear'd in heart, and lone, and blighted,
More than this I scarce can die.

There is, of course, a good deal more of it, in similar lachrymose vein and equally unworthy of its predecessors. Caroline was not impressed.

'You will surely never publish this?' she said to Murray, who replied that he would publish anything Byron cared to give him.

That decided her. She wrote again to Byron imploring him not to allow those verses to be published. It would do him untold harm. If she could see him for one moment she would explain why. She offered darkest hints of some knowledge she possessed that would 'draw ruin on his head and on that of his wife if she should read those verses'.

Why such doggerel should be thought to draw ruin on the head of Byron and his wife, other than not unlikely attacks from the critics, was, and does remain, inexplicable.

He, meanwhile, heartily sick of himself, his liver, and the bailiffs drinking his wine, guzzling his food and rifling his precious books and *objets d'art*, had returned to his chambers in Albany.

Now, notwithstanding his repeated hymns of hate against Caroline and their mutual resolve never to meet or to speak with each other again, the two absurd creatures did meet again to speak at much length, if with little purpose, before the curtain fell on the last act of their tragicomedy.

She has left a record of that scene which may be reconstructed something in this wise:

She: *Byron, I implore you to return to your wife. You cannot have the heart to leave her. She loves you as deeply, though, God forbid, not so profanely as I did and do and shall until death.*

He (in a broken voice): *Caro, my poor Caro, you, I see, will never change.*

She (tearlessly sobbing): *But I am changed. My heart, once so warm for you, is frozen. Yet it has one corner left wherein its wintered ashes spring to life again in hope — not for myself — for her, your wife, the sweet unsoiled girl to whom you write these verses that, if given to the world, will ring the death knell of your marriage. I beg you not to publish them.*

At which, forgetful of his lines, he rapped out, 'What do you mean, not publish them? They're good enough, aren't they? Murray thinks so, anyway.'

'Good, bad or indifferent is immaterial to me.' She too had lost her lines and in attempt to extemporise succeeded only in calling him, 'You beast! You *can't* do that to her. You can't afford to let her go.'

'How right you are,' was the glum reply. 'I've the bums in my parlour and not a penny in my purse.'

'You should know by now that I abhor alliteration. Nor do I allude to your financial liabilities. It is your reputation that concerns me — and not your literary reputation, though that will be an easy target for the mud-slingers if you hand them out this "Farewell" slop.' And, watching the colour rush up to his face, she added, with ever so little a grin, 'It is your good name I would guard from assault. If you could only know,' mustering another sob, 'the evil reports that are associated with —'

'Wait a minute!' came the heated interruption. 'You forced your way in here to tell me why I should not publish my heart-wringing farewell to Annabella. There is no possible connection between those verses and the death knell, as you call it, of my good name, which is now so bad a name since it was linked with yours that I'm waiting for the hangman. Give a dog, etcetera. It's obvious to me you don't care a row of pins that she and I have come to grief.'

'As you were bound to do. You could never pull together with a girl in high-necked gowns who talks statistics by the hour and has the face and figure of a dumpling.'

'If you came to tell me that you tell me nothing I don't know,' he muttered, picking at his thumb. 'As for your winks and nods and hints of diabolical excesses in which your over-ripe imagination suggests that I indulge — all moonshine — a pretext, admit it, to gain access to me. It is clear as daylight that you want me on my knees, you persistent little gadfly. Well, you waste your words, your powers of invention and my time, so I suggest you go before I put you out.'

At which, taking fire, 'To hell with you!' she flung at him. 'You may stew before I'll lift a finger to drag you from the pit.'

'Why not the pot?' he drawled. 'They used to boil all-alive-o miscreants, vagabonds and villains such as I in the Middle Ages.'

'This is not the Middle Ages, it is the nineteenth century, but you are born four hundred or four thousand years too late. Your peculiar attractions and unusual code of morals would have flourished with the Borgias or the Pharaohs.' And with typical inconsequence she added, 'I cannot say that married life has improved your looks. You still bite your nails, are yellow as a guinea and have developed quite a mayoral corporation.'

He gave a shout of laughter and caught her in his arms. 'This is how I love you best — when you give me back as good as I have given.' He fastened his mouth on her lips that parted from his in a sigh.

'Is this to be the end of our romance? It is too sad an end.'

'Not sad. The only happy end to a romance,' said he, 'is to leave it as ours is … unfinished.'

NINE

When Byron, having signed a deed of separation from his wife, left England never to return, it was hoped that Caroline would now pacifically adapt herself to married life. Not at all. More frequent were her outbursts of hysteria and her tempers so ebullient that the Thorn no longer doubted she was mentally deranged. But medical opinion gave insomnia as the primary cause of her condition, although the sedatives prescribed had small effect.

Gossip seized upon to circulate all kinds of torrid tales from which might have been deducted a modicum of truth. That she and her husband no longer shared a bedroom allowed full rein to rumour. William, disturbed by her nocturnal rambles, locked himself in his dressing room and plugged his ears. She, fortified against the cold with the contents of a bottle, pounded away at her organ all night and took to her bed all day.

An incident that ran like wildfire from the servants' hall to the salons of their ladies was reported by Caroline's maid, awakened in the early hours of the morning to hear her ladyship banging on the master's door entreating him to let her in.

'I'm your wife. You can't turn me out. I demand my rights to sleep with you or I'll drag you through the courts. How dare you lock me out! Open — I say open! Let me in.'

To which the door was opened, but not to let her in.

'I'll not have you in my bed, you drunken little whore. You stink of brandy.' So the maid declared she heard the master say; and in her lady's face was slammed the door. We have only the maid's word for it.

On another occasion, when playing cricket in the corridor with Augustus and one of her young pages, the boy missed a catch, the ball bounced on a table and broke a valuable vase. Whereupon she raged at him, 'You clumsy spawn of Satan; I'll have the hide off you for this.' And flung the ball with all her force — it was a hard one — at his head. It hit him on the nose, blood spurted, the youngster yelled, 'My lady, you've killed me!' and she: 'Oh no, oh yes! Oh God, I have murdered the page. Help! Help!'

The racket above brought the Thorn from below to find Augustus crouching in a corner and Caro, white-faced, supporting on her knees a gory child.

'I've killed him!' she cried. 'I'll have to fly the country — escape to France at once before they take me. I didn't mean to do it but that is no excuse. They can hang me for boyslaughter. William is a barrister. He must get me out of this.'

It was Lady Melbourne who got her out of that. Once assured the page had suffered nothing worse than a fright and a crack on his nose, she had it in a plaster and Caro in a coach bound for Brocket Hall within the hour.

The gossips were enchanted. Here was food to fill them for a month. The Lambs, in agitated conference, decided that William and Caroline must part. William surely now must realise he had a *prima facie* case against his wife as a homicidal lunatic. This savage attack on a defenceless little boy, her favourite page whom she professed to love, was symptomatic of her maniacal mind.

'The mother of your child,' the Thorn declared, 'is not fit to have care of or access to Augustus. Who knows but that in her frenzies she may turn on him who, I fear me, inherits her taint.'

William, poor devil, was not proof against such argument. He succumbed to persuasion. Lawyers were consulted and arrangements for a legal separation went apace.

Caro, meanwhile, in the custody of one Mrs. Welsh, Lady Melbourne's trusted maid, showed herself to be remarkably docile. Reports from Welsh told of visits to villagers with soups and delicacies taken to the ailing and the old; of her daily rides and her interest in the horses. She was breaking in a new young colt but still complained of sleeplessness. She would be writing, Welsh recounted, half the night.

Yes, she was writing. The novel she submitted to Murray had not been accepted. It had been returned with suggestions for improvement. She was working now on its revision, adding chapters, scenes and characters, newly created. That kept her busy; and Welsh, who slept at her mistress's command in a room adjoining her ladyship's bedchamber, may have relaxed her vigilance.

Winningly invited to sup with Lady Caroline, 'for I do detest to eat alone. I am confident that if I stay up talking and eat a heavy meal I shall sleep much better,' Welsh, nothing loth, was gratified to sit at table with her lady and partake of dainties such as never would be offered in the servants' hall; and with a mild dose of laudanum slipped into her wine she fell to nodding.

'Poor dear, you're tired,' commented Caro on a yawn. 'I too am ready for my bed. I know I shall sleep well tonight.'

So did Welsh, and soundly, undisturbed till daybreak to find her lady gone.

Wearing a page's suit, of which a choice were kept at Brocket, she left at midnight, tiptoeing down the stairs and out at the back door, unseen, unheard.

She had to foot it to St Albans, not daring to saddle a horse lest she rouse the men who slept over the stables.

The night was fine and clear with a moon to light her way; but when she came to St Albans, the little town and all its inns were close shuttered and in darkness, no horse or chaise obtainable, so she would have to walk, begging lifts of wagoners along the road to London. She had her tale pat for those who picked her up. She had been sent on an urgent message from Brocket Hall, where Lady Caroline — known by name to them and all the county — lay sick unto death. Mr. Lamb, the doctor said, must be informed. Her horse went lame so she had to leave him at St Albans with the farrier. She parted lavishly with largesse and was dropped at Covent Garden by a farmer driving in to market.

Arriving at Melbourne House she found the family in early-morning conclave with their lawyer. She walked in on the Lambs and stood at the door, dirty, dishevelled, and, with her urchin's grin, announced, 'I've footed it most of the way, but I did the last lap of the journey in a cartload of vegetables. I've not had any breakfast and I'm starving.'

A stupor of astonishment fell upon the Melbournes, who, with William, his brother George, and Emily, looked, at Caro's entrance, to have been turned to stone. The lawyer, from under elevated eyebrows, cast a searching glance around and hemmed behind his hand. His clerk was pop-eyed, staring.

Lady Melbourne was the first to speak. 'You were left at Brocket under lock and key. How come you here in this ridiculous disguise?'

'It isn't a disguise. You've seen me in it scores of times, and I've told you how I came here — on Shanks's pony. I know I'm dirty, so would you be if you'd been sitting on a bushel of potatoes.' She made a dash at William. 'Darling! forgive me if I smell of onions. There were stacks of them around me.' And deliciously she kissed him, saying plaintively, 'I do so want my breakfast, devilled kidneys, mutton chops and coffee good and strong.'

'You shall have it!' William cried, and, to the lawyer: 'Sir, I sign no deeds. You may destroy them for they will not now be wanted.' And with Caro on his arm he marched away.

It was the signal for a stampede from the family below to the apartments of the Lambs above, leaving the attorney and his clerk to dispose of the carefully documented deeds of separation. 'But I shall not,' he told his clerk, 'destroy them, for they may certainly be wanted at some future date again.'

A prophecy that proved to be correct.

Lady Melbourne was followed up the stairs by her puffing lord, who proclaimed that he would wring the hussy's neck for making fools of them; while Emily and George were loud in their insistence that William could not possibly withdraw at this last minute. 'Such a waste,' urged Emily, 'of lawyers' fees, Papa. He'll charge you double knowing William will refuse to pay. He'll say, as for this last week he has been saying, that he was coerced against his will to these "extremes" as he calls them.'

'I'm damned,' his lordship shouted, 'if I'll pay! I'll send the bill to Bessborough. Caroline's his pigeon, not mine.'

The door of her boudoir was flung open. The Melbournes, with their young, all but fell into the room to find Caro on William's knee, her arms around his neck, being fed with bread and butter.

Unsurprised by the invaders she explained to them with smiles, 'An *hors-d'oeuvre* to my breakfast. I do love bread and butter. They used to call me "Bread-and-butter Caro" at Miss Rowden's school. Not that I was ever bread-and-buttery.'

'Unless,' suggested William, 'you were flavoured with cayenne.'

'Aha, my clever one! However did you guess?' She scrambled down from off his knee. 'I thank you, my lord and sir and ladies, for your kind attention.' She made them an impudent leg. 'Your most obedient. And now if you'll excuse me —'

'Your ladyship's breakfast,' announced the butler at the door, 'is served.'

War having been openly declared between Melbourne House and Caroline, the victory in this first battle went to her. While the enemy retreated to reinforce their arms, she laid in a store of ammunition to meet their next attack. No longer did she keep the house awake by tramping up and down the corridors or playing on the organ. At her desk she would sit correcting the proofs of her novel — rejected, not surprisingly, by Murray, but accepted by Colburn to set her world aflame.

This sensational absurd extravaganza, *Glenarvon,* was to be her wooden horse, bristling with javelins to bear upon the Melbournes.

It success was instantaneous: not for its literary merit, but for its diabolically clever, satirical portraits of all in her intimate circle. Although there are some striking passages of descriptive narrative, distinctly reminiscent of her visit to Ireland and Lismore, it is a deplorable medley of melodrama, fantasy and farce in which murder, kidnappings of rightful heirs, changelings, spectres, maniacs and corpses are jumbled together in bewildering confusion.

From an overburdened hotch-potch of exaggerated verbiage, Caro, the innocent and exquisite Calantha, presents herself as deified with all the virtues. The husband of this paragon is the austere and lofty-minded Lord Avondale (William), whose cynical acceptance of an amoral society drives her to the arms of Lord Glenarvon (alias Lord Byron). To his protestations of imperishable love she is tempted to yield when neglected by her still adoring if somewhat frigid spouse.

Alas, she soliloquises, *'I am as a child — as a mistress to my husband, but never his friend, his companion. Oh for a heart's friend in whom I could confide every thought and feeling … Such friend was Lord Avondale. By what means have I lost him?*

Means that are not far to seek, since, during his ardent courtship, she has the grace to warn him, *'I am like one uncivilized and savage.'* The deity, apparently, is not without a blemish even though the portrait is self-flattered. *'If you place me in society you will have to blush for the faults that I commit … My temper — I am more violent — Oh that it were not so!'*

'You are all that is noble, frank and generous. I will protect you. Be mine.' Thus Lord Avondale to *that strange uncertain being, for whom he was about to sacrifice so much.*

How much exactly he was about to sacrifice is to the reader a trifle obscure, but eminently satisfactory to Calantha. The wedding bells ring out, all is set for happiness thereafter, with the bride *in a dream of enchantment.* Her only regret is that her husband *seemed not to partake as she would have wished in her delight.*

When Lord Avondale suggests they return to their home in Ireland after a long honeymoon in London, he is *surprised at her ready acquiescence.*

'You are then still the same?' he asks her. *'I am the same,'* she replies, *'but you are changed. Everyone tells me you neglect me — you treat me like a child, like a fool — you forget I am a reasonable creature.'*

'You so seldom do anything to remind me of it.' (Oh, William!)

And so on, and on, to end of volume one.

Vol. Two
Enter Lord Glenarvon:

...leaning against the trunk of a tree, playing at intervals upon a flute or breathing, as if from a suffering heart, the sweet melody of his untaught song. He started not when she approached: — he neither saw nor heard her — so light was her airy step. She gazed for one moment upon his countenance: — She marked it. It was one of those faces which having once beheld we never afterwards forget ... The eye beamed with life as it threw up its dark ardent gaze, while the proud curl of the upper lip expressed haughtiness and bitter contempt ... Yet an air of melancholy and dejection shaded and softened every harsher expression. Such a countenance spoke to the heart ... Calantha felt the power not then alone but evermore.

Thus the affair begins and soars to its frenzied climax.

'I love you to madness,' Byron-Glenarvon tells Caro-Calantha. *'You distract me. Avondale may find another wife but the world contains for me but one Calantha.'*

All this is heavenly until ... Glenarvon cools. He goes abroad pursued by frantic letters from the stricken deserted Calantha.

I have seen — have heard of cruelty and falsehood but you, Glenarvon, oh you who are so young and beautiful. Can you be so inhuman? Jest not with my sufferings...

Pages of it, more and more and more. And then ... that fatal letter, sealed and directed to Lady (Oxford) Mandeville:

...but the hand that wrote it was Lord Glenarvon's ... When the very soul is annihilated by sudden and unexpected evil the outward frame is calm. Oh did the aunt who loved her (a composite portrait of Lady

Bessborough and Georgiana Devonshire) *as she read that barbarous letter exhibit equal marks of fortitude? 'No. In tears, in reproaches she vented her indignation but still Calantha moved not.*

She falls into a decline and eventually dies of a broken heart. There is a holocaust of dying. Everybody dies. Lord Avondale dies, also broken-hearted, at the loss of his Calantha. Glenarvon commits suicide, having joined the British Navy that appears to be at war, in the nineteenth century, and for some unfathomable reason with the Dutch. As commander of a frigate, he, with no previous maritime experience, *was the soul and spirit which actuated and moved every other... Victory having been decided in favour of the British flag, this splendid success was obtained by the heroic valour of their brave commander.*

But Glenarvon is not to be let off so lightly. He is taken ill and carried on deck, where *visions of death and horror*, he cries, *persecute me!* A phantom vessel, manned by a gigantic figure in the habit of a monk, looms up before him. *At his feet kneels a form, so beautiful, so fair, a pitying angel*, the ghost of Calantha. *Ah, but see! With a relentless hand the friar dashed the fragile being clinging round him for mercy into the deep dark water. 'Monster!'* shrieks Glenarvon. *'I will revenge that deed!'*

He was spared the pains. *The monk drew slowly from his bosom the black covering that enshrouded his form ... that bosom was gored with deadly wounds, black spouting streams of blood.* Unable to endure the horrid sight, *his brain burning, his eye darting forward, lost not for one moment of that terrific vision,* the hag-ridden, haunted Glenarvon plunges headlong into the sea, and *as he closed his eyes in death a voice, loud, terrible from beneath, thus seemed to address him: — 'Hardened unpenitent* (sic) *sinner. The measure of your iniquity is full...'*

So much for, and quite enough of, the Byronic flavour; but few could have read to the end of this preposterous farrago, all being eager to read about themselves; loudly indignant if they were recognisable and greatly disappointed if they weren't. And what has the author to say of Lady Melbourne?

Under the semblance of youthful gaiety, she concealed a dark intriguing spirit which could neither remain at rest nor satisfy itself in the pursuit of great and noble objects... She had been hurried on by the evil activity of her own mind until the habit of crime had overcome every scruple... Even to the annexing of one Count Viviani, a youthful admirer (Byron in another guise) many years younger than herself. In this career she had improved to such a degree her natural talent for dissimulation that under its impenetrable veil she was able to carry on securely her *darkest machinations ... that are nothing short of murder.*

As for Lady Holland, she is the Princess of Madagascar, wife of the 'Great Nabob'... *And who so ignorant as not to know that this Lady resides in an old-fashioned Gothic building called Barbary House three miles beyond the turnpike?*

Who indeed? To give the author full scope to draw a witty and mischievous caricature of Lady Holland and her entourage, with here and there a crack at *sallow complexioned poets and critics sneering and simpering behind her chair,* among whom is Rogers, as a 'yellow hyena'. But it is the Melbourne House contingent who come in for more than their share of the poison from her pen: a weapon in the nature of a boomerang to rebound upon herself.

Loud were the laments of the Melbournes and their young. How could she do this to *them,* her husband's family whom she so wickedly had wronged and by whom, with godlike clemency, had been forgiven? But not now, oh, no! Not now. William could not, they insisted, forgive her this treacherous assault calculated deliberately to wound and destroy. The whole fantastic hocus-pocus had been contrived from her demented brain for one sole purpose only: to hold him and them in ridicule. Such utter disloyalty could not be overlooked. This *must* be the end of William's disastrous marriage. If not divorce — and heaven knew there was evidence enough for that — then a legal separation should and most certainly could be enforced. Surely he must see that she was unworthy of his misplaced love and his indulgence? She was unfit to be the wife of him or any man.

Yes, he saw, and he agreed. She had forfeited all right to his name and his protection.

Urged by persistent hammer blows from his outraged family, to say nothing of complaints from Holland House and others she had pilloried, William allowed himself to be persuaded. This, then, was the end.

But was it?

With the book in his hand he confronted Caroline to find her completely unabashed.

'If this novel is published,' William told her in great heat, 'as I understand it is, and without my knowledge or consent, though I cannot believe any reputable publisher would print such paltry rubbish, I will never see you again. I am done with you now and for ever.'

She gazed up at him in startled incredulous dismay.

'William! You think it *paltry?* And rubbish? My book, my first novel? Colburn says it is a masterpiece of satire, worthy of Swift. Can you not understand, if you have read it with any intelligence, that apart from my descriptions of Ireland, which everyone says are quite beautiful — and even Rogers, who doesn't mind being called a yellow hyena — at least, not very much — that it is a fantasia, a pastiche of the melodramatic blood-curdling romances churned out by the dozen today? I'll admit it has been my joyous revenge on those odious persons, your mama not excluded, who have tormented and maligned me until I, poor worm, have turned — to bring about a *succès fou*. It is already reprinting after one week. Colburn says the demand is phenomenal.'

William stared back, baffled, dumbfounded.

'Good God!' He found tongue to lash at her. 'Are you so lost to all reason and sense of loyalty to me and mine, and to those whom you call your friends, that your inflated self-esteem and vanity can applaud this revolting exhibition which you are pleased to designate a "joyous revenge"?'

Her face crumpled; she covered it. Her shoulders heaved. She sank back among the cushions of her couch, her head turned sideways, so that he could see only the delicate articulation of her cheek. He stepped hesitatingly forward to lean over her. Had he gone too far, said too much, too harshly?

His hand went out to the tumbled curls, and suddenly she twisted round, caught that hand to her mouth and bit it.

'Damn you!' He snatched his hand away smartly to slap her cheek. She sprang up, her face aflame.

'You — you hit me!'

'I'll do more than that,' said he. 'I'll thrash you, backside up, across my knee, failing the cart's tail to which you should be tied and dragged from here to Newgate... Oh, no, you don't!' For she was ready, claws out, to come at him again, her eyes tear-brightened, her mouth a little open; but, instead of the inevitable cascade of screams, burst forth a ripple of laughter.

'I'm sorry — I am — I *am* sorry, I do,' she gasped, 'apologise. You and all of you have been most wrongfully abused.' She held her side. 'Oh, dear!'

Was her laughter genuine, hysterical, or trickery? He couldn't know. With her and her devilish enchantment there was never any knowing.

'You are,' she spluttered, 'so very Avondale-ish. I'm a clever little weasel, am I not? I have drawn you, my own heart's life, and all of you, with so sure and cunning a touch that I touch *you* — on the raw! But I didn't mean to hurt. Truly, honest, no, I didn't. Forgive and laugh with me.'

She snuggled up to him; and he recoiled. His lips were white. He looked down at the imprint of her teeth on his hand.

'Forgive?' he uttered grimly. 'Yes, we can forgive a wildcat that mauls in self-defence or fear of men, but you, to whom I have rendered everything that is most dear to me, my honour and my love —'

'If you had rendered less honour and more love,' she flashed, 'I might have told a better tale.'

'It couldn't have been worse. You will be hearing from my lawyer.' And ramrod straight, nose pointed to the door, out he went.

At his club, sunk in gloom and brandy, he sat and brooded on his wrongs. Fellow members wandered in, saw him there, and hastily withdrew. But Lord Holland, *Calantha*'s 'Great Nabob', stayed. In his white waistcoat and looking more than ever, as a contemporary remarked, *like a turbot standing on its tail*, he hailed the dejected William in a foghorn voice to make him jump.

'Sir, were it not for the regard in which you are held by us all as a future asset to our party, I would be constrained to demand reparation from you on behalf of your wife, from whom I would not deign to extract the apology that she rightfully should offer.'

William raised his head; his eyes were bloodshot. 'If to challenge me would satisfy yourself, your wife, and those who are the objects of such wanton and unwarranted attack, I will meet your lordship when and where you please.'

Holland lowered his heavy bulk into a chair, brushed his chins with sausage fingers, and said uncomfortably, 'Now, now, let's have no talk of challenge as between us, William, hey? What? We must take a sensible view of this unfortunate — hum — this misdirected publication. Although my wife — and your good mother, too — must feel not unnaturally aggrieved, the fault —' Aware of William's haggard gaze, *The poor brute,* reflected Holland, *has had a bellyful of this. I'll not pile it on lest he should vomit.* And clearing his throat he added weightily, 'The fault lies with this publisher fellow, this — what's his name? — Colburn. If the ladies insist, as well they may, on a lawsuit for libel it is the publishers and printers who should be held responsible.'

'None is responsible,' was the hollow answer, 'save myself. Had I guarded her more closely, shown more interest in her activities — she has always been so active —' he bent and flexed his knuckles till they cracked like little pistol shots — 'always *doing,* writing, painting, and she's musical, you know. She plays the organ, has a pretty flair for it. She taught herself. She has unbounded energy which drives her to these rash impetuosities, and, of course, she is unusually gifted, but I should have supervised — there's no excuse —' His head drooped down. The glossy black hair showed streaks of grey.

Holland stretched out a hand to clamp it on his shoulder. 'Take heart. It will soon blow over. The women'll forget it when they've chewed it to rags. You can't be inculpated for Caro's indiscretions, but my advice to you is the same as your mother's. She has reason to tell you to sever the knot, but do it legally. Have deeds drawn up and stamped and sealed, and this time no eleventh-hour wheedling for your capitulation as before, if you remember.'

Well did he remember.

He gave the hearty Holland a wan smile; refused another brandy and got upon his feet. 'I realise now I have come to the Rubicon. There is no turning back. I must cross it.'

'Mind you do, and don't stick in the mud mid-stream.' To a hovering waiter Holland said, 'Half a pint of champagne. Sure you won't join me, William?'

'I think not — thank you. No.' And he took himself off.

It did not blow over quite so soon as Holland had predicted. The ladies, apart from those of Melbourne House, were rampant. In the park, at dinners, in their drawing rooms when the men were at their port, the one topic that engaged them was *Glenarvon*. Not only had Caro Lamb made fools of and insulted them, her so-called 'friends', but she had cruelly exposed the intimacies of her married life and that of William's family. His mother, sister, brother, were displayed in so unfavourable and mischievous a light that by unanimous opinion she must be ostracised. All were of one mind on that sore point. She had forfeited her right to be received.

Lady Jersey, doyenne of Almack's, had her name removed from the list of members. When out driving in the park, should her carriage halt at the barriers, occupants of other vehicles, their noses upturned as at a smell, at once commanded their coachmen to drive on. Her greetings were stonily ignored. Men feigned not to see her; none bowed as she passed. She was cut.

Newspaper articles, the product of those same minor poets and critics she had vilified, poured forth vituperation which dismayed neither her nor her publisher one whit. The sales of the book were fabulous with three editions called for in three weeks.

She put a bold front on it, supported by her mother. Lady Bessborough, though shocked at the reaction to Caroline's first novel, could not but be proud of its success and furious with William for his ready agreement to seize this opportunity for the breaking of his marriage.

'I have no friend in the world but Mama, and Hart, and you,' Caro cried to the faithful Trimmer, who had come from Chiswick where she 'kept house' for the duke. 'Even my own brothers have turned on me. Dun thinks he sees himself as Lord Dartford in my book, who is enamoured of the Thorn — I mean Lady Margaret. But of course he is not the model for Dartford. How they all turn on me! But you, Selina, you won't turn on me, will you?'

'Always your ladyship may count ... I am so deeply distressed, and having read the ... having read it,' was Miss Trimmer's staunch reply. 'I am confident you have been most wickedly misjudged. As a literary effort it is a remarkable ... I might say brilliant satire on our modern depraved society, and your descriptive powers are quite...'

'Ah, my own most kind and generous Selina!' Caroline submitted to Miss Trimmer's breathless pause. 'You deserve a halo. You are an angel. So is Hart. He is coming from Chatsworth to support me. I had a letter from him this morning and meant to tell you but forgot. He should be arriving today. He is determined to vanquish the Lambs, who are now transformed into Gadarene swine, and my own beloved William is turned into an effete and tuskless boar — boar, not the other kind, for he never could be that. He is far too good a speechifier. I have always said, and I'm as good as a witch, that he'll make his mark in politics. You'll see. He'll be prime minister one day, when I am ... out of his life.' Her eyes filled.

Miss Trimmer murmured, 'I am sure Mr. Lamb and you will never ... he is utterly devoted to ... it is but a storm in a tea —'

'Cup? It will have to be a very large cup to take the deluge that pours into it. At this very moment down below,' Caro pointed, 'the Melbournes' attorney is in conference with William, the Thorn and my papa-in-law. I expect the original documents, drawn up a year ago, will be brought out again. Do you think my novel good? You do? You are not just saying it to cheer me?'

'Indeed, no,' came the stout denial in an unusually lengthy effort. 'You have always shown an aptitude for the *mot juste*. I ... I admit it seems to me a trifle too ... shall we say hyperbolic? But I am confident your lamented grandmother, Lady Spencer, would have appreciated its worth and flow of...' Clasping and unclasping her small mouse hands, Miss Trimmer's voice dwindled away.

'I wonder what Byron will say,' reflected Caroline, 'if he has read it yet, which is doubtful, for it would have to follow him to his latest love, the Jungfrau, or somewhere in the Alps. I hear he is in Switzerland. I must send him a copy.'

But she did not send him a copy. When Hart arrived from Chatsworth he came straight to her at Melbourne House, dusty, hot and 'starving, Selina,' he told her, 'having eaten nothing since eight o'clock this morning.'

'Dear, dear, this is very distress...' twittered Miss Trimmer. 'I will order Your Grace ... at once...' She hurried off.

'My own Caro!' Hart hugged her. 'How lovely you are! Authorship agrees with you. I have brought with me a case of pistols and the choice of swords to call out every man jack of those foul and filthy critics of the gutter press who carve you up and roll you in the kennel.'

'Darling Hart! Did you see *The Satirist?* Wasn't it beastly?' She wound her arms round his neck. 'I adore you. If William divorces me shall we be married?'

'Don't,' he groaned, 'don't bring reality into my dreams. He will not divorce you, rot him, but — give me the nod and I'll make him. Shall we elope? Ha! Here's our Selina,' who, having given an order to the butler to pass on to the chef, had unobtrusively returned to stand in the doorway smiling, eye-blinking, fluttering, and, overhearing Hart's remark, had blanched. 'How pale you look, Selina. Don't swoon away, will you? We were only discussing a most improbable eventuality.'

'I hope … I beg Your Grace,' trembled Miss Trimmer, 'will not be persuaded by your chivalry to…'

'Allow our Caro to be taken in adultery? You need have no fear on that score,' Hart assured her. 'William will never let her go. What are you giving me to eat? All I've had in these six hours is a sandwich, and I'm empty as a drum.'

'There's mutton collops and a chicken on the spit, but if Your Grace … so that you will not have to wait … cold beef to begin with and…'

'By all means. A whole ox if you have one cooked and cold and ready.'

And when Miss Trimmer hurried off again, Hart seated himself and, stretching his legs, said, 'I was not joking, Caro, when I told you I am out to fight any blackguardly sod who dares to libel you — yes, Selina?' who had put her little grey head round the door.

'Will Your Grace be served here or in the dining room?'

'Oh, bring it here. I can't wait. And tell the chef I'll have a syllabub to finish with.'

Caro gave a little crow of laughter. 'Dear Hart, you have never left the nursery, nor have I. We were always gluttons for syllabubs and cream buns, weren't we? I still am. Yes, I too will share the syllabub, Selina. Run along and tell them — and a bottle of champagne.' And when Selina ran along to tell them, 'Hart,' she asked him, 'have you heard anything at all of Byron? I long to know if he has read *Glenarvon* and what he thinks of it.'

Hart jerked up his chin. 'It's odd you should ask me that because I did hear, while at Chatsworth, in some roundabout way from Madame de Staël, who was so fond of — you recollect? — of my mother, and still writes to me, that Byron is at some place near Chillon in Switzerland, and is so struck with the chateau there he is writing a poem about it in between stanzas of the *Childe* — and she tells me he said your portrait of him is not good because he didn't sit long enough for it.'

'How typically Byronic! There is so much to love in him, and so very much to hate. His conceit and egomania is such he is likely to be peeved that I didn't fill my whole canvas with him in the foreground and all subsidiary characters dwarfed to pygmy size. Well, it's good to know that he, for one, is not out to kill me. Hart, I can't tell you how happy I am to have you here, my champion! But I would rather you do not tilt at windmills for my sake. Put up your lance, and leave all who rend me to stew... Ah, here comes your dinner, or is it your breakfast?'

Preceded by Miss Trimmer came a footman to set a cloth; another followed with dishes, and a butler brought up the rear with a bottle.

Hart fell to gustily, urging Caro, 'And you, Selina, sit with me while I eat.'

'Your Grace is too … but I must just go and tell them … be sure of syllabub … if Your Grace will excuse…' Miss Trimmer faded away.

'Though your whole world rocks,' said Hart between mouthfuls, 'and you, my Car, are blown sky-high to fall and be devoured by a ravening pack of yellow hyenas —'

'Oh, so you have read it? You didn't tell me that.'

'You have hardly given me a chance. I was about to say that 'spite of these earthquakes and eruptions you have brought upon yourself, Selina remains serene, untroubled, devoted — the Martha of your house and mine.'

'Sherry, Your Grace?' intoned the butler at his elbow.

And while Hart did full justice to the four-course meal provided by Miss Trimmer, he told of his main object in coming to London, 'which is to make certain that William who is so completely Thorn-riddled, will provide you with an adequate allowance in this separation deed that I insist I see and will submit to my lawyer for his approval and advice. You shall not be deprived of your rights, my love, and since your father and brother appear to have no voice in these proceedings, I take it upon me to guard your interests. I presume your mother is far too shocked by recent events to —'

'Not in the least,' interposed Caro. 'She is disgusted at the way the Thorn and all of them have coerced William into leaving me, but at the same time I think that Mama is rather cock-a-hoop at the tremendous success of my first novel. Papa, of course, never reads a book, so he dismisses this domestic crisis as women's fiddle-faddle, and I don't think either he or Mama believe that William and I have arrived at the parting of our ways. Nor, to tell the truth, do I.'

And nor, in his heart, did William; yet with constant pressure brought to bear upon him from his family he could not face the outcry that would ensue should he retract. He also had taken bitterly to heart that Caro had so wilfully maligned those he loved: his mother more than any. She had given him the book to read with the passages concerning her and the rest of them marked in red ink.

Once again the legal formalities were set in motion, the deeds drawn up. Hart, acting on Caroline's behalf, demanded a substantial settlement that William felt he could ill afford, but to which, at Hart's insistence, he agreed.

The summer was well advanced by the time all the documents were completed to the satisfaction of the duke. During these proceedings Caro, with Augustus, had left Melbourne House and was staying at Cavendish Square.

On the night before the final signing of the deeds William drove down to Brocket. He arrived towards sundown, and after a lonely meal went out on to the terrace. It was a glorious evening. The westering sky, rich with the sun's cremation, looked to be draped in fiery banners. And gazing out across green lawns to ripe meadowland beyond, he seemed to see again a small boyish shape astride a galloping pony, the forward thrust of the young body rising to take the jump, to hear the far-off echo of an eager child's voice to sear his heart.

The sun sank lower; the gentle hills were dark against the rose-flushed clouds that parted slowly for the coming of a moon like a golden coin, high above the tree-tops. All was still; the fields, bereft of workers, lay bathed in gilded light; the evensong of birds sank to silence. Then, as dusk mantled the drowsy trees, the first owl's night-cry pierced the listening quiet.

'Life,' muttered William, 'holds no more than memories for me.'

Candleshine from within fell across the paving stones. A footman was busy with a taper in the library that opened on to the terrace; and all colours faded out of things under the whitening sky. The unruffled lake shone like a pewter shield.

William shivered, turned and went inside, took himself early to bed and read Aristotle until he fell uneasily to sleep. He was aroused by a scuffling sound … a rat in the wainscot or starlings in the chimney? Or something at the door?

He sat up. A moonbeam slid through the window, silvering the room; a slight breeze stirred the unclosed curtains. It must have been the rising wind he heard. But as he lay down again that little furtive sound was repeated, not from the window nor the chimney but certainly near at hand, as of a sigh, a whisper…

'William.'

Slowly the door opened. She stood there on the threshold. Light from a lamp behind her in the corridor made of her head an aureole and lent a luminous transparency to the pallor of her face. Her eyes were shadowed pools of dark.

He left his bed and stood there in his nightshirt. He thought his sight betrayed him, that he dreamed, or saw what could not be. But when she ran to him his arms received and held no ghostly vision, conjured from his longing for just this, her warm little body, her soft yielding mouth and the breath of her words on his lips.

'My William, I had to come this once to see you … just this once before the end.'

'No!' His voice rang out as if in challenge to unseen forces. 'No, there will never be an end for us, nor of this, our love … together.' And, lifting her, he carried her to bed.

TEN

The long clouded life of George the Third had come to its merciful end, but the death of the king brought to his successor no change of circumstance other than that of title. For almost nine years he had reigned supreme as deputy sovereign of his father's subjects; and those lesser beings who had suffered bitter privation from the Napoleonic wars and resultant economic disaster saw no hope of relief in the regent's accession to the throne. Indeed, more than ever, as protest to the monarch's extravagance and debts, did riots, rick-burnings, outbreaks and monster meetings persist all over the country, prompted by radical firebrand leaders of industrial revolt.

Yet events were moving rapidly to change, not the face of history alone but the fortunes of William Lamb.

On May 24th, 1819, in a country palace at Kensington, some months before the passing of a king, unmourned, unseen, forgotten by vast numbers of his people, a new life was born to the House of his name. Yet the birth of a daughter to the Duke of Kent, fourth son of George III, was to the nation of small significance; still less to William Lamb.

Little could he know that his destiny was interlocked with that of an exceedingly fat baby crowing in her crib at Kensington; and that he, as queen's pawn on the chequerboard of fate, was to fulfil his wildest youthful ambitions long ago submerged in the quicksands of time. That for the future; for the present his outlook was dreary.

When he and Caroline were reunited on the eve of a second separation, the uproar at Melbourne House surpassed all previous crises. The Thorn, rabid with disappointment, drove post-haste to Brocket and found the renegade William seated on the parapet of the terrace in fits of laughter while Caro, in a *chaise longue,* read him passages 'from her atrocious novel', so to her daughter Emily she tearfully relayed it.

'And he had the effrontery to tell me,' sobbed his mother, 'that he had only skimmed the scum of it at my insistence, and that in his opinion it was a devilish clever burlesque on society in general and all of us in particular — of us!' The lady smote her breast. 'Can you conceive it? And he was laughing. He said — he said it was "damned comical"!'

It had been a shattering blow to the Thorn, who had set her heart on rescuing her son from his deplorable marriage; and now to find that Caroline had won him back — 'by what beguilement or witchery,' she wailed, 'we shall never know.'

And there was more to it than that.

'Can you believe this monstrous infamy?' she appealed to her son George, her daughter and her husband who, consequent upon this latest agitation, was in a state of stupor induced by persistent resort to a mixture of wines and supplemental brandy. 'He accused me — me!' ranted Lady Melbourne, 'of being the primary cause of this "strife" as he called it, between them! I, his mother, who have suffered innumerable indignities and insults from that wretched woman since the ill-fated day when he took her to wife. And for all the misery she has brought upon him and on us he blames himself. Not only *me,* but himself! He said her portrait of Lord Avondale in that awful book of hers holds a mirror to his faults, his cynicism, his lack of guidance in their early days of marriage, and his selfishness. No word of *her* selfishness — oh, dear, no. "She was a child then," he said, "and is a child still if not in years, in immaturity." So does he excuse her wanton violation of every moral code. I am too old,' sobbed her ladyship, 'for this.'

It proved to be her death blow. She fell into a swift decline and died within the year.

It must be confessed that Caro grieved no more than in sympathy for William, who mourned his mother deeply. Nor can it be said that the loss of her dominating influence offered, as she might have hoped, a happier prospect for their married life. William, bereft of the one being in the world on whom he could rely to sustain, support, advise him, felt himself to be a ship adrift on an uncharted sea. With middle age approaching, his only son showing developmental difficulties, his wife irresponsible as ever, he was charged with a sense of frustration and failure.

He had wished for a political career, which he, of his own volition, had renounced; but it was not too late to re-enter the lists. Urged by Lord Holland he decided to accept the offer of a seat, and, before his mother's death, had been elected member for Northampton. Yet, still a cypher among the backbenchers, he was not particular in his attendance at the House. He spent much of his time at Brocket, reading, translating Homer and the classics, or writing despondent verse in which he bemoaned his vanished youth: *Give me back that fervid soul which love inflamed with strange delight.*

'You are no poet,' Caro told him bluntly, 'although if you had sufficient driving force you could rise to political heights, but you are too lazy to scale them. Whereas I...'

Ignoring his glowering look she left it at that; for if his star had been eclipsed in its ascension, hers shone with sporadic luminosity, only with a difference from the days when her tableaux were received with acclamation. Although, as ever, she could command an audience, those who came to watch and applaud her performances were no longer of the elegant privileged world that had nurtured her, and where she once had reigned as 'Fairie Queen'.

Now she gathered round her a heterogeneous crowd of intellectuals, artists, writers, and a sprinkling of those minor poets, some of whom in *Glenarvon* she had ridiculed and who hoped to garner profitable crumbs from her literary table, where she sat surrounded by fawning sycophants. Among the more prominent notabilities drawn into her circle was William Godwin, whose *Political Justice*, published in 1793, had won him fame and a thousand guineas.

Calmly subversive of everything that had hitherto been sacrosanct, this dynamic doctrinaire of free thought, free speech, free love — as expounded in one of his oft-quoted shockers, *Marriage is the worst of all laws* — was caviar to Caroline. In Godwin's beatified aura, where the revolutionary and progressive intelligentsia met to discourse on metaphysics, philosophy, democracy, theology, pantheism, atheism and every other 'ism', including egoism — as directed to themselves — Caro found her Mecca.

Discarded by the mediocrities of fashion, she basked in her own effulgence, which, if less dazzling than heretofore, did reflect a glimmer of the unique capricious personality that had enslaved the heart of William, had lured to captive the transient passion of a Byron, and could now engage the interest of a Godwin in his sixties and a boy, scarcely out of his teens, cramming for a double First and Cambridge. He and his name, as yet unknown to her and to the world, was to be linked with hers and inscribed, as is Byron's, on the scroll of immortality.

Since the production of *Glenarvon* she had published two more novels: *Graham Hamilton* and *Ada Reis*. Neither created a furore but both are more competent and distinctly better written than *Glenarvon*. Those who rushed to buy them, hoping for more libellous scandals with which to attack her, were baulked. There was nothing, no incident that could be traced to any recognisable source.

William, having read, revised and corrected the manuscripts for her deplorable spelling, wrote to Murray, who had accepted *Ada Reis,* pointing out certain faults of structure and design; but on the whole he found *much beauty of sentiment and effective situations*.

His encouragement of and interest in her work are significant of his altered attitude to their relationship. For although she occupied herself with various activities at Melbourne House and Brocket there were ominous signs of recurrent instability. And William went haunted, believing he was in part responsible for their disrupted marriage. Had he shown a firmer hand from the first and held her back when she took the bit between her teeth, he might have broken her in as she would break an untamed colt. And now it was too late. Yet he loved her still and the more, perhaps, for the knowledge that in their early days together he had been too preoccupied with his own conflicting enthusiasms and ambitions to appreciate her creative individuality, which, at the time of their marriage, had been centred less in herself than in him. Had he sought to plumb the depths that lay beneath her emotional superficialities, he might have dragged her from the perilous brink of that border line which needed just the least unwary step to topple her over into an abyss of mental and moral disintegration.

All he could do to ease the nagging reminder of that which he had left undone to save her broken life was to exercise infinite patience, tact, and guardianship in his care of her; and to him she turned as a sick child to its father for her comfort, and of him she wrote to Godwin, *I have one faithful friend in William Lamb.*

That was true enough, yet there were other friends, more sincere than any of those who, in the heyday of her popularity, had flocked to her dinners, routs and waltzing parties at Melbourne House, and now had closed their doors to her. But in that circle of literary lights where she had found a footing, she was given right of entry by virtue of three published novels and a few indifferent poems. One of these she dedicated to her husband: *Yes, I adore thee, William Lamb, but hate to hear thee say God damn!* — which is slightly anomalous in view of her own predilection to words not commonly used by well-brought-up young ladies. Among the women who welcomed her to their selective band of 'Blues', were Lady Morgan and Miss Benger.

Lady Morgan, under the pseudonym 'Sydney Owenson', had made something of a stir with her first novel, *The Wild Irish Girl.* The daughter of a Shrewsbury grocer who had migrated with his family to Dublin, she attracted the attention of a fashionable physician, Sir Charles Morgan. When, after her marriage, she came to London, she hovered on the fringe of that exclusive society from which Caroline Lamb had been banned.

Miss Benger, who had made her mark as an historian, forerunner of Agnes Strickland, lodged in Doughty Street, the centre of authorship, where the ten-year-old Charles Dickens, sticking labels on bottles in a blacking factory, was eventually to live.

Up three flights of dingy stairs, in a dingy room, a fur tippet and mob cap, Miss Benger entertained her lady guests to tea and ratafias, with negus for the gentlemen and instructive genteel talk. On the erudite Miss Benger Caroline was wont to call at all untimely hours, and on one occasion in the early morning when Miss Benger, whose means were limited to the inconsiderable sales of her books, was engaged in counting the week's washing for the laundrywoman to collect.

Hastily shoving the articles under the sofa when her one little scrubby maid announced with awe the distinguished visitor's arrival, Miss Benger received her with rapturous curtsies. Begging her ladyship 'Be seated — here', she indicated the sofa where certain feminine necessities were hidden.

Unfortunately Caroline had brought her dog; not Edgar, long deceased, but his successor. Nosing round the room this second, or third, Edgar, scenting savoury odours to excite him, dived beneath the couch where the ladies sat ensconced, and dragged forth — oh, horrors! — a pair of soiled drawers. In vain did poor Miss Benger, by backward application of her heels to Edgar's inquisitive muzzle, strive to circumvent further discovery. A nightgown, a petticoat, chemise and other garments privy to Miss Benger, were dragged forth and strewn about the floor.

'He thinks he's found a covey of partridges,' laughed Caro.

When afterwards, in fainting voice, Miss Benger recalled to her intimates this harrowing experience, 'I declare,' she assured her hearers, 'I thought to die of heart failure, but Lady C. is so very much the lady, she made light of it to cover my unutterable shame.'

It was to these two friends — the boisterous large-hearted Lady Morgan and the modest retiring Miss Benger — when Lady Bessborough, while on a continental tour, died suddenly at Florence, that Caro in her desolation turned to find their sympathy unstinted. William, supported by medical advice, decided it were better she should not attend the funeral, and sent for Miss Trimmer, who stayed with her till called away to the sick-bed of a sister.

Letters from Caroline to Hart and her brother Duncannon show her, though prostrate with shock, too stunned for realisation.

While my poor brothers are deeply affected, she wrote to Hart, *I do not know whether I am or not. I feel a calm I never felt before...*

And that unnatural calm persisted when a few weeks later in a valiant effort to face her loss with fortitude and to win, as pathetically she hoped, William's approval, she occupied herself with household management, not, however, with very much success. Her attempt to reorganise Brocket under more economical conditions than had prevailed since the death of Lady Melbourne, resulted only in the losing of her staff.

'The servants,' complained Emily to William, 'come and go like figures in a magic lantern. She can never keep a chef. She has had four in as many months. Each one that departs without warning forfeits his wages of fifty pounds a year sooner than put up with Caro's interference and ridiculous orders how to serve a dish. And when it is served she refuses to eat it. During the few days I was there I saw plates of food left in every room, at her insistence, that she may help herself when she feels inclined. But there's one thing to be thankful for: she can't get any worse, so she may get better.'

She did not get better and she did get worse. Her attempts to readjust her life to William's ways and means resulted in lamentable failure.

'I have written a short book — a sort of treatise — about stables, of which I know much, and domestic economy, of which I know nothing,' she confessed to Lady Morgan, 'only it was so different from my usual style that Murray and others refused it. Yet I did think that William would encourage my efforts to study his — or rather his father's — bank balance, but all he could say was "What's the use of saving in one place" — meaning Brocket — "if you throw it away in another?" — meaning Melbourne. If it comes to that, what is the use of anything, and I often wonder what is the use of me?'

Yet she was happier and more content at Brocket than anywhere else. She would wander off with her sketchbook making drawings of Augustus or herself, of which one is a delightful little study that she whimsically entitled *I was the last rose of summer.* Or she would spend hours in the stables or riding about the country on her favourite black mare or in company with Mr. Walker, engaged by William as tutor for Augustus.

Mr. Walker had taken a medical degree and could therefore answer the purpose both of resident doctor and instructor to Augustus, who at seventeen could scarcely read or write.

Caro, who could never resist exerting her wiles on any personable young gentleman with whom she came in contact, made no exception in the case of Mr. Walker. Needless to say he soon was victimised, evincing all the usual symptoms of amorous response to her advances; blushed when she addressed him, sulked when she didn't, and slept with one of her stockings under his pillow. How he came by her stocking is hypothetical. He may have found it lying about in her boudoir, in her salon — she had always been untidy and could never keep a maid since none but Mrs. Peterson, now in retirement, would put up with her tantrums. Or he may have come across it in the garden. She would often take off her shoes and stockings to dance or play ring-a-ring-o'-roses barefoot with Augustus on the lawn. Be that as it may, a stocking had been discovered by a housemaid in Mr. Walker's bed.

It was in the servants' hall in a jiffy; in the mouths of the whole village the same day, brought to London as hot news and handed out to Emily, who made the very worst of it to William when Caro, Mr. Walker and Augustus came to town.

'How could you be such a fool, lost to all sense of proportion, as to countenance Caroline's misconduct with the tutor?' cried Emily. 'Harriet Leveson-Gower saw you at a concert laughing in the foyer with the pair of them, and you, she said, were looking pleased as Punch with yourself. Harriet thinks you must be as mad as Caro to consent without a murmur to this — your latest cuckoldry. As for her, Harriet describes her appearance as disgusting, in a dirty white gown that by the look of it had been rolled in the mud, where she belongs.'

To this amiable address William found no answer more than curtly to say, 'If you can believe the jealous spite of Harriet, you are welcome to believe my head has sprouted horns.'

In truth he was thankful that Caro could find diversion in flirting with the tutor. Her fits of depression had increased, alternating with repetition of her brainstorms and scenes in which she would turn and abuse the servants, William, the hapless Mr. Walker or anyone within her range.

In order to give her something other to engross her than herself, William encouraged her to entertain at Melbourne House and Brocket her new friends of both sexes, and in particular one, a disciple of Godwin.

He, just down from Cambridge, was easy prey for the youth-greedy Caroline Lamb.

On a blue-and-golden morning in 1824, her brief interlude with Mr. Walker was abruptly terminated, not wholly due to a stormy scene in which she dismissed him and afterwards retracted, but because of a more entrancing engrossment.

The hapless Mr. Walker was confronted with the accusation of neglecting Augustus 'to make sheep's eyes at me! You have taught him as much as will sit on a farthing, and as little worth. As for religious instruction he actually asked me today if God is married and if so to whom? A fine tutor you, for all your credentials and MAs, MBs and whatever.'

Poor Mr. Walker. His services, she told him, were redundant. She demanded the return of a watch she had given him and the stocking he had stolen to compromise and make a fool of her. And when, in abject misery, he returned not the stocking but the watch, she threw it at his head and flung out of the room, calling over her shoulder, 'You can pack your bags and go!'

But he did not go; she was back the next minute, tearfully apologetic.

'I didn't mean it! Did I break the watch? Show me… Oh, 'tis only the glass. Have the works stopped? If so I'll have it mended. I didn't intend you to go. You should know me by now. When I'm possessed it is Satan who speaks out of my mouth, not I. You do know that, don't you? Only it is such agony when my boy — who is almost a man in years and a baby still, he'll always be my baby — but you can't — how can you? — understand what I suffer when I see him with others of his — of his age.' Sobbing wildly she rushed away, yelling to her maid, 'I want my riding habit!'

Refusing the attendance of a groom, she rode alone through the comforting Hertfordshire lanes. Primroses were starry in the high-banked hedges swathed in April green. Birdsong was clamorous, the sky a gentle blue tufted with a flurry of white clouds driven by a breeze that, like a mischievous urchin, played with the glossy black mane of her mare; then scampered off to kick up a dust from the road and into her eye.

Softly cursing at an obstinate grit lodged under her eyelid, she did not see the limping approach of an old man known to the villagers as 'Wanting Jake', being senile, simple, or both. What he at that moment might have been wanting was a crutch to support an injured foot. She, riding on a loose rein, pulled up just in time to save him from her horse's hooves.

'Hi, there, old fellow!' she leaned from the saddle to shout. 'Why don't you look where you're going? Or I should have looked, were my eye not closed up with a rock in it and pouring water.' She applied a handkerchief and told him, 'You never used to be lame, Jake. What have you done to yourself?'

''Tis my ankle, m'lady. I fell in the ditch when searching for the bogle.'

'Searching for the *what?*'

'The bogle. There's one 'ereabouts what sours the cream and dries the milk in cows' udders, an' 'tis spawned of old Thirza the witch, down beyond.' He jerked his head in the direction of grey huddled roof-tops clustered at the foot of the low hill-land. 'We be after duckin' 'er to see if she'll sink or she'll swim.'

'A witch hunt, is it? Fine doings in this year of God's grace. Time was two centuries ago when such barbarity would have been an everyday event. Here, let me have a look at that ankle of yours.'

Dismounting, she looped the bridle rein over her arm, bade the old man take off his shoe — he wore no stockings — and with a shudder at his filth-begrimed foot, and a retch at the stench of it, her fingers, expert at examining a horse, carefully explored to pronounce her verdict. 'A beauty of a sprain, or it might be a splintered bone. That's for the surgeon to say. Now you sit here — yes, here, on this bank, *whereon the wild thyme blows* —'

'— *Where oxslips and the nodding violet grows* —' cut in a voice from above.

Caro, kneeling in the dust, looked up to see him looking down; a youth, bare-headed, his nut-brown hair swept back from a high-domed forehead. His eyes, laughter-filled, gazed into hers as he solemnly continued, *There sleeps Titania some time of the night* —'

'But not habited for riding,' she interposed, 'I fancy.'

'Should you wave your wand, madame, you could ride upon a moonbeam, may I make so bold to say?' And, as in after years he said of her, 'With whose delicate fairy-like proportions a Phidias —' or Shakespeare? — 'might have found no fault.'

So there they were all set for an idyll in a pastoral scene that could not have been bettered had she staged it herself.

Welcome, wanderer!' she laughed back at him. 'I don't know who you are, but were you Oberon you could not come more timely. Will you keep guard on this old man who also has been hunting fairies — or, as not so prettily he calls them, bogles — while I ride back for a conveyance to carry him? He cannot walk.' She got upon her feet, rubbing her eye. 'I have a something in it, a mote, a beam — can you perhaps…' She pulled off her hat. Her curls glinting in the sun shone gold.

He caught his breath. 'I will be with you instanter.' And scrambling through the hedge, beating back the blackthorn, unmindful of scratches and pricks, he gained her side. 'My ophthalmic assistance is at your service, madame.'

'How kind of you — Jake! I told you to sit, so *sit*. Now, sir, if you please.' Tilting her chin she submitted her eye to the young stranger's ardent scrutiny. 'It might be an eyelash,' he murmured, 'since they are at least an inch long. Will you look to the right ... now to the left...?'

There followed an interval while their faces, drawn together in the process of operation, almost met. At last, 'Is — is it out?' he stammered with what little breath was left to him.

'O, excellent young man! — most wonderfully out. Are you, sir, an oculist? If not, you ought to be."

'There is much I ought to be and, alas, may never be, but what I hope to be is — always at your service, ma'am. My name is Bulwer, Edward Bulwer. Am I allowed to ask yours?'

'You may ask,' she gleamed up at him, 'and you will know my name when I send the carriage back here for old Jake. Will you come with him to Brocket Hall? For that is where I live.'

And that, or in some such fashion, is how it all began.

Edward Bulwer, later to be known to the world as Bulwer-Lytton, was from that day a constant visitor at Brocket. Living with his mother at Knebworth House, no distance in a crow's flight, made it possible for him to ride almost daily during the next week or so to enquire after old Jake, installed at Brocket in the care of Lady Caroline. So touched was Mr. Bulwer at her consideration of the needy that he, an enthusiastic radical, was moved to write a poem in praise of her beauty and her.

Poor Mr. Walker! His existence now forgotten, he suffered agonies of jealousy and unrequited love. Unable to endure the torment of watching from his window the mistress of his heart walking in the garden, and sometimes in the moonlight, with that 'prosy fellow, Bulwer', whom he had known at Cambridge, Mr. Walker was compelled and of his own decision now, to 'pack his bags and go'.

And Caroline, basking in the adoration of a new admirer, had again become emotionally involved. It mattered not to her that she was forty and he but twenty-one, 'for love,' she sighed, 'is ageless.'

'And you, Titania,' was his fatuous reply, 'are an immortal.'

Those spring weeks sped lightly into summer and brought to her a second blooming. They walked and rode together. He read to her his poems, she read hers to him; and he was ravished, moved with pity for her lovely wasted womanhood, as in this, her latest role of the neglected wife, she saw herself.

'I am like the wreck of a little boat,' she told him, 'a once-gay merry little boat that has been left stranded on an arid beach — or perhaps a butterfly that has burned its wings in a tallow candle.' Nor did he know that she had written almost those very words that day to Godwin. 'You must not overrate me. I can never pass from the ridiculous to the sublime.'

'You have passed beyond the stars,' he answered idiotically, 'to clip Elysium.' For love had caught him badly and she played him like a fish upon a line. He swallowed all the tempting bait she offered, drank in her every word, and was ready to fight any man who dared slander her name.

While still the doors of the elect refused her entry, she did not discriminate and kept open house to every chance acquaintance. Edward Bulwer, to his anguish, found he was not the only one on whom she bestowed favours to be snatched away and offered to another when the charm of conquest faded.

She wore a ring given her by Byron, and this she lent to Edward to wear in memory of him. He wore it till she asked for its return, and saw it the next morning on the finger of a certain Mr. Russell, a newcomer to Brocket and a natural son of the Duke of Bedford.

It was now the turn of Edward to suffer the same torment of jealousy as had the cast-off Mr. Walker.

At dinner that same evening, to which Edward was invited, the girlish, long-haired, pretty, and — to Edward's jaundiced eye — nauseating Mr. Russell was seated on the right hand of his hostess. Edward found himself beside Miss Benger who, throughout the meal, engaged him in discussion on the 'Rights of Women'.

The subject taken up by Caroline, she gave it as her opinion — to horrify the green-eyed Mr. Bulwer — that 'husband and wife should live in separate houses and sleep never in one bed after the first year.'

To which William, sitting silent, drinking much and eating little, unexpectedly agreed. 'Man and wife who live together confined to the same rooms, are like two pigeons in one basket and must invariably fight.'

'As do we,' laughed Caro, kissing fingertips to him across the table.

After dinner there was music in the drawing room. Mr. Russell, with soulful eyes upon his hostess, played, and Mr. Bulwer, reclining on the sofa, was found to be in tears.

'Pray stop that melancholy air,' Caro interrupted Mr. Russell's mournful rendering of Bach. 'It is making Mr. Bulwer cry.'

Apart from its ill taste it was deliberately unkind and inexcusable. Edward, who loved her as much as William ever did in his first blinding passion, could forgive, but he could not forget. All his life the thought of her remained with him like the petals of a flower pressed within the pages of a book, so frail that the merest touch would crumble it to dust where it lay resting. And often, even after, the shade of her recurred, a nostalgic echo through his verses.

All thy woes have sprung from feeling;
Thine only guilt was not concealing.

Yes, her only guilt, as Bulwer-Lytton of them all could understand.

ELEVEN

Life, she wrote to Godwin, *is very, very long...* Did she feel it so, as slowly, imperceptibly her own life ebbed away? None saw, none guessed, that her febrile vitality was draining her heart's blood. Her mental condition had worsened. Her insomnia increased, and now, as when the curtain fell upon the Byron drama, did she revert to her nocturnal habits of pounding the organ, waking the household and William with her screaming fits; or if, after copious sedation, she was induced to sleep, she would rouse the house again with her nightmares.

On one occasion she swore she had seen Byron standing at the foot of her bed. When William, hearing her terror-stricken shrieks, came from his room to investigate he found her shaking as if with an ague. 'He looked horrible, fatter than he used and not handsome any more. He stood and mocked me, gibbering...'

'It was a dream, my love.' William strove to soothe her, holding her in his arms, stroking the damp tendrils of hair from her forehead.

'It was *no* dream! I have seen his ghost. He is dead, or dying, and he comes to tell me so. He broke my heart and will haunt me to my death and afterwards.'

But whether dream or ghost or premonition, when, a few weeks later, the news of Byron's death in Greece was conveyed to her carefully by William, she collapsed. She was put to bed, cupped, purged, dosed, and lay in a state diagnosed as 'hysterical fever'. Her recovery was slow; and when, convalescent, the doctor attending her at Brocket pronounced her well enough to take a drive, another greater shock than any yet awaited her.

As the carriage left the gates on its way towards Welwyn it was halted by a funeral cortège with all the pomp and grisly circumstance of black-plumed horses, black-velveted hearse, followed by mourners in a line of coaches winding through the narrow lanes.

William, who accompanied her, riding at her carriage wheels, on this, her first outing, rode ahead to ask whose funeral it was; they told him, 'Lord Byron's'. Whereupon he gave orders that the carriage should be driven back to Brocket. Not for the world would he have Caroline know, at that grim moment, for fear of fatal consequences. When, however, she read in the news sheet the next day that his body had been taken to Welwyn *en route* for his burial in Westminster Abbey, it was too much for her and she collapsed again.

From that time forth her frenzies became increasingly violent. William's nerves were frayed to breaking point. Urged by Emily and his brother George, he decided she could no longer be trusted to live at Brocket in charge of the house and Augustus. The same fears of what she might do to their son or the pages in her 'fits of madness', which Emily continuously voiced, were once more brought forward; and this time his decision would not, he promised, be revoked. He agreed that he and Caroline must part. There would be no half measures, no relenting. She must go.

'But *where* am I to go?' she cried to Hart, who had come to her appeal to act for her. 'They talk of an amicable separation. How can any separation from him — who for twenty years has been a part of me, my better self — be amicable? Oh, I know — I know what they are saying. That I am a lunatic and should be kept in a padded cell, as Emily for years has been saying, the snake! A viper who has wormed her way between us as her mother did before her. Why — why do they do this to me? I am not mad … I'm not, I'm not!'

'My poor Caro.' Hart took her little feverish hand in his and held it close. 'Emily and such as she cannot understand you who are as different from them as —' he groped for a metaphor to achieve, rather proud of himself — 'as a firefly is to a black beetle.'

'How true! My clever Hart. Of course! They — not William, but the Lambs — swarm with hate for me in the dark cellars of their minds and scuttle away when my light shines on them. Fireflies carry lights in their heads, I believe, or is it glow-worms? The beasts, the loathsome vermin that they are! May their souls rot in hell!' Snatching her hand from his she dug her teeth savagely into the tender flesh to draw blood.

'Don't!' cried Hart. 'Don't do that to yourself. Bite me if you want to. My skin is tough.'

'Oh, see,' she looked ruefully down at her hand, 'it's bleeding. Why do you go on loving me when no one else does or can, not even William, whom I love with all my might and strength and always have, and yet at a word from them he casts me off. He and they are always searching for my faults to lay them out on slabs like fish in the market stalls until they stink as they have made me and my name stink!'

She fell to crying. Hart took her on his knees and wiped her eyes with a very clean starched handkerchief and she tucked her head under his chin and told him dreamily, 'But I can't altogether blame them, and certainly not William, who has borne with me too long. And I can't blame myself either. You know my upbringing, and your own too. Wonder it is you are as you are, so sane and sensible — except about me — but then you went to school, and so did I, for five minutes. But after I left Miss Rowden's I had no guidance and no care except from dear Miss Trimmer. You know how we used to believe that horses were fed on roast beef and that bread and butter was a plant that grew out of the ground?'

Hart tweaked a lock of her hair. 'Which bread is, silly, or rather the wheat from which it is made is a plant.'

'Of course — if you go back to its beginnings. And you,' she slid an arm round his neck and laid her cheek to his, 'you only, of all the children at Devonshire House, loved me.'

'As I love you still,' he mumbled, 'and for ever will — till death.'

'Which for me is not far off, I hope. No, don't imagine I am play-acting now, or that I fear what comes to all of us. My life has been so full and yet so empty. There is nothing more empty, Hart, than to make an image of — or should I say a portrait of — oneself and another, as I did of me and William, and of Byron too, to find it out of drawing, the colours all wrong, too many highlights, no half-tones, no shadows. Life is full of light and shade. You can't live always in the light any more than you can live in shadowed corners, though many do. Selina, for instance, only she sheds a gentle light around her for the comfort of all, but that is not my way of life. I must always stand in the glare of a torch until I sizzle in its flame…'

So on and on she would talk in that soft lisping voice of hers until exhausted; but on the whole she was more subdued and rational than she had been before her illness, though physically she weakened.

William, who had not dared to face her with this final ultimatum, took himself to Brighton and wrote to her from there to say a private separation was impossible. Their case must be settled in court; to which at first she consented, then refused. On no account would she have their names dragged into court, which, in view of her craving for any form of notoriety, surprised him. She suggested that William should meet Hart and her brother, William Ponsonby, who would make all arrangements for a settlement on her behalf.

Emily Cowper, determined that William should not change his mind this time, began to be uneasy at his lethargic attitude to the whole proceedings. Could it be that even now he wavered?

He had returned to London, and, to his sister's dismay, had gone down to Brocket. 'Only to discuss with her,' was the excuse he offered, 'the allowance that her brother and Devonshire demand.'

'They are asking far too much,' demurred Emily. 'Papa says two thousand a year is quite enough. She is pressing for more and on no account must you give it her. Be firm.'

But, contrary to Emily's expectations, at the meeting, where neither Hart nor Ponsonby were present, he found her tractable, docile, ready to agree to any allowance he thought proper if he would let her live at Brocket with Augustus.

'That is all I ask. I won't be parted from Augustus. You can't be so cruel as to take him from me, you can't! I will, of course, pay for his keep and mine, and my horses.'

'Don't!' He buried his face in his hands. 'Don't talk like that — it breaks me.'

'It is rather late in the day for you to be broken,' said she with the ghost of a grin, 'but I've no doubt Emily will plaster up your cracks. As for bringing our case to court, you surely wouldn't, would you? Can you see us throwing verbal brickbats at each other? Or if I could lay hands on an inkpot I might hurl it at you when my evil spirit moves me. My poor darling, how many ornaments have I smashed in all these years! And what purgatory have I made you suffer! Never mind, you won't have to suffer any more. You will live in heavenly peace when you are done with me. As to these proceedings you propose to bring against me, I'll be so gentle, quiet, calm, when you tell the judge what a harridan you've married, how she has disgraced your name — you must pile on the wickedness and my infidelities, although I tell you now, and will swear it on oath, that whatever else I am I have never been unfaithful to you according to the law of man, even if by the law of God. For *Whosoever looketh on a woman* — or a man — *to lust after her* — or him — *hath committed adultery in his heart,* of which I cannot plead guiltless. I was saying that my demeanour in court will be so exemplary that the judge will tell the jury — I suppose there'll be a jury? — "This poor young wife —" you may be sure I'll be at pains to make myself look twenty years younger than I am — "this poor young wife has been most cruelly abused. I award her a maintenance allowance of ten thousand pounds a year. As for the plaintiff —" no, what are you? — the appellant? — with a basilisk look at your squirming in the witness box, "I pass judgment that he eats dust at the feet of the defendant —" or whatever I am — "for the rest of his life."'

At this glimpse of that engaging whimsicality which with lightning touch illumined her most tragic performances, how, William asked himself, could he go on with it? But he had to go on with it having gone so far. And she, sensing his uncertainty, aware that she held the whip hand should she choose to use it, made no effort to dissuade him. She was wise enough to know that unless he came to her with his whole heart they could never live together in peace and amity.

'I have read somewhere in some old book,' she said, 'an Indian legend of Twashtri, the elephant god, who, after he created man, made woman and gave her to him to love and cherish. But in a very little while man came to Twashtri and spoke thus: "Sir, this creature you have given me — she will drive me mad. She chatters incessantly, has the temper of a tigress, the softness of the dove, the cunning of the serpent, the fidelity of the dog and the sweetness of the sugarcane, but she is always making rows, is utterly selfish, cries and screams for nothing, scratches me and bites me, and O, please, Sir, take her back again, for I cannot live with her." So Twashtri took her back again, and after three days man came to him and said, "Sir, I find my life is very lonely since I gave you back that creature. I remember how she used to dance and sing to me and she was beautiful to look at and soft to touch and her laughter was as the music of a fountain and her heart was like a pearl, and O, please, Sir, give her back to me again." So Twashtri gave her back to him again, and the very next morning man came to him and said, "Lord, it is no use. I cannot live with her, so, if you please —"

'Then Twashtri, who had by that time lost his patience, said, "Away with you, begone! I've had enough of this. I will *not* take her back." And the man raised eyes and hands to heaven, crying, "What am I to do, for I can neither live with her nor without her?" Don't you think that's very true of us?'

'Caro!' He made a step forward; his arms engulfed her and his mouth sought hers.

'No.' She shook her head and gently drew away from him, 'you must not weaken now. You must be strong, for my sake and your own. I love you too much to let you sacrifice your life to me. You have your future, that great political career which I know will be yours if I am not there to harass and distract you from your life's work. I'll never stand in your light. All I ask is that we may meet sometimes and be ... good friends.'

He tried to speak but no words came and, turning, he went from her blindly.

Their case, as she had known it would be, was settled out of court. She had hoped to live at Brocket, but under the deed of separation no home for her had been provided, and she was legally bound to bide by the terms agreed, which gave William the custody of their son.

It was a great wrench to leave the house she loved and where, as a child, she had first met William. Only she could know the deadening anguish she endured on that last day when she must be severed not only from Augustus but from all that had been dear to her in childhood. Her letters to Lady Morgan show her valiant efforts to adjust herself to circumstances *that might*, she wrote, *try anybody. Every tree, every flower will waken my bitter reflections. O, God, it is a punishment severe enough… I have rushed forward to my own destruction.*

Yet while her world darkened she still retained that sense of puckish humour which could laugh in defiance of fate. And to Hart she said, 'While my rich relations spurn me with a pittance —'

'The two thousand five hundred a year,' he interposed, 'that I've managed to squeeze out of old Melbourne, is hardly a pittance, would you say?'

'Yes, for me it is, I would say, though for some, a fortune. What am I to do? Shall I go abroad, to Paris, to Rome? Or shall I live over a cheap little shop in the City Road or Shoreditch and sell stockings? Or shall I open a seminary for young ladies and teach them much that is not good for them and all they shouldn't know? Or shall I throw myself on those who do not want me?'

'I,' muttered Hart, 'will always want you.'

'Darling, you are like a Greek chorus the way you take up your cue and chime in so aptly. What a thing Euripides could have made of my life… Well, when all others fail me I'll throw myself on you.'

But she did not throw herself on anyone. Her farewell to Brocket might have given opportunity for sentimental drama; yet her parting from the servants and the villagers who loved her was the more affecting for its simplicity. She moved among them with a restraint that none could guess was the courage of despair. The butler wept. Miss Trimmer, who was to go with her to London, wept. The servants wept. The villagers, who thronged the gates to see her pass, they wept; but not a tear was shed by her on that last morning, not even when she visited the stables. Her black mare thrust her head over the door of her loose-box to nuzzle her. Caro laid her cheek against the soft dark lips, and whispered. 'We will meet again, my beautiful, if not here, hereafter … I can't believe in life everlasting without you.'

On a mounting block in the stable yard where she sat awaiting the coach that would take her away, she was moved to improvise part of a poem later to be scribbled in her notebook:

My joyous days with youth are fled,
My friends are either changed or dead,
Where'er I go, God bless you all,
And thus I leave thee, Brocket Hall.

And three months later: 'William! Did you know she has come back?' Emily, in a state of agitation, rushed at him in his library at Melbourne House. 'I thought we were quit of her for ever.'

'You may be quit of her but I am not,' he answered quietly. 'I never will be quit of her. And yes, she has, thank God, come back.'

Emily stared at him in horrified dismay. 'Do you mean — you *knew*? I thought it was understood that she should live in Paris. She seemed content enough to go, and now — what do you propose to do?'

William rose from his desk and, with a cold steady look at his sister, said, 'What I propose to do is to place Brocket at my wife's disposal, for I —'

'You can't!' broke in Emily. 'You can't be so weak. Why are you doing this to bring misery on yourself and all of us again?'

'For I,' continued William, as if deaf to interruption, 'have accepted office as Chief Secretary to Ireland. I leave my wife and son at Brocket, in their home.'

The autumn days were drawing in at the close of an Indian summer. The wistful sunless mornings brightened to breeze-swept afternoons when the trees of Brocket, decked in ambered green, tossed wild arms in the dance of the winds under skies of muted crimson.

In her room overlooking the garden she would gaze out at the dear familiar landmarks of cornfields and wooded hills and valleys where the winding coil of the River Lea shone. 'Like a silver thread in golden hair,' she murmured, 'but my hair never will be silver.' She would talk often to herself, having none to talk to other than the servants, Hart on brief visits from Chatsworth, and the faithful Trimmer anxiously beside her, watching, fearing, hoping, when all hope was gone.

In the Ladies' Mile whispers circled on the wings of gossip.

'They say she's dying of a dropsy.' Lips were pursed, laughter bubbled, spiced with malice. 'I've heard from Lady Cowper that she looks like a balloon!'

A few were moved to pity; conscience pricked perhaps, when they remembered her as once she was, their 'Fairie Queen', a 'Sprite', an 'Ariel', flitting wraith-like through their drawing rooms with her short boyish curls, her irrepressible gaiety and elusive charm that none who most decried her had been able to resist. And in this, her last performance, when the inexorable slow advance of a remorseless enemy was sapping her defences, she was in truth the heroine she had always seen herself. All the fervid warmth and strength of her nature rose to meet her ordeal fearlessly: nor did she now demand an audience. Her auditorium was empty. There were no curtain calls. Even the harshness of Emily melted before a courage that still could laugh in the face of death as if she hid a chuckle in her shroud.

I shall no doubt go with an Almack ticket to heaven, she wrote to Lady Morgan; and, to her sister-in-law, Maria Duncannon:

I consider my illness a great blessing. I feel returned to my God and my duty and my dearest husband … I broke that horrible spell which prevented me saying my prayers … I say all this, dearest Maria, lest you should think I flew to religion because I was in danger — it is no such thing, my heart is softened … I am quite resigned to die.

She had no wish to live. Her unquenchable spirit went forward gallantly to meet 'what, after all,' she said to the grave-faced doctor at her bedside, 'comes soon or late to all of us. How glum you look! You mustn't let my husband know how ill I am. I would not have him worried. He has so much to do and to think of over there in Ireland of more importance than my ailments and me. I will not have him told.'

But when they brought her to London for a consultation with eminent physicians it was decided that her husband must be told.

Propped on her pillows in her room at Melbourne House she could watch the sky in all its changes: the misted blue of mornings; the copper glow of sunsets clouded with grey London smoke; or the starred canopy of night lit by a great gold moon with a halo of bronze around it.

She was tired, glad to rest, content to lie and see, gathered about her, the faces of those she had loved and whom she never thought to see again: her mother, her grandmother and her aunt, the lovely duchess... And she saw him, no longer 'horrible' as in her dream, but as she had known him whose *beautiful pale face will be my fate* — so she had written in her journal after their first meeting long ago — he who had taught her the dark witchery of passion and the ache of passion's emptiness. All were here in one last yearning glimpse of love and youth returned in the dawn of her awakening from that short spell of sleep which men call life.

She knew no pain, no fever, only a quiet drifting on a slow untroubled tide of memories. And when to them who watched beside her she whispered, 'William... send for William...' he was there, his hand in hers to guide her through the falling darkness into light.

EPILOGUE (1839)

'My dear, my very dear Lord Melbourne, you must be the first to hear. I have spoken to Albert and we are to be married.'

The homely little face with its forward teeth and backward chin was radiant with happiness. The slightly protuberant blue eyes were raised in *schwärmerisch* devotion to the courtly figure with its silvered hair, jet-black eyebrows and sensitive mouth. How handsome he was, her dear Lord M.! — but not so handsome as her dearest Albert.

She held out her hand; he bowed over it, his sight a trifle dimmed. To him, this young girl, who had stepped from a schoolroom to a throne, was the symbol of rebirth, regeneration. The dissolute years of her predecessors with their mistresses, debaucheries and debts were gone, forgotten. It was as if a dead orchard, blighted by long winter frosts, had blossomed overnight.

And for her, never had spring danced so gladly as in this second year of her reign, with her dear 'Lord M' always at her side, protective, advising, her guardian and her servant, First Lord of the Treasury, Prime Minister of England.

Straightening his back where he felt a twinge of his rheumatics, he murmured, 'Allow me, ma'am, to be the first to offer Your Majesty my warmest felicitations. May your marriage bring you all your heart desires, now and ever more.'

'Oh, it will, it will! It is you to whom I owe this supreme joy of my betrothal. As you know, I did not want to marry anyone and was loth to meet my cousin Albert until you advised me to invite him here, and when I saw him again, not having seen him since my accession, I knew there was *none* other in all the *world* for me!'

Lord Melbourne cleared away some slight obstruction affecting his voice; she was so young, so fresh, so innocent. He, the cynic, who had said, 'Wealth is the greatest gift that fortune can bring'; he, who in this last decade had attained the highest peak of his political career, whose paradoxical quips had enlivened the tables of his ladies and their lords, and who, in his widowed years, had skated on thinnest ice to bring him to the verge of the divorce court, could now, with old age upon him, be moved to tears by a gushful young girl's romance.

'Pray, Lord Melbourne, be seated.' She waved him to a chair; and seating herself, her small plump hands folded in her lap, she said, with a touching mixture of artlessness and dignity, 'We did so dread a change of government. I don't know *what* we would have done if the Tories had won the election with Sir Robert Peel in office. How thankful I am it is *you*!'

'Your Majesty may rest assured that I am ever at your service to command.'

Her lips parted in a gratified smile to show her gums. 'Dear Lord Melbourne, you are such a comfort to me. I rely on you implicitly. We dare not contemplate any other prime minister, especially now in view of our approaching marriage.' Then the shining look faded. She said softly, 'You too have been married, but you … have lost.'

'No, ma'am,' his gaze slipped past her and away, 'not lost… She is still more to me than anyone was or ever will be, saving you, ma'am,' with the gallantry of the trained courtier he added, 'to whom I dedicate my life.'

That evening the girl Queen Victoria wrote in her diary: *As for 'the confidence of the Crown', God knows! No MINISTER, NO*

FRIEND, EVER possessed it so entirely as this truly excellent Lord Melbourne possesses mine!

Dismissing his carriage, he walked home through the gathering dusk to Melbourne House. At his desk he sat, opened a drawer and took out an ivory casket. It contained every letter, every scrap of verse his wife had written to him through the years. And when he found what he sought, though he knew each line by heart, he read again a fragment of the very last poem she wrote:

> *To William*
> *Passion and pride and flattery strove*
> *They made a wreck of me,*
> *But O, I never ceased to love*
> *I never loved but thee.*

A NOTE TO THE READER

If you have enjoyed this novel enough to leave a review on **Amazon** and **Goodreads**, then we would be truly grateful.

Sapere Books

Sapere Books is an exciting new publisher of brilliant fiction and popular history.

To find out more about our latest releases and our monthly bargain books visit our website: **saperebooks.com**